HENRY JAMES

Daisy Miller and Other Tales

Edited and with an Introduction and Notes by
STEPHEN FENDER

PENGUIN BOOKS

PENGUIN CLASSICS

UK | USA | Canada | Ireland | Australia
India | New Zealand | South Africa

Penguin Books is part of the Penguin Random House group of companies
whose addresses can be found at global.penguinrandomhouse.com.

This edition first published in Penguin Classics 2016
001

Set in 10.25/12.25 pt Sabon
Typeset by Jouve (UK), Milton Keynes
Printed in Great Britain by Clays Ltd, St Ives plc

ISBN: 978-0-141-38977-6

www.greenpenguin.co.uk

MIX
Paper from
responsible sources
FSC® C018179

Penguin Random House is committed to a
sustainable future for our business, our readers
and our planet. This book is made from Forest
Stewardship Council® certified paper.

Contents

DAISY MILLER AND
OTHER TALES

Chronology

1843 *15 April*: Henry James born at 21 Washington Place in New York City, second of five children of Henry James (1811–82), speculative theologian and social thinker, whose strict entrepreneur father had amassed wealth estimated at $3 million, one of the top ten American fortunes of his time, and his wife Mary (1810–82), daughter of James Walsh, a New York cotton merchant of Scottish origin.

1843–5 Accompanies parents to Paris and London.

1845–7 James family returns to USA and settles in Albany, New York.

1847–55 Family settles in New York City; HJ taught by tutors and in private schools.

1855–8 Family travels in Europe: Geneva, London, Paris, Boulogne-sur-Mer. Returns to USA and settles in Newport, Rhode Island.

1859–60 Family in Europe again: HJ attends scientific school, then the Academy (later the University) in Geneva. Learns German in Bonn.

September 1860: Family returns to Newport. HJ makes friends with future critic T. S. Perry (who records that HJ 'was continually writing stories, mainly of a romantic kind') and artist John La Farge.

1861–3 Injures his back helping to extinguish a fire in Newport and is exempted from military service in American Civil War (1861–5).

Autumn 1862: Enters Harvard Law School for a term. Begins to send stories to magazines.

1864 *February*: First short story, 'A Tragedy of Error', published anonymously in *Continental Monthly*.

May: Family moves to 13 Ashburton Place, Boston, Massachusetts.

October: Unsigned review published in *North American Review*.

1865 *March*: First signed tale, 'The Story of a Year', appears in *Atlantic Monthly*. HJ's criticism published in first number of the *Nation* (New York).

1866–8 Continues reviewing and writing stories.

Summer 1866: W. D. Howells, novelist, critic and influential editor, becomes a friend.

November 1866: Family moves to 20 Quincy Street, beside Harvard Yard, in Cambridge, Massachusetts.

1869 Travels for his health to England, where he meets John Ruskin, William Morris, Charles Darwin and George Eliot; also visits Switzerland and Italy.

1870 *March*: Death in USA of his much-loved cousin Minny Temple.

May: HJ, still unwell, is reluctantly back in Cambridge.

1871 *August–December*: First short novel, *Watch and Ward*, serialized in *Atlantic Monthly*.

1872–4 Accompanies invalid sister Alice and aunt Catherine Walsh ('Aunt Kate') to Europe in May. Writes travel pieces for the *Nation*. Between October 1872 and September 1874 spends periods of time in Paris, Rome, Switzerland, Homburg and Italy without his family.

Spring 1874: Begins first long novel, *Roderick Hudson*, in Florence.

September 1874: Returns to USA.

1875 *January*: Publishes *A Passionate Pilgrim, and Other Tales*, his first work to appear in book form. It is followed by *Transatlantic Sketches* (travel pieces) and then by *Roderick Hudson* in November. Spends six months in New York City (111 East 25th Street), then three in Cambridge.

11 *November*: Arrives at 29 rue de Luxembourg, Paris, as correspondent for the *New York Tribune*.

December: Begins new novel, *The American*.

1876 Meets Gustave Flaubert, Ivan Turgenev, Edmond de Goncourt, Alphonse Daudet, Guy de Maupassant and Émile Zola.

December: Moves to London and settles at 3 Bolton Street, just off Piccadilly.

1877 Visits Paris, Florence and Rome.

May: *The American* is published.

1878 Meets William Gladstone, Alfred Tennyson and Robert Browning.

February: Collection of essays, *French Poets and Novelists*, is the first book HJ publishes in London.

July: Novella 'Daisy Miller' serialized in *The Cornhill Magazine*; in November *Harper's* publish it in the USA, establishing HJ's reputation on both sides of the Atlantic.

September: Publishes novel *The Europeans*.

1879 *December*: Publishes novel *Confidence* and *Hawthorne* (critical study).

1880 *December*: Publishes novel *Washington Square*.

1881 *October*: Returns to USA; visits Cambridge.

November: Publishes novel *The Portrait of a Lady*.

1882 *January*: Death of mother. Visits New York and Washington, DC.

May: Travels back to England but returns to USA on death of father in December.

1883 *Summer*: Returns to London.

November: Fourteen-volume collected edition of fiction published by Macmillan.

December: Publishes *Portraits of Places* (travel writings).

1884 Sister Alice moves to London and settles near HJ.

September: Publishes *A Little Tour in France* (travel writings) and *Tales of Three Cities*; his important artistic statement 'The Art of Fiction' appears in *Longman's Magazine*. Becomes a friend of R. L. Stevenson and Edmund Gosse. Writes to his American friend Grace Norton: 'I shall never marry ... I am both happy enough and miserable enough, as it is.'

1885–6 Publishes two serial novels, *The Bostonians* and *The Princess Casamassima*.

6 March 1886: Moves into flat at 34 de Vere Gardens.

1887 *Spring and summer*: Visits Florence and Venice. Continues friendship (begun in 1880) with American novelist Constance Fenimore Woolson.

1888 Publishes novel *The Reverberator*, novella 'The Aspern Papers' and *Partial Portraits* (criticism).

1889 Collection of tales *A London Life* published.

1890 Novel *The Tragic Muse* published.

1891 Play version of *The American* has a short run in the provinces and London.

1892 *February*: Publishes *The Lesson of the Master* (story collection).

    March: Death of Alice James in London.

1893 Three volumes of tales published: *The Real Thing* (March), *The Private Life* (June), *The Wheel of Time* (September).

1894 Deaths of Constance Fenimore Woolson and R. L. Stevenson.

1895 *5 January*: Play *Guy Domville* is greeted by boos and applause on its premiere at St James's Theatre; HJ abandons playwriting for many years. Visits Ireland. Takes up cycling. Publishes two volumes of tales, *Terminations* (May) and *Embarrassments* (June).

1896 Publishes novel *The Other House*.

1897 Two novels, *The Spoils of Poynton* and *What Maisie Knew*, published.

    February: Starts dictating, due to wrist problems.

    September: Takes lease on Lamb House, Rye, Sussex.

1898 *June*: Moves into Lamb House. Sussex neighbours include the writers Joseph Conrad, H. G. Wells and Ford Madox Hueffer (Ford).

    August: Publishes *In the Cage* (short novel).

    October: 'The Turn of the Screw', ghost story included in *The Two Magics*, proves his most popular work since 'Daisy Miller'.

1899 *April*: Novel *The Awkward Age* published.

    August: Buys the freehold of Lamb House.

1900 Shaves off his beard.

    August: Publishes collection of tales *The Soft Side*. Friendship with American novelist Edith Wharton develops.

1901 *February*: Publishes novel *The Sacred Fount*.

1902 *August*: Publishes novel *The Wings of the Dove*.

1903 *February*: Publishes collection of tales *The Better Sort*.
September: Publishes novel *The Ambassadors*.
October: Publishes memoir *William Wetmore Story and his Friends*.

1904 *August*: Sails to USA, his first visit for twenty-one years. Travels to New England, New York, Philadelphia, Washington, the South, St Louis, Chicago, Los Angeles and San Francisco.
November: Publishes novel *The Golden Bowl*.

1905 *January*: Is President Theodore Roosevelt's guest at the White House. Elected to the American Academy of Arts and Letters.
July: Back in Lamb House, begins revising works for the New York Edition of *The Novels and Tales of Henry James*.
October: Publishes *English Hours* (travel essays).

1906–8 Selects, arranges, writes prefaces and has illustrations made for New York Edition (published 1907–9, twenty-four volumes).

1907 *January*: Publishes *The American Scene* (travel essays).

1908 *March*: Play *The High Bid* produced at Edinburgh.

1909 *October*: Publishes *Italian Hours* (travel essays). Health problems.

1910 *August*: Travels to USA with brother William, who dies a week after their return.
October: Publishes *The Finer Grain* (tales).

1911 *August*: Returns to England.
October: Publishes *The Outcry* (novel adapted from play). Begins work on autobiography.

1912 *June*: Receives honorary doctorate from Oxford University.
October: Takes flat at 21 Carlyle Mansions, Cheyne Walk, Chelsea; suffers from shingles.

1913 *March*: Publishes *A Small Boy and Others* (first volume of autobiography). Portrait painted by John Singer Sargent for seventieth birthday.

1914 *March*: Publishes *Notes of a Son and Brother* (second volume of autobiography).

August: Outbreak of First World War; HJ becomes passionately engaged with the British cause and helps Belgian refugees and wounded soldiers.

October: Publishes *Notes on Novelists*.

1915 Is made honorary president of the American Volunteer Motor Ambulance Corps.

July: Becomes a British citizen. Writes essays about the war (collected in *Within the Rim* (1919)) and the Preface to *Letters from America* (1916) by the poet Rupert Brooke, who had died the previous year.

2 December: Suffers a stroke.

1916 Awarded the Order of Merit in New Year Honours.

28 February: Dies. After his funeral in Chelsea Old Church, his ashes are smuggled back to America by sister-in-law and buried in the family plot in Cambridge.

Philip Horne, 2008

Introduction

I

The stories collected and edited here represent various explorations of the 'international theme', or what Henry James called 'the Americano-European legend'. They appear in the same order in which they were published, from 1870 to 1904, and so give a good idea of how the topic developed.

It was a subject, as he wrote in his notebook on 20 June 1887, 'which really, without forcing the matter or riding the horse to death, strikes me as an inexhaustible mine'. And so it turned out, since not just these and other tales but much of his longest, most ambitious fiction – *The Portrait of a Lady* (1881) and his three late, great novels, *The Wings of the Dove* (1902), *The Ambassadors* (1903) and *The Golden Bowl* (1904), are wound round the armature of the international theme.

Briefly, the international theme focuses on the social, emotional, aesthetic and moral responses of Americans in Europe – usually American women, though Christopher Newman in *The American* (1877) and Lambert Strether in *The Ambassadors* are notable exceptions – and also (more rarely) Europeans in America. In comparing the cultural assumptions and political conventions of great civilizations, it studied not only the extent to which national differences conditioned social behaviour, but also how the conflict had an impact upon the consciousness of those engaged in it, and those observing it. James's interest in and treatment of the theme was, therefore, both that of an imaginative sociologist and that of a profoundly insightful novelist.

Typically the comparison, to put it in the terms established by William Blake, was between (American) innocence and (European) experience. Other cognate antitheses could be American local democracy as against European centralized oligarchy; the American egalitarian impulse versus the European love of hierarchy; American spontaneity and European respect for convention; the Americans' imagination fired by the future as against the Europeans' by the past, and so on.

James's own upbringing had positively pitched him into the middle of 'Americano-European' comparisons. Born in New York City in 1843, by his eighteenth year he had already been to Europe three times, on family tours and to study. Ten years later he went again on his own, as an avid traveller and budding author, a 'passionate pilgrim' (as the title of one of his first tales in the theme would have it) to the cultural shrines of England and Italy. After that his life and work took him to Europe on increasingly long periods of residence – in Paris, in London, then Rye, Sussex, where in his beloved Lamb House he wrote his last three great novels.

But life in different countries offered more than social and cultural variety; for James the country he lived in had profound aesthetic and moral – hence professional – implications. As Kendall Johnson has put it, James's concept of culture, like that of the British intellectuals Matthew Arnold and John Ruskin, was based on the belief that literature and painting were 'forces of moral instruction' that had brought mankind out of savagery, through barbarism to civilization. Against the background of this belief, Johnson continues, 'James capitalized on a collective anxiety over how the United States would measure up against the nations of Europe'.[1] Perhaps his best-known expression of this anxiety appeared in James's critical study of Nathaniel Hawthorne in 1879, in which he listed the 'items of high civilization' absent from American life: 'No State, in the European sense of the word . . . no sovereign, no court, no personal loyalty . . . no castles, nor manors, nor old country-houses . . . nor thatched cottages nor ivied ruins . . . no Oxford, nor Eton . . . no political society, no sporting class – no Epsom nor Ascot!'

In expressing America's presumed deficiencies in the form of a long negative catalogue James was latching onto an already familiar trope. In the preface to *The Marble Faun* (1860), quoted by James only a page before his own reiteration of the lament, Hawthorne had complained that America had 'no shadow, no antiquity, no mystery, no picturesque and gloomy wrong, nor anything but a common-place prosperity'. Long before that, in his non-fictional *Notions of the Americans* (1828), James Fenimore Cooper had written that America challenged the 'man of genius' in having 'no follies (beyond the most vulgar and commonplace) for the satirist; no manners for the dramatist; no obscure fictions for the writer of romance . . . There is no costume for the peasant (there is scarcely a peasant at all), no wig for the judge, no baton for the general.'

Reviewing *Hawthorne* in *The Atlantic Monthly* for February 1880, James's friend, the novelist and literary editor William Dean Howells, commented that 'After leaving out all those novelistic "properties" . . . by the absence of which Mr James suggests our poverty to the English conception, we have the whole of human life remaining.' As for Hawthorne, 'No man would have known less what to do with that dreary and worn-out paraphernalia.' James answered Howells in a letter of 31 January 1880, making his case, if anything, more emphatically, that 'it takes an old civilization to set a novelist in motion – a proposition that seems to me so true as to be a truism. It is on manners, customs, usages, habits, forms, upon all these things matured & established, that a novelist lives – they are the very stuff his work is made of.'[2]

Of course there were things American writers could do, especially in the way of romance. Cooper was able to mine the (in fact, already) quite rich deposits of American history, together with the allure of the disappearing tribe, in the magisterial series of his five *Leatherstocking Tales* written between 1823 and 1841, and Hawthorne was able to reinvent the New England past as a fanciful arena in which Puritan self-analysis could be turned to the project of questioning the truth value of narrative itself – historical as well as fictional.

But realistic novels of manners were something else. In the

Declaration of Independence and the Constitution of the United States, the new republic had identified itself as both egalitarian and democratic. It was proud of having abolished distinctions of class and wealth based on hereditary advantage. Of course the actuality had never lived up to the grand proclamations. There were then, and still are, plenty of class strata in America, from old money and new money, down through white-collar and blue-collar workers to poor whites and poor white trash – and that's not to mention the distinctions of race that have bedevilled the country. But the abolition of inherited privilege was and remains central to America's sense of itself.

American fiction that defined its characters and plotted their fortunes through marks of rank, status or unearned income, therefore, could hardly be read as realistic, however accurate they might be. Readers would simply not have the ideological and emotional conditioning to take these distinctions seriously, to believe in the triumph or pathos of characters caught in such matrices. Beyond that, the American audience would be likely to read novels about castles, manor houses or old abbeys as a bit on the grand side – unless they were set in Europe, of course – and wigs, batons, Epsom and Ascot would be taken as little more than absurd stage props. So the American equivalent of the novel of manners was best done by having your characters go to Europe, as Hawthorne does with Hilda in *The Marble Faun* (1860), surely the prototype of James's American girl abroad. In the European setting distinctions and markers of rank and privilege may be deplored, but at least they could be believed in.

II

James didn't invent the international theme; rather, he was tapping into a perennial fascination with the contrast between New World and Old. Even before they first stepped on American soil Europeans were fantasizing about its apparent state of nature. Living in innocence, the natives would surely live

happily without the constraints of European cultural institutions. And so it followed after America was actually discovered.
In a letter home of 1502 Amerigo Vespucci, after whom the
great continent was named, noted that the natives seemed to
have no law; 'they use no trade, they neither buy nor sell'.
What we in Europe hoard as wealth, he observed, 'they hold as
nothing'. It was like creation before the Fall, or life in Ovid's
Golden Age.

By just over a century later New World nature meant not
so much the natives' benign way of life as the raw materials
awaiting exploitation. Writing in 1616, the English explorer
(and settler of the Jamestown Colony in 1608) Captain John
Smith, trying to promote settlement in what *he* had named
as New England, expressed his awe at the abundant natural
profusion – all ready for eating, chopping down, shooting,
catching and shipping home – in endless catalogues:

> Oake is the chiefe wood . . . firre, pyne, walnut, chesnut, birch,
> ash, elme, cypresse, ceder . . . Eagles, Gripes [vultures], diverse
> sorts of Hawkes, Cranes, Geese . . . Meawes, Guls, Turkies . . .
> and many other sorts whose names I knowe not.

Because New England nature was so profuse and outlandish,
it defied the formalities of syntax (Smith's catalogues have little shape, and could go on more or less indefinitely), and outran
the store of Old World vocabulary, since there were so many
things he couldn't name.

So from early on the polarities of the transatlantic contrast
were set: America had the nature, Europe the culture. After
the United States broke free from Great Britain, some Americans were happy to embrace the comparison. 'The English,
when they sneer at our country,' wrote the American explorer
Timothy Flint in *Recollections of the Last Ten Years* (1826),
'speak of it as sterile in moral interest. It has . . . no castles, no
mouldering abbeys, no baronial towers and dungeons, nothing
to connect the imagination and the heart with the past.' But we
have the Mississippi River, 'which runs the length of [our] continent, and to which all but two or three of the rivers of Europe

are but rivulets', and massive 'lakes which could find a place for the Cumberland lakes in the hollow of one of their islands'.

But despite Flint's boast it wasn't only the English who deplored the American lack of castles, abbeys and baronial towers; it was the Americans themselves. And this anxiety both preceded and was more general than that of Cooper, Hawthorne and James, because of its unease that materials were lacking not only for novels of manners but also for the more fundamental project of constructing a national identity. 'I visited the various parts of my own country,' wrote the American essayist and historian Washington Irving in his 'Author's Account' prefacing *The Sketchbook of Geoffrey Crayon, Gent.* (1819–20), a collection of tales and sketches written in and largely about Europe, 'and had I been merely a lover of fine scenery, I should have felt little desire to seek elsewhere its gratification, for on no country have the charms of nature been more prodigally lavished.' He then goes on to cite America's 'mighty lakes, like oceans of liquid silver; her mountains, with their bright aerial tints . . . her tremendous cataracts thundering in their solitude', and so on, concluding that 'never need an American look beyond his own country for the sublime and beautiful of natural scenery'.

What was missing from the American scene was a third aesthetic term, not on the same categorical level as the sublime and the beautiful, but rather an enabler, a sort of trigger to the imagination. This was association, or the mental power to connect the perceptions of diverse things, scenes and ideas over periods in time, on the principles of similarity, contrast or contiguity. This is what Europe 'had' and America didn't. Irving again:

> But Europe held forth the charms of storied [that is, historical] and poetical association. There were to be seen the masterpieces of art, the refinements of highly cultivated society, the quaint peculiarities of ancient and local custom. My native country was full of youthful promise; Europe was rich in the accumulated treasures of age. Her very ruins told the history of times gone by, and every mouldering stone was a chronicle.

So despite their revolutionary breach with the mother country, Americans weren't quite ready to abandon those artefacts that 'connect the imagination and the heart with the past', as Flint had put it. And James shared this more general anxiety about what native materials would feed the American imagination. This perceived absence helps to explain Charlotte Evans's overwhelmed response to Tintoretto's *Crucifixion* in 'Travelling Companions', Caroline Spencer's hunger for the picturesque in 'Four Meetings', and in 'An International Episode' Bessie Alden's search for charming associations in London.

III

How did that revolutionary breach with the mother country condition the European attitude to America? For mainstream British opinion in the first half of the nineteenth century the United States was an affront, an errant dinghy broken loose from the main vessel – unattached, un-navigated. So British travellers' reports of the young republic, always eagerly reviewed by the metropolitan quarterly magazines, speak of degeneration and falling away. 'Retrograding and barbarizing is an easy process,' wrote William Faux in *Memorable Days in America* (1823), a book allocated no fewer than thirty-three admiring pages in the august *Quarterly Review* for July 1823. 'Far from the laws and restraints of society, and having no servants to do that for us which was once daily done, we become too idle in time to do any thing but that which nature and necessity require.' Here men are returning 'to that state of nature,' wrote a reviewer in the *Quarterly*, this time of Morris Birkbeck's *Notes on a Journey in America* (1818), 'in which he is accountable to no earthly tribunal for his actions.' Once he has thrown off the 'restraints which a state of civilization and a sense of religion impose, he feels little inclination to re-assume them'.

Hogs in the street were a favourite trope among travellers to the States. So were the incessant smoking of 'seegars' in hotels, spitting phlegm and tobacco juice out of the windows of trains, and the aggressive habits of eating in rooming houses, where the diners lunge to the middle of the long communal table to spear potatoes, cabbages and even whole chickens before the other boarders could get to them. More thoughtful denunciations included America's lack of serious literature, poor schools, bad architecture and universal colour prejudice.

Frances Trollope, mother of the novelist, was another disappointed emigrant. Having tried and failed to make a go of an exclusive 'emporium' of ladies' fashions in the then frontier settlement of Cincinnati, she fell back on the one thing she could do well – write – and on her connections in the London book world. The result was *Domestic Manners of the Americans* (1832), a travel report that begins with a voyage up the Mississippi fuller of images of decay and fragmentation than an old-fashioned apocalyptic sermon. She railed against the unhealthy climate of Cincinnati, the emotional turmoil of evangelical camp meetings, hogs in the street (again) and the slovenly deportment of the audience in a New York theatre, where elegant women breastfed their infants and the men in boxes lounged so far back with their legs up on the front railing that they showed their rear ends. The book was a huge success on both sides of the Atlantic. Some Americans were amused by it, most were outraged, but everyone read it. 'Old Madame Vinegar', they called her. For many years afterwards people in the pit of a theatre would shout, 'A Trollope! A Trollope!' if they espied someone in a box with his legs up over the railing.

In other words, by mid-century the international theme, or at least the Anglo-American branch of it, had moved on from the vexations of American novelists and the disputes between the British and American quarterlies, into the realm of popular culture. A case in point was *Our American Cousin* (1858), a three-act farce, enormously popular on both sides of the Atlantic, by the British playwright and editor of *Punch*, Tom Taylor. Now (sadly) best remembered as the play that President Abraham Lincoln was watching for light relief on the night of his assassination, *Our American Cousin* is about an American

from Vermont, called Asa Trenchard, who crosses the Atlantic
to claim his inheritance in the form of an English country
estate. Asa is descended from a branch of the family that had
emigrated to America two centuries earlier, so of course he has
degenerated into a coarse country bumpkin, who both appals
and amuses his aristocratic English relatives, though he turns
out to have a heart of gold. Mixed into the action is Lord Dundreary, an idle, dim, comically be-whiskered nobleman with a
monocle and a lisp, who says things like:

> Dundreary: Now, I want to put your brains to the test. I want
> to ask you a whime.
> Florence: A whime, what's that?
> Dundreary: A whime is a widdle, you know.
> Florence: A widdle!
> Dundreary: Yeth; one of those things, like – why is so and so
> or somebody like somebody else?
> Florence: Oh, I see, you mean a conundrum.
> Dundreary: Yeth, a drum, that's the idea.

Edward Askew Southern, who played Dundreary, worked the
part up with an increasing number of ad libs and additional
stage business, until he became the main reason why audiences
came to see the play on both sides of the Atlantic. The play
itself prompted various imitations, like *Our Female American
Cousin* (1859), *Our American Cousin at Home, or, Lord
Dundreary Abroad* (1860) and *Dundreary Married and Done
For* (1862).

Henry James was just fifteen years old when *Our American
Cousin* premiered at Laura Keene's theatre in New York; so
despite his early fascination with the stage and his admiration
for Laura Keene in her Shakespearean roles, as described in
Chapter Nine of *A Small Boy and Others* (1913), there is
no record of his having seen *Our American Cousin*. So if
the character of Lord Lambeth seems to carry more than a
faint trace of Lord Dundreary, perhaps that is because by the
time he came to write 'An International Episode' the popular

stereotype of the bumbling English aristocrat had become so well established as to be inescapable.

But popular stereotypes – let alone stage farce – didn't go deep enough for Henry James. He was determined to treat the topic more seriously. On 8 November 1894, with 'Madame de Mauves', 'Daisy Miller', *The American* and *The Portrait of a Lady* already a decade behind him, he recalled being asked by the publisher Henry Harper if he wanted to do yet another story in the international theme, this time on the snobbishness of Americans abroad. 'The thing is not worth doing at all,' he wrote in his notebook for that date:

> unless something tolerably big and strong is got out of it. But the only way that's at all luminous to look at it is to see what there may be in it of most eloquent, most illustrative and most human – most characteristic and essential: what is its real, innermost, dramatic, tragic, comic, pathetic, ironic *note*. The primary interest is not in any mere grotesque picture of follies and misadventures, of successes and sufferings: it's in the experience of some creature that sees it and knows and judges and feels it all, that has a part to play in the episode, that is tried and tested and harrowed and exhibited by it and that forms the glass, as it were, through which we look at the diorama.

So much is packed into this paragraph that it can act as a key to the stories collected here. The international theme is not simply to be a matter of externals, of clashes of behaviour observed from outside, but of internals – the feelings of those caught up in the drama. But there's more to it than that. James cannot conceive of the 'innermost' conflict without positing an observer, one who is both part of the action and also conveying it to the reader. So the third-person narrative is increasingly saturated by the point of view of one of the characters, a consciousness that comes to shape the reader's reactions to the tale.

IV

What kind of Americans went to Europe, and why did they go? James noted two main categories, the Europhobes and the Europhiles. The hostiles – these were mainly tourists – were a bit like Randolph in 'Daisy Miller', only less funny, bearing a 'stingy grudging defiant attitude towards everything European', as James wrote to his mother from Florence on 13 October 1869, and a 'perpetual reference of all things to some American standard'. As for this lot, he thought, 'It's the absolute & incredible lack of <u>culture</u> that strikes you in common travelling Americans.'[3]

Then there were the Americans who were avid for Europe, who settled there for varying amounts of time, 'for culture or for music, for art, for the languages, for economy, for the education of [their] children' – as Henry James Senior had for his. Or more often, it was 'the unattached young American lady – the young lady travelling for culture, or relaxation, or economy', as James explained in an essay for the *Nation*. Yet even Europhile 'Americans in Europe are *outsiders*', he cautioned. Even those who settle there are denied the society of the natives. 'The compensation that comes from shops and theatres and restaurants seems insufficient to the average European mind, preoccupied as that mind is with the belief that nothing can be so agreeable as the *life* of one's native land.'[4]

It was 'the growing divorce between the American woman (with her comparative leisure, culture, grace, social instincts, artistic ambitions)', as James put it in a notebook entry of 26 November 1892, 'and the male American immersed in the ferocity of business' that made the 'unattached American woman' more likely to visit Europe than the man. Even if married, as is Mrs Westgate in 'An International Episode', their husbands' business in town kept them from coming too.

For the men, this was probably a relief. Culture was a luxury, but also a chore, something best left to the women. As Benjamin Franklin had put it in *Information to Those Who Would Remove to America* (1782), in the business of building a nation, 'Belles-lettres, . . . Paintings, Statues, Architecture, and other Works of Art . . . are more curious than useful.' Later Mark Twain and other western humorists would make a good living selling sketches to newspapers lampooning grand opera and productions of classic drama.

Charged with the urgent project of building a new nation, why were so many of James's Americans almost literally dying to immerse themselves in European culture, so determined to stay there for as long as possible, and considering it a virtual death sentence to be sent back to the States, like poor Charlotte Verver in *The Golden Bowl* (1904)? Just what was this 'culture' for which they were desperate? Surely not just what the negative cataloguers lamented the lack of. If the longed-for Europe had consisted solely of high art in museums, high learning in universities and the picturesque charms of thatched cottages and ivied ruins, then it would be very hard for the reader to empathize with James's yearning Americans for whom Europe is such an emotional inevitability.

The point that doesn't come out in the negative catalogues but does in James's fiction is that European culture isn't just *Kunst*, or art, but something closer to the sociological end of the definition of 'culture'. (James's imagination, especially when first piqued by a potential plot, often ran to the sociological, an aspect sometimes overlooked by critics). In other words, 'the masterpieces of art' and so forth are not just artefacts roped off in an art gallery.

The first story collected here makes this point well. 'Travelling Companions' was inspired by James's first tour of Europe in 1869, not as a son and brother, but as an independent adult. Having gone by ship and train from London, through Paris to Geneva, he hiked around Switzerland, then over the Alps into Italy. His itinerary through the Italian lake district, then Milan, Pavia, Brescia and Verona to Venice, was soon to be retraced by Mr Brooke, the narrator and protagonist of

'Travelling Companions' (James composed the story in the May and June immediately following his continental tour), and the ecstatic tone of his letters home to his mother, father and sister (see Notes) anticipates Brooke's reactions to his first sight of Italy.

Yet even in this most travelogue-like of the stories, the rhapsodies of Brooke and Charlotte Evans when confronted by Michelangelo, Tintoretto, Correggio, Raphael, Veronese and Giotto don't occur in art galleries (apart from the Titian in the Galleria Borghese) but in churches, cathedrals, public buildings, where the art functions in the ordinary life of these places. Note that James includes snapshots of various kinds of ordinary worshippers – a copyist, the woman in the mantilla, the 'young woman of the middle class and a man of her own rank', Charlotte herself, the Protestant half praying in the Catholic cathedral, and what old Mr Evans calls 'pretty Italian ladies saying their prayers' – as though to show that these great works are integral to the living culture, that everyone can value them on one or another level, more or less seriously, with the piety either of aesthetic appreciation or of devout belief in what they represent.

By contrast, the worst thing about Charlotte Verver's sentence is that she will become the curator of her husband's museum in American City, a frontier town west of the Mississippi. Inside this *Kunsthaus* there will be only acolytes, devotees of Art, or hapless yokels. Outside and around it there will be no bustling square overlooked by drowsy beauties gazing from balconies at 'slim young officers ... glorious with their clanking swords', as Brooke and Charlotte see from the balustrade of Milan Cathedral, no cafés, humble or fancy, in which ordinary people can meet to exchange and receive news and greetings, in which they might eat a meal, or order coffee or an alcoholic drink at any time of the day or night. That focus of sociability is also part of the culture. In the States the consumption of food and drink was segregated, if not actually regulated by law. You drank alcohol in saloons frequented by men only; you ate in restaurants, where there were any, or at home.

In fact Brooke mentions cafés almost as often as he does paintings. In his gushing descriptions of the inside of cathedrals he may be a long way from Ernest Hemingway's Jake Barnes (compare Jake's deliberately inarticulate 'It seemed like a nice cathedral, nice and dim, like Spanish churches' in *The Sun Also Rises* (1926)), but he is every bit as pleased to show off his inwardness with continental cafés and bars: the Quadri, Florian's, the Caffè Dante, the Caffè Pedrocchi.

To speak of Hemingway is to recall that Americans never flocked to Europe more than in the 1920s. What did Hemingway, Gertrude Stein, Scott Fitzgerald and others of the so-called lost generation seek in Paris? True, their dollar went a lot further (James's 'economy'). Stein was attracted by the art – seeing it, encouraging its production. But more generally Paris also offered them not just the anonymity of the metropolis, but also relative – relative, that is, to Prohibition America – liberality in matters of drinking, loving and other forms of self-expression, including writing of course.

V

So for reasons of cultural and economic verisimilitude James's treatment of the international theme centred on young American women in Europe. These are of two kinds. First, there are those who, though bright and independent, are intellectually naive, not especially ambitious to enjoy the cultural openings on offer. Daisy Miller occupies almost the whole of this field; also present, though more marginally and tentatively, is Euphemia before her marriage in 'Madame de Mauves', in her convent dreams and susceptibility to the temptations of an aristocratic attachment. Then there is the class of what James, in a notebook entry for 29 January 1884, was to call 'the self-made girl', which he intended to make 'a rival to D[aisy] M[iller]'. By 'self-made' he meant self-motivating, well read, well educated, already interested in widening her cultural experience through travel, open to new experience, curious, intellectually ambitious.

These women turned out to be more numerous, more complex and more interesting than the Daisy Millers, not least
because their very attractions often provoke their exploitation.
In time the type would develop into James's great, psychologic-
ally complex heroines, like Isabel Archer in *The Portrait of a
Lady* and Milly Theale in *The Wings of the Dove*. In this volume it is represented by Charlotte Evans, determined to grasp
the whole European experience, if not the adult human condition, through visual art; by Caroline Spencer of 'Four Meetings',
with her thirst for the picturesque; and by Bessie Alden in 'An
International Episode', who – following Irving's train of
thought as well as his terminology – 'expected the "associations" [of England] would be very charming'. Bessie dutifully
treks around the tourist sights of London, but she is more than
a tourist. In her intellectual curiosity 'she especially prized the
privilege of meeting certain celebrated persons – authors and
artists, philosophers and statesmen – of whose renown she had
been a humble and distant beholder'. As for Lord Lambeth,
she is not content to bask in the glamour of his aristocratic
company, but wants to know what he thinks, what he does in
the House of Lords (precious little, as it turns out) and how he
votes there (he doesn't).

The dramatic energy of the international theme comes from
the dialectic between the manners of the Old World and the
New. So crucial is this thematic tension that sometimes verisimilitude itself is sacrificed to keep it at concert pitch. In
revisiting *The American* (1877) for the New York Edition of
1907, James famously acknowledged that the Bellegardes, the
French aristocratic family that objected so strongly in the novel
to their daughter marrying Christopher Newman, 'would positively have jumped . . . at my rich and easy American, and not
have "minded" in the least any drawback – especially as, after
all, given the pleasant palette from which I have painted him,
there were few drawbacks to mind'. Something of the same
might be said of Lord Lambeth's mother and sister, those
august personages named faintly comically after down-market
districts of London, the Duchess of Bayswater and Lady Pimlico. Why do they intrigue to get their son and brother back

home from Newport, and why are they so snooty to Bessie and Mrs Westgate when they show up on their home turf? Their motives are irrelevant; this hostility is one of the hazards forced on the American visitors by the logic of the transatlantic theme, even if Mrs Westgate resents it more for the ladies' thinking they have scared them off than Bessie is hurt by their rejection of her as a daughter and sister-in-law.

Right on cue, the English reviewers played their part by objecting strenuously to the portrait of England in 'An International Episode'. 'We feel bound to protest against the manners of Lord Lambeth and Mr Percy Beaumont . . . being received as typical of the manners of English gentlemen', wrote Mrs F. H. Hill in her husband's *Daily News* shortly after the story appeared. 'Nor are the manners of his English fine ladies pretty.' On 21 March 1879 James wrote her a long letter defending his portraits. Lord Lambeth's repeated 'I say' she claimed to be the speech of the street, but James pointed out politely that he had heard more 'I says' in the St James's Club than he had ever heard elsewhere. In any case, he added pointedly, a novelist 'may make figures & figures without intending generalizations – generalizations of which I have a horror'.[5]

VI

Sometimes the alleged aesthetic advantages of Europe could prove dangerous. Take the picturesque, for instance. For poor Caroline Spencer it's a trap – psychically speaking, a fatal one. 'Four Meetings' opens with a cultural evening in Grimwinter, the almost-too-appropriately named town in New England.[6] They are meeting to look at photographs of Switzerland, Italy and Spain. Entranced by a view of the Castle of Chillon, Caroline Spencer asks the narrator if he has seen it for real (many times, he says), then quotes Byron's 'The Prisoner of Chillon' (1816) more accurately than he.

Jean Gooder's notes on 'Four Meetings' refer the reader to James's *Hawthorne*, about an evening at Elizabeth Peabody's, at which Hawthorne and his sisters were invited to examine a portfolio of illustrations to Dante's *Inferno* by the sculptor and illustrator John Flaxman (1755–1826). This little vignette, wrote James, expresses 'the lonely frigidity which characterized most attempts at social recreation in the New England world some forty years ago'. Here they were looking at reproductions of a European artist's designs: pictures of pictures. 'There was at that time,' James continues, 'a great desire for culture, a great interest in knowledge, in art, in aesthetics, together with a very scanty supply of the materials for such pursuits.'[7]

Sensing Caroline's hunger for these materials, the narrator says, 'I understand your case . . . You have the native American passion – the passion for the picturesque. With us, I think, it is primordial – antecedent to experience. Experience comes and only shows us something we have dreamt of.'[8] Before long, Caroline will test this proposition (as they say, to destruction), when she lands at Le Havre. The narrator is strolling with his brother-in-law along 'a wide, pleasant street, which lay half in sun and half in shade – a French provincial street, that looked like an old water-colour drawing', when they come across 'a nice little, quiet, old-fashioned café', outside which Caroline is sitting, enraptured. ' "Oh, I can't tell you," she said; "I feel as if I were in a dream. I have been sitting here for an hour, and I don't want to move. Everything is so picturesque. I don't know whether the coffee has intoxicated me; it's so delicious." '

What follows is an almost diabolical play on the idea of the picturesque. Her cousin arrives, the would-be painter in 'Byronic' velvet doublet and 'picturesque hat', with a quick eye for a 'nice bit of colour' in a 'red cloth hung out of an old window', and an even quicker eye for the main chance of Caroline's savings, which he proceeds to unlock with his picturesque tale of a poor French wife, a countess disinherited by her father. ' "My dear young lady," ' the narrator exclaims, ' "you don't want to be ruined for picturesqueness' sake?" ' But she can't shirk her family obligation. He next meets her five years later (though she seems to him to have aged a decade), easily recognizing her cottage in Grimwinter as 'the abode of a frugal old maid with a taste for the picturesque'. At this point, Caroline's only intoxicating coffee is the cup spiked with cognac that she is forced to serve the 'countess', now settled cuckoo-like in her picturesque nest.

A more notorious hazard for young American women in Europe was the loss of their reputations. As Protestants brought up in a democracy and expected to have their own opinions, they seemed 'to listen to the murmur of [their] own young spirit', as the older Madame de Mauves comments to the young Euphemia, 'rather than to the voice from behind the confessional'. Yet Old World formalities spring up to bite them unawares. One of these is the European convention inherited from aristocratic families that an unmarried daughter must always be chaperoned by a respectable relative, must never be allowed alone with an eligible man not contracted to be her husband. Any suspicion, however remote, of an earlier, un-supervised relationship that might have produced illegitimate children who might lay claims to the family's property would reduce the girl's commodity value in a marriage exchange.

So Charlotte Evans is allowed to go to Padua with Mr Brooke un-chaperoned; they miss the last train back to Venice and have to spend the night in a hotel. Thus compromised, Charlotte is the talk of the guests in her Venice hotel, and her father expects to be told that Brooke has proposed to his daughter. Reassured on this point, he walks Brooke arm-in-arm through the hotel to demonstrate that he's satisfied that the form has been observed.

Daisy Miller scandalizes everyone. With Winterbourne she goes un-chaperoned to Chillon. Later she swans about Rome on the arm of a no-account *cicerone*, a little Italian 'barber's block', as Winterbourne's aunt, Mrs Costello, calls him.

Yet just who are the onlookers so outraged by such behaviour? The guests in the Evans's hotel, Mrs Costello, Mrs Walker. Not the natives, as it happens, but other Americans on tour or living in Europe. So another hazard faced by the unwary American woman in Europe is that of other Americans. This irony is most fully developed, of course, in *The Portrait of a Lady*, where those who plot against Isabel's money and her independent spirit are the denaturalized, over-Europeanized Americans Gilbert Osmond and Serena Merle.

Mrs Costello is less cunning and sophisticated than they, less aware of her own contradictions (she finds Victor Cherbuliez's *Paule Méré* a 'pretty novel', but isn't so amused when its story plays out in real life), but equally snobbish. Without having met the Miller family, she dismisses them at Vevey as 'the sort of Americans that one does one's duty by not – not accepting'. Later, when Daisy takes up with Giovanelli, she thinks he must assume that Daisy is 'a young lady *qui se passe ses fantaisies*! [who acts according to her whims!]'.

Mrs Walker, who – as the narrator describes her, 'was one of those American ladies who, while residing abroad, make a point, in their own phrase, of studying European society' – tries to persuade Daisy not to stroll in the Pincian Gardens, and when she comes across her there, tries (again vainly) to prise her away from Giovanelli. Later, when Daisy arrives very late at her party, she explodes, ' "*Elle s'affiche* [She is making a spectacle of herself]. It's her revenge for my having ventured to remonstrate with her. When she comes I shall not speak to her." ' So Daisy Miller, an American, is confronted with the irony of two American women in Italy, first condemning, then snubbing her *in French*. That is why it's wrong to claim, as the otherwise excellent Fred Kaplan does, that '[Daisy] seems an American innocent on her own in a small-minded European culture'.[9] No, the small-mindedness belongs to the socially and culturally anxious European wannabes, the American expatriates. It's only in a foreign setting that they can dare to delineate such distinctions of class between Americans.

VII

Almost from the start of his career James's fictional men are passive and/or indecisive. In whetting Caroline Spencer's appetite for the picturesque, the first-person narrator of 'Four Meetings' may be said to have precipitated her downfall, yet respecting her privacy, he is unable to help her. Winterbourne can't work out whether Daisy's piquant wit and unconventional behaviour are evidence of brave independence or of moral laxity. He sees her as one of a type.[10] 'How pretty they are!' he thinks when he first catches sight of her. 'Were they all like that, the pretty girls who had a good deal of gentlemen's society? Or was she also a designing, an audacious, an unscrupulous young person?' Having failed to answer his own question in matching it up against an individual human being, he fails in his love, or affection, or just simple loyalty to Daisy, and thus in a sense contributes to her death. His name says it all: he is born in, and has been borne (carried) in by, winter. He is Hamlet's 'undiscovered country, from whose bourne/No traveller returns'. His problem is not just that he has been too long out of touch with his American social instincts (his and his aunt's flattering construction on the tragedy's denouement) but that although an honest and sensitive man, open to new experience, he dare not risk committing to his own emotions.

Longmore is another revealing name. His attraction to Madame de Mauves is more like longing than the passion he imagines it to be, or as David Lodge has put it, 'he longs for desire, while at the same time being fearful of it'. His powerful sympathy for Euphemia is brought to a head when he accidentally sees the Comte de Mauves with his mistress in the Paris restaurant, at which point (Lodge again) 'the young man hastens chivalrously to Madame de Mauves to offer her – what? Nothing, it seems, except the assurance of his friendship and moral support'.[11]

It's not as though this aristocratic family are putting up barriers against the fuller union of Longmore and Euphemia – quite the contrary. The Comte would be glad of his wife's affair to cover his own philandering, and his sister Madame Clairin adds to the temptation when she taunts Longmore, ' "But for Heaven's sake, if it is to lead anywhere, don't come back with that *visage de croquemort* [undertaker's face]. You look as if you were going to bury your heart – not to offer it to a pretty woman. You are much better when you smile – you are very nice then. Come, do yourself justice." '

This is, it has to be said, a challenge to the modern reader's sympathies. Of course, from the vantage point of the honourable Americans the de Mauves family are unspeakably cynical and wicked. Euphemia is determined to deny her and Long-more's delight and perhaps happiness out of faith to her marriage vows, even though vitiated by her husband. In any case, Longmore now sees it as his duty to support her. But from Madame Clairin's perspective Longmore is a timid Puritan, endlessly caught up in abstract values like purity and duty and dignity – words he applies approvingly to Euphemia – and there's a touch of priggishness to these upright (or is it uptight?) Americans.

These wavering men are treatments of that 'creature' posed by James in his 1894 notebook entry, who 'sees . . . and knows and judges and feels . . . all, that has a part to play in the episode'. As such they are part of a narrative procedure growing increasingly complex. 'Daisy Miller' is told almost throughout in the third person, but not conventionally to establish an omniscient point of view, since the reader knows almost nothing about Daisy or any other character in the drama apart from what Winterbourne perceives and thinks he knows. Endlessly flummoxed by Daisy's moral status, this sensitive 'central intelligence' (to use the Jamesian phrase) is finally disabused by the least substantial figure in the story, Giovanelli, who declares, authoritatively (because he has the first-hand experience from which Winterbourne has shied away), that 'she was the most innocent'.

In 'Madame de Mauves' the narrative moves more fluidly between points of view, because the number of central intelligences is doubled. For the most part events are seen, known, judged and felt by Longmore. But on page 68, where old Madame de Mauves advises the young, as yet unmarried Euphemia to continue to be herself, just who is hearing this in order to report it? Is it strict third-person narrative? Or something told to Longmore, or surmised by him?

Most likely, it is what Euphemia remembers of the process by which she had been snared – 'Euphemia remembered this speech in after years' – as she goes on to reflect that the occasion has since taken on a fateful portent for her. So in 'Madame de Mauves' the third-person point of view becomes multiple, reflecting the two chief consciousnesses in the tale, while still remaining partial and so never approximating the omniscient third person. It is a most remarkable technical achievement for an author who had yet to publish a full-length novel in book form.

VIII

In the last two stories in this collection, ' "Europe" ' and 'Fordham Castle', the narratives are compressed to the point of stasis. No one crosses the Atlantic to America or Europe. No one goes anywhere, let alone to the places announced in the titles. Abel Taker, alias Mr C. P. Addard, parked in a Swiss hotel like a refractory relative in a rest home, is positively forbidden from going to Fordham Castle. True, Mrs Magaw is allowed there temporarily (though we don't go with her), and Jane goes to Europe, but the narrative doesn't follow her there either, and throughout the story 'Europe' retains its quotation marks as a place in the mind only, to be assigned an increasingly darker meaning as the story evolves. If there was (in fact) little interaction between Europeans and Americans in the earlier stories, now there is none at all. For that matter, where are the Europeans? The only characters in play are American, and once again the Americans' only antagonists are other Americans.

These late tales also rework themes raised in the earlier stories, only to push them to inoperable absurdity. In ' "Europe" ' there is that old hunger for the complex aesthetic and sensuous adventure offered by Europe, as evoked in 'Travelling Companions', 'Four Meetings' and 'An International Episode'. There is also that New England moral courage to renounce immediate pleasure for duty, as Caroline renounces her life-long thirst for the European picturesque in order to help her cousin, and Euphemia renounces Longmore in order to honour her marriage vows.

But in ' "Europe" ' the quality of renunciation apparently required of old Mrs Rimmle's daughters destroys them. If Caroline's sacrifice in 'Four Meetings' kills her metaphorically, Becky's giving up 'Europe' out of loyalty to and to care for her mother kills her literally. She dies of old age, while her mother lives on. Old Mrs Rimmle, now disorientated, thinks that Jane's absence means that she has died in Europe. The tale is so compressed that, as Pierre Han has noted,[12] it fits within one long sentence articulated by Mrs Rimmle (who controls the action in other ways too), beginning with 'Our feeling is, you know, that Becky *should* go' and ending with 'to Europe'. During the course of that sentence 'Europe' has gone from promising life to signifying death.

'Fordham Castle' is even more compressed, as James intended it to be. 'Would the little idea of the "suppressed (American) mother" be feasible in 5000 words?' he asked himself in a notebook entry on 15 February 1899. 'It wd. be worth trying – for I seem to see I shall never do it in any other way.' Now the business of signifying names (Longmore, Winterbourne, and so forth) is pushed to the point almost of a parlour game – but one played in deadly earnest so as to serve the social ambitions of the absent women. Mrs Magaw must become Mrs Vanderplank. Sue, Mrs Abel Taker, has been reborn as Mrs Sherrington Reeve in order to gain entrance to Fordham Castle, forcing on her husband the moniker Mr C. P. Addard. As for his 'real' name, as Philip Horne has written, 'the husband is Abel, implying his wife is a murderous Cain; he should be "able", but has been proved incompetent, especially *as* a "taker" in the capitalist system, the reason for his wife's disgust at him; as a sacrificial stooge he is instead a helpless "giver".'[13]

And Abel accepts the role of the passive male to the point of renouncing life itself. When Mrs Magaw is allowed back, temporarily, into her daughter's circle, Taker is left, not just alone, but devastated. As her train pulls out of the station, he feels 'left, in his solitude, to the sense of his extinction. He faced it completely now, and to himself at least could express it without fear of protest. "Why certainly I'm dead."'

James wrote 'Fordham Castle' in 1904, after completing his three late, great masterpieces in the international theme, *The Wings of the Dove*, *The Ambassadors* and *The Golden Bowl*, and on the eve of his long-planned return to the United States. How did he now look on the topic? In his preface to the 'Daisy

Miller' volume (1909) of the New York Edition James said that 'Fordham Castle' had been prompted by a desire to escape from his 'appointed thematic doom' of 'too unbroken an eternity of mere international young ladies'. Had he, by now, grown weary of the topic? Bored by it? It may be that the sense one gets in reading 'Fordham Castle' and ' "Europe" ' of the international theme painting itself into a corner, if not imploding altogether, may be a sign of exhaustion, if not in the author himself, then of one of his favourite fields of imaginative play.

What else had he grown weary of? Europe? Had he, in his late years, come to regret his expatriation, as some critics allege? His 'The Jolly Corner' (1908), in which his persona returns to his childhood home in New York, only to encounter the ghost of what he might have been had he never left, suggests he was thinking along those lines. In *Roadside Meetings* (1930) Hamlin Garland, the novelist of the American Midwest, remembered visiting James in Rye in 1906. Though he found his host fit and well, and totally at ease in his physical and social surroundings, he recalls James telling him that 'If I were to live my life over again . . . I would be an American.' James's dear friend and fellow novelist Edith Wharton was having none of this. She thought it was nonsense to claim, as had some 'critics of a later generation', that James regretted having 'thwarted his genius by living in Europe'. What he missed was the old America, she wrote in *A Backward Glance* (1934); in the new 'he was never really happy or at home'.

The contrast between *The American Scene* (1907), in which James shudders at the crass materialism of contemporary America, and *A Small Boy and Others* (1913), which takes us back to a world of American notables like Emerson and Irving who were friends of the family, would seem to confirm Wharton's judgement. But there was one Americano-European comparison that James did recant in his later years: his dismissal of the native materials available to Hawthorne. This came in a letter written to commemorate the centenary of the author's birth in 1904. Now his nostalgia for the old America prompted him to reconsider Hawthorne's Salem as a 'blissfully homogenous community', providing the author with 'romance near at hand, and where it grows thick and true, rather than on the other side of the globe and in the Dictionary of Dates'.[14]

NOTES

1. Kendall Johnson, 'Henry James, 1843–1916: A Brief Biography', in John Carlos Rowe and Eric Haralson, eds., *A Historical Guide to Henry James*. Oxford: Oxford University Press, 2012, pp. 14–52.

2. *HJLL*, p. 118.

3. *CLHJ*, II, pp. 144–5.

4. Henry James, 'Americans Abroad'. *The Nation*, 3 October 1878; reprinted in *Great Britain and America*, pp. 786–92, *passim*.

5. *HJLL*, pp. 101–5, *passim*.

6. James later changed this town's name to North Verona.

7. *LCAEW*, p. 371.

8. For the New York Edition James revised this passage to 'You've the great American disease and you've got it "bad" – the appetite, morbid and monstrous, for colour and form, for the picturesque and the romantic at any price. I don't know whether we come into the world with it – with the germs implanted and antecedent to experience; rather perhaps we catch it early, almost before developed consciousness.'

9. Fred Kaplan, *Henry James: The Imagination of Genius*, (New York: Morrow, 1992), p. 196.

10. Winterbourne seeing Daisy as a 'type' is consonant with the story's half title 'A Study' on first publication. James deleted this for the New York Edition.

11. David Lodge, 'Innocent Abroad', *Guardian*, Saturday, 2 July 2005.

12. Pierre Han, 'Organic Unity in "Europe"', *South Atlantic Bulletin* 35 (1970), pp. 40–1.

13. Philip Horne, 'They Are Not Lost: The Jamesian "Note"', an unpublished paper given in Rome, 10 July 2011, at 'Transforming Henry James', a conference of the Henry James Society.

14. *LCAEW*, pp. 468–74, 470; Joseph Timothy Haydn's *Dictionary of Dates* (1841, and many subsequent editions) was an encyclopaedia of historical dates 'and Universal Reference Relating to all Ages and Nations . . .'

Further Reading

NB: *where the following are quoted in the notes and introduction, they are cited by the words, phrases or acronyms in square brackets*

GENERAL

Dover, Adrian, *The Ladder: A Henry James Website. http://www.henryjames.org.uk.*

Edel, Leon and Laurence, Dan H., *A Bibliography of Henry James*, third edn, revised with the assistance of James Rambeau (Oxford: Oxford University Press, 1982).

BIOGRAPHICAL

Edel, Leon, *Henry James: A Life* (New York: Harper & Row, 1985).

Kaplan, Fred, *Henry James: The Imagination of Genius* (London: Hodder & Stoughton, 1992).

BY HENRY JAMES

Letters

Henry James: Letters, ed. Leon Edel, 4 vols. (Cambridge, MA, and London: Belknap Press, 1974–84).

Horne, Philip (ed.), *Henry James: A Life in Letters* (London: Penguin, 1999) [*HJLL*].

The Complete Letters of Henry James, ed. Pierre A. Walker and Greg Zacharias (Lincoln, NE: University of Nebraska, 2006–) [*CLHJ*].

The Complete Letters of Henry James, 1880–1882, ed. Michael Anesko and Greg W. Zacharias (Lincoln, NE: University of Nebraska, forthcoming October 2016).

Other Writing

Collected Travel Writings, ed. Richard Howard, 2 vols. (New York: Library of America, 1993). (Includes 'Americans Abroad') [*Great Britain and America*].

The Complete Notebooks of Henry James, ed. Leon Edel and Lyall H. Powers (New York and Oxford: Oxford University Press, 1987).

The Complete Plays of Henry James, ed. Leon Edel (London: Rupert Hart-Davis, 1949).

Complete Stories, 5 vols. (New York and Cambridge: Library of America, 1996–9).

Literary Criticism: Essays on Literature, American Writers, English Writers, ed. Leon Edel and Mark Wilson (New York: Library of America, 1984) [*LCAEW*].

Literary Criticism: French Writers, Other European Writers, Prefaces to the New York Edition, ed. Leon Edel and Mark Wilson (New York: Library of America, 1984) [*LCFW*].

Notes of a Son and Brother and *The Middle Years: A Critical Edition*, ed. Peter Collister (Charlottesville, VA and London: University of Virginia Press, 2011).

A Small Boy and Others: A Critical Edition, ed. Peter Collister (Charlottesville, VA and London: University of Virginia Press, 2011).

The Tales of Henry James, ed. Maqbool Aziz, 3 vols (Oxford: The Clarendon Press, 1973–84) [*THJ1, THJ2, THJ3*].

SELECTED CRITICISM

Albers, Christina E., *A Reader's Guide to the Short Stories of Henry James* (New York: G. K. Hall, 1997).

Anesko, Michael, *'Friction with the Market': Henry James and the Profession of Authorship* (New York: Oxford University Press, 1986).

Aziz, Maqbool, 'Introduction' to *The Tales of Henry James, Volume 3, 1875–1879*, ed. Maqbool Aziz (Oxford: Oxford University Press, 1984).

Bell, Millicent, *Meaning in Henry James* (Cambridge, MA and London: Harvard University Press, 1991).

Bouraoui, H. A., 'Henry James and the French Mind: The International Theme in "Madame de Mauves"', *Novel: A Forum on Fiction* 4 (1970), pp. 69–76.

Buzard, James, *The Beaten Track: European Tourism, Literature, and the Ways to 'Culture', 1800–1918* (Oxford: Oxford University Press, 1993).

Fogel, Daniel Mark, *A Companion to Henry James Studies* (Westport, CT: Greenwood Press, 1993).

―――― *Daisy Miller: A Dark Comedy of Manners* (Boston: Twayne, 1990).

Fowler, Virginia, *Henry James's American Girl: The Embroidery on the Canvas* (Madison: University of Wisconsin, 1984).

Gooder, Jean (ed.), *Daisy Miller and Other Stories* (Oxford: Oxford University Press, World's Classics, 1985) [Gooder].

Hocks, Richard A., *Henry James: A Study of the Short Fiction* (New York: Twayne, 1990).

Horne, Philip, 'The Biography of "Daisy Miller"', in K. Reed and P. G. Beidler, eds., *Approaches to Teaching Henry James's 'Daisy Miller' and 'The Turn of the Screw'*, Approaches to Teaching World Literature, series ed. J. Gibaldi (New York: The Modern Language Association of America, 2005), pp. 46–52.

―――― *Henry James and Revision: The New York Edition* (Oxford: Oxford University Press, 1990) [*HJR*].

————, 'Henry James at Work: The Question of Our Texts', chapter in *The Cambridge Companion to Henry James*, ed. Jonathan Freedman (Cambridge: Cambridge University Press, 1998), pp. 63–78.

Leslie, Louis, ' "Writing Consciously for a Small Audience": An Exploration of the Relationship between American Magazine Culture and Henry James's Italian Fiction,1870–1875', unpublished Ph.D. thesis (University College London, n.d.) [Leslie].

Lodge, David (ed.), *Daisy Miller* (New York: Penguin, 2007).

———— 'Innocent Abroad,' *Guardian*, 2 July 2005.

McWhirter, David, *Henry James in Context* (Cambridge: Cambridge University Press, 2010).

Poole, Adrian (ed.), *Daisy Miller and An International Episode* (Oxford: Oxford University Press, World's Classics, 2013) [Poole].

Reeve, N. H. (ed.), *Henry James: The Shorter Fiction Reassessment* (Basingstoke: Palgrave Macmillan, 1997).

———— (ed.), *'The Jolly Corner' and Other Stories* (a volume of *The Complete Fiction of Henry James* (Cambridge: Cambridge University Press), forthcoming) [Reeve].

Roberts, Priscilla, 'The Geopolitics of Literature: The Shifting International Theme in the Works of Henry James', *International History Review* 34 (2012), pp. 89–114.

Tintner, Adeline R., ' "An International Episode": A Centennial Review of a Centennial Story', *Henry James Review* 1 (1979), pp. 24–56 [Tintner].

Wardley, Lynn, 'Reassembling Daisy Miller', *American Literary History* 3 (1991), pp. 232–55.

Wrenn, Angus, *Henry James and the Second Empire* (Oxford: Legenda, 2009).

A Note on the Text

Typically James would publish a tale first in a magazine like *The Atlantic Monthly*, *The Galaxy* or *The Cornhill*, then revise it for publication in successive collections of his shorter fiction, finally revising it for the twenty-four-volume New York Edition comprising almost all his fiction – novels as well as novellas and short stories – that appeared in 1907–1909. A rare exception to this rule is the first of the stories collected here, 'Travelling Companions', which appeared in serial form only and was never revised for collection later.

The texts in this collection are, where relevant, the first book version of the tale. The principle behind this selection is that it preserves the benefit of James's (almost always improving) revisions, while still preserving the chronological development of his thoughts around the international theme. What appears below is a list showing the periodical in which each tale appeared, followed by its first publication in book form.

'Travelling Companions', *The Atlantic Monthly*, November, December 1870; no book form.

'Madame de Mauves', *The Galaxy*, February, March 1874; first book form, *A Passionate Pilgrim and Other Tales* (Boston: James R. Osgood, 1875).

'Four Meetings', *Scribner's Monthly*, November 1877; first book form, *Daisy Miller: A Study, An International Episode, Four Meetings*, 2 vols. (London: Macmillan, 1879).

'Daisy Miller', *The Cornhill Magazine*, June, July 1878; first book form, *Daisy Miller* (as above).

'An International Episode', *The Cornhill Magazine*, December
    1878, January 1879; first book form, *Daisy Miller* (as above).
' "Europe" ', *Scribner's Magazine*, June 1899; first book form,
    The Soft Side (London: Methuen, 1900).
'Fordham Castle', *Harper's Magazine*, December 1904; first
    book form, the New York Edition (New York: Scribner;
    London: Macmillan, 1907–1909), 24 vols., vol 16.

Since the stories come from various sources and are somewhat
inconsistent in spelling and punctuation, these have been
standardized throughout this volume. In addition, some errors,
mostly the printers', have been corrected by reference to earlier
and later texts; some minor adjustments have been made to
punctuation, including the substitution of n-rule dashes for
m-rule except for broken-off speech and sentences. Contrac-
tions opened up by James (e.g. could n't) have been closed up
(couldn't). Single quotation marks replace double ones, and for
a single word or phrase in quotation marks, the closing mark
is placed before a comma or full stop. In accordance with Penguin Classics style, spelling has been anglicized and 'ise'
spellings have been standardized throughout to 'ize'. There has
been no attempt to regularize James's use of italics for foreign
words and expressions.

Daisy Miller
and Other Tales

TRAVELLING COMPANIONS

I

The most strictly impressive picture in Italy is incontestably the Last Supper of Leonardo at Milan.[1] A part of its immense solemnity is doubtless due to its being one of the first of the great Italian masterworks that you encounter in coming down from the North. Another secondary source of interest resides in the very completeness of its decay. The mind finds a rare delight in filling each of its vacant spaces, effacing its rank defilement, and repairing, as far as possible, its sad disorder. Of the essential power and beauty of the work there can be no better evidence than this fact that, having lost so much, it has yet retained so much. An unquenchable elegance lingers in those vague outlines and incurable scars; enough remains to place you in sympathy with the unfathomable wisdom of the painter. The fresco covers a wall, the reader will remember,[2] at the end of the former refectory of a monastery now suppressed, the precinct of which is occupied by a regiment of cavalry. Horses stamp, soldiers rattle their oaths, in the cloisters which once echoed to the sober tread of monastic sandals and the pious greetings of meek-voiced friars.

It was the middle of August, and summer sat brooding fiercely over the streets of Milan. The great brick-wrought dome of the church of St Mary of the Graces rose black with the heat against the brazen sky. As my *fiacre* drew up in front of the church, I found another vehicle in possession of the little square of shade which carpeted the glaring pavement before the adjoining convent. I left the two drivers to share this advantage as they could, and made haste to enter the cooler presence of the Cenacolo.[3] Here I found the occupants of the *fiacre* without, a young lady and an elderly man. Here also, besides the official who takes your tributary franc, sat a long-haired copyist, wooing back the silent secrets of the great fresco into the cheerfullest commonplaces of yellow and blue. The gentleman was earnestly watching this ingenious operation; the young lady sat with her eyes fixed on the picture, from which she failed to move them when I took my place on a line with her. I too, however, speedily became as unconscious of her presence as she of mine, and lost myself in the study of the work before us. A single glance[4] had assured me that she was an American.

Since that day, I have seen all the great art treasures of Italy: I have seen Tintoretto at Venice, Michael Angelo at Florence and Rome, Correggio[5] at Parma; but I have looked at no other picture with an emotion equal to that which rose within me as this great creation of Leonardo slowly began to dawn upon my intelligence from the tragical twilight of its ruin. A work so nobly conceived can never utterly die, so long as the half-dozen main lines of its design remain. Neglect and malice are less cunning than the genius of the great painter. It has stored away with masterly skill such a wealth of beauty as only perfect love and sympathy can fully detect. So, under my eyes, the restless ghost of the dead fresco returned to its mortal abode. From the beautiful central image of Christ I perceived its radiation right and left along the sadly broken line of the disciples. One by one, out of the depths of their grim dismemberment, the figures trembled into meaning and life, and the vast, serious beauty of the work stood revealed. What is the ruling force of this magnificent design? Is it art? is it science? is it sentiment? is it knowledge? I am sure I can't say; but in moments of doubt and depression I find it of excellent use to recall the great picture with all possible distinctness. Of all the works of man's hands it is the least superficial.

The young lady's companion finished his survey of the copyist's work and came and stood behind his chair. The reader will remember that a door[6] has been rudely cut in the wall, a part of it entering the fresco.

'He hasn't got in that door,' said the old gentleman, speaking apparently of the copyist.

The young lady was silent. 'Well, my dear,' he continued. 'What do you think of it?'

The young girl gave a sigh. 'I see it,' she said.

'You see it, eh? Well, I suppose there is nothing more to be done.'

The young lady rose slowly, drawing on her glove. As her eyes were still on the fresco, I was able to observe her. Beyond doubt she was American. Her age I fancied to be twenty-two. She was of middle stature, with a charming slender figure. Her hair was brown, her complexion fresh and clear. She wore a white piqué[7] dress and a black lace shawl, and on her thick dark braids a hat with a purple feather.[8] She was largely characterized by that physical delicacy and that personal elegance (each of them sometimes excessive) which seldom fail to betray my young countrywomen in Europe. The gentleman, who was obviously her father, bore the national stamp as plainly as she. A shrewd, firm, generous face, which told of many dealings with many men, of stocks and shares and current prices, – a face, moreover, in which there lingered the mellow afterglow of a sense of excellent claret. He was bald and grizzled, this perfect American, and he wore a short-bristled white moustache between the two hard wrinkles forming the sides of a triangle of which his mouth was the base and the ridge of his nose, where his eye-glass sat, the apex. In deference perhaps to this exotic growth, he was better dressed than is common with the typical American citizen, in a blue necktie, a white waistcoat, and a pair of grey trousers. As his daughter still lingered, he looked at me with an eye of sagacious conjecture.

'Ah, that beautiful, beautiful, beautiful Christ,' said the young lady, in a tone which betrayed her words in spite of its softness. 'O father, what a picture!'

'Hum!' said her father. 'I don't see it.'

'I must get a photograph,' the young girl rejoined. She turned away and walked to the farther end of the hall, where the custodian presides at a table of photographs and prints. Meanwhile her father had perceived my Murray.[9]

'English, sir?' he demanded.

'No, I'm an American, like yourself, I fancy.'

'Glad to make your acquaintance, sir. From New York?'

'From New York. I have been absent from home, however, for a number of years.'

'Residing in this part of the world?'

'No. I have been living in Germany. I have only just come into Italy.'

'Ah, so have we. The young lady is my daughter. She is crazy about Italy. We were very nicely fixed at Interlaken,[10] when suddenly she read in some confounded book or other that Italy should be seen in summer. So she dragged me over the mountains into this fiery furnace. I'm actually melting away. I have lost five pounds in three days.'

I replied that the heat was indeed intense, but that I agreed with his daughter that Italy should be seen in summer. What could be pleasanter than the temperature of that vast cool hall?

'Ah, yes,' said my friend; 'I suppose we shall have plenty of this kind of thing. It makes no odds to me, so long as my poor girl has a good time.'

'She seems,' I remarked, 'to be having a pretty good time with the photographs.' In fact, she was comparing photographs with a great deal of apparent energy, while the salesman lauded his wares in the Italian manner. We strolled over to the table. The young girl was seemingly in treaty for a large photograph of the head of Christ, in which the blurred and fragmentary character of the original was largely intensified, though much of its exquisite pathetic beauty was also preserved. 'They'll not think much of that at home,' said the old gentleman.

'So much the worse for them,' said his daughter, with an accent of delicate pity. With the photograph in her hand, she walked back to the fresco. Her father engaged in an English dialogue with the custodian. In the course of five minutes, wishing likewise to compare the copy and the original, I returned to the great picture. As I drew near it the young lady turned away. Her eyes then for the first time met my own. They were deep and dark and luminous, – I fancied streaming with tears. I watched her as she returned to the table. Her walk

seemed to me peculiarly graceful; light, and rapid, and yet full
of decision and dignity. A thrill of delight passed through my
heart as I guessed at her moistened lids.

'Sweet fellow-countrywoman,' I cried in silence, 'you have
the divine gift of feeling.' And I returned to the fresco with a
deepened sense of its virtue. When I turned around, my companions had left the room.

In spite of the great heat, I was prepared thoroughly to 'do'
Milan. In fact, I rather enjoyed the heat; it seemed to my
Northern senses to deepen the Italian, the Southern, the local
character of things. On that blazing afternoon, I have not forgotten, I went to the church of St Ambrose, to the Ambrosian
Library,[11] to a dozen minor churches. Every step distilled a
richer drop into the wholesome cup of pleasure. From my earli-
est manhood, beneath a German sky, I had dreamed of this
Italian pilgrimage, and, after much waiting and working and
planning, I had at last undertaken it in a spirit of fervent devotion. There had been moments in Germany when I fancied
myself a clever man; but it now seemed to me that for the first
time I really *felt* my intellect. Imagination, panting and
exhausted, withdrew from the game; and Observation stepped
in to her place, trembling and glowing with open-eyed desire.

I had already been twice to the Cathedral,[12] and had wandered through the clustering inner darkness of the high arcades
which support those light-defying pinnacles and spires.
Towards the close of the afternoon I found myself strolling
once more over the great column-planted, altar-studded pavement, with the view of ascending to the roof. On presenting
myself at the little door in the right transept, through which
you gain admission to the upper regions, I perceived my late
fellow-visitors of the fresco preparing apparently for an upward
movement, but not without some reluctance on the paternal
side. The poor gentleman had been accommodated with a
chair, on which he sat fanning himself with his hat and looking painfully apoplectic. The sacristan meanwhile held open
the door with an air of invitation. But my corpulent friend,
with his thumb in his Murray, balked at the ascent. Recognizing me, his face expressed a sudden sense of vague relief.

'Have you been up, sir?' he inquired, groaningly.

I answered that I was about to ascend; and recalling then the fact, which I possessed rather as information than experience, that young American ladies may not improperly detach themselves on occasion from the parental side, I ventured to declare that, if my friend was unwilling to encounter the fatigue of mounting to the roof in person, I should be most happy, as a fellow-countryman, qualified already perhaps to claim a traveller's acquaintance, to accompany and assist his daughter.

'You're very good, sir,' said the poor man; 'I confess that I'm about played out. I'd far rather sit here and watch these pretty Italian ladies saying their prayers. Charlotte, what do you say?'

'Of course if you're tired I should be sorry to have you make the effort,' said Charlotte. 'But I believe the great thing is to see the view from the roof. I'm much obliged to the gentleman.'

It was arranged accordingly that we should ascend together. 'Good luck to you,' cried my friend, 'and mind you take good care of her.'

Those who have rambled among the marble immensities of the summit of Milan Cathedral will hardly expect me to describe them. It is only when they have been seen as a complete concentric whole that they can be properly appreciated. It was not as a whole that I saw them; a week in Italy had assured me that I have not the architectural *coup d'œil*. In looking back on the scene into which we emerged from the stifling spiral of the ascent, I have chiefly a confused sense of an immense skyward elevation and a fierce blinding efflorescence of fantastic forms of marble. There, reared for the action of the sun, you find a vast marble world. The solid whiteness lies in mighty slabs along the iridescent slopes of nave and transept, like the lonely snow-fields of the higher Alps. It leaps and climbs and shoots and attacks the unsheltered blue with a keen and joyous incision. It meets the pitiless sun with a more than equal glow; the day falters, declines, expires, but the marble shines forever, unmelted and unintermittent. You will know what I mean if you have looked upward from the Piazza at midnight. With confounding frequency too, on some uttermost point of a pinnacle, its plastic force explodes into satisfied rest in some perfect flower of a figure. A myriad carven statues, known only to the circling air, are poised and niched beyond reach of human vision, the loss of which to mortal eyes is, I suppose, the gain of the Church and the Lord. Among all the jewelled shrines and overwrought tabernacles of Italy, I have seen no such magnificent waste of labour, no such glorious synthesis of cunning secrets. As you wander, sweating and blinking, over the changing levels of the edifice, your eye catches at a hundred points the little profile of a little saint, looking out into the dizzy air, a pair of folded hands praying to the bright immediate heavens, a sandalled monkish foot planted on the edge of the white abyss. And then, besides this mighty world of the great Cathedral itself, you possess the view of all green Lombardy, – vast, lazy Lombardy, resting from its Alpine upheavals.

My companion carried a little white umbrella, with a violet lining. Thus protected from the sun, she climbed and gazed with abundant courage and spirit. Her movements, her glance, her voice, were full of intelligent pleasure. Now that I could observe her closely, I saw that, though perhaps without regular beauty, she was yet, for youth, summer, and Italy, more than pretty enough. Owing to my residence in Germany, among Germans, in a small university town, Americans had come to have for me, in a large degree, the interest of novelty and remoteness. Of the charm of American women, in especial, I had formed a very high estimate, and I was more than ready to be led captive by the far-famed graces of their frankness and freedom. I already felt that in the young girl beside me there was a different quality of womanhood from any that I had recently known; a keenness, a maturity, a conscience, which deeply stirred my curiosity. It was positive, not negative maidenhood.

'You're an American,' I said, as we stepped to look at the distance.

'Yes; and you?' In her voice alone the charm faltered. It was high, thin, and nervous.

'O, happily, I'm also one.'

'I shouldn't have thought so. I should have taken you for a German.'

'By education I am a German. I knew you were an American the moment I looked at you.'

'I suppose so. It seems that American women are easily recognized. But don't talk about America.' She paused and swept her dark eye over the whole immensity of prospect. 'This is Italy,' she cried, 'Italy, Italy!'

'Italy indeed. What do you think of the Leonardo?'

'I fancy there can be only one feeling about it. It must be the saddest and finest of all pictures. But I know nothing of art. I have seen nothing yet but that lovely Raphael in the Brera.'[13]

'You have a vast deal before you. You're going southward, I suppose.'

'Yes, we are going directly to Venice. There I shall see Titian.'

'Titian and Paul Veronese.'[14]

'Yes, I can hardly believe it. Have you ever been in a gondola?'

'No; this is my first visit to Italy.'

'Ah, this is all new, then, to you as well.'

'Divinely new,' said I, with fervour.

She glanced at me, with a smile – a ray of friendly pleasure in my pleasure. 'And you are not disappointed!'

'Not a jot. I'm too good a German.'

'I'm too good an American. I live at Araminta, New Jersey!'[15]

We thoroughly 'did' the high places of the church, concluding with an ascent into the little gallery of the central spire. The view from this spot is beyond all words, especially the view toward the long mountain line which shuts out the North. The sun was sinking: clear and serene upon their blue foundations, the snow-peaks sat clustered and scattered, and shrouded in silence and light. To the south the long shadows fused and multiplied, and the bosky Lombard flats melted away into perfect Italy. This prospect offers a great emotion to the Northern traveller. A vague, delicious impulse of conquest stirs in his heart. From his dizzy vantage-point, as he looks down at her, beautiful, historic, exposed, he embraces the whole land in the far-reaching range of his desire. 'That is Monte Rosa,' I said; 'that is the Simplon pass;[16] there is the triple glitter of those lovely lakes.'

'Poor Monte Rosa,' said my companion.

'I'm sure I never thought of Monte Rosa as an object of pity.'

'You don't know what she represents. She represents the genius of the North. There she stands, frozen and fixed, resting her head upon that mountain wall, looking over at this lovely southern world and yearning towards it forever in vain.'

'It is very well she can't come over. She would melt.'

'Very true. She is beautiful, too, in her own way. I mean to fancy that I am her chosen envoy, and that I have come up here to receive her blessing.'

I made an attempt to point out a few localities. 'Yonder lies Venice, out of sight. In the interval are a dozen divine little towns. I hope to visit them all. I shall ramble all day in their streets and churches, their little museums, and their great palaces. In the evening I shall sit at the door of a café in the little piazza, scanning some lovely civic edifice in the moonlight, and saying, "Ah! this is Italy!"'

'You gentlemen are certainly very happy. I'm afraid we must go straight to Venice.'

'Your father insists upon it?'

'He wishes it. Poor father! in early life he formed the habit of being in a hurry, and he can't break it even now, when, being out of business, he has nothing on earth to do.'

'But in America I thought daughters insisted as well as fathers.'

The young girl looked at me, half serious, half smiling. 'Have you a mother?' she asked; and then, blushing the least bit at her directness and without waiting for an answer, 'This is not America,' she said. 'I should like to think I might become for a while a creature of Italy.'

Somehow I felt a certain contagion in her momentary flash of frankness.

'I strongly suspect,' I said, 'that you are American to the

depths of your soul, and that you'll never be anything else; I hope not.'

In this hope of mine there was perhaps a little impertinence; but my companion looked at me with a gentle smile, which seemed to hint that she forgave it. 'You, on the other hand,' she said, 'are a perfect German, I fancy; and you'll never be anything else.'

'I am sure I wish with all my heart,' I answered, 'to be a good American. I'm open to conversion. Try me.'

'Thank you; I haven't the ardour; I'll make you over to my father. We mustn't forget, by the way, that he is waiting for us.'

We did forget it, however, awhile longer. We came down from the tower and made our way to the balustrade which edges the front of the edifice, and looked down on the city and the piazza below. Milan had, to my sense, a peculiar charm of temperate gayety – the softness of the South without its laxity; and I felt as if I could gladly spend a month there. The common life of the streets was beginning to stir and murmur again, with the subsiding heat and the approaching night. There came up into our faces a delicious emanation as from the sweetness of Transalpine life. At the little balconies of the windows, beneath the sloping awnings, with their feet among the crowded flower-pots and their plump bare arms on the iron rails, lazy, dowdy Italian beauties would appear, still drowsy with the broken *siesta*. Beautiful, slim young officers had begun to dot the pavement, glorious with their clanking swords, their brown moustaches, and their legs of azure. In gentle harmony with these, various ladies of Milan were issuing forth to enjoy the cool; elegant, romantic, provoking, in short black dresses and lace mantillas[17] depending from their *chignons*, with a little cloud of powder artfully enhancing the darkness of their hair and eyes. How it all wasn't Germany! How it couldn't have been Araminta, New Jersey! 'It's the South, the South,' I kept repeating, – 'the South in nature, in man, in manners.' It was a brighter world. 'It's the South,' I said to my companion. 'Don't you feel it in all your nerves?'

'O, it's very pleasant,' she said.

'We must forget all our cares and duties and sorrows. We

must go in for the beautiful. Think of this great trap for the sunbeams, in this city of yellows and russets and crimsons, of liquid vowels and glancing smiles being, like one of our Northern cathedrals, a temple to Morality and Conscience. It doesn't belong to heaven, but to earth – to love and light and pleasure.'

My friend was silent a moment. 'I'm glad I'm not a Catholic,' she said at last. 'Come, we must go down.'

We found the interior of the Cathedral delightfully cool and shadowy. The young lady's father was not at our place of ingress, and we began to walk through the church in search of him. We met a number of Milanese ladies, who charmed us with their sombre elegance and the Spanish romance of their veils. With these pale penitents and postulants my companion had a lingering sisterly sympathy.

'Don't you wish you were a Catholic now?' I asked. 'It would be so pleasant to wear one of those lovely mantillas.'

'The mantillas are certainly becoming,' she said. 'But who knows what horrible old-world sorrows and fears and remorses they cover? Look at this person.' We were standing near the great altar. As she spoke, a woman rose from her knees, and as she drew the folds of her lace mantle across her bosom, fixed her large dark eyes on us with a peculiar significant intensity. She was of less than middle age, with a pale, haggard face, a certain tarnished elegance of dress, and a remarkable nobleness of gesture and carriage. She came towards us, with an odd mixture, in her whole expression, of decency and defiance. 'Are you English?' she said in Italian. 'You are very pretty. Is he a brother or a lover?'

'He is neither,' said I, affecting a tone of rebuke.

'Neither? Only a friend! You are very happy to have a friend, Signorina. Ah, you are pretty! You were watching me at my prayers just now; you thought me very curious, apparently. I don't care. You may see me here any day. But I devoutly hope you may never have to pray such bitter, bitter prayers as mine. A thousand excuses.' And she went her way.

'What in the world does she mean?' said my companion.

'Monte Rosa,' said I, 'was the genius of the North. This

poor woman is the genius of the Picturesque.[18] She shows us the essential misery that lies behind it. It's not an unwholesome lesson to receive at the outset. Look at her sweeping down the aisle. What a poise of the head! The picturesque is handsome, all the same.'

'I do wonder what is her trouble,' murmured the young girl. 'She has swept away an illusion in the folds of those black garments.'

'Well,' said I, 'here is a solid fact to replace it.' My eyes had just lighted upon the object of our search. He sat in a chair, half tilted back against a pillar. His chin rested on his shirt-bosom, and his hands were folded together over his waistcoat, where it most protruded. Shirt and waistcoat rose and fell with visible, audible regularity. I wandered apart and left his daughter to deal with him. When she had fairly aroused him, he thanked me heartily for my care of the young lady, and expressed the wish that we might meet again. 'We start to-morrow for Venice,' he said. 'I want awfully to get a whiff of the sea-breeze and to see if there is anything to be got out of a gondola.'

As I expected also to be in Venice before many days, I had little doubt of our meeting. In consideration of this circumstance, my friend proposed that we should exchange cards; which we accordingly did, then and there, before the high altar, above the gorgeous chapel which enshrines the relics of St Charles Borromeus.[19] It was thus that I learned his name to be Mr Mark Evans.

'Take a few notes for us!' said Miss Evans, as I shook her hand in farewell.

I spent the evening, after dinner, strolling among the crowded streets of the city, tasting of Milanese humanity. At the door of a café I perceived Mr Evans seated at a little round table. He seemed to have discovered the merits of absinthe. I wondered where he had left his daughter. She was in her room, I fancied, writing her journal.

The fortnight which followed my departure from Milan was in all respects memorable and delightful. With an interest that hourly deepened as I read, I turned the early pages of the

enchanting romance of Italy. I carried out in detail the programme which I had sketched for Miss Evans. Those few brief
days, as I look back on them, seem to me the sweetest, fullest,
calmest of my life. All personal passions, all restless egotism,
all worldly hopes, regrets, and fears were stilled and absorbed
in the steady perception of the material present. It exhaled the
pure essence of romance. What words can reproduce the picture
which these Northern Italian towns project upon a sympathetic
retina? They are shabby, deserted, dreary, decayed, unclean. In
those August days the southern sun poured into them with a
fierceness which might have seemed fatal to any lurking shadow
of picturesque mystery. But taking them as cruel time had made
them and left them, I found in them an immeasurable instruction and charm. My perception seemed for the first time to live
a sturdy creative life of its own. How it fed upon the mouldy
crumbs of the festal past! I have always thought the observant
faculty a windy impostor, so long as it refuses to pocket pride
and doff its bravery and crawl on all-fours, if need be, into the
unillumined corners and crannies of life. In these dead cities of
Verona, Mantua, Padua, how life had revelled and postured in
its strength! How sentiment and passion had blossomed and
flowered! How much of history had been performed! What a
wealth of mortality had ripened and decayed! I have never elsewhere got so deep an impression of the social secrets of mankind.
In England, even, in those verdure-stifled haunts of domestic
peace which muffle the sounding chords of British civilization,
one has a fainter sense of the possible movement and fruition of
individual character. Beyond a certain point you fancy it merged
in the general medium of duty, business, and politics. In Italy,
in spite of your knowledge of the strenuous public conscience
which once unflamed these compact little states, the unapplied,
spontaneous moral life of society seems to have been more
active and more subtle. I walked about with a volume of Stendahl[20] in my pocket; at every step I gathered some lingering
testimony to the exquisite vanity of ambition.

But the great emotion, after all, was to feel myself among
scenes in which art had ranged so freely. It had often enough
been bad, but it had never ceased to be art. An invincible

instinct of beauty had presided at life, – an instinct often ludi-
crously crude and primitive. Wherever I turned I found a vital
principle of grace, – from the smile of a chambermaid to the
curve of an arch. My memory reverts with an especial tenderness to certain hours in the dusky, faded saloons of those
vacant, ruinous palaces which boast of 'collections'. The pictures are frequently poor, but the visitor's impression is
generally rich. The brick-tiled floors are bare; the doors lack
paint; the great windows, curtains; the chairs and tables have
lost their gilding and their damask drapery; but the ghost of a
graceful aristocracy treads at your side and does the melancholy honours of the abode with a dignity that brooks no
sarcasm. You feel that art and piety here have been blind, generous instincts. You are reminded in persuasive accents of the
old personal regimen in human affairs. Certain pictures are
veiled and curtained *virginibus puerisque*.[21] Through these
tarnished halls lean and patient abbés led their youthful virginal pupils. Have you read Stendahl's *Chartreuse de Parme*?[22]
There was such a gallery in the palace of the Duchess of San
Severino. After a long day of strolling, lounging, and staring, I
found a singularly perfect pleasure in sitting at the door of a
café in the warm starlight, eating an ice and making an occasional experiment in the way of talk with my neighbours. I
recall with peculiar fondness and delight three sweet sessions
in the delicious Piazza die Signori[23] at Verona. The Piazza is
small, compact, private almost, accessible only to pedestrians,
paved with great slabs which have known none but a gentle
human tread. On one side of it rises in elaborate elegance and
grace, above its light arched *loggia*, the image-bordered mass
of the ancient palace of the Council; facing this stand two
sterner, heavier buildings, dedicated to municipal offices and
to the lodgement of soldiers. Step through the archway which
leads out of the Piazza and you will find a vast quadrangle
with a staircase climbing sunward, along the wall, a row of
gendarmes sitting in the shade, a group of soldiers cleaning
their muskets, a dozen persons of either sex leaning downward
from the open windows. At one end of the little square rose
into the pale darkness the high slender shaft of a brick

campanile; in the centre glittered steadily a colossal white statue of Dante.[24] Behind this statue was the Caffè Dante, where on three successive days I sat till midnight, feeling the scene, learning its sovereign 'distinction'. But of Verona I shall not pretend to speak. As I drew near Venice I began to feel a soft impatience, an expectant tremor of the heart. The day before reaching it I spent at Vicenza. I wandered all day through the streets, of course, looking at Palladio's palaces and enjoying them in defiance of reason and Ruskin.[25] They seemed to me essentially rich and palatial. In the evening I resorted, as usual, to the city's generous heart, the decayed ex-glorious Piazza. This spot at Vicenza affords you a really soul-stirring premonition of Venice. There is no Byzantine Basilica and no Ducal Palace; but there is an immense impressive hall of council, and a soaring campanile, and there are two discrowned columns telling of defeated Venetian dominion. Here I seated myself before a café door, in a group of gossiping votaries of the Southern night. The tables being mostly occupied, I had some difficulty in finding one. In a short time I perceived a young man walking through the crowd, seeking where he might bestow himself. Passing near me, he stopped and asked me with irresistible grace if he might share my table. I cordially assented; he sat down and ordered a glass of sugar and water. He was of about my own age, apparently, and full of the opulent beauty of the greater number of young Italians. His dress was simple even to shabbiness: he might have been a young prince in disguise, a Haroun-al-Raschid.[26] With small delay we engaged in conversation. My companion was boyish, modest, and gracious; he nevertheless discoursed freely on the things of Vicenza. He was so good as to regret that we had not met earlier in the day; it would have given him such pleasure to accompany me on my tour of the city. He was passionately fond of art: he was in fact an artist. Was I fond of pictures? Was I inclined to purchase? I answered that I had no desire to purchase modern pictures, that in fact I had small means to purchase any. He informed me that he had a beautiful ancient work which, to his great regret, he found himself compelled to sell; a most divine little

Correggio. Would I do him the favour to look at it? I had small belief in the value of this unrenowned masterpiece; but I felt a kindness for the young painter. I consented to have him call for me the next morning and take me to his house, where for two hundred years, he assured me, the work had been jealously preserved.

He came punctually, beautiful, smiling, shabby, as before. After a ten minutes' walk we stopped before a gaudy half-palazzo which rejoiced in a vague Palladian air. In the basement, looking on the court, lived my friend; with his mother, he informed me, and his sister. He ushered me in, through a dark antechamber, into which, through a gaping kitchen door, there gushed a sudden aroma of onions. I found myself in a high, half-darkened saloon. One of the windows was open into the court, from which the light entered verdantly through a row of flowering plants. In an arm-chair near the window sat a young girl in a dressing-gown, empty-handed, pale, with wonderful eyes, apparently an invalid. At her side stood a large elderly woman in a rusty black silk gown, with an agreeable face, flushed a little, apparently with the expectation of seeing me. The young man introduced them as his mother and his sister. On a table near the window, propped upright in such a way as to catch the light, was a small picture in a heavy frame. I proceeded to examine it. It represented in simple composition a Madonna and Child; the mother facing you, pressing the infant to her bosom, faintly smiling, and looking out of the picture with a solemn sweetness. It was pretty, it was good; but it was not Correggio. There was indeed a certain suggestion of his exquisite touch; but it was a likeness merely, and not the precious reality. One fact, however, struck swiftly home to my consciousness: the face of the Madonna bore a singular resemblance to that of Miss Evans. The lines, the character, the expression, were the same; the faint half-thoughtful smile was hers, the feminine frankness and gentle confidence of the brow, from which the dark hair waved back with the same even abundance. All this, in the Madonna's face, was meant for heaven; and on Miss Evans's in a fair degree, probably, for earth. But the mutual likeness was, nevertheless, perfect, and it quickened my interest in the picture to a point which the intrinsic merit of the work would doubtless have failed to justify; although I confess that I was now not slow to discover a great deal of agreeable painting in it.

'But I doubt of its being a Correggio,' said I.

'A Correggio, I give you my word of honour, sir!' cried my young man.

'*Ecco!* my son's word of honour,' cried his mother.

'I don't deny,' I said, 'that it is a very pretty work. It is perhaps Parmigianino.'[27]

'O no, sir,' the elder insisted, 'a true Correggio! We have had it two hundred years! Try another light; you will see. A true Correggio! Isn't it so, my daughter?'

The young man put his arm in mine, played his fingers airily over the picture, and whispered of a dozen beauties.

'O, I grant you,' said I, 'it's a very pretty picture.' As I looked at it I felt the dark eyes of the young girl in the arm-chair fixed upon me with almost unpleasant intensity. I met her gaze for a moment: I found in it a strange union of defiant pride and sad despondent urgency.

'What do you ask for the picture?' I said.

There was a silence.

'Speak, *madre mia*,' said the young man.

'*La senta!*' and the lady played with her broken fan. 'We should like you to name a price.'

'O, if I named a price, it would not be as for a Correggio. I can't afford to buy Correggios. If this were a real Correggio, you would be rich. You should go to a duke, a prince, not to me.'

'We would be rich! Do you hear, my children? We are very poor, sir. You have only to look at us. Look at my poor daughter. She was once beautiful, fresh, gay. A year ago she fell ill: a long story, sir, and a sad one. We have had doctors; they have ordered five thousand things. My daughter gets no better. There it is, sir. We are very poor.'

The young girl's look confirmed her mother's story. That she had been beautiful I could easily believe; that she was ill was equally apparent. She was still remarkable indeed for a touching, hungry, unsatisfied grace. She remained silent and motionless, with her eyes fastened upon my face. I again examined the pretended Correggio. It was wonderfully like Miss Evans. The young American rose up in my mind with irresistible vividness and grace. How she seemed to glow with strength, freedom, and joy, beside this sombre, fading, Southern sister! It was a happy thought that, under the benediction of her image, I might cause a ray of healing sunshine to fall at this poor girl's feet.

'Have you ever tried to sell the picture before?'

'Never!' said the old lady, proudly. 'My husband had it from his father. If we have made up our minds to part with it now – most blessed little Madonna! – it is because we have had an intimation from heaven.'

'From heaven?'

'From heaven, Signore. My daughter had a dream. She dreamed that a young stranger came to Vicenza, and that he wandered about the streets saying, "Where, ah where, is my blessed Lady?" Some told him in one church, and some told him in another. He went into all the churches and lifted all the curtains, giving great fees to the sacristans! But he always came out shaking his head and repeating his question, "Where is my blessed Lady? I have come from over the sea, I have come to Italy to find her!"' The woman delivered herself of this recital with a noble florid unction and a vast redundancy, to my Northern ear, of delightful liquid sounds. As she paused momentarily, her daughter spoke for the first time.

'And then I fancied,' said the young girl, 'that I heard his voice pausing under my window at night. "His blessed Lady is here," I said, "we must not let him lose her." So I called my brother and bade him go forth in search of you. I dreamed that he brought you back. We made an altar with candles and lace and flowers, and on it we placed the little picture. The stranger had light hair, light eyes, a flowing beard like you. He kneeled down before the little Madonna and worshipped her. We left him at his devotions and went away. When we came back the candles on the altar were out: the Madonna was gone, too; but in its place there burned a bright pure light. It was a purse of gold!'

'What a very pretty story!' said I. 'How many pieces were there in the purse?'

The young man burst into a laugh. 'Twenty thousand!' he said.

I made my offer for the picture. It was esteemed generous apparently; I was cordially thanked. As it was inconvenient, however, to take possession of the work at that moment, I agreed to pay down but half the sum, reserving the other half to the time of delivery. When I prepared to take my departure the young girl rose from her chair and enabled me to measure at once her weakness and her beauty. 'Will you come back for the picture yourself?' she asked.

'Possibly. I should like to see you again. You must get better.'

'O, I shall never get better.'

'I can't believe that. I shall perhaps have a dream to tell you!'

'I shall soon be in heaven. I shall send you one.'

'Listen to her!' cried the mother. 'But she is already an angel.'

With a farewell glance at my pictured Madonna I departed. My visit to this little Vicenza household had filled me with a painful, indefinable sadness. So beautiful they all were, so civil, so charming, and yet so mendacious and miserable! As I hurried along in the train toward the briny cincture of Venice, my heart was heavy with the image of that sombre, dying Italian maiden. Her face haunted me. What fatal wrong had she suffered? What hidden sorrow had blasted the freshness of her youth? As I began to smell the nearing Adriatic, my fancy bounded forward to claim asylum in the calmer presence of my bright American friend. I have no space to tell the story of my arrival in Venice and my first impressions. Mr Evans had not mentioned his hotel. He was not at the Hotel de l'Europe,[28] whither I myself repaired. If he was still in Venice, however, I foresaw that we should not fail to meet. The day succeeding my arrival I spent in a restless fever of curiosity and delight, now lost in the sensuous ease of my gondola, now lingering in charmed devotion before a canvas of Tintoretto or Paul Veronese. I exhausted three gondoliers and saw all Venice in a passionate fury and haste. I wished to probe its fulness and learn at once the best – or the worst. Late in the afternoon I disembarked at the Piazzetta²⁹ and took my way haltingly and gazingly to the many-domed Basilica³⁰ – that shell of silver with a lining of marble. It was that enchanting Venetian hour when the ocean-touching sun sits melting to death, and the whole still air seems to glow with the soft effusion of his golden substance. Within the church, the deep brown shadow-masses, the heavy thick-tinted air, the gorgeous composite darkness, reigned in richer, quainter, more fantastic gloom than my feeble pen can reproduce the likeness of. From those rude concavities of dome and semi-dome, where the multitudinous facets of pictorial mosaic shimmer and twinkle in their own dull brightness; from the vast antiquity of innumerable marbles, incrusting the walls in roughly mated slabs, cracked and polished and triple-tinted with eternal service; from the wavy carpet of compacted stone, where a thousand once-bright fragments glimmer through the long attrition of idle feet and devoted knees; from sombre gold and mellow alabaster, from porphyry and malachite, from long dead crystal and the sparkle of undying lamps, there proceeds a dense rich atmosphere of splendour and sanctity which transports the half-stupefied traveller to the age of a simpler and more awful faith. I wandered for half an hour beneath those reverted cups of scintillating darkness, stumbling on the great stony swells of the pavement as I gazed upward at the long mosaic saints who curve gigantically with the curves of dome and ceiling. I had left Europe; I was in the East. An overwhelming sense of the sadness of man's spiritual history took possession of my heart. The clustering picturesque shadows about me seemed to represent the darkness of a past from which he had slowly and painfully struggled. The great mosaic images, hideous, grotesque, inhuman, glimmered like the cruel spectres of early superstitions and terrors. There came over me, too, a poignant conviction of the ludicrous folly of the idle spirit of travel. How with Murray and an opera-glass it strolls and stares where omniscient angels stand diffident and sad! How blunted and stupid are its senses! How trivial and superficial its imaginings! To this builded sepulchre of trembling hope and dread, this monument of mighty passions, I had wandered in search of pictorial effects. O vulgarity! Of course I remained, nevertheless, still curious of effects. Suddenly I perceived a very agreeable one. Kneeling on a low *prie-dieu*, with her hands clasped, a lady was gazing upward at the great mosaic Christ in the dome of the choir.[31] She wore a black lace shawl and a purple hat. She was Miss Evans. Her attitude slightly puzzled me. Was she really at her devotions, or was she only playing at prayer? I walked to a distance, so that she might have time to move before I addressed her. Five minutes afterwards, however, she was in the same position. I walked slowly towards her, and as I approached her attracted her attention. She immediately recognized me and smiled and bowed, without moving from her place.

'I saw you five minutes ago,' I said, 'but I was afraid of interrupting your prayers.'

'O, they were only half-prayers,' she said.

'Half-prayers are pretty well for one who only the other day was thanking Heaven that she was not a Catholic.'

'Half-prayers are no prayers. I'm not a Catholic yet.'

Her father, she told me, had brought her to the church, but had returned on foot to the hotel for his pocket-book. They were to dine at one of the restaurants in the Piazza. Mr Evans was vastly contented with Venice, and spent his days and nights in gondolas. Awaiting his return, we wandered over the church. Yes, incontestably, Miss Evans resembled my little Vicenza picture. She looked a little pale with the heat and the constant nervous tension of sight-seeing; but she pleased me now as effectually as she had pleased me before. There was an even deeper sweetness in the freedom and breadth of her utterance and carriage. I felt more even than before that she was an example of woman active, not of woman passive. We strolled through the great Basilica in serious, charmed silence. Miss Evans told me that she had been there much: she seemed to know it well. We went into the dark Baptistery and sat down on a bench against the wall, trying to discriminate in the vaulted dimness the harsh mediæval reliefs behind the altar and the mosaic Crucifixion above it.[32]

'Well,' said I, 'what has Venice done for you?'

'Many things. Tired me a little, saddened me, charmed me.'

'How have you spent your time?'

'As people spend it. After breakfast we get into our gondola and remain in it pretty well till bedtime. I believe I know every canal, every canaletto, in Venice. You must have learned already how sweet it is to lean back under the awning, to feel beneath you that steady, liquid lapse, to look out at all this bright, sad elegance of ruin. I have been reading two or three of George Sand's novels. Do you know *La Dernière Aldini*?[33] I fancy a romance in every palace.'

'The reality of Venice seems to me to exceed all romance. It's romance enough simply to be here.'

'Yes; but how brief and transient a romance!'

'Well,' said I, 'we shall certainly cease to be here, but we shall never cease to have been here. You are not to leave directly, I hope.'

'In the course of ten days or a fortnight we go to Florence.'

'And then to Rome?'

'To Rome and Naples, and then by sea, probably, to Genoa, and thence to Nice and Paris. We must be at home by the new year. And you?'

'I hope to spend the winter in Italy.'

'Are you never coming home again?'

'By no means. I shall probably return in the spring. But I wish you, too, were going to remain.'

'You are very good. My father pronounces it impossible. I have only to make the most of it while I'm here.'

'Are you going back to Araminta?'

Miss Evans was silent a moment. 'O, don't ask!' she said.

'What kind of a place is Araminta?' I asked, maliciously.

Again she was silent. 'That is John the Baptist on the cover of the basin,'[34] she said, at last, rising to her feet, with a light laugh.

On emerging from the Baptistery we found Mr Evans, who greeted me cordially and insisted on my coming to dine with them. I think most fondly of our little dinner. We went to the Caffè Quadri[35] and occupied a table beside an open window, looking out into the Piazza, which was beginning to fill with evening loungers and listeners to the great band of music in the centre. Miss Evans took off her hat and sat facing me in friendly silence. Her father sustained the larger burden of conversation. He seemed to feel its weight, however, as the dinner proceeded and when he had attacked his second bottle of wine. Miss Evans then questioned me about my journey from Milan. I told her the whole story, and felt that I infused into it a great deal of colour and heat. She sat charming me forward with her steady, listening smile. For the first time in my life I felt the magic of sympathy. After dinner we went down into the Piazza and established ourselves at one of Florian's[36] tables. Night had become perfect; the music was magnificent. At a neighbouring table was a group of young Venetian gentlemen, splendid in dress, after the manner of their kind, and glorious with the wondrous physical glory of the Italian race.

'They only need velvet and satin and plumes,' I said, 'to be subjects for Titian and Paul Veronese.'

They sat rolling their dark eyes and kissing their white hands at passing friends, with smiles that were like the moon-flashes on the Adriatic.

'They are beautiful exceedingly,' said Miss Evans; 'the most beautiful creatures in the world, except—'

'Except, you mean, this other gentleman.'

She assented. The person of whom I had spoken was a young man who was just preparing to seat himself at a vacant table. A lady and gentleman, elderly persons, had passed near him and recognized him, and he had uncovered himself and now stood smiling and talking. They were all genuine Anglo-Saxons. The young man was rather short of stature, but firm and compact. His hair was light and crisp, his eye a clear blue, his face and neck violently tanned by exposure to the sun. He wore a pair of small blond whiskers.

'Do you call him beautiful?' demanded Mr Evans. 'He reminds me of myself when I was his age. Indeed, he looks like you, sir.'

'He's not beautiful,' said Miss Evans, 'but he is handsome.'

The young man's face was full of decision and spirit; his

whole figure had been moulded by action, tempered by effort. He looked simple and keen, upright, downright.

'Is he English?' asked Miss Evans, 'or American?'

'He is both,' I said, 'or either. He is made of that precious clay that is common to the whole English-speaking race.'

'He's American.'

'Very possibly,' said I; and indeed we never learned. I repeat the incident because I think it has a certain value in my recital. Before we separated I expressed the hope that we might meet again on the morrow.

'It's very kind of you to propose it,' said Miss Evans; 'but you'll thank us for refusing. Take my advice, as for an old Venetian, and spend the coming three days alone. How can you enjoy Tintoretto and Bellini,[37] when you are racking your brains for small talk for me?'

'With you, Miss Evans, I shouldn't talk small. But you shape my programme with a liberal hand. At the end of three days, pray, where will you be?'

They would still be in Venice, Mr Evans declared. It was a capital hotel, and then those jolly gondolas! I was unable to impeach the wisdom of the young girl's proposition. To be so wise, it seemed to me, was to be extremely charming.

For three days, accordingly, I wandered about alone. I often thought of Miss Evans and I often fancied I should enjoy certain great pictures none the less for that deep associated contemplation and those fine emanations of assent and dissent which I should have known in her society. I wandered far; I penetrated deep, it seemed to me, into the heart of Venetian power. I shook myself free of the sad and sordid present, and embarked on that silent contemplative sea whose irresistible tides expire at the base of the mighty canvases in the Scuola di San Rocco.[38] But on my return to the hither shore, I always found my sweet young countrywoman waiting to receive me. If Miss Evans had been an immense coquette, she could not have proceeded more cunningly than by this injunction of a three days' absence. During this period, in my imagination, she increased tenfold in value. I don't mean to say that there were not hours together when I quite forgot her, and when I

had no heart but for Venice and the lessons of Venice, for the
sea and sky and the great painters and builders. But when my
mind had executed one of these great passages of appreciation,
it turned with a sudden sense of solitude and lassitude to those
gentle hopes, those fragrant hints of intimacy, which clustered
about the person of my friend. She remained modestly un-
eclipsed by the women of Titian.[39] She was as deeply a woman
as they, and yet so much more of a person; as fit as the broadest
and blondest to be loved for herself, yet full of serene superiority as an active friend. To the old, old sentiment what an
exquisite modern turn she might give! I so far overruled her
advice as that, with her father, we made a trio every evening,
after the day's labours, at one of Florian's tables. Mr Evans
drank absinthe and discoursed upon the glories of our common country, of which he declared it was high time I should
make the acquaintance. He was not the least of a bore: I relished him vastly. He was in many ways an excellent
representative American. Without taste, without culture or
polish, he nevertheless produced an impression of substance in
character, keenness in perception, and intensity in will, which
effectually redeemed him from vulgarity. It often seemed to
me, in fact, that his good-humoured tolerance and easy morality, his rank self-confidence, his nervous decision and vivacity,
his fearlessness of either gods or men, combined in proportions
of which the union might have been very fairly termed aristocratic. His voice, I admit, was of the nose, nasal; but possibly,
in the matter of utterance, one eccentricity is as good as
another. At all events, with his clear, cold grey eye, with that
just faintly impudent, more than level poise of his ample chin,
with those two hard lines which flanked the bristling wings of
his grey moustache, with his general expression of unchal-
lenged security and practical aptitude and incurious scorn of
tradition, he impressed the sensitive beholder as a man of
incontestable force. He was entertaining, too, partly by wit
and partly by position. He was weak only in his love of
absinthe. After his first glass he left his chair and strolled about
the piazza, looking for possible friends and superbly unconscious of possible enemies. His daughter sat back in her chair,

her arms folded, her ungloved hands sustaining them, her prettiness half defined, her voice enhanced and subdued by the
gas-tempered starlight. We had infinite talk. Without question,
she had an admirable feminine taste: she was worthy to know
Venice. I remember telling her so in a sudden explosion of
homage. 'You are really worthy to know Venice, Miss Evans.
We must learn to know it together. Who knows what hidden
treasures we may help each other to find?'

H. James, Jr

II

At the end of my three days' probation, I spent a week constantly with my friends. Our mornings were, of course, devoted
to churches and galleries, and in the late afternoon we passed
and repassed along the Grand Canal or betook ourselves to the
Lido.[40] By this time Miss Evans and I had become thoroughly
intimate; we had learned to know Venice together, and the
knowledge had helped us to know each other. In my own mind,
Charlotte Evans and Venice had played the game most effec-
tively into each other's hands. If my fancy had been called upon
to paint her portrait, my fancy would have sketched her with a
background of sunset-flushed palace wall, with a faint reflected
light from the green lagoon playing up into her face. And if I
had wished to sketch a Venetian scene, I should have painted it
from an open window, with a woman leaning against the case-
ment, – as I had often seen her lean from a window in her hotel.
At the end of a week we went one afternoon to the Lido, timing
our departure so as to allow us to return at sunset. We went
over in silence, Mr Evans sitting with reverted head, blowing
his cigar-smoke against the dazzling sky, which told so fiercely
of sea and summer; his daughter motionless and thickly veiled;
I facing them, feeling the broken swerve of our gondola, and
watching Venice grow level and rosy beyond the liquid interval. Near the landing-place on the hither side of the Lido is a
small *trattoria* for the refreshment of visitors. An arbour outside the door, a horizontal vine checkering still further a dirty

table-cloth, a pungent odour of *frittata*, an admiring circle of gondoliers and beggars, are the chief attractions of this suburban house of entertainment – attractions sufficient, however, to have arrested the inquisitive steps of an elderly American gentleman, in whom Mr Evans speedily recognized a friend of early years, a comrade in affairs. A hearty greeting ensued. This worthy man had ordered dinner: he besought Mr Evans at least to sit down and partake of a bottle of wine. My friend vacillated between his duties as a father and the prospect of a rich old-boyish revival of the delectable interests of home; but his daughter graciously came to his assistance. 'Sit down with Mr Munson, talk till you are tired, and then walk over to the beach and find us. We shall not wander beyond call.'

She and I accordingly started slowly for a stroll along the barren strand which averts its shining side from Venice and takes the tides of the Adriatic. The Lido has for me a peculiar melancholy charm, and I have often wondered that I should have felt the presence of beauty in a spot so destitute of any exceptional elements of beauty. For beyond the fact that it knows the changing moods and hues of the Adriatic, this narrow strip of sand-stifled verdure has no very rare distinction. In my own country I know many a sandy beach, and many a stunted copse, and many a tremulous ocean line ot little less purity and breadth ot composition, with far less magical interest. The secret of the Lido is simply your sense of adjacent Venice. It is the salt-sown garden of the city of the sea. Hither came short-paced Venetians for a meagre taste of *terra firma*, or for a wider glimpse of their parent ocean. Along a narrow line in the middle of the island are market-gardens and breeze-twisted orchards, and a hint of hedges and lanes and inland greenery. At one end is a series of low fortifications duly embanked and moated and sentinelled. Still beyond these, half over-drifted with sand and over-clambered with rank grasses and coarse thick shrubbery, are certain quaintly lettered funereal slabs, tombs of former Jews of Venice. Toward these we slowly wandered and sat down in the grass. Between the sand-heaps, which shut out the beach, we saw in a dozen places the blue agitation of the sea. Over all the scene there brooded

the deep bright sadness of early autumn. I lay at my companion's feet and wondered whether I was in love. It seemed to me
that I had never been so happy in my life. They say, I know, that
to be in love is not pure happiness; that in the mood of the
unconfessed, unaccepted lover there is an element of poignant
doubt and pain. Should I at once confess myself and taste of the
perfection of bliss? It seemed to me that I cared very little for
the meaning of her reply. I only wanted to talk of love; I wanted
in some manner to enjoy in that atmosphere of romance the
woman who was so blessedly fair and wise. It seemed to me
that all the agitation of fancy, the excited sense of beauty, the
fervour and joy and sadness begotten by my Italian wander-
ings, had suddenly resolved themselves into a potent demand
for expression. Miss Evans was sitting on one of the Hebrew
tombs,[41] her chin on her hand, her elbow on her knee, watching
the broken horizon. I was stretched on the grass on my side,
leaning on my elbow and on my hand, with my eyes on her face.
She bent her own eyes and encountered mine; we neither of us
spoke or moved, but exchanged a long steady regard; after
which her eyes returned to the distance. What was her feeling
toward me? Had she any sense of my emotion or of any answering trouble in her own wonderful heart? Suppose she should
deny me: should I suffer, would I persist? At any rate, I should
have struck a blow for love. Suppose she were to accept me;
would my joy be any greater than in the mere translation of my
heart-beats? Did I in truth long merely for a bliss which should
be of that hour and that hour alone? I was conscious of an
immense respect for the woman beside me. I was unconscious
of the least desire even to touch the hem of her garment as it lay
on the grass, touching my own. After all, it was but ten days
that I had known of her. How little I really knew of her! How
little else than her beauty and her wit! How little she knew of
me, of my vast outlying, unsentimental, spiritual self! We knew
hardly more of each other than had appeared in this narrow
circle of our common impressions of Venice. And yet if into
such a circle Love had forced his way, let him take his way! Let
him widen the circle! Transcendent Venice! I rose to my feet

with a violent movement, and walked ten steps away. I came back and flung myself again on the grass.

'The other day at Vicenza,' I said, 'I bought a picture.'

'Ah? an "original"?'

'No, a copy.'

'From whom?'

'From you!'

She blushed. 'What do you mean?'

'It was a little pretended Correggio; a Madonna and Child.'

'Is it good?'

'No, it's rather poor.'

'Why, then, did you buy it?'

'Because the Madonna looked singularly like you.'

'I'm sorry, Mr Brooke, you hadn't a better reason. I hope the picture was cheap.'

'It was quite reason enough. I admire you more than any woman in the world.'

She looked at me a moment, blushing again. 'You don't know me.'

'I have a suspicion of you. It's ground enough for admiration.'

'O, don't talk about admiration. I'm tired of it all before-hand.'

'Well, then,' said I, 'I'm in love.'

'Not with me, I hope.'

'With you, of course. With whom else?'

'Has it only just now occurred to you?'

'It has just occurred to me to say it.'

Her blush had deepened a little; but a genuine smile came to its relief. 'Poor Mr Brooke!' she said.

'Poor Mr Brooke indeed, if you take it in that way.'

'You must forgive me if I doubt of your love.'

'Why should you doubt?'

'Love, I fancy, doesn't come in just this way.'

'It comes as it can. This is surely a very good way.'

'I know it's a very pretty way, Mr Brooke; Venice behind us, the Adriatic before us, these old Hebrew tombs! Its very prettiness makes me distrust it.'

'Do you believe only in the love that is born in darkness and pain? Poor love! It has trouble enough, first and last. Allow it a little ease.'

'Listen,' said Miss Evans, after a pause. 'It's not with me you're in love, but with that painted picture. All this Italian beauty and delight has thrown you into a romantic state of mind. You wish to make it perfect. I happen to be at hand, so you say, "Go to, I'll fall in love." And you fancy me, for the purpose, a dozen fine things that I'm not.'

'I fancy you beautiful and good. I'm sorry to find you so dogmatic.'

'You mustn't abuse me, or we shall be getting serious.'

'Well,' said I, 'you can't prevent me from adoring you.'

'I should be very sorry to. So long as you "adore" me, we're safe! I can tell you better things than that I'm in love with you.'

I looked at her impatiently. 'For instance?'

She held out her hand. 'I like you immensely. As for love, I'm in love with Venice.'

'Well, I like Venice immensely, but I'm in love with you.'

'In that way I am willing to leave it. Pray don't speak of it again to-day. But my poor father is probably wandering up to his knees in the sand.'

I had been happy before, but I think I was still happier for the words I had spoken. I had cast them abroad at all events; my heart was richer by a sense of their possible fruition. We walked far along the beach. Mr Evans was still with his friend.

'What is beyond that horizon?' said my companion.

'Greece, among other things.'

'Greece! only think of it! Shall you never go there?'

I stopped short. 'If you will believe what I say, Miss Evans, we may both go there.' But for all answer she repeated her request that I should forbear. Before long, retracing our steps, we met Mr Evans, who had parted with his friend, the latter having returned to Venice. He had arranged to start the next morning for Milan. We went back over the lagoon in the glow of the sunset, in a golden silence which suffered us to hear the far-off ripple in the wake of other gondolas, a golden clearness so perfect that the rosy flush on the marble palaces seemed as

light and pure as the life-blood on the forehead of a sleeping
child. There is no Venice like the Venice of that magical hour.
For that brief period her ancient glory returns. The sky arches
over her like a vast imperial canopy crowded with its clustering
mysteries of light. Her whole aspect is one of unspotted splendour. No other city takes the crimson evanescence of day with
such magnificent effect. The lagoon is sheeted with a carpet of
fire. All torpid, pallid hues of marble are transmuted to a
golden glow. The dead Venetian tone brightens and quickens
into life and lustre, and the spectator's enchanted vision seems
to rest on an embodied dream of the great painter who wrought
his immortal reveries into the ceilings of the Ducal Palace.[42]

It was not till the second day after this that I again saw Miss
Evans. I went to the little church of San Cassiano,[43] to see a
famous Tintoretto, to which I had already made several vain
attempts to obtain access. At the door in the little bustling
campo[44] which adjoins the church I found her standing expectant. A little boy, she told me, had gone for the sacristan and his
key. Her father, she proceeded to explain, had suddenly been
summoned to Milan by a telegram from Mr Munson, the friend
whom he had met at the Lido, who had suddenly been taken ill.

'And so you're going about alone? Do you think that's altogether proper? Why didn't you send for me?' I stood lost in
wonder and admiration at the exquisite dignity of her
self-support. I had heard of American girls doing such things;
but I had yet to see them done.

'Do you think it less proper for me to go about alone than
to send for you? Venice has seen so many worse improprieties
that she'll forgive me mine.'

The little boy arrived with the sacristan and his key, and we
were ushered into the presence of Tintoretto's Crucifixion.
This great picture is one of the greatest of the Venetian school.
Tintoretto, the travelled reader will remember, has painted
two masterpieces on this tremendous theme. The larger and
more complex work is at the Scuola di San Rocco; the one of
which I speak is small, simple, and sublime. It occupies the left
side of the narrow choir of the shabby little church which we
had entered, and is remarkable as being, with two or three

exceptions, the best preserved work of its incomparable author. Never, in the whole range of art, I imagine, has so powerful an effect been produced by means so simple and select; never has the intelligent choice of means to an effect been pursued with such a refinement of perception. The picture offers to our sight the very central essence of the great tragedy which it depicts. There is no swooning Madonna, no consoling Magdalen, no mockery of contrast, no cruelty of an assembled host. We behold the silent summit of Calvary. To the right are the three crosses, that of the Saviour foremost. A ladder pitched against it supports a turbaned executioner, who bends downward to receive the sponge offered him by a comrade. Above the crest of the hill the helmets and spears of a line of soldiery complete the grimness of the scene. The reality of the picture is beyond all words: it is hard to say which is more impressive, the naked horror of the fact represented, or the sensible power of the artist. You breathe a silent prayer of thanks that you, for your part, are without the terrible clairvoyance of genius. We sat and looked at the picture in silence. The sacristan loitered about; but finally, weary of waiting, he retired to the *campo* without. I observed my companion: pale, motionless, oppressed, she evidently felt with poignant sympathy the commanding force of the work. At last I spoke to her; receiving no answer, I repeated my question. She rose to her feet and turned her face upon me, illumined with a vivid ecstasy of pity. Then passing me rapidly, she descended into the aisle of the church, dropped into a chair, and, burying her face in her hands, burst into an agony of sobs. Having allowed time for her feeling to expend itself, I went to her and recommended her not to let the day close on this painful emotion. 'Come with me to the Ducal Palace,' I said; 'let us look at the Rape of Europa.'[45] But before departing we went back to our Tintoretto, and gave it another solemn half-hour. Miss Evans repeated aloud a dozen verses from St Mark's Gospel.

'What is it here,' I asked, 'that has moved you most, the painter or the subject?'

'I suppose it's the subject. And you?'

'I'm afraid it's the painter.'

We went to the Ducal Palace, and immediately made our way to that transcendent shrine of light and grace, the room which contains the masterpiece of Paul Veronese, and the Bacchus and Ariadne of his solemn comrade.[46] I steeped myself with unprotesting joy in the gorgeous glow and salubrity of that radiant scene, wherein, against her bosky screen of immortal verdure, the rosy-footed, pearl-circled, nymph-flattered victim of a divine delusion rustles her lustrous satin against the ambrosial hide of bovine Jove. 'It makes one think more agreeably of life,' I said to my friend, 'that such visions have blessed the eyes of men of mortal mould. What has been may be again. We may yet dream as brightly, and some few of us translate our dreams as freely.'

'This, I think, is the brighter dream of the two,' she answered, indicating the Bacchus and Ariadne. Miss Evans, on the whole, was perhaps right. In Tintoretto's picture there is no shimmer of drapery, no splendour of flowers and gems; nothing but the broad, bright glory of deep-toned sea and sky, and the shining purity and symmetry of deified human flesh. 'What do you think,' asked my companion, 'of the painter of that tragedy at San Cassiano being also the painter of this dazzling idyl; of the great painter of darkness being also the great painter of light?'

'He was a colourist! Let us thank the great man, and be colourists too. To understand this Bacchus and Ariadne we ought to spend a long day on the lagoon, beyond sight of Venice. Will you come to-morrow to Torcello?'[47] The proposition seemed to me audacious; I was conscious of blushing a little as I made it. Miss Evans looked at me and pondered. She then replied with great calmness that she preferred to wait for her father, the excursion being one that he would probably enjoy. 'Will you come, then – somewhere?' I asked.

Again she pondered. Suddenly her face brightened. 'I should very much like to go to Padua.[48] It would bore my poor father to go. I fancy he would thank you for taking me. I should be almost willing,' she said with a smile, 'to go alone.'

It was easily arranged that on the morrow we should go for the day to Padua. Miss Evans was certainly an American to perfection. Nothing remained for me, as the good American which I aspired to be, but implicitly to respect her confidence. To Padua, by an early train, we accordingly went. The day stands out in my memory delightfully curious and rich. Padua is a wonderful little city. Miss Evans was an excellent walker, and, thanks to the broad arcades which cover the footways in the streets, we rambled for hours in perpetual shade. We spent an hour at the famous church of St Anthony,[49] which boasts one of the richest and holiest shrines in all church-burdened Italy. The whole edifice is nobly and darkly ornate and pictur- esque, but the chapel of its patron saint – a wondrous combination of chiselled gold and silver and alabaster and per- petual flame – splendidly outshines and outshadows the rest. In all Italy, I think, the idea of palpable, material sanctity is nowhere more potently enforced.

'O the Church, the Church!' murmured Miss Evans, as we stood contemplating.

'What a real pity,' I said, 'that we are not Catholics; that that dazzling monument is not something more to us than a mere splendid show! What a different thing this visiting of churches would be for us, if we occasionally felt the prompting to fall on our knees. I begin to grow ashamed of this perpetual attitude of bald curiosity. What a pleasant thing it must be, in such a church as this, for two good friends to say their prayers together!'

'*Ecco!*' said Miss Evans. Two persons had approached the glittering shrine, a young woman of the middle class and a man of her own rank, some ten years older, dressed with a good deal of cheap elegance. The woman dropped on her knees; her com- panion fell back a few steps, and stood gazing idly at the chapel. 'Poor girl!' said my friend, 'she believes; he doubts.'

'He doesn't look like a doubter. He's a vulgar fellow. They're a betrothed pair, I imagine. She is very pretty.' She had turned round and flung at her companion a liquid glance of entreaty. He appeared not to observe it; but in a few moments he slowly approached her, and bent a single knee at her side. When pres- ently they rose to their feet, she passed her arm into his with a beautiful, unsuppressed lovingness. As they passed us, looking at us from the clear darkness of their Italian brows, I keenly envied them. 'They are better off than we,' I said. 'Be they husband and wife, or lovers, or simply friends, we, I think, are rather vulgar beside them.'

'My dear Mr Brooke,' said Miss Evans, 'go by all means and say your prayers.' And she walked away to the other side of the church. Whether I obeyed her injunction or not, I feel under no obligation to report. I rejoined her at the beautiful frescoed chapel in the opposite transept. She was sitting listlessly turning over the leaves of her Murray. 'I suppose,' she said, after a few moments, 'that nothing is more vulgar than to make a noise about having been called vulgar. But really, Mr Brooke, don't call me so again. I have been of late so fondly fancying I am not vulgar.'

'My dear Miss Evans, you are—'

'Come, nothing vulgar!'

'You're divine!'

'*A la bonne heure!* Divinities needn't pray. They are prayed to.'

I have no space and little power to enumerate and describe the various curiosities of Padua. I think we saw them all. We left the best, however, for the last, and repaired in the late afternoon, after dining fraternally at a restaurant, to the Chapel of Giotto.[50] This little empty church, standing un-shaded and forlorn in the homely market-garden which was once a Roman arena, offers one of the deepest lessons of Italian travel. Its four walls are covered, almost from base to ceiling, with that wonderful series of dramatic paintings which usher in the golden prime of Italian art. I had been so ill-informed as to fancy that to talk about Giotto was to make more or less of a fool of one's self, and that he was the especial property of the mere sentimentalists of criticism. But you no sooner cross the threshold of that little ruinous temple – a mere empty shell, but coated as with the priceless substance of fine pearls and vocal with a murmured eloquence as from the infinite of art – than you perceive with whom you have to deal: a complete painter of the very strongest sort. In one respect, assuredly, Giotto has never been surpassed, – in the art of presenting a story. The amount of dramatic expression compressed into those quaint little scenic squares would equip a thousand later masters. How, beside him, they seem to fumble and grope and trifle! And he, beside them, how direct he seems, how essential, how masculine! What a solid simplicity, what an immediate purity and grace! The exhibition suggested to my friend and me more wise reflections than we had the skill to utter. 'Happy, happy art,' we said, as we seemed to see it beneath Giotto's hand tremble and thrill and sparkle, almost, with a presentiment of its immense career, 'for the next two hundred years what a glorious felicity will be yours!' The chapel door stood open into the sunny corn-field, and the lazy litter of verdure enclosed by the crumbling oval of Roman masonry. A loutish boy who had come with the key lounged on a bench, awaiting tribute, and gazing at us as we gazed. The ample light flooded the inner precinct, and lay hot upon the coarse, pale surface of the painted wall. There seemed an irresistible pathos in such a combination of shabbiness and beauty. I thought of this subsequently at the beautiful Museum at Bologna, where mediocrity is so richly enshrined. Nothing that we had yet seen together had filled us with so deep a sense of enjoyment. We stared, we laughed, we wept almost, we raved with a decent delight. We went over the little compartments one by one: we lingered and returned and compared; we studied; we melted together in unanimous homage. At last the light began to fade and the little saintly figures to grow quaint and terrible in the gathering dusk. The loutish boy had transferred himself significantly to the door-post: we lingered for a farewell glance.

'Mr Brooke,' said my companion, 'we ought to learn from all this to be *real*; real even as Giotto is real; to discriminate between genuine and factitious sentiment; between the substantial and the trivial; between the essential and the superfluous; sentiment and sentimentality.'

'You speak,' said I, 'with appalling wisdom and truth. You strike a chill to my heart of hearts.'

She spoke unsmiling, with a slightly contracted brow and an apparent sense of effort. She blushed as I gazed at her.

'Well,' she said, 'I'm extremely glad to have been here.

Good, wise Giotto! I should have liked to know you. Nay, let
me pay the boy.' I saw the piece she put into his hand; he was
stupefied by its magnitude.

'We shall not have done Padua,' I said, as we left the garden,
'unless we have been to the Caffè Pedrocchi.[51] Come to the
Caffè Pedrocchi. We have more than an hour before our train,
time to eat an ice.' So we drove to the Caffè Pedrocchi, the
most respectable *café* in the world; a *café* monumental, scho-
lastic, classical.

We sat down at one of the tables on the cheerful external
platform, which is washed by the gentle tide of Paduan life.
When we had finished our ices, Miss Evans graciously allowed
me a cigar. How it came about I hardly remember, but,
prompted by some happy accident of talk, and gently encouraged
perhaps by my smoke-wreathed quietude, she lapsed, with an
exquisite feminine reserve, into a delicate autobiographical
strain. For a moment she became egotistical; but with a modesty, a dignity, a lightness of touch which filled my eyes with
admiring tears. She spoke of her home, her family, and the few
events of her life. She had lost her mother in her early years;
her two sisters had married young; she and her father were
equally united by affection and habit. Upon one theme she
touched, in regard to which I should be at loss to say whether
her treatment told more, by its frankness, of our friendship, or,
by its reticence, of her modesty. She spoke of having been
engaged, and of having lost her betrothed in the Civil War. She
made no story of it; but I felt from her words that she had
tasted of sorrow. Having finished my cigar, I was proceeding
to light another. She drew out her watch. Our train was to
leave at eight o'clock. It was now a quarter past. There was no
later evening train.

The reader will understand that I tell the simple truth when
I say that our situation was most disagreeable and that we
were deeply annoyed. 'Of course,' said I, 'you are utterly
disgusted.'

She was silent. 'I am extremely sorry,' she said, at last, just
vanquishing a slight tremor in her voice.

'Murray says the hotel is good,' I suggested.

She made no answer. Then, rising to her feet, 'Let us go immediately,' she said. We drove to the principal inn and bespoke our rooms. Our want of luggage provoked, of course, a certain amount of visible surprise. This, however, I fancy, was speedily merged in a more flattering emotion, when my companion, having communed with the chambermaid, sent her forth with a list of purchases.

We separated early. 'I hope,' said I, as I bade her good-night, 'that you will be fairly comfortable.'

She had recovered her equanimity. 'I have no doubt of it.'

'Good-night.'

'Good-night.' Thank God, I silently added, for the dignity of American women. Knowing to what suffering a similar accident would have subjected a young girl of the orthodox European training, I felt devoutly grateful that among my own people a woman and her reputation are more indissolubly one. And yet I was unable to detach myself from my Old-World associations effectually enough not to wonder whether, after all, Miss Evans's calmness might not be the simple calmness of despair. The miserable words rose to my lips, 'Is she Compromised?' If she were, of course, as far as I was concerned, there was but one possible sequel to our situation.[52]

We met the next morning at breakfast. She assured me that she had slept, but I doubted it. I myself had not closed my eyes, – not from the excitement of vanity. Owing partly, I suppose, to a natural reaction against our continuous talk on the foregoing day, our return to Venice was attended with a good deal of silence. I wondered whether it was a mere fancy that Miss Evans was pensive, appealing, sombre. As we entered the gondola to go from the railway station to the Hotel Danieli,[53] she asked me to request the gondoliers to pass along the Canalezzo[54] rather than through the short cuts of the smaller canals. 'I feel as if I were coming home,' she said, as we floated beneath the lovely façade of the Ca' Doro.[55] Suddenly she laid her hand on my arm. 'It seems to me,' she said, 'that I should like to stop for Mrs L—,' and she mentioned the wife of the American Consul. 'I have promised to show her some jewellery. This is a particularly good time. I shall ask her to come home with me.'

We stopped accordingly at the American Consulate. Here we found, on inquiry, to my great regret, that the Consul and his wife had gone for a week to the Lake of Como. For a moment my companion meditated. Then, 'To the hotel,' she said with decision. Our arrival attracted apparently little notice. I went with Miss Evans to the door of her father's sitting-room, where we met a servant, who informed us with inscrutable gravity that Monsieur had returned the evening before, but that he had gone out after breakfast and had not reappeared.

'Poor father,' she said. 'It was very stupid of me not to have left a note for him.' I urged that our absence for the night was not to have been foreseen, and that Mr Evans had in all likelihood very plausibly explained it. I withdrew with a handshake and permission to return in the evening.

I went to my hotel and slept, a long, sound, dreamless sleep. In the afternoon I called my gondola, and went over to the Lido. I crossed to the outer shore and sought the spot where a few days before I had lain at the feet of Charlotte Evans. I stretched myself on the grass and fancied her present. To say that I *thought* would be to say at once more and less than the literal truth. I was in a tremulous glow of feeling. I listened to the muffled rupture of the tide, vaguely conscious of my beating heart. Was I or was I not in love? I was able to settle nothing. I wandered musingly further and further from the point. Every now and then, with a deeper pulsation of the heart, I would return to it, but only to start afresh and follow some wire-drawn thread of fancy to a nebulous goal of doubt. That she was a most lovely woman seemed to me of all truths the truest, but it was a hard-featured fact of the senses rather than a radiant mystery of faith. I felt that I was not possessed by a passion; perhaps I was incapable of passion. At last, weary of self-bewilderment, I left the spot and wandered beside the sea. It seemed to speak more musingly than ever of the rapture of motion and freedom. Beyond the horizon was Greece, beyond and below was the wondrous Southern world which blooms about the margin of the Midland Sea. To marry, somehow, meant to abjure all this, and in the prime of youth and manhood to sink into obscurity and care. For a moment there stirred in my heart a feeling of anger and pain. Perhaps, after all, I *was* in love!

I went straight across the lagoon to the Hotel Danieli, and as I approached it I became singularly calm and collected. From below I saw Miss Evans alone on her balcony, watching the sunset. She received me with perfect friendly composure. Her father had again gone out, but she had told him of my coming, and he was soon to return. He had not been painfully alarmed at her absence, having learned through a chamber-maid, to whom she had happened to mention her intention, that she had gone for the day to Padua.

'And what have you been doing all day?' I asked.

'Writing letters, long, tiresome, descriptive letters. I have also found a volume of Hawthorne, and have been reading 'Rappacini's Daughter'.[56] You know the scene is laid in Padua.' And what had I been doing?

Whether I was in a passion of love or not, I was enough in love to be very illogical. I was disappointed, Heaven knows why!, that she should have been able to spend her time in this wholesome fashion. 'I have been at the Lido, at the Hebrew tombs, where we sat the other day, thinking of what you told me there.'

'What I told you?'

'That you liked me immensely.'

She smiled; but now that she smiled, I fancied I saw in the movement of her face an undercurrent of pain. Had the peace of her heart been troubled? 'You needn't have gone so far away to think of it.'

'It's very possible,' I said, 'that I shall have to think of it, in days to come, farther away still.'

'Other places, Mr Brooke, will bring other thoughts.'

'Possibly. This place has brought that one.' At what prompting it was that I continued I hardly know; I *would* tell her that I loved her. 'I value it beyond all other thoughts.'

'I do like you, Mr Brooke. Let it rest there.'

'It may rest there for you. It can't for me. It begins there! Don't refuse to understand me.'

She was silent. Then, bending her eyes on me, 'Perhaps,' she said, 'I understand you too well.'

'O, in Heaven's name, don't play at coldness and scepticism!'

She dropped her eyes gravely on a bracelet which she locked and unlocked on her wrist. 'I think,' she said, without raising them, 'you had better leave Venice.' I was about to reply, but the door opened and Mr Evans came in. From his hard, grizzled brow he looked at us in turn; then, greeting me with an extended hand, he spoke to his daughter.

'I have forgotten my cigar-case. Be so good as to fetch it from my dressing-table.'

For a moment Miss Evans hesitated and cast upon him a faint protesting glance. Then she lightly left the room. He stood holding my hand, with a very sensible firmness, with his eyes on mine. Then, laying his other hand heavily on my shoulder, 'Mr Brooke,' he said, 'I believe you are an honest man.'

'I hope so,' I answered.

He paused, and I felt his steady grey eyes. 'How the devil,' he said, 'came you to be left at Padua?'

'The explanation is a very simple one. Your daughter must have told you.'

'I have thought best to talk very little to my daughter about it.'

'Do you regard it, Mr Evans,' I asked, 'as a very serious calamity?'

'I regard it as an infernally disagreeable thing. It seems that the whole hotel is talking about it. There is a little beast of an Italian down-stairs—'

'Your daughter, I think, was not seriously discomposed.'

'My daughter is a d—d proud woman!'

'I can assure you that my esteem for her is quite equal to your own.'

'What does that mean, Mr Brooke?' I was about to answer, but Miss Evans reappeared. Her father, as he took his cigar-case from her, looked at her intently, as if he were on the point of speaking, but the words remained on his lips, and, declaring that he would be back in half an hour, he left the room.

His departure was followed by a long silence.

'Miss Evans,' I said, at last, 'will you be my wife?'

She looked at me with a certain firm resignation. 'Do you *feel* that, Mr Brooke? Do you know what you ask?'

'Most assuredly.'

'Will you rest content with my answer?'

'It depends on what your answer is.'

She was silent.

'I should like to know what my father said to you in my absence.'

'You had better learn from himself.'

'I think I know.[57] Poor father!'

'But you give me no answer,' I rejoined, after a pause.

She frowned a little. 'Mr Brooke,' she said, 'you disappoint me.'

'Well, I'm sorry. Don't revenge yourself by disappointing me.'

'I fancied that I had answered your proposal; that I had, at least, anticipated it, the other day at the Lido.'

'O, that was very good for the other day; but do give me something different now.'

'I doubt of your being more in earnest to-day than then.'

'It seems to suit you wonderfully well to doubt!'

'I thank you for the honour of your proposal: but I can't be your wife, Mr Brooke.'

'That's the answer with which you ask me to remain satisfied!'

'Let me repeat what I said just now. You had better leave Venice, otherwise we must leave it.'

'Ah, that's easy to say!'

'You mustn't think me unkind or cynical. You have done your duty.'

'My duty, – what duty?'

'Come,' she said, with a beautiful blush and the least attempt at a smile, 'you imagine that I have suffered an injury by my being left with you at Padua. I don't believe in such injuries.'

'No more do I.'

'Then there is even less wisdom than before in your

proposal. But I strongly suspect that if we had not missed the train at Padua, you would not have madc it. There is an idea of reparation in it. – O sir!' And she shook her head with a deepening smile.

'If I had flattered myself that it lay in my power to do you an injury,' I replied, 'I should now be rarely disenchanted. As little almost as to do you a benefit!'

'You have loaded me with benefits. I thank you from the bottom of my heart. I may be very unreasonable, but if I had doubted of my having to decline your offer three days ago, I should have quite ceased to doubt this evening.'

'You are an excessively proud woman. I can tell you that.'

'Possibly. But I'm not as proud as you think. I believe in my common sense.'

'I wish that for five minutes you had a grain of imagination!'

'If only for the same five minutes you were without it. You have too much, Mr Brooke. You imagine you love me.'

'Poor fool that I am!'

'You imagine that I'm charming. I assure you I'm not in the least. Here in Venice I have not been myself at all. You should see me at home.'

'Upon my word, Miss Evans, you remind me of a German philosopher.[58] I have not the least objection to seeing you at home.'

'Don't fancy that I think lightly of your offer. But we have been living, Mr Brooke, in poetry. Marriage is stern prose. Do let me bid you farewell!'

I took up my hat. 'I shall go from here to Rome and Naples,' I said. 'I must leave Florence for the last. I shall write you from Rome and of course see you there.'

'I hope not. I had rather not meet you again in Italy. It perverts our dear good old American truth!'

'Do you really propose to bid me a final farewell?'

She hesitated a moment. 'When do you return home?'

'Some time in the spring.'

'Very well. If a year hence, in America, you are still of your present mind, I shall not decline to see you. I feel very safe! If you are not of your present mind, of course I shall be still more happy. Farewell.' She put out her hand; I took it.

'Beautiful, wonderful woman!' I murmured.

'That's rank poetry! Farewell!'

I raised her hand to my lips and released it in silence. At this point Mr Evans reappeared, considering apparently that his half-hour was up. 'Are you going?' he asked.

'Yes. I start to-morrow for Rome.'

'The deuce! Daughter, when are we to go?'

She moved her hand over her forehead, and a sort of nervous tremor seemed to pass through her limbs. 'O, you must take me home!' she said. 'I'm horribly home-sick!' She flung her arms round his neck and buried her head on his shoulder. Mr Evans with a movement of his head dismissed me.

At the top of the staircase, however, he overtook me. 'You made your offer!' And he passed his arm into mine.

'Yes!'

'And she refused you?' I nodded. He looked at me, squeezing my arm. 'By Jove, sir, if she had accepted—'

'Well!' said I, stopping.

'Why, it wouldn't in the least have suited me! Not that I don't esteem you. The whole house shall see it.' With his arm in mine we passed downstairs, through the hall, to the landing place, where he called his own gondola and requested me to use it. He bade me farewell with a kindly handshake, and the assurance that I was too 'nice a fellow not to keep as a friend'.

I think, on the whole, that my uppermost feeling was a sense of freedom and relief. It seemed to me on my journey to Florence that I had started afresh, and was regarding things with less of nervous rapture than before, but more of sober insight. Of Miss Evans I forbade myself to think. In my deepest heart I admitted the truth, the partial truth at least, of her assertion of the unreality of my love. The reality I believed would come. The way to hasten its approach was, meanwhile, to study, to watch, to observe, doubtless even to enjoy. I certainly enjoyed Florence and the three days I spent there. But I shall not attempt to deal with Florence in a parenthesis. I subsequently saw that divine little city under circumstances which peculiarly coloured and shaped it. In Rome, to begin with, I spent a week and went down to Naples, dragging the heavy Roman chain which she rivets about your limbs forever. In Naples I discovered the real South – the Southern South, – in art, in nature, in man, and the least bit in woman. A German lady, an old kind friend, had given me a letter to a Neapolitan lady whom she assured me she held in high esteem. The Signora B— was at Sorrento, where I presented my letter. It seemed to me that 'esteem' was not exactly the word; but the Signora B— was charming. She assured me on my first visit that she was a 'true Neapolitan', and I think, on the whole, she was right. She told me that I was a true German, but in this she was altogether wrong. I spent four days in her house; on one of them we went to Capri, where the Signora had an infant – her only one – at nurse. We saw the Blue Grotto, the Tiberian ruins, the tarantella[59] and the infant, and returned late in the evening by moonlight. The Signora sang on the water in a magnificent contralto. As I looked upward at Northern Italy, it seemed, in contrast, a cold, dark hyperborean clime, a land of order, conscience, and virtue. How my heart went out to that brave, rich, compact little Verona! How there Nature seemed to have mixed her colours with potent oil, instead of as here with crystalline water, drawn though it was from the Neapolitan Bay! But in Naples, too, I pursued my plan of vigilance and study. I spent long mornings at the Museum and learned to know Pompei; I wrote once to Miss Evans, about the statues in the Museum, without a word of wooing, but received no answer. It seemed to me that I returned to Rome a wiser man. It was the middle of October when I reached it. Unless Mr Evans had altered his programme, he would at this moment be passing down to Naples.

A fortnight elapsed without my hearing of him, during which I was in the full fever of initiation into Roman wonders. I had been introduced to an old German archaeologist, with whom I spent a series of memorable days in the exploration of ruins and the study of the classical topography. I thought, I lived, I ate and drank, in Latin, and German Latin at that. But I remember with especial delight certain long lonely rides on the Campagna.[60] The weather was perfect. Nature seemed only to slumber, ready to wake far on the hither side of wintry death. From time to time, after a passionate gallop, I would pull up my horse on the slope of some pregnant mound and embrace with the ecstasy of quickened senses the tragical beauty of the scene; strain my ear to the soft low silence, pity the dark dishonoured plain, watch the heavens come rolling down in tides of light, and breaking in waves of fire against the massive stillness of temples and tombs. The aspect of all this sunny solitude and haunted vacancy used to fill me with a mingled sense of exaltation and dread. There were moments when my fancy swept that vast funereal desert[61] with passionate curiosity and desire, moments when it felt only its potent sweetness and its high historic charm. But there were other times when the air seemed so heavy with the exhalation of unburied death, so bright with sheeted ghosts, that I turned short about and galloped back to the city. One afternoon after I had indulged in one of these supersensitive flights on the Campagna, I betook myself to St Peter's.[62] It was shortly before the opening of the recent Council[63] and the city was filled with foreign ecclesiastics, the increase being of course especially noticeable in the churches. At St Peter's they were present in vast numbers; great armies encamped in prayer on the marble plains of its pavement: an inexhaustible physiognomical study. Scattered among them were squads of little tonsured neophytes, clad in scarlet, marching and counter-marching, and ducking and flapping, like poor little raw recruits for the heavenly host. I had never before, I think, received an equal impression of the greatness of this church of churches, or, standing beneath the dome, beheld such a vision of erected altitude – of the builded sublime. I lingered awhile near the brazen image of St Peter, observing the steady procession of his devotees. Near me stood a lady in mourning, watching with a weary droop of the head the grotesque deposition of kisses. A peasant-woman advanced with the file of the faithful and lifted up her little girl to the well-worn toe. With a sudden movement of impatience the lady turned away, so that I saw her face to face. She was strikingly pale, but as her eyes met mine the blood rushed into her cheeks. This lonely mourner was Miss Evans. I advanced to her

with an outstretched hand. Before she spoke I had guessed at
the truth.

'You're in sorrow and trouble!'

She nodded, with a look of simple gravity.

'Why in the world haven't you written to me?'

'There was no use. I seem to have sufficed to myself.'

'Indeed, you have not sufficed to yourself. You are pale and
worn; you look wretchedly.' She stood silent, looking about
her with an air of vague unrest. 'I have as yet heard nothing,' I
said. 'Can you speak of it?'

'O Mr Brooke!' she said with a simple sadness that went to
my heart. I drew her hand through my arm and led her to the
extremity of the left transept of the church. We sat down
together, and she told me of her father's death. It had happened
ten days before, in consequence of a severe apoplectic stroke.
He had been ill but a single day, and had remained unconscious from first to last. The American physician had been
extremely kind, and had relieved her of all care and responsibility. His wife had strongly urged her to come and stay in
their house, until she should have determined what to do; but
she had preferred to remain at her hotel. She had immediately
furnished herself with an attendant in the person of a French
maid, who had come with her to the church and was now at
confession. At first she had wished greatly to leave Rome, but
now that the first shock of grief had passed away she found it
suited her mood to linger on from day to day. 'On the whole,'
she said, with a sober smile, 'I have got through it all rather
easily than otherwise. The common cares and necessities of
life operate strongly to interrupt and dissipate one's grief. I
shall feel my loss more when I get home again.' Looking at her
while she talked, I found a pitiful difference between her words
and her aspect. Her pale face, her wilful smile, her spiritless
gestures, spoke most forcibly of loneliness and weakness. Over
this gentle weakness and dependence I secretly rejoiced; I felt
in my heart an immense uprising of pity, – of the pity that goes
hand in hand with love. At its bidding I hastily, vaguely
sketched a magnificent scheme of devotion and protection.

'When I think of what you have been through,' I said, 'my

heart stands still for very tenderness. Have you made any plans?'
She shook her head with such a perfection of helplessness that I
broke into a sort of rage of compassion: 'One of the last things
your father said to me was that you are a very proud woman.'

She coloured faintly. 'I may have been! But there is not
among the most abject peasants who stand kissing St Peter's
foot a creature more bowed in humility than I.'

'How did you expect to make that weary journey home?'

She was silent a moment and her eyes filled with tears. 'O
don't cross-question me, Mr Brooke!' she softly cried. 'I
expected nothing. I was waiting for my stronger self.'

'Perhaps your stronger self has come.' She rose to her feet as
if she had not heard me, and went forward to meet her maid.
This was a decent, capable-looking person, with a great deal of
apparent deference of manner. As I rejoined them, Miss Evans
prepared to bid me farewell. 'You haven't yet asked me to come
and see you,' I said.

'Come, but not too soon?'

'What do you call too soon? This evening?'

'Come to-morrow.' She refused to allow me to go with her to
her carriage. I followed her, however, at a short interval, and
went as usual to my restaurant to dine. I remember that my dinner cost me ten francs – it usually cost me five. Afterwards, as
usual, I adjourned to the Caffè Greco,[64] where I met my German
archaeologist. He discoursed with even more than his wonted
sagacity and eloquence; but at the end of half an hour he rapped
his fist on the table and asked me what the deuce was the matter;
he would wager I hadn't heard a word of what he said.

I went forth the next morning into the Roman streets, doubt-
ing heavily of my being able to exist until evening without seeing
Miss Evans. I felt, however, that it was due to her to make the
effort. To help myself through the morning, I went into the
Borghese Gallery. The great treasure of this collection is a certain masterpiece of Titian.[65] I entered the room in which it hangs
by the door facing the picture. The room was empty, save that
before the great Titian, beside the easel of an absent copyist,
stood a young woman in mourning. This time, in spite of her
averted head, I immediately knew her and noiselessly approached

her. The picture is one of the finest of its admirable author, – rich and simple and brilliant with the true Venetian fire. It unites the charm of an air of latent symbolism with a steadfast splendour and solid perfection of design. Beside a low sculptured well sit two young and beautiful women: one richly clad, and full of mild dignity and repose; the other with unbound hair, naked, ungirdled by a great reverted mantle of Venetian purple, and radiant with the frankest physical sweetness and grace. Between them a little winged cherub bends forward and thrusts his chubby arm into the well. The picture glows with the inscrutable chemistry of the prince of colourists.

'Does it remind you of Venice?' I said, breaking a long silence, during which she had not noticed me.

She turned and her face seemed bright with reflected colour. We spoke awhile of common things; she had come alone. 'What an emotion, for one who has loved Venice,' she said, 'to meet a Titian in other lands.'

'They call it,' I answered, – and as I spoke my heart was in my throat, – 'a representation of Sacred and Profane Love. The name perhaps roughly expresses its meaning. The serious, stately woman is the likeness, one may say, of love as an experience, – the gracious, impudent goddess of love as a sentiment; this of the passion that fancies, the other of the passion that knows.' And as I spoke I passed my arm, in its strength, around her waist. She let her head sink on my shoulders and looked up into my eyes.

'One may stand for the love I denied,' she said; 'and the other—'

'The other,' I murmured, 'for the love which, with this kiss, you accept.' I drew her arm into mine, and before the envious eyes that watched us from gilded casements we passed through the gallery and left the palace. We went that afternoon to the Pamfili-Doria Villa.[66] Saying just now that my stay in Florence was peculiarly coloured by circumstances, I meant that I was there with my wife.

H. James Jr.

MADAME DE MAUVES

I

The view from the terrace at Saint-Germain-en-Laye[1] is immense and famous. Paris lies spread before you in dusky vastness, domed and fortified, glittering here and there through her light vapours, and girdled with her silver Seine. Behind you is a park of stately symmetry, and behind that a forest, where you may lounge through turfy avenues and light-checkered glades, and quite forget that you are within half an hour of the boulevards. One afternoon, however, in mid-spring, some five years ago, a young man seated on the terrace had chosen not to forget this. His eyes were fixed in idle wistfulness on the mighty human hive before him. He was fond of rural things, and he had come to Saint-Germain a week before to meet the spring half-way; but though he could boast of a six months' acquaintance with the great city, he never looked at it from his present standpoint without a feeling of painfully unsatisfied curiosity. There were moments when it seemed to him that not to be there just then was to miss some thrilling chapter of experience. And yet his winter's experience had been rather fruitless, and he had closed the book almost with a yawn. Though not in the least a cynic, he was what one may call a disappointed observer; and he never chose the right-hand road without beginning to suspect after an hour's wayfaring that the left would have been the interesting one. He now had a dozen minds to go to Paris for the evening, to dine at the Café Brébant,[2] and to repair afterwards to the Gymnase[3] and listen to the latest exposition of the duties of the injured husband. He would probably have risen to execute this project, if he had not observed a little girl who, wandering along the terrace, had suddenly stopped short and begun to gaze at him with round-eyed frankness. For a moment he was simply amused, for the child's face denoted helpless wonderment; the next he was agreeably surprised. 'Why, this is my friend Maggie,' he said; 'I see you have not forgotten me.'

Maggie, after a short parley, was induced to seal her remembrance with a kiss. Invited then to explain her appearance at Saint-Germain, she embarked on a recital in which the general, according to the infantine method, was so fatally sacrificed to the particular, that Longmore looked about him for a superior source of information. He found it in Maggie's mamma, who was seated with another lady at the opposite end of the terrace; so, taking the child by the hand, he led her back to her companions.

Maggie's mamma was a young American lady, as you would immediately have perceived,[4] with a pretty and friendly face and an expensive spring toilet. She greeted Longmore with surprised cordiality, mentioned his name to her friend, and bade him bring a chair and sit with them. The other lady, who, though equally young and perhaps even prettier, was dressed more soberly, remained silent, stroking the hair of the little girl, whom she had drawn against her knee. She had never heard of Longmore, but she now perceived that her companion had crossed the ocean with him, had met him afterwards in travelling, and (having left her husband in Wall Street)[5] was indebted to him for various small services.

Maggie's mamma turned from time to time and smiled at her friend with an air of invitation; the latter smiled back, and continued gracefully to say nothing.

For ten minutes Longmore felt a revival of interest in his interlocutress; then (as riddles are more amusing than commonplaces) it gave way to curiosity about her friend. His eyes wandered; her volubility was less suggestive than the latter's silence.

The stranger was perhaps not obviously a beauty nor obviously an American; but she was essentially both, on a closer scrutiny. She was slight and fair, and, though naturally pale, delicately flushed, apparently with recent excitement. What chiefly struck Longmore in her face was the union of a pair of beautifully gentle, almost languid grey eyes, with a mouth peculiarly expressive and firm. Her forehead was a trifle more expansive than belongs to classic types, and her thick brown hair was dressed out of the fashion, which was just then very ugly. Her throat and bust were slender, but all the more in harmony with certain rapid, charming movements of the head, which she had a way of throwing back every now and then, with an air of attention and a sidelong glance from her dove-like eyes. She seemed at once alert and indifferent, contemplative and restless; and Longmore very soon discovered that if she was not a brilliant beauty, she was at least an extremely interesting one. This very impression made him magnanimous. He perceived that he had interrupted a confidential conversation, and he judged it discreet to withdraw, having first learned from Maggie's mamma – Mrs Draper – that she was to take the six o'clock train back to Paris. He promised to meet her at the station.

He kept his appointment, and Mrs Draper arrived betimes, accompanied by her friend. The latter, however, made her farewells at the door and drove away again, giving Longmore time only to raise his hat. 'Who is she?' he asked with visible ardour, as he brought Mrs Draper her tickets.

'Come and see me to-morrow at the Hôtel de l'Empire,'[6] she answered, 'and I will tell you all about her.' The force of this offer in making him punctual at the Hôtel de l'Empire Longmore doubtless never exactly measured; and it was perhaps well that he did not, for he found his friend, who was on the point of leaving Paris, so distracted by procrastinating milliners and perjured lingères that she had no wits left for disinterested narrative. 'You must find Saint-Germain dreadfully dull,' she said, as he was going. 'Why won't you come with me to London?'

'Introduce me to Madame de Mauves,' he answered, 'and Saint-Germain will satisfy me.' All he had learned was the lady's name and residence.

'Ah! she, poor woman, will not make Saint-Germain cheerful for you. She's very unhappy.'

Longmore's further inquiries were arrested by the arrival of a young lady with a bandbox; but he went away with the promise of a note of introduction, to be immediately despatched to him at Saint-Germain.

He waited a week, but the note never came; and he declared that it was not for Mrs Draper to complain of her milliner's treachery. He lounged on the terrace and walked in the forest, studied suburban street life, and made a languid attempt to investigate the records of the court of the exiled Stuarts,[7] but he spent most of his time in wondering where Madame de Mauves lived, and whether she ever walked on the terrace. Sometimes, he finally discovered; for one afternoon towards dusk he perceived her leaning against the parapet, alone. In his momentary hesitation to approach her, it seemed to him that there was almost a shade of trepidation; but his curiosity was not diminished by the consciousness of this result of a quarter of an hour's acquaintance. She immediately recognized him, on his drawing near, with the manner of a person unaccustomed to encounter an embarrassing variety of faces. Her dress, her expression, were the same as before; her charm was there, like that of sweet music on a second hearing. She soon made conversation easy by asking him for news of Mrs Draper. Longmore told her that he was daily expecting news, and, after a pause, mentioned the promised note of introduction.

'It seems less necessary now,' he said – 'for me, at least. But for you – I should have liked you to know the flattering things Mrs Draper would probably have said about me.'

'If it arrives at last,' she answered, 'you must come and see me and bring it. If it doesn't, you must come without it.'

Then, as she continued to linger in spite of the thickening twilight, she explained that she was waiting for her husband, who was to arrive in the train from Paris, and who often passed along the terrace on his way home. Longmore well remembered that Mrs Draper had pronounced her unhappy, and he found it convenient to suppose that this same husband made her so. Edified by his six months in Paris— 'What else is possible,' he asked himself, 'for a sweet American girl who marries an unclean Frenchman?'

But this tender expectancy of her lord's return undermined his hypothesis, and it received a further check from the gentle eagerness with which she turned and greeted an approaching figure. Longmore beheld in the fading light a stoutish gentleman, on the fair side of forty, in a high light hat, whose countenance, indistinct against the sky, was adorned by a fantastically pointed moustache. M. de Mauves saluted his wife with punctilious gallantry, and having bowed to Longmore, asked her several questions in French. Before taking his proffered arm to walk to their carriage, which was in waiting at the gate of the terrace, she introduced our hero as a friend of Mrs Draper, and a fellow-countryman, whom she hoped to see at home. M. de Mauves responded briefly, but civilly, in very fair English, and led his wife away.

Longmore watched him as he went, twisting his picturesque moustache, with a feeling of irritation which he certainly would have been at a loss to account for. The only conceivable cause was the light which M. de Mauves's good English cast upon his own bad French. For reasons involved apparently in the very structure of his being, Longmore found himself unable to speak the language tolerably. He admired and enjoyed it, but the very genius of awkwardness controlled his phraseology. But he reflected with satisfaction that Madame de Mauves and he had a common idiom, and his vexation was effectually dispelled by his finding on his table that evening a letter from Mrs Draper. It enclosed a short, formal missive to Madame de Mauves, but the epistle itself was copious and confidential. She had deferred writing till she reached London, where for a week, of course, she had found other amusements.

'I think it is the sight of so many women here who don't look at all like her, that has reminded me by the law of contraries of my charming friend at Saint-Germain and my promise to introduce you to her,' she wrote. 'I believe I told you that she was unhappy, and I wondered afterwards whether I had not been guilty of a breach of confidence. But you would have found it out for yourself, and besides, she told me no secrets. She declared she was the happiest creature in the world, and then, poor thing, she burst into tears, and I prayed to be delivered from such happiness. It's the miserable story of an American girl, born to be neither a slave nor a toy, marrying a profligate Frenchman, who believes that a woman must be one or the other. The silliest American woman is too good for the best foreigner, and the poorest of us have moral needs that the cleverest Frenchman is quite unable to appreciate. She was romantic and perverse – she thought Americans were vulgar. Matrimonial felicity perhaps *is* vulgar; but I think nowadays she wishes she were a little less elegant. M. de Mauves cared, of course, for nothing but her money, which he is spending royally on his *menus plaisirs*. I hope you appreciate the compliment I pay you when I recommend you to go and console an unhappy wife. I have never given a man such a proof of esteem, and if you were to disappoint me I should renounce the world. Prove to Madame de Mauves that an American friend may mingle admiration and respect better than a French husband. She avoids society and lives quite alone, seeing no one but a horrible French sister-in-law. Do let me hear that you have drawn some of the sadness from that desperate smile of hers. Make her smile with a good conscience.'

These zealous admonitions left Longmore slightly disturbed. He found himself on the edge of a domestic tragedy from which he instinctively recoiled. To call upon Madame de Mauves with his present knowledge seemed a sort of fishing in troubled waters. He was a modest man, and yet he asked himself whether the effect of his attentions might not be to add to her discomfort. A flattering sense of unwonted opportunity, however, made him, with the lapse of time, more confident – possibly more reckless. It seemed a very inspiring idea to draw the sadness from his fair countrywoman's smile, and at least he hoped to persuade her that there was such a thing as an agreeable American. He immediately called upon her.

II

She had been placed for her education, fourteen years before, in a Parisian convent, by a widowed mamma who was fonder

of Homburg[8] and Nice[9] than of letting out tucks in the frocks
of a vigorously growing daughter. Here, besides various elegant accomplishments – the art of wearing a train, of composing
a bouquet, of presenting a cup of tea – she acquired a certain
turn of the imagination which might have passed for a sign of
precocious worldliness. She dreamed of marrying a title – not
for the pleasure of hearing herself called Madame la
Vicomtesse[10] (for which it seemed to her that she should never
greatly care), but because she had a romantic belief that the
best birth is the guarantee of an ideal delicacy of feeling.
Romances are rarely constructed in such perfect good faith,
and Euphemia's[11] excuse was the primitive purity of her imagination. She was profoundly incorruptible, and she cherished
this pernicious conceit as if it had been a dogma revealed by a
white-winged angel. Even after experience had given her a
hundred rude hints, she found it easier to believe in fables,
when they had a certain nobleness of meaning, than in well
attested but sordid facts. She believed that a gentleman with a
long pedigree must be of necessity a very fine fellow, and that
the consciousness of a picturesque family tradition imparts an
exquisite tone to the character. *Noblesse oblige*, she thought,
as regards yourself, and insures, as regards your wife. She had
never spoken to a nobleman in her life, and these convictions
were but a matter of transcendent theory. They were the fruit,
in part, of the perusal of various Ultramontane[12] works of
fiction – the only ones admitted to the convent library – in
which the hero was always a Legitimist[13] vicomte who fought
duels by the dozen, but went twice a month to confession; and
in part of the perfumed gossip of her companions, many of
them *filles de haut lieu*, who in the convent garden, after Sundays at home, depicted their brothers and cousins as Prince
Charmings and young Paladins.[14] Euphemia listened and said
nothing; she shrouded her visions of matrimony under a coro-
net in religious mystery. She was not of that type of young lady
who is easily induced to declare that her husband must be six
feet high and a little near-sighted, part his hair in the middle,
and have amber lights in his beard. To her companions she
seemed to have a very pallid fancy, and even the fact that she

was a sprig of the transatlantic democracy never sufficiently explained her apathy on social questions. She had a mental image of that son of the Crusaders who was to suffer her to adore him, but like many an artist who has produced a master-piece of idealization, she shrank from exposing it to public criticism. It was the portrait of a gentleman rather ugly than handsome, and rather poor than rich. But his ugliness was to be nobly expressive, and his poverty delicately proud.

Euphemia had a fortune of her own, which, at the proper time, after fixing on her in eloquent silence those fine eyes which were to soften the feudal severity of his visage, he was to accept with a world of stifled protestations. One condition alone she was to make – that his blood should be of the very finest strain. On this she would stake her happiness.

It so chanced that circumstances were to give convincing colour to this primitive logic.

Though little of a talker, Euphemia was an ardent listener, and there were moments when she fairly hung upon the lips of Mademoiselle Marie de Mauves. Her intimacy with this chosen schoolmate was, like most intimacies, based on their points of difference. Mademoiselle de Mauves was very positive, very shrewd, very ironical, very French – everything that Euphemia felt herself unpardonable in not being. During her Sundays *en ville* she had examined the world and judged it, and she imparted her impressions to our attentive heroine with an agreeable mixture of enthusiasm and scepticism. She was moreover a handsome and well-grown person, on whom Euphemia's ribbons and trinkets had a trick of looking better than on their slender proprietress. She had, finally, the supreme merit of being a rigorous example of the virtue of exalted birth, having, as she did, ancestors honourably mentioned by Join-ville and Commines[15] and a stately grandmother with a hooked nose, who came up with her after the holidays from a veritable *castel* in Auvergne.[16] It seemed to Euphemia that these attrib-utes made her friend more at home in the world than if she had been the daughter of even the most prosperous grocer. A certain aristocratic impudence Mademoiselle de Mauves abundantly possessed, and her raids among her friend's finery were quite in the spirit of her baronial ancestors in the twelfth century – a spirit which Euphemia considered but a large way of understanding friendship – a freedom from small deference to the world's opinions which would sooner or later justify itself in acts of surprising magnanimity. Mademoiselle de Mauves herself perhaps was but partially conscious of that sweet security which Euphemia envied her. She proved herself later in life such an accomplished schemer that her sense of having further heights to scale must have awakened early. Our heroine's ribbons and trinkets had much to do with the other's sisterly patronage, and her appealing pliancy of character even more; but the concluding motive of Marie's writing to her grandmamma to invite Euphemia for a three weeks' holiday to the *castel* in Auvergne involved altogether superior considerations. Mademoiselle de Mauves was indeed at this time seventeen years of age, and presumably capable of general views; and Euphemia, who was hardly less, was a very well-grown subject for experiment, besides being pretty enough almost to pre-assure success. It is a proof of the sincerity of Euphemia's aspirations that the *castel* was not a shock to her faith. It was neither a cheerful nor a luxurious abode, but the young girl found it as delightful as a play. It had battered towers and an empty moat, a rusty drawbridge and a court paved with crooked, grass-grown slabs, over which the antique coach-wheels of the old lady with the hooked nose seemed to awaken the echoes of the seventeenth century. Euphemia was not frightened out of her dream; she had the pleasure of seeing it assume the consistency of a flattering presentiment. She had a taste for old servants, old anecdotes, old furniture, faded household colours, and sweetly stale odours – musty treasures in which the Château de Mauves[17] abounded. She made a dozen sketches in water-colours, after her conventual pattern; but sentimentally, as one may say, she was for ever sketching with a freer hand.

Old Madame de Mauves had nothing severe but her nose, and she seemed to Euphemia, as indeed she was, a graciously venerable relic of an historic order of things. She took a great fancy to the young American, who was ready to sit all day at her feet and listen to anecdotes of the *bon temps* and quotations

from the family chronicles. Madame de Mauves was a very
honest old woman, and uttered her thoughts with antique
plainness. One day, after pushing back Euphemia's shining
locks and blinking at her with some tenderness from under her
spectacles, she declared with an energetic shake of the head
that she didn't know what to make of her. And in answer to
the young girl's startled blush – 'I should like to advise you,'
she said, 'but you seem to me so all of a piece that I am afraid
that if I advise you, I shall spoil you. It's easy to see that you
are not one of us. I don't know whether you are better, but you
seem to me to listen to the murmur of your own young spirit,
rather than to the voice from behind the confessional or to the
whisper of opportunity. Young girls, in my day, when they
were stupid, were very docile, but when they were clever, were
very sly. You are clever enough, I imagine, and yet if I guessed
all your secrets at this moment, is there one I should have to
frown at? I can tell you a wickeder one than any you have discovered for yourself. If you expect to live in France, and you
wish to be happy, don't listen too hard to that little voice I just
spoke of – the voice that is neither the curé's nor the world's.
You will fancy it saying things that it won't help your case to
hear. They will make you sad, and when you are sad you will
grow plain, and when you are plain you will grow bitter, and
when you are bitter you will be very disagreeable. I was brought
up to think that a woman's first duty is to please, and the happiest women I have known have been the ones who performed
this duty faithfully. As you are not a Catholic, I suppose you
can't be a *dévote*; and if you don't take life as a fifty years'
mass, the only way to take it is as a game of skill. Listen to this.
Not to lose at the game of life, you must – I don't say cheat, but
not be too sure your neighbour won't, and not be shocked
out of your self-possession if he does. Don't lose, my dear; I
beseech you, don't lose. Be neither suspicious nor credulous,
and if you find your neighbour peeping, don't cry out, but very
politely wait your own chance. I have had my *revanche* more
than once in my day, but I really think that the sweetest I could
take against life as a whole would be to have your blessed
innocence profit by my experience.'

This was rather bewildering advice, but Euphemia understood it too little to be either edified or frightened. She sat listening to it very much as she would have listened to the speeches of an old lady in a comedy, whose diction should picturesquely correspond to the pattern of her mantilla and the fashion of her head-dress. Her indifference was doubly dangerous, for Madame de Mauves spoke at the prompting of coming events, and her words were the result of a somewhat troubled conscience – a conscience which told her at once that Euphemia was too tender a victim to be sacrificed to an ambition, and that the prosperity of her house was too precious a heritage to be sacrificed to a scruple. The prosperity in question had suffered repeated and grievous breaches, and the house of De Mauves had been pervaded by the cold comfort of an establishment in which people were obliged to balance dinner-table allusions to feudal ancestors against the absence of side-dishes; a state of things the more regrettable as the family was now mainly represented by a gentleman whose appetite was large and who justly maintained that its historic glories had not been established by underfed heroes.

Three days after Euphemia's arrival, Richard de Mauves came down from Paris to pay his respects to his grandmother, and treated our heroine to her first encounter with a gentilhomme[18] in the flesh. On coming in he kissed his grandmother's hand, with a smile which caused her to draw it away with dignity, and set Euphemia, who was standing by, wondering what had happened between them. Her unanswered wonder was but the beginning of a life of bitter perplexity, but the reader is free to know that the smile of M. de Mauves was a reply to a certain postscript affixed by the old lady to a letter promptly addressed to him by her granddaughter, after Euphemia had been admitted to justify the latter's promises. Mademoiselle de Mauves brought her letter to her grandmother for approval, but obtained no more than was expressed in a frigid nod. The old lady watched her with a sombre glance as she proceeded to seal the letter, and suddenly bade her open it again and bring her a pen.

'Your sister's flatteries are all nonsense,' she wrote; 'the young lady is far too good for you, *mauvais sujet*. If you have a particle of conscience you will not come and disturb the repose of an angel of innocence.'

The young girl, who had read these lines, made up a little face as she re-directed the letter; but she laid down her pen with a confident nod which might have seemed to mean that, to the best of her belief, her brother had not a conscience.

'If you meant what you said,' the young man whispered to his grandmother on the first opportunity, 'it would have been simpler not to let her send the letter!'

It was perhaps because she was wounded by this cynical insinuation that Madame de Mauves remained in her own apartment during a greater part of Euphemia's stay, so that the latter's angelic innocence was left entirely to the Baron's mercy. It suffered no worse mischance, however, than to be prompted to intenser communion with itself. M. de Mauves was the hero of the young girl's romance made real, and so completely accordant with this creature of her imagination, that she felt afraid of him, very much as she would have been of a super-natural apparition. He was now thirty-five – young enough to suggest possibilities of ardent activity, and old enough to have formed opinions which a simple woman might deem it an intel-lectual privilege to listen to. He was perhaps a trifle handsomer than Euphemia's rather grim, Quixotic[19] ideal, but a very few days reconciled her to his good looks, as effectually they would have reconciled her to his ugliness. He was quiet, grave, emi-nently distinguished. He spoke little, but his speeches, without being sententious, had a certain nobleness of tone which caused them to re-echo in the young girl's ears at the end of the day. He paid her very little direct attention, but his chance words – if he only asked her if she objected to his cigarette – were accompan-ied by a smile of extraordinary kindness.

It happened that shortly after his arrival, riding an unruly horse which Euphemia with shy admiration had watched him mount in the castle yard, he was thrown with a violence which, without disparaging his skill, made him for a fortnight an inter-esting invalid, lounging in the library with a bandaged knee. To beguile his confinement, Euphemia was repeatedly induced to sing to him, which she did with a little natural tremor in her voice which might have passed for an exquisite refinement of art. He never overwhelmed her with compliments, but he listened with unwandering attention, remembered all her melodies, and sat humming them to himself. While his imprisonment lasted, indeed, he passed hours in her company, and made her feel not unlike some unfriended artist who has suddenly gained the opportunity to devote a fortnight to the study of a great model. Euphemia studied with noiseless diligence what she supposed to be the 'character' of M. de Mauves, and the more she looked, the more fine lights and shades she seemed to behold in this masterpiece of nature. M. de Mauves's character, indeed, whether from a sense of being generously scrutinized, or for reasons which bid graceful defiance to analysis, had never been so amiable; it seemed really to reflect the purity of Euphemia's interpretation of it. There had been nothing especially to admire in the state of mind in which he left Paris – a hard determination to marry a young girl whose charms might or might not justify his sister's account of them, but who was mistress, at the worst, of a couple of hundred thousand francs a year. He had not counted out sentiment; if she pleased him, so much the better; but he had left a meagre margin for it, and he would hardly have admitted that so excellent a match could be improved by it. He was a placid sceptic, and it was a singular fate for a man who believed in nothing to be so tenderly believed in. What his original faith had been he could hardly have told you; for as he came back to his childhood's home to mend his fortunes by pretending to fall in love, he was a thoroughly perverted creature, and overlaid with more corruptions than a summer day's questioning of his conscience would have put to flight. Ten years' pursuit of pleasure, which a bureau full of unpaid bills was all he had to show for, had pretty well stifled the natural lad whose violent will and generous temper might have been shaped by other circumstances to a result which a romantic imagination might fairly accept as a late-blooming flower of hereditary honour. The Baron's violence had been subdued, and he had learned to be irreproachably polite; but he had lost the fineness of his generosity, and his politeness, which in the long run society paid for, was hardly more than a form of luxurious egotism, like his fondness for cambric handkerchiefs, lavender gloves, and other fopperies by which shopkeepers remained out of pocket. In after years he was terribly polite to his wife. He had formed himself, as the phrase was, and the form prescribed to him by the society into which his birth and his tastes introduced him was marked by some peculiar features. That which mainly concerns us is its classification of the fairer half of humanity as objects not essentially different – say from the light gloves one soils in an evening and throws away. To do M. de Mauves justice, he had in the course of time encountered such plentiful evidence of this pliant, glove-like quality in the feminine character, that idealism naturally seemed to him a losing game.

Euphemia, as he lay on his sofa, seemed by no means a refutation; she simply reminded him that very young women are generally innocent, and that this, on the whole, is the most charming stage of their development. Her innocence inspired him with profound respect, and it seemed to him that if he shortly became her husband it would be exposed to a danger the less. Old Madame de Mauves, who flattered herself that in this whole matter she was very laudably rigid, might have learned a lesson from his gallant consideration. For a fortnight the Baron was almost a blushing boy again. He watched from behind the *Figaro*,[20] and admired, and held his tongue. He was not in the least disposed towards a flirtation; he had no desire to trouble the waters he proposed to transfuse into the golden cup of matrimony. Sometimes a word, a look, a movement of Euphemia's, gave him the oddest sense of being, or of seeming at least, almost bashful; for she had a way of not dropping her eyes, according to the mysterious virginal mechanism – of not fluttering out of the room when she found him there alone, of treating him rather as a benignant than as a pernicious influence – a radiant frankness of demeanour, in fine, in spite of an evident natural reserve, which it seemed equally graceless not to make the subject of a compliment and indelicate not to take for granted. In this way there was wrought in the Baron's mind a vague, unwonted resonance of soft impressions, as we may call it, which indicated the transmutation of 'sentiment' from a contingency into a fact. His imagination enjoyed it; he was very fond of music, and this reminded him of some of the best he had ever heard. In spite of the bore of being laid up with a lame knee, he was in a better humour than he had known for months; he lay smoking cigarettes and listening to the nightingales, with the comfortable smile of one of his country neighbours whose big ox should have taken the prize at a fair. Every now and then, with an impatient suspicion of the resemblance, he declared that he was pitifully *bête*; but he was under a charm which braved even the supreme penalty of seeming ridiculous. One morning he had half an hour's *tête-à-tête* with his grandmother's confessor, a soft-voiced old Abbé, whom, for reasons of her own, Madame de Mauves had suddenly summoned, and had left waiting in the drawing-room while she rearranged her curls. His reverence, going up to the old lady, assured her that M. le Baron[21] was in a most edifying state of mind, and a promising subject for the operation of grace. This was a theological interpretation of the Baron's momentary good-humour. He had always lazily wondered what priests were good for, and he now remembered, with a sense of especial obligation to the Abbé, that they were excellent for marrying people.

A day or two after this he left off his bandages, and tried to walk. He made his way into the garden and hobbled successfully along one of the alleys; but in the midst of his progress he was seized with a spasm of pain which forced him to stop and call for help. In an instant Euphemia came tripping along the path and offered him her arm with the frankest solicitude.

'Not to the house,' he said, taking it; 'further on, to the bosquet.' This choice was prompted by her having immediately confessed that she had seen him leave the house, had feared an accident, and had followed him on tiptoe.

'Why didn't you join me?' he had asked, giving her a look in which admiration was no longer disguised, and yet felt itself half at the mercy of her replying that a *jeune fille* should not be seen following a gentleman. But it drew a breath which filled its lungs for a long time afterwards, when she replied simply that if she had overtaken him he might have accepted her arm out of politeness, whereas she wished to have the pleasure of seeing him walk alone.

The bosquet was covered with an odorous tangle of blossoming creepers, and a nightingale overhead was shaking out love-notes with a profuseness which made the Baron consider his own conduct the perfection of propriety.

'In America,' he said, 'I have always heard that when a man wishes to marry a young girl, he offers himself simply, face to face, without any ceremony – without parents, and uncles, and cousins sitting round in a circle.'

'Why, I believe so,' said Euphemia, staring, and too surprised to be alarmed.

'Very well, then,' said the Baron, 'suppose our bosquet here to be America. I offer you my hand, à l'Américaine. It will make me intensely happy to see you accept it.'

Whether Euphemia's acceptance was in the American manner is more than I can say; I incline to think that for fluttering, grateful, trustful, softly-amazed young hearts, there is only one manner all over the world.

That evening, in the little turret chamber which it was her happiness to inhabit, she wrote a dutiful letter to her mamma and had just sealed it when she was sent for by Madame de Mauves. She found this ancient lady seated in her boudoir, in a lavender satin gown, with all her candles lighted, as if to celebrate her grandson's betrothal. 'Are you very happy?' Madame de Mauves demanded, making Euphemia sit down before her.

'I am almost afraid to say so,' said the young girl, 'lest I should wake myself up.'

'May you never wake up, *belle enfant*,' said the old lady, solemnly. 'This is the first marriage ever made in our family in this way – by a Baron de Mauves proposing to a young girl in an arbour, like Jeannot and Jeannette.[22] It has not been our way of doing things, and people may say it wants frankness. My grandson tells me he considers it the perfection of frankness. Very good. I am a very old woman, and if your differences should ever be as marked as your agreement, I should not like to see them. But I should be sorry to die and think you were going to be unhappy. You can't be, beyond a certain point; because, though in this world the Lord sometimes makes light of our expectations, He never altogether ignores our deserts. But you are very young and innocent, and easy to deceive. There never was a man in the world – among the saints themselves – as good as you believe the Baron. But he's a *galant homme* and a gentleman, and I have been talking to him to-night. To you I want to say this – that you're to forget the worldly rubbish I talked the other day about frivolous women being happy. It's not the kind of happiness that would suit you. Whatever befalls you, promise me this: to be yourself. The Baronne de Mauves[23] will be none the worse for it. Yourself, understand, in spite of everything – bad precepts and bad examples, bad usage, even. Be persistently and patiently yourself, and a De Mauves will do you justice!'

Euphemia remembered this speech in after years, and more than once, wearily closing her eyes, she seemed to see the old woman sitting upright in her faded finery and smiling grimly, like one of the Fates[24] who sees the wheel of fortune turning up her favourite event. But at the moment it seemed to her simply to have the proper gravity of the occasion; this was the way, she supposed, in which lucky young girls were addressed on their engagement by wise old women of quality.

At her convent, to which she immediately returned, she found a letter from her mother, which shocked her far more than the remarks of Madame de Mauves. Who were these people, Mrs Cleve demanded, who had presumed to talk to her daughter of marriage without asking her leave? Questionable gentlefolk, plainly; the best French people never did such things. Euphemia would return straightway to her convent, shut herself up, and await her own arrival.

It took Mrs Cleve three weeks to travel from Nice to Paris, and during this time the young girl had no communication with her lover beyond accepting a bouquet of violets, marked with his initials and left by a female friend. 'I have not brought you up with such devoted care,' she declared to her daughter at their first interview, 'to marry a penniless Frenchman. I will take you straight home, and you will please to forget M. de Mauves.'

Mrs Cleve received that evening at her hotel a visit from the Baron which mitigated her wrath, but failed to modify her decision. He had very good manners, but she was sure he had horrible morals; and Mrs Cleve, who had been a very good-natured censor on her own account, felt a genuine spiritual need to sacrifice her daughter to propriety. She belonged to that large class of Americans who make light of their native land in familiar discourse, but are startled back into a sense of moral responsibility when they find Europeans taking them at their word. 'I know the type, my dear,' she said to her daughter with a sagacious nod. 'He will not beat you; sometimes you will wish he would.'

Euphemia remained solemnly silent; for the only answer she felt capable of making her mother was that her mind was too small a measure of things, and that the Baron's type was one which it took some mystical illumination to appreciate. A person who confounded him with the common throng of her watering-place acquaintance was not a person to argue with. It seemed to Euphemia that she had no cause to plead; her cause was in the Lord's hands and her lover's.

M. de Mauves had been irritated and mortified by Mrs Cleve's opposition, and hardly knew how to handle an adversary who failed to perceive that a De Mauves of necessity gave more than he received. But he had obtained information on his return to Paris which exalted the uses of humility. Euphemia's fortune, wonderful to say, was greater than its fame, and in view of such a prize, even a De Mauves could afford to take a snubbing.

The young man's tact, his deference, his urbane insistence, won a concession from Mrs Cleve. The engagement was to be put off and her daughter was to return home, be brought out and receive the homage she was entitled to, and which would but too surely take a form dangerous to the Baron's suit. They were to exchange neither letters, nor mementos, nor messages; but if at the end of two years Euphemia had refused offers enough to attest the permanence of her attachment, he should receive an invitation to address her again.

This decision was promulgated in the presence of the parties interested. The Baron bore himself gallantly, and looked at the young girl, expecting some tender protestation. But she only looked at him silently in return, neither weeping, nor smiling, nor putting out her hand. On this they separated; but as the Baron walked away, he declared to himself that, in spite of the confounded two years, he was a very happy fellow – to have a fiancée who, to several millions of francs, added such strangely beautiful eyes.

How many offers Euphemia refused but scantily concerns us – and how the Baron wore his two years away. He found that he needed pastimes, and, as pastimes were expensive, he added heavily to the list of debts to be cancelled by Euphemia's millions. Sometimes, in the thick of what he had once called pleasure with a keener conviction than now, he put to himself the case of their failing him after all; and then he remembered that last mute assurance of her eyes, and drew a long breath of such confidence as he felt in nothing else in the world save his own punctuality in an affair of honour.

At last, one morning, he took the express to Havre[25] with a letter of Mrs Cleve's in his pocket, and ten days later made his bow to mother and daughter in New York. His stay was brief, and he was apparently unable to bring himself to view what Euphemia's uncle, Mr Butterworth, who gave her away at the altar, called our great experiment in democratic self-government, in a serious light. He smiled at everything, and seemed to regard the New World as a colossal *plaisanterie*. It is true that a perpetual smile was the most natural expression of countenance for a man about to marry Euphemia Cleve.

III

Longmore's first visit seemed to open to him so large an opportunity for tranquil enjoyment that he very soon paid a second, and, at the end of a fortnight, had spent a great many hours in the little drawing-room which Madame de Mauves rarely quitted except to drive or walk in the forest. She lived in an old-fashioned pavilion,[26] between a high-walled court and an

excessively artificial garden, beyond whose enclosure you saw
a long line of tree-tops. Longmore liked the garden, and in the
mild afternoons used to move his chair through the open window to the little terrace which overlooked it, while his hostess
sat just within. After a while she came out and wandered
through the narrow alleys and beside the thin-spouting fountain, and at last introduced him to a little gate in the
garden-wall, opening upon a lane which led to the forest.
Hitherward, more than once, she wandered with him, bareheaded
and meaning to go but twenty rods²⁷ but always strolling
good-naturedly further, and often taking a generous walk.
They discovered many things to talk about, and to the pleasure
of finding the hours tread inaudibly away, Longmore was able
to add the satisfaction of suspecting that he was a 'resource'
for Madame de Mauves. He had made her acquaintance with
the sense, not altogether comfortable, that she was a woman
with a painful secret, and that seeking her acquaintance would
be like visiting at a house where there was an invalid who
could bear no noise. But he very soon perceived that her sorrow, since sorrow it was, was not an aggressive one; that it was
not fond of attitudes and ceremonies, and that her earnest wish
was to forget it. He felt that even if Mrs Draper had not
told him she was unhappy, he would have guessed it; and yet
he could hardly have pointed to his evidence. It was chiefly
negative – she never alluded to her husband. Beyond this it
seemed to him simply that her whole being was pitched on a
lower key than harmonious Nature meant; she was like a
powerful singer who had lost her high notes. She never drooped
nor sighed nor looked unutterable things; she indulged in no
dusky sarcasms against fate; she had, in short, none of the
coquetry of unhappiness. But Longmore was sure that her gentle gaiety was the result of strenuous effort, and that she was
trying to interest herself in his thoughts to escape from her
own. If she had wished to irritate his curiosity and lead him to
take her confidence by storm, nothing could have served her
purpose better than this ingenuous reserve. He declared to
himself that there was a rare magnanimity in such ardent
self-effacement, and that but one woman in ten thousand was

capable of merging an intensely personal grief in thankless
outward contemplation. Madame de Mauves, he instinctively
felt, was not sweeping the horizon for a compensation or a
consoler; she had suffered a personal deception which had disgusted her with persons. She was not striving to balance her
sorrow with some strongly seasoned joy; for the present, she
was trying to live with it, peaceably, reputably, and without
scandal – turning the key on it occasionally, as you would on
a companion liable to attacks of insanity. Longmore was a
man of fine senses and of an active imagination, whose
leading-strings had never been slipped. He began to regard his
hostess as a figure haunted by a shadow which was somehow
her intenser, more authentic self. This hovering mystery came
to have for him an extraordinary charm. Her delicate beauty
acquired to his eye the serious cast of certain blank-browed
Greek statues; and sometimes, when his imagination, more
than his ear, detected a vague tremor in the tone in which she
attempted to make a friendly question seemed to have behind
it none of the hollow resonance of absent-mindedness, his
marvelling eyes gave her an answer more eloquent, though
much less to the point, than the one she demanded.

    She gave him indeed much to wonder about, and, in his
ignorance he formed a dozen experimental theories on the subject of her marriage. She had married for love and staked her
whole soul on it; of that he was convinced. She had not married a Frenchman to be near Paris and her base of supplies of
millinery; he was sure she had seen conjugal happiness in a
light of which her present life, with its conveniences for shopping and its moral aridity, was the absolute negation. But by
what extraordinary process of the heart – through what mysterious intermission of that moral instinct which may keep
pace with the heart, even when this organ is making unprecedented time – had she fixed her affections on an arrogantly
frivolous Frenchman? Longmore needed no telling; he knew M.
de Mauves was frivolous; it was stamped on his eyes, his nose,
his mouth, his carriage. For Frenchwomen Longmore had but
a scanty kindness, or at least (what with him was very much
the same thing) but a scanty gallantry; they all seemed to

belong to the type of a certain fine lady to whom he had ventured to present a letter of introduction, and whom, directly
after his first visit to her, he had set down in his note book as
'metallic'. Why should Madame de Mauves have chosen a
Frenchwoman's lot – she whose character had a perfume which
is absent from even the brightest metals? He asked her one day
frankly if it had cost her nothing to transplant herself – if she
were not oppressed with a sense of irreconcilable difference
from 'all these people'. She was silent a while, and he fancied
that she was hesitating as to whether she should resent so
unceremonious an allusion to her husband. He almost wished
she would; it would seem a proof that her deep reserve of sorrow had a limit.

'I almost grew up here,' she said at last, 'and it was here for
me that those dreams of the future took shape that we all have
when we cease to be very young. As matters stand, one may be
very American and yet arrange it with one's conscience to live
in Europe. My imagination perhaps – I had a little when I was
younger – helped me to think I should find happiness here. And
after all, for a woman, what does it signify? This is not America, perhaps, about me, but it's quite as little France. France is
out there, beyond the garden, in the town, in the forest; but
here, close about me, in my room and' – she paused a
moment – 'in my mind, it's a nameless country of my own. It's
not her country,' she added, 'that makes a woman happy or
unhappy.'

Madame Clairin, Euphemia's sister-in-law, might have been
supposed to have undertaken the graceful task of making
Longmore ashamed of his uncivil jottings about her sex and
nation. Mademoiselle de Mauves, bringing example to the
confirmation of precept, had made a remunerative match and
sacrificed her name to the millions of a prosperous and aspir-
ing wholesale druggist – a gentleman liberal enough to consider
his fortune a moderate price for being towed into circles
unpervaded by pharmaceutic odours. His system, possibly, was
sound, but his own application of it was unfortunate. M. Clairin's head was turned by his good luck. Having secured an
aristocratic wife, he adopted an aristocratic vice and began to

gamble at the Bourse. In an evil hour he lost heavily, and then staked heavily to recover himself. But he overtook his loss only by a greater one. Then he let everything go – his wits, his courage, his probity – everything that had made him what his ridiculous marriage had so promptly unmade. He walked up the Rue Vivienne one day with his hands in his empty pockets, and stood for half an hour staring confusedly up and down the glittering Boulevard. People brushed against him, and half a dozen carriages almost ran over him, until at last a policeman, who had been watching him for some time, took him by the arm and led him gently away. He looked at the man's cocked hat and sword with tears in his eyes; he hoped he was going to interpret to him the wrath of Heaven – to execute the penalty of his dead-weight of self-abhorrence. But the *sergent de ville* only stationed him in the embrasure of a door, out of harm's way, and walked away to supervise a financial contest between an old lady and a cabman. Poor M. Clairin had only been married a year, but he had had time to measure the lofty spirit of a De Mauves. When night had fallen, he repaired to the house of a friend and asked for a night's lodging; and as his friend, who was simply his old head book-keeper, and lived in a small way, was put to some trouble to accommodate him – 'You must excuse me,' Clairin said, 'but I can't go home. I am afraid of my wife!' Towards morning he blew his brains out. His widow turned the remnants of his property to better account than could have been expected, and wore the very handsomest mourning. It was for this latter reason, perhaps, that she was obliged to retrench at other points, and accept a temporary home under her brother's roof.

Fortune had played Madame Clairin a terrible trick, but had found an adversary and not a victim. Though quite without beauty, she had always had what is called the grand air, and her air from this time forward was grander than ever. As she trailed about in her sable furbelows[28] tossing back her well-dressed head, and holding up her vigilant eye-glass, she seemed to be sweeping the whole field of society and asking herself where she should pluck her revenge. Suddenly she espied it, ready made to her hand, in poor Longmore's wealth and amiability. American dollars and American complaisance had made her brother's fortune; why should they not make hers? She over-estimated Longmore's wealth and misinterpreted his amiability; for she was sure that a man could not be so contented without being rich, nor so unassuming without being weak. He encountered her advances with a formal politeness which covered a great deal of unflattering discomposure. She made him feel acutely uncomfortable; and though he was at a loss to conceive how he could be an object of interest to a shrewd Parisienne, he had an indefinable sense of being enclosed in a magnetic circle, like the victim of an incantation. If Madame Clairin could have fathomed his Puritanic soul, she would have laid by her wand and her book and admitted that he was an impossible subject. She gave him a kind of moral chill, and he never mentally alluded to her save as that dreadful woman – that terrible woman. He did justice to her grand air, but for his pleasure he preferred the small air of Madame de Mauves; and he never made her his bow, after standing frigidly passive for five minutes to one of her gracious overtures to intimacy, without feeling a peculiar desire to ramble away into the forest, fling himself down on the warm grass, and, staring up at the blue sky, forget that there were any women in nature who didn't please like the swaying tree-tops. One day, on his arrival, she met him in the court and told him that her sister-in-law was shut up with a headache, and that his visit must be for her. He followed her into the drawing-room with the best grace at his command, and sat twirling his hat for half an hour. Suddenly he understood her; the caressing cadence of her voice was a distinct invitation to solicit the incomparable honour of her hand. He blushed to the roots of his hair and jumped up with uncontrollable alacrity; then, dropping a glance at Madame Clairin, who sat watching him with hard eyes over the edge of her smile, as it were, perceived on her brow a flash of unforgiving wrath. It was not becoming, but his eyes lingered a moment, for it seemed to illuminate her character. What he saw there frightened him and he felt himself murmuring, 'Poor Madame de Mauves!' His departure was abrupt, and this time he really went into the forest and lay down on the grass.

After this he admired Madame de Mauves more than ever;
she seemed a brighter figure, with a darker shadow appended
to it. At the end of a month he received a letter from a friend
with whom he had arranged a tour through the Low Countries, reminding him of his promise to meet him promptly at
Brussels. It was only after his answer was posted that he fully
measured the zeal with which he had declared that the journey
must either be deferred or abandoned – that he could not possibly leave Saint-Germain. He took a walk in the forest, and
asked himself if this were irrevocably true. If it were, surely his
duty was to march straight home and pack his trunk. Poor
Webster, who, he knew, had counted ardently on this excursion, was an excellent fellow; six weeks ago he would have
gone through fire and water to join Webster. It had never been
in his books to throw overboard a friend whom he had loved
for ten years for a married woman whom for six weeks he
had – admired. It was certainly beyond question that he was
lingering at Saint-Germain because this admirable married
woman was there; but in the midst of all this admiration, what
had become of prudence? This was the conduct of a man drift-
ing rapidly into passion. If she were as unhappy as he believed,
the passion of such a man would help her very little more than
his indifference; if she were less so, she needed no help, and
could dispense with his friendly offices. He was sure, moreover, that if she knew he was staying on her account she would
be extremely annoyed. But this very feeling had much to do
with making it hard to go; her displeasure would only enhance
the gentle stoicism which touched him to the heart. At
moments, indeed, he assured himself that to linger was simply
impertinent; it was indelicate to make a daily study of such a
shrinking grief. But inclination answered that some day her
self-support would fail, and he had a vision of this admirable
creature calling vainly for help. He would be her friend, to any
length; it was unworthy to both of them to think about consequences. But he was a friend who carried about with him a
muttering resentment that he had not known her five years
earlier, and a brooding hostility to those who had anticipated
him. It seemed one of fortune's most mocking strokes, that she

should be surrounded by persons whose only merit was that they threw the charm of her character into radiant relief.

Longmore's growing irritation made it more and more difficult for him to see any other merit than this in the Baron de Mauves. And yet, disinterestedly, it would have been hard to give a name to the portentous vices which such an estimate implied, and there were times when our hero was almost persuaded against his finer judgement that he was really the most considerate of husbands, and that his wife liked melancholy for melancholy's sake. His manners were perfect, his urbanity was unbounded, and he seemed never to address her but, sentimentally speaking, hat in hand. His tone to Longmore (as the latter was perfectly aware) was that of a man of the world to a man not quite of the world; but what it lacked in deference it made up in easy friendliness. 'I can't thank you enough for having overcome my wife's shyness,' he more than once declared. 'If we left her to do as she pleased, she would bury herself alive. Come often, and bring some one else. She will have nothing to do with my friends, but perhaps she will look at yours.'

The Baron made these speeches with a remorseless placidity very amazing to our hero, who had an innocent belief that a man's head may point out to him the shortcomings of his heart, and make him ashamed of them. He could not fancy him capable both of neglecting his wife and taking an almost humorous view of her suffering. Longmore had, at any rate, an exasperating sense that the Baron thought rather the less of his wife on account of that very same fine difference of nature which so deeply stirred his own sympathies. He was rarely present during Longmore's visits, and he made a daily journey to Paris, where he had 'business', as he once mentioned – not in the least with a tone of apology. When he appeared, it was late in the evening, and with an imperturbable air of being on the best of terms with every one and everything, which was peculiarly annoying if you happened to have a tacit quarrel with him. If he was a good fellow, he was surely a good fellow spoiled. Something he had, however, which Longmore vaguely envied – a kind of superb positiveness – a manner rounded and polished

by the traditions of centuries – an urbanity exercised for his
own sake and not his neighbours' – which seemed the result of
something better than a good conscience – of a vigorous and
unscrupulous temperament. The Baron was plainly not a
moral man, and poor Longmore, who was, would have been
glad to learn the secret of his luxurious serenity. What was it
that enabled him, without being a monster with visibly cloven
feet, exhaling brimstone, to misprize so cruelly a lovely wife,
and to walk about the world with a candid smile under his
moustache? It was the essential grossness of his imagination,
which had nevertheless helped him to turn so many neat compliments. He could be very polite, and he could doubtless be
supremely impertinent; but he was as unable to draw a moral
inference of the finer strain as a school-boy who has been playing truant for a week to solve a problem in algebra. It was ten
to one he did not know his wife was unhappy; he and his brilliant sister had doubtless agreed to consider their companion a
Puritanical little person, of meagre aspirations and slender
accomplishments, contented with looking at Paris from the
terrace, and, as an especial treat, having a countryman very
much like herself to supply her with homely transatlantic gossip. M. de Mauves was tired of his companion; he relished a
higher flavour in female society. She was too modest, too simple, too delicate; she had too few arts, too little coquetry, too
much charity. M. de Mauves, some day, lighting a cigar, had
probably decided she was stupid. It was the same sort of taste,
Longmore moralized, as the taste for Gérôme in painting, and
for M. Gustave Flaubert in literature.[29] The Baron was a pagan
and his wife was a Christian, and between them, accordingly,
was a gulf. He was by race and instinct a *grand seigneur*.
Longmore had often heard of this distinguished social type,
and was properly grateful for an opportunity to examine it
closely. It had certainly a picturesque boldness of outline, but
it was fed from spiritual sources so remote from those of which
he felt the living gush of his own soul, that he found himself
gazing at it, in irreconcilable antipathy, across a dim historic
mist. 'I am a modern *bourgeois*,' he said, 'and not perhaps so
good a judge of how far a pretty woman's tongue may go at

supper without prejudice to her reputation. But I have not met one of the sweetest of women without recognizing her, and discovering that a certain sort of character offers better entertainment than Thérésa's songs, sung by a dissipated duchess. Wit for wit, I think mine carries me further.' It was easy indeed to perceive that, as became a *grand seigneur,* M. de Mauves had a stock of social principles. He would not especially have desired, perhaps, that his wife should compete in amateur operettas with the duchesses in question, chiefly of recent origin; but he held that a gentleman may take his amusement where he finds it, that he is quite at liberty not to find it at home, and that the wife of a De Mauves who should hang her head and have red eyes, and allow herself to make any other response to officious condolence than that her husband's amusements were his own affair, would have forfeited every claim to having her finger-tips bowed over and kissed. And yet in spite of this definite faith, Longmore fancied that the Baron was more irritated than gratified by his wife's irreproachable reserve. Did it dimly occur to him that it was self-control and not self-effacement? She was a model to all the inferior matrons of his line, past and to come, and an occasional 'scene' from her at a convenient moment would have something reassuring – would attest her stupidity a trifle more forcibly than her inscrutable tranquillity.

Longmore would have given much to know the principle of her submissiveness, and he tried more than once, but with rather awkward timidity, to sound the mystery. She seemed to him to have been long resisting the force of cruel evidence, and, though she had succumbed to it at last, to have denied herself the right to complain, because if faith was gone, her heroic generosity remained. He believed even that she was capable of reproaching herself with having expected too much, and of trying to persuade herself out of her bitterness by saying that her hopes had been illusions and that this was simply – life. 'I hate tragedy,' she once said to him; 'I have a really pusillanimous dread of moral suffering. I believe that – without base concessions – there is always some way of escaping from it. I would almost rather never smile all my life than have a single violent explosion of grief.' She lived evidently in nervous appre-hension of being fatally convinced – of seeing to the end of her deception. Longmore, when he thought of this, felt an immense longing to offer her something of which she could be as sure as of the sun in heaven.

IV

His friend Webster lost no time in accusing him of the basest infidelity, and asking him what he found at Saint-Germain to prefer to Van Eyck and Memling, Rubens and Rembrandt.[30] A day or two after the receipt of Webster's letter, he took a walk with Madame de Mauves in the forest. They sat down on a fallen log, and she began to arrange into a bouquet the anem-ones and violets she had gathered. 'I have a letter,' he said at last, 'from a friend whom I some time ago promised to join at Brussels. The time has come – it has passed. It finds me terribly unwilling to leave Saint-Germain.'

She looked up with the candid interest which she always displayed in his affairs, but with no disposition, apparently, to make a personal application of his words. 'Saint-Germain is pleasant enough,' she said; 'but are you doing yourself justice? Shall you not regret in future days that instead of travelling and seeing cities and monuments and museums and improving your mind, you sat here – for instance – on a log, pulling my flowers to pieces?'

'What I shall regret in future days,' he answered after some hesitation, 'is that I should have sat here and not spoken the truth on the matter. I am fond of museums and monuments and of improving my mind, and I am particularly fond of my friend Webster. But I can't bring myself to leave Saint-Germain without asking you a question. You must forgive me if it's indiscreet, and be assured that curiosity was never more respectful. Are you really as unhappy as I imagine you to be?'

She had evidently not expected his question, and she greeted it with a startled blush. 'If I strike you as unhappy,' she said, 'I have been a poorer friend to you than I wished to be.'

'I, perhaps, have been a better friend of yours than you have supposed. I have admired your reserve, your courage, your studied gaiety. But I have felt the existence of something beneath them that was more *you* – more you as I wished to know you – than they were; something that I have believed to be a constant sorrow.'

She listened with great gravity, but without an air of offence, and he felt that while he had been timorously calculating the last consequences of friendship, she had serenely accepted them. 'You surprise me,' she said slowly, and her blush still lingered. 'But to refuse to answer you would confirm an impression on your part which is evidently already too strong. An unhappiness that one can sit comfortably talking about is an unhappiness with distinct limitations. If I were examined before a board of commissioners for investigating the felicity of mankind, I am sure I should be pronounced a very fortunate woman.' There was something delightfully gentle to him in her tone, and its softness seemed to deepen as she continued. 'But let me add, with all gratitude for your sympathy, that it's my own affair altogether. It need not disturb you, Mr Longmore, for I have often found myself in your company a very contented person.'

'You are a wonderful woman,' he said, 'and I admire you as I never have admired any one. You are wiser than anything I, for one, can say to you; and what I ask of you is not to let me advise or console you, but simply thank you for letting me know you.' He had intended no such outburst as this, but his voice rang loud, and he felt a kind of unfamiliar joy as he uttered it.

She shook her head with some impatience. 'Let us be friends – as I supposed we were going to be – without protestations and fine words. To have you paying compliments to my wisdom – that would be real wretchedness. I can dispense with your admiration better than the Flemish painters can – better than Van Eyck and Rubens, in spite of all their worshippers. Go join your friend – see everything, enjoy everything, learn everything, and write me an excellent letter, brimming over with your impressions. I am extremely fond of the Dutch painters,' she added, with a slight faltering of the voice, which Longmore had noticed once before, and which he had interpreted as the sudden weariness of a spirit self-condemned to play a part.

'I don't believe you care a button about the Dutch painters,' he said, with an unhesitating laugh. 'But I shall certainly write you a letter.'

She rose and turned homeward, thoughtfully rearranging her flowers as she walked. Little was said; Longmore was asking himself, with a tremor in the unspoken words, whether all this meant simply that he was in love. He looked at the rooks wheeling against the golden-hued sky, between the tree-tops, but not at his companion, whose personal presence seemed lost in the felicity she had created. Madame de Mauves was silent and grave, because she was painfully disappointed. A sentimental friendship she had not desired; her scheme had been to pass with Longmore as a placid creature with a good deal of leisure, which she was disposed to devote to profitable conversation of an impersonal sort. She liked him extremely, and felt that there was something in him to which, when she made up her girlish mind that a needy French baron was the ripest fruit of time, she had done very scanty justice. They went through the little gate in the garden-wall and approached the house. On the terrace Madame Clairin was entertaining a friend – a little elderly gentleman with a white moustache, and an order in his button-hole. Madame de Mauves chose to pass round the house into the court; whereupon her sister-in-law, greeting Longmore with a commanding nod, lifted her eye-glass and stared at them as they went by. Longmore heard the little old gentleman uttering some old-fashioned epigram about 'la vieille galanterie Française', and then, by a sudden impulse, he looked at Madame de Mauves and wondered what she was doing in such a world. She stopped before the house, without asking him to come in. 'I hope you will act upon my advice,' she said, 'and waste no more time at Saint-Germain.'

For an instant there rose to his lips some faded compliment about his time not being wasted, but it expired before the simple sincerity of her look. She stood there as gently serious as the angel of disinterestedness, and Longmore felt as if he should insult her by treating her words as a bait for flattery. 'I shall start in a day or two,' he answered, 'but I will not promise you not to come back.'

'I hope not,' she said, simply. 'I expect to be here a long time.'

'I shall come and say good-bye,' he rejoined; on which she nodded with a smile, and went in.

He turned away, and walked slowly homeward by the terrace. It seemed to him that to leave her thus, for a gain on which she herself insisted, was to know her better and admire her more. But he was in a vague ferment of feeling which her evasion of his question half an hour before had done more to deepen than to allay. Suddenly, on the terrace, he encountered M. de Mauves, who was leaning against the parapet, finishing a cigar. The Baron, who, he fancied, had an air of peculiar affability, offered him his fair, plump hand. Longmore stopped; he felt a sudden angry desire to cry out to him that he had the loveliest wife in the world; that he ought to be ashamed of himself not to know it; and that for all his shrewdness he had never looked into the depths of her eyes. The Baron, we know, considered that he had; but there was something in Euphemia's eyes now that was not there five years before. They talked for a while about various things, and M. de Mauves gave a humorous account of his visit to America. His tone was not soothing to Longmore's excited sensibilities. He seemed to consider the country a gigantic joke, and his urbanity only went so far as to admit that it was not a bad one. Longmore was not, by habit, an aggressive apologist for his native institutions; but the Baron's narrative confirmed his worst impressions of French superficiality. He had understood nothing, he had felt nothing, he had learned nothing; and our hero, glancing askance at his aristocratic profile, declared that if the chief merit of a long pedigree was to leave one so fatuously stupid, he thanked his stars that the Longmores had emerged from obscurity in the present century, in the person of an enterprising timber-merchant. M. de Mauves dwelt of course on that prime oddity of ours – the liberty allowed to young girls; and related the history of his researches into the 'opportunities' it presented to French noblemen – researches in which, during a fortnight's stay, he seemed to have spent many agreeable hours. 'I am bound to admit,' he said, 'that in every case I was disarmed by the extreme candour of the young lady, and that they took care of themselves to better purpose than I have seen some mammas in France take care of them.' Longmore greeted this handsome concession with the grimmest of smiles, and damned his impertinent patronage.

Mentioning at last that he was about to leave Saint-Germain, he was surprised, without exactly being flattered, by the Baron's quickened attention. 'I am so very sorry!' the latter cried. 'I hoped we had you for the whole summer.' Longmore murmured something civil, and wondered why M. de Mauves should care whether he stayed or went. 'You were a distraction to Madame de Mauves,' the Baron added; 'I assure you I mentally blessed your visits.'

'They were a great pleasure to me,' Longmore said, gravely. 'Some day I expect to come back.'

'Pray do;' and the Baron laid his hand urgently on his arm. 'You see I have confidence in you.' Longmore was silent for a moment, and the Baron puffed his cigar reflectively and watched the smoke. 'Madame de Mauves,' he said at last, 'is a rather singular person.'

Longmore shifted his position, and wondered whether he were going to 'explain' Madame de Mauves.

'Being, as you are, her fellow-countryman,' the Baron went on, 'I don't mind speaking frankly. She's just a little morbid – the most charming woman in the world, as you see, but a little fanciful – a little *entêtée*. Now you see she has taken this extraordinary fancy for solitude. I can't get her to go anywhere – to see any one. When my friends present themselves she is perfectly polite, but she is simply freezing. She doesn't do herself justice, and I expect every day to hear two or three of them say to me, "Your wife is *jolie à croquer*: what a pity she hasn't a little *esprit*." You must have found out that she has really a great deal. But to tell the whole truth, what she needs is to forget herself. She sits alone for hours poring over her English

books and looking at life through that terrible brown fog
which they always seem to me to fling over the world. I doubt
if your English authors,' the Baron continued, with a serenity
which Longmore afterwards characterized as sublime, 'are
very sound reading for young married women. I don't pretend
to know much about them; but I remember that, not long after
our marriage, Madame de Mauves undertook to read me one
day a certain Wordsworth – a poet highly esteemed, it appears,
chez vous. It seemed to me that she took me by the nape of the
neck and held my head for half an hour over a basin of *soupe
aux choux*, and that one ought to ventilate the drawing-room
before any one called. But I suppose you know him – *ce
génie-là*. I think my wife never forgave me, and that it was a
real shock to her to find she had married a man who had very
much the same taste in literature as in cookery. But you are a
man of general culture – a man of the world,' said the Baron,
turning to Longmore and fixing his eyes on the seal of his
watchguard. 'You can talk about everything, and I am sure
you like Alfred de Musset[31] as well as Monsieur Wordsworth.
Talk to her about everything, Alfred de Musset included. Bah!
I forgot that you are going. Come back then as soon as possible
and talk about your travels. If Madame de Mauves too would
make a little voyage, it would do her good. It would enlarge
her horizon' – and M. de Mauves made a series of short nervous jerks with his stick in the air – 'it would wake up her
imagination. She's too rigid, you know – it would show her
that one may bend a trifle without breaking.' He paused a
moment and gave two or three vigorous puffs. Then, turning
to his companion again, with a little nod and a confidential
smile – 'I hope you admire my candour. I wouldn't say all this
to one of *us*!'

Evening was coming on, and the lingering light seemed to
float in the air in faintly golden motes. Longmore stood gazing
at these luminous particles; he could almost have fancied them
a swarm of humming insects, murmuring as a refrain, 'She has
a great deal of *esprit* – she has a great deal of *esprit*.' 'Yes, she
has a great deal,' he said, mechanically, turning to the
Baron. M. de Mauves glanced at him sharply, as if to ask what

the deuce he was talking about. 'She has a great deal of intelligence,' said Longmore, deliberately, 'a great deal of beauty, a
great many virtues.'

M. de Mauves busied himself for a moment in lighting
another cigar, and when he had finished, with a return of his
confidential smile, 'I suspect you of thinking that I don't do my
wife justice,' he said. 'Take care – take care, young man; that's
a dangerous assumption. In general a man always does his wife
justice. More than justice,' cried the Baron with a laugh – 'that
we keep for the wives of other men!'

Longmore afterwards remembered it in favour of the Baron's
fine manner that he had not measured at this moment the dusky
abyss over which it hovered. But a sort of deepening subterranean echo lingered on his spiritual ear. For the present his
keenest sensation was a desire to get away and cry aloud that
M. de Mauves was an arrogant fool. He bade him an abrupt
good-night, which was to serve also, he said, as good-bye.

'Decidedly, then, you go?' said M. de Mauves, almost
peremptorily.

'Decidedly.'

'Of course you will come and say good-bye to Madame de
Mauves?' His tone implied that the omission would be very
uncivil; but there seemed to Longmore something so ludicrous
in his taking a lesson in consideration from M. de Mauves,
that he burst into a laugh. The Baron frowned, like a man for
whom it was a new and most unpleasant sensation to be perplexed. 'You are a queer fellow,' he murmured, as Longmore
turned away, not foreseeing that he should think him a very
queer fellow indeed before he had done with him.

Longmore sat down to dinner at his hotel with his usual
good intentions; but as he was lifting his first glass of wine to
his lips, he suddenly fell to musing and set down his wine
untasted. His reverie lasted long, and when he emerged from
it, his fish was cold; but this mattered little, for his appetite
was gone. That evening he packed his trunk with a kind of
indignant energy. This was so effective that the operation was
accomplished before bedtime, and as he was not in the least
sleepy, he devoted the interval to writing two letters; one was

a short note to Madame de Mauves, which he intrusted to a
servant, to be delivered the next morning. He had found it
best, he said, to leave Saint-Germain immediately, but he
expected to be back in Paris in the early autumn. The other
letter was the result of his having remembered a day or two
before that he had not yet complied with Mrs Draper's injunction to give her an account of his impressions of her friend. The
present occasion seemed propitious, and he wrote half a dozen
pages. His tone, however, was grave, and Mrs Draper, on
receiving them, was slightly disappointed – she would have
preferred a stronger flavour of rhapsody. But what chiefly concerns us is the concluding sentences.

'The only time she ever spoke to me of her marriage,' he
wrote, 'she intimated that it had been a perfect love-match.
With all abatements, I suppose most marriages are; but in her
case, I think, this would mean more than in that of most
women; for her love was an absolute idealization. She believed
her husband was a hero of rose-coloured romance, and he
turns out to be not even a hero of very sad-coloured reality. For
some time now she has been sounding her mistake, but I don't
believe she has touched the bottom of it yet. She strikes me as
a person who is begging off from full knowledge – who has
struck a truce with painful truth, and is trying a while the
experiment of living with closed eyes. In the dark she tries to
see again the gilding on her idol. Illusion of course is illusion,
and one must always pay for it; but there is something truly
tragical in seeing an earthly penalty levied on such divine folly
as this. As for M. de Mauves, he's a Frenchman to his fingers'
ends; and I confess I should dislike him for this if he were a
much better man. He can't forgive his wife for having married
him too sentimentally and loved him too well; for in some
uncorrupted corner of his being he feels, I suppose, that as she
saw him, so he ought to have been. It is a perpetual vexation to
him that a little American bourgeoise should have fancied him
a finer fellow than he is, or than he at all wants to be. He has
not a glimmering of real acquaintance with his wife; he can't
understand the stream of passion flowing so clear and still. To
tell the truth, I hardly can understand it myself; but when I see

the spectacle I can admire it furiously. M. de Mauves, at any rate, would like to have the comfort of feeling that his wife is as corruptible as himself; and you will hardly believe me when I tell you that he goes about intimating to gentlemen whom he deems worthy of the knowledge, that it would be a convenience to him that they should make love to her.'

V

On reaching Paris, Longmore straightway purchased a Murray's *Belgium*, to help himself to believe that he would start on the morrow for Brussels; but when the morrow came, it occurred to him that, by way of preparation, he ought to acquaint himself more intimately with the Flemish painters in the Louvre. This took a whole morning, but it did little to hasten his departure. He had abruptly left Saint-Germain, because it seemed to him that respect for Madame de Mauves demanded that he should allow her husband no reason to suppose that he had understood him; but now that he had satisfied the behest of delicacy, he found himself thinking more and more ardently of Euphemia. It was a poor expression of ardour to be lingering irresolutely on the deserted Boulevards, but he detested the idea of leaving Saint-Germain five hundred miles behind him. He felt very foolish, nevertheless, and wandered about nervously, promising himself to take the next train; but a dozen trains started, and Longmore was still in Paris. This sentimental tumult was more than he had bargained for, and, as he looked at the shop windows, he wondered whether it was a 'passion'. He had never been fond of the word, and had grown up with a kind of horror of what it represented. He had hoped that when he should fall in love, he should do it with an excellent conscience, with no greater agitation than a mild suffusion of cheerfulness. But here was a sentiment concocted of pity and anger, as well as of admiration, and bristling with scruples and doubts. He had come abroad to enjoy the Flemish painters and all others; but what fair-tressed saint of Van Eyck or Memling was so interesting a figure as Madame de Mauves? His restless steps carried him at last out of the long villa-bordered avenue which leads to the Bois de Boulogne.[32]

Summer had fairly begun, and the drive beside the lake was empty, but there were various loungers on the benches and chairs, and the great café had an air of animation. Longmore's walk had given him an appetite, and he went into the establishment and demanded a dinner, remarking for the hundredth time, as he observed the smart little tables disposed in the open air, how much better they ordered this matter in France.

'Will monsieur dine in the garden, or in the saloon?' asked the waiter. Longmore chose the garden; and observing that a great cluster of June roses was trained over the wall of the house, placed himself at a table near by, where the best of dinners was served him on the whitest of linen, in the most shining of porcelain. It so happened that his table was near a window, and that as he sat he could look into a corner of the saloon. So it was that his attention rested on a lady seated just within the window, which was open, face to face apparently with a companion who was concealed by the curtain. She was a very pretty woman, and Longmore looked at her as often as was consistent with good manners. After a while he even began to wonder who she was, and to suspect that she was one of those ladies whom it is no breach of good manners to look at as often as you like. Longmore, too, if he had been so disposed, would have been the more free to give her all his attention, that her own was fixed upon the person opposite to her. She was what the French call a *belle brune*, and though our hero, who had rather a conservative taste in such matters, had no great relish for her bold outlines and even bolder colouring, he could not help admiring her expression of basking contentment.

She was evidently very happy, and her happiness gave her an air of innocence. The talk of her friend, whoever he was, abundantly suited her humour, for she sat listening to him with a broad, lazy smile, and interrupted him occasionally, while she crunched her bon-bons, with a murmured response, presumably as broad, which seemed to deepen his eloquence. She drank a great deal of champagne and ate an immense number of strawberries, and was plainly altogether a person with an impartial relish for strawberries, champagne, and what she would have called *bêtises*.

They had half finished dinner when Longmore sat down, and he was still in his place when they rose. She had hung her bonnet on a nail above her chair, and her companion passed round the table to take it down for her. As he did so, she bent her head to look at a wine-stain on her dress, and in the movement exposed the greater part of the back of a very handsome neck. The gentleman observed it, and observed also, apparently, that the room beyond them was empty; that he stood within eyeshot of Longmore, he failed to observe. He stooped suddenly and imprinted a gallant kiss on the fair expanse. Longmore then recognized M. de Mauves. The recipient of this vigorous tribute put on her bonnet, using his flushed smile as a mirror, and in a moment they passed through the garden, on their way to their carriage.

Then, for the first time, M. de Mauves perceived Longmore. He measured with a rapid glance the young man's relation to the open window, and checked himself in the impulse to stop and speak to him. He contented himself with bowing with great gravity as he opened the gate for his companion.

That evening Longmore made a railway journey, but not to Brussels. He had effectually ceased to care about Brussels; the only thing he now cared about was Madame de Mauves. The atmosphere of his mind had had a sudden clearing up; pity and anger were still throbbing there, but they had space to rage at their pleasure, for doubts and scruples had abruptly departed. It was little, he felt, that he could interpose between her resignation and the indignity of her position; but that little, if it involved the sacrifice of everything that bound him to the tranquil past, he could offer her with a rapture which at last made reflection appear a wofully halting substitute for faith. Nothing in his tranquil past had given such a zest to consciousness as this happy sense of choosing to go straight back to Saint-Germain. How to justify his return, how to explain his ardour, troubled him little. He was not sure, even, that he wished to be understood; he wished only to feel that it was by no fault of his that Madame de Mauves was alone with the ugliness of fate. He was conscious of no distinct desire to 'make love' to her; if he could have uttered the essence of his longing, he would have said that he wished her to remember that in a world coloured grey to her vision by disappointment, there was one vividly honest man. She might certainly have remembered it, however, without his coming back to remind her; and it is not to be denied that, as he waited for the morrow he wished immensely to hear the sound of her voice.

He waited the next day till his usual hour of calling – the late afternoon; but he learned at the door that Madame de Mauves was not at home. The servant offered the information that she was walking in the forest. Longmore went through the garden and out of the little door into the lane, and, after half an hour's vain exploration, saw her coming toward him at the end of a green by-path. As he appeared, she stopped for a moment, as if to turn aside; then recognizing him, she slowly advanced, and he was soon shaking hands with her.

'Nothing has happened,' she said, looking at him fixedly. 'You are not ill?'

'Nothing, except that when I got to Paris I found how fond I had grown of Saint-Germain.'

She neither smiled nor looked flattered; it seemed indeed to Longmore that she was annoyed. But he was uncertain, for he immediately perceived that in his absence the whole character of her face had altered. It told him that something momentous had happened. It was no longer self-contained melancholy that he read in her eyes, but grief and agitation which had lately struggled with that passionate love of peace of which she had spoken to him, and forced him to know that deep experience is never peaceful. She was pale, and she had evidently been shedding tears. He felt his heart beating hard; he seemed now to know her secrets. She continued to look at him with a contracted brow, as if his return had given her a sense of responsibility too great to be disguised by a commonplace welcome. For some moments, as he turned and walked beside her, neither spoke; then abruptly – 'Tell me truly, Mr Longmore,' she said, 'why you have come back.'

He turned and looked at her with an air which startled her

into a certainty of what she had feared. 'Because I have learned
the real answer to the question I asked you the other day. You
are not happy – you are too good to be happy on the terms
offered you. Madame de Mauves,' he went on with a gesture
which protested against a gesture of her own, 'I can't be happy
if you are not! I don't care for anything so long as I see such an
unfathomable sadness in your eyes. I found during three dreary
days in Paris that the thing in the world I most care for is this
daily privilege of seeing you. I know it's very brutal to tell you
I admire you; it's an insult to you to treat you as if you had
complained to me or appealed to me. But such a friendship as
I waked up to there' – and he tossed his head toward the distant city – 'is a potent force, I assure you; and when forces are
compressed they explode. But if you had told me every trouble
in your heart, it would have mattered little; I couldn't say
more than I must say now – that if that in life from which you
have hoped most has given you least, this devoted respect of
mine will refuse no service and betray no trust.'

She had begun to make marks in the earth with the point of
her parasol; but she stopped and listened to him in perfect
immobility. Rather, her immobility was not perfect; for when
he stopped speaking a faint flush had stolen into her cheek. It
told Longmore that she was moved, and his first perceiving it
was the happiest instant of his life. She raised her eyes at last,
and looked at him with what at first seemed a pleading dread
of excessive emotion.

'Thank you – thank you!' she said, calmly enough; but the
next moment her own emotion overcame her calmness, and
she burst into tears. Her tears vanished as quickly as they
came, but they did Longmore a world of good. He had always
felt indefinably afraid of her; her being had somehow seemed
fed by a deeper faith and a stronger will than his own; but her
half-dozen smothered sobs showed him the bottom of her
heart, and assured him that she was weak enough to be
grateful.

'Excuse me,' she said; 'I am too nervous to listen to you. I
believe I could have encountered an enemy to-day, but I can't
endure a friend.'

'You are killing yourself with stoicism – that is what is the matter with you!' he cried. 'Listen to a friend for his own sake, if not for yours. I have never ventured to offer you an atom of compassion, and you can't accuse yourself of an abuse of charity.'

She looked about her with a kind of weary confusion which promised a reluctant attention. But suddenly perceiving by the wayside the fallen log on which they had rested a few evenings before, she went and sat down on it in impatient resignation, and looked at Longmore, as he stood silent, watching her, with a glance which seemed to urge that, if she was charitable now, he must be very wise.

'Something came to my knowledge yesterday,' he said as he sat down beside her, 'which gave me an intense impression of your loneliness. You are truth itself, and there is no truth about you. You believe in purity and duty and dignity, and you live in a world in which they are daily belied. I sometimes ask myself with a kind of rage how you ever came into such a world – and why the perversity of fate never let me know you before.'

'I like my "world" no better than you do, and it was not for its own sake I came into it. But what particular group of people is worth pinning one's faith upon? I confess it sometimes seems to me that men and women are very poor creatures. I suppose I am romantic. I have an unfortunate taste for poetic fitness. Life is hard prose, and one must learn to read prose contentedly. I believe I once thought that all the prose was in America, which was very foolish. What I thought, what I believed, what I expected, when I was an ignorant girl, fatally addicted to fall-ing in love with my own theories, is more than I can begin to tell you now. Sometimes, when I remember certain impulses, certain illusions of those days, they take away my breath, and I wonder that my false point of view has not led me into troubles greater than any I have now to lament. I had a conviction which you would probably smile at if I were to attempt to express it to you. It was a singular form for passionate faith to take, but it had all of the sweetness and the ardour of passionate faith. It led me to take a great step, and it lies behind me now in the distance, like a shadow melting slowly in the light of experience. It has faded, but it has not vanished. Some feelings, I am sure, die only with ourselves; some illusions are as much the condition of our life as our heart-beats. They say that life itself is an illusion – that this world is a shadow of which the reality is yet to come. Life is all of a piece, then, and there is no shame in being miserably human. As for my loneliness, it doesn't greatly matter; it is the fault, in part, of my obstinacy. There have been times when I have been frantically distressed, and, to tell you the truth, wretchedly homesick, because my maid – a jewel of a maid – lied to me with every second breath. There have been moments when I have wished I was the daughter of a poor New England minister, living in a little white house under a couple of elms, and doing all the housework.'

She had begun to speak slowly, with an air of effort; but she went on quickly, as if talking were a relief. 'My marriage introduced me to people and things which seemed to me at first very strange and then very horrible, and then, to tell the truth, very contemptible. At first I expended a great deal of sorrow and dismay and pity on it all; but there soon came a time when I began to wonder whether it were worth one's tears. If I could tell you the eternal friendships I have seen broken, the inconsolable woes consoled, the jealousies and vanities scrambling for precedence, you would agree with me that tempers like yours and mine can understand neither such troubles nor such compensations. A year ago, while I was in the country, a friend of mine was in despair at the infidelity of her husband; she wrote me a most dolorous letter, and on my return to Paris I went immediately to see her. A week had elapsed, and, as I had seen stranger things, I thought she might have recovered her spirits. Not at all; she was still in despair – but at what? At the conduct, the abandoned, shameless conduct of Madame de T. You'll imagine, of course, that Madame de T. was the lady whom my friend's husband preferred to his wife. Far from it; he had never seen her. Who, then, was Madame de T.? Madame de T. was cruelly devoted to M. de V. And who was M. de V.? M. de V. – in two words, my friend was cultivating two jealousies at once. I hardly know what I said to her; something, at any rate, that she found unpardonable, for she quite gave me up. Shortly afterward my husband proposed we should cease to live in Paris, and I gladly assented, for I believe I was falling into a state of mind that made me a detestable companion. I should have preferred to go quite into the country, into Auvergne, where my husband has a house. But to him, Paris, in some degree, is necessary, and Saint-Germain has been a sort of compromise.'

'A sort of compromise!' Longmore repeated. 'That's your whole life.'

'It's the life of many people, of most people of quiet tastes, and it is certainly better than acute distress. One is at a loss theoretically to defend a compromise; but if I found a poor creature who had managed to invent one, I should think it questionable friendship to expose its weak side.' Madame de Mauves had no sooner uttered these words than she smiled faintly, as if to mitigate their personal application.

'Heaven forbid that one should do that unless one has something better to offer,' said Longmore. 'And yet I am haunted by a vision of a life in which you should have found no compromises, for they are a perversion of natures that tend only to goodness and rectitude. As I see it, you should have found happiness serene, profound, complete; a *femme de chambre* not a jewel perhaps, but warranted to tell but one fib a day; a society possibly rather provincial, but (in spite of your poor opinion of mankind) a good deal of solid virtue; jealousies and vanities very tame, and no particular iniquities and adulteries. A husband,' he added after a moment – 'a husband of your own faith and race and spiritual substance, who would have loved you well.'

She rose to her feet, shaking her head. 'You are very kind to go to the expense of visions for me. Visions are vain things; we must make the best of the reality.'

'And yet,' said Longmore, provoked by what seemed the very wantonness of her patience, 'the reality, if I am not mistaken, has very recently taken a shape that keenly tests your philosophy.'

She seemed on the point of replying that his sympathy was too zealous; but a couple of impatient tears in his eyes proved that it was founded on a devotion of which it was impossible to make light. 'Philosophy?' she said. 'I have none. Thank Heaven!' she cried, with vehemence. 'I have none. I believe, Mr Longmore,' she added in a moment, 'that I have nothing on earth but a conscience – it's a good time to tell you so – nothing but a dogged, obstinate, clinging conscience. Does that prove me to be indeed of your faith and race, and have you one for which you can say as much? I don't say it in vanity, for I believe that if my conscience will prevent me from doing anything very base, it will effectually prevent me from doing anything very fine.'

'I am delighted to hear it,' cried Longmore. 'We are made for each other. It's very certain I too shall never do anything fine. And yet I have fancied that in my case this unaccommodating organ might be blinded and gagged a while, in a fine cause, if not turned out of doors. In yours,' he went on with the same appealing irony, 'is it absolutely inexpugnable?'

But she made no concession to his sarcasm. 'Don't laugh at your conscience,' she answered gravely; 'that's the only blasphemy I know.'

She had hardly spoken when she turned suddenly at an unexpected sound, and at the same moment Longmore heard a footstep in an adjacent by-path which crossed their own at a short distance from where they stood.

'It's M. de Mauves,' said Euphemia directly, and moved slowly forward. Longmore, wondering how she knew it, had overtaken her by the time her husband advanced into sight. A solitary walk in the forest was a pastime to which M. de Mauves was not addicted, but he seemed on this occasion to have resorted to it with some equanimity. He was smoking a fragrant cigar, and his thumb was thrust into the armhole of his waistcoat, with an air of contemplative serenity. He stopped short with surprise on seeing his wife and her companion, and to Longmore his surprise seemed impertinent. He glanced rapidly from one to the other, fixed Longmore's eye sharply for a single instant, and then lifted his hat with formal politeness.

'I was not aware,' he said, turning to Madame de Mauves, 'that I might congratulate you on the return of monsieur.'

'You should have known it,' she answered gravely, 'if I had expected Mr Longmore's return.'

She had become very pale, and Longmore felt that this was a first meeting after a stormy parting. 'My return was unexpected to myself,' he said. 'I came last evening.'

M. de Mauves smiled with extreme urbanity. 'It is needless for me to welcome you. Madame de Mauves knows the duties of hospitality.' And with another bow he continued his walk.

Madame de Mauves and her companion returned slowly home, with few words, but, on Longmore's part at least, many thoughts. The Baron's appearance had given him an angry chill; it was a dusky cloud reabsorbing the light which had begun to shine between himself and his companion.

He watched Euphemia narrowly as they went, and wondered what she had last had to suffer. Her husband's presence had checked her disposition to talk, but nothing indicated that she had acknowledged the insulting meaning of his words. Matters were evidently at a crisis between them, and Longmore wondered vainly what it was on Euphemia's part that prevented an absolute rupture. What did she suspect? – how much did she know? To what was she resigned? – how much had she forgiven? How, above all, did she reconcile with knowledge, or with suspicion, that ineradicable tenderness of which she had just now all but assured him? 'She has loved him once,' Longmore said with a sinking of the heart, 'and with her to love once is to commit one's self for ever. Her husband thinks her too stiff! What would a poet call it?'

He relapsed with a kind of aching impotence into the sense of her being somehow beyond him, unattainable, immeasurable by his own fretful logic. Suddenly he gave three passionate switches in the air with his cane, which made Madame de Mauves look round. She could hardly have guessed that they meant that where ambition was so vain, it was an innocent compensation to plunge into worship.

Madame de Mauves found in her drawing-room the little elderly Frenchman, M. de Chalumeau, whom Longmore had observed a few days before on the terrace. On this occasion, too, Madame Clairin was entertaining him, but as her sister-in-law came in she surrendered her post and addressed herself to our hero. Longmore, at thirty, was still an ingenuous youth, and there was something in this lady's large coquetry which had the power of making him blush. He was surprised at finding he had not absolutely forfeited her favour by his deportment at their last interview, and a suspicion of her being prepared to approach him on another line completed his uneasiness.

'So you have returned from Brussels by way of the forest?' she said.

'I have not been to Brussels. I returned yesterday from Paris by the only way – by the train.'

Madame Clairin stared and laughed. 'I have never known a young man to be so fond of Saint-Germain. They generally declare it's horribly dull.'

'That's not very polite to you,' said Longmore, who was vexed at his blushes, and determined not to be abashed.

'Ah, what am I?' demanded Madame Clairin, swinging open her fan. 'I am the dullest thing here. They have not had your success with my sister-in-law.'

'It would have been very easy to have it. Madame de Mauves is kindness itself.'

'To her own countrymen!'

Longmore remained silent; he hated the tone of this conversation. Madame Clairin looked at him a moment, and then turned her head and surveyed Euphemia, to whom M. de Chalumeau was serving up another epigram, which she was receiving with a slight droop of the head and her eyes absently wandering through the window. 'Don't pretend to tell me,' she murmured suddenly, 'that you are not in love with that pretty woman.'

'*Allons donc!*' cried Longmore, in the best French he had ever uttered. He rose the next minute, and took a hasty farewell.

VI

He allowed several days to pass without going back; it seemed delicate to appear not to regard Madame de Mauves' frankness during their last interview as a general invitation. This

cost him a great effort, for hopeless passions are not the most
deferential; and he had, moreover, a constant fear that if, as he
believed, the hour of supreme explanations had come, the
magic of her magnanimity might convert M. de Mauves.
Vicious men, it was abundantly recorded, had been so converted as to be acceptable to God, and the something divine in
Euphemia's temper would sanctify any means she should
choose to employ. Her means, he kept repeating, were no business of his, and the essence of his admiration ought to be to
allow her to do as she liked; but he felt as if he should turn
away into a world out of which most of the joy had departed,
if she should like, after all, to see nothing more in his interest
in her than might be repaid by a murmured 'Thank you.'

When he called again he found to his vexation that he was
to run the gauntlet of Madame Clairin's officious hospitality.
It was one of the first mornings of perfect summer, and the
drawing-room, through the open windows, was flooded with
a sweet confusion of odours and bird-notes which filled him
with the hope that Madame de Mauves would come out and
spend half the day in the forest. But Madame Clairin, with her
hair not yet dressed, emerged like a brassy discord in a maze of
melody.

At the same moment the servant returned with Euphemia's
regrets; she was 'indisposed', and was unable to see Mr Longmore. The young man knew that he looked disappointed and
that Madame Clairin was observing him, and this consciousness impelled him to give her a glance of almost aggressive
frigidity. This was apparently what she desired. She wished to
throw him off his balance, and, if she was not mistaken, she
had the means.

'Put down your hat, Mr Longmore,' she said, 'and be polite
for once. You were not at all polite the other day when I asked
you that friendly question about the state of your heart.'

'I have no heart – to talk about,' said Longmore,
uncompromisingly.

'As well say you have none at all. I advise you to cultivate a
little eloquence; you may have use for it. That was not an idle
question of mine; I don't ask idle questions. For a couple of

months now that you have been coming and going among us, it seems to me that you have had very few to answer of any sort.'

'I have certainly been very well treated,' said Longmore.

Madame Clairin was silent a moment, and then –

'Have you never felt disposed to ask any?' she demanded.

Her look, her tone, were so charged with roundabout meanings that it seemed to Longmore as if even to understand her would savour of dishonest complicity. 'What is it you have to tell me?' he asked, frowning and blushing.

Madame Clairin flushed. It is rather hard, when you come bearing yourself very much as the sibyl when she came to the Roman king,[33] to be treated as something worse than a vulgar gossip. 'I might tell you, Mr Longmore,' she said, 'that you have as bad a *ton* as any young man I ever met. Where have you lived – what are your ideas? I wish to call your attention to a fact which it takes some delicacy to touch upon. You have noticed, I suppose, that my sister-in-law is not the happiest woman in the world.'

Longmore assented with a gesture.

Madame Clairin looked slightly disappointed at his want of enthusiasm. Nevertheless – 'You have formed, I suppose,' she continued, 'your conjectures on the causes of her – dissatisfaction.'

'Conjecture has been superfluous. I have seen the causes – or at least a specimen of them – with my own eyes.'

'I know perfectly what you mean. My brother, in a single word, is in love with another woman. I don't judge him; I don't judge my sister-in-law. I permit myself to say that in her position I would have managed otherwise. I would either have kept my husband's affection, or I would have frankly done without it. But my sister is an odd compound; I don't profess to understand her. Therefore it is, in a measure, that I appeal to you, her fellow-countryman. Of course you will be surprised at my way of looking at the matter, and I admit that it's a way in use only among people whose family traditions compel them to take a superior view of things.' Madame Clairin paused, and Longmore wondered where her family traditions were going to lead her.

'Listen,' she went on. 'There has never been a De Mauves who has not given his wife the right to be jealous. We know our history for ages back, and the fact is established. It's a shame if you like, but it's something to have a shame with such a pedigree. Our men have been real Frenchmen, and their wives – I may say it – have been worthy of them. You may see all their portraits at our house in Auvergne; every one of them an "injured" beauty, but not one of them hanging her head. Not one of them had the bad taste to be jealous, and yet not one in a dozen was guilty of an escapade – not one of them was talked about. There's good sense for you! How they managed – go and look at the dusky, faded canvases and pastels, and ask. They were femmes d'esprit! When they had a headache, they put on a little rouge and came to supper as usual; and when they had a heart-ache, they put a little rouge on their hearts. These are great traditions, and it doesn't seem to me fair that a little American bourgeoise should come in and pretend to alter them, and should hang her photograph, with her obstinate little *air penché*, in the gallery of our shrewd fine ladies. A De Mauves must be of the old race. When she married my brother, I don't suppose she took him for a member of a *société de bonnes œuvres*. I don't say we are right; who is right? But we are as history has made us, and if any one is to change, it had better be my sister-in-law herself.' Again Madame Clairin paused, and opened and closed her fan. 'Let her conform!' she said, with amazing audacity.

Longmore's reply was ambiguous; he simply said, 'Ah!'

Madame Clairin's historical retrospect had apparently imparted an honest zeal to her indignation. 'For a long time,' she continued, 'my sister has been taking the attitude of an injured woman, affecting a disgust with the world, and shutting herself up to read free-thinking books. I have never permitted myself any observation on her conduct, but I have quite lost patience with it. When a woman with her prettiness lets her husband stray away, she deserves her fate. I don't wish you to agree with me – on the contrary; but I call such a woman a goose. She must have bored him to death. What has passed between them for many months needn't concern us, what provocation my sister has had – monstrous, if you wish – what ennui my brother has suffered. It's enough that a week ago, just after you had ostensibly gone to Brussels, something happened to produce an explosion. She found a letter in his pocket – a photograph – a trinket – *que sais-je?* At any rate, the scene was terrible. I didn't listen at the keyhole, and I don't know what was said; but I have reason to believe that my brother was called to account as I fancy none of his ancestors have ever been – even by injured mistresses!'

Longmore had leaned forward in silent attention with his elbows on his knees; and now instinctively he dropped his face into his hands. 'Ah, poor woman!' he groaned.

'Voilà!' said Madame Clairin. 'You pity her.'

'Pity her?' cried Longmore, looking up with ardent eyes and forgetting the spirit of Madame Clairin's narrative in the miserable facts. 'Don't you?'

'A little. But I am not acting sentimentally; I am acting politically. We have always been a political family. I wish to arrange things – to see my brother free to do as he chooses – to see Euphemia contented. Do you understand me?'

'Very well, I think. You are the most immoral person I have lately had the privilege of conversing with.'

Madame Clairin shrugged her shoulders. 'Possibly. When was there a great politician who was not immoral?'

'Ah no,' said Longmore in the same tone. 'You are too superficial to be a great politician. You don't begin to know anything about Madame de Mauves.'

Madame Clairin inclined her head to one side, eyed Longmore sharply, mused a moment, and then smiled with an excellent imitation of intelligent compassion. 'It's not in my interest to contradict you.'

'It would be in your interest to learn, Madame Clairin,' the young man went on with unceremonious candour, 'what honest men most admire in a woman – and to recognize it when you see it.'

Longmore certainly did injustice to her talents for diplomacy, for she covered her natural annoyance at this sally with a pretty piece of irony. 'So you *are* in love!' she quietly exclaimed.

Longmore was silent a while. 'I wonder if you would understand me,' he said at last, 'if I were to tell you that I have for Madame de Mauves the most devoted friendship?'

'You underrate my intelligence. But in that case you ought to exert your influence to put an end to these painful domestic scenes.'

'Do you suppose that she talks to me about her domestic scenes?' cried Longmore.

Madame Clairin stared. 'Then your friendship isn't returned?' And as Longmore turned away, shaking his head – 'Now, at least,' she added, 'she will have something to tell you. I happen to know the upshot of my brother's last interview with his wife.' Longmore rose to his feet as a sort of protest against the indelicacy of the position in which he found himself; but all that made him tender made him curious, and she caught in his averted eyes an expression which prompted her to strike her blow. 'My brother is monstrously in love with a certain person in Paris; of course he ought not to be; but he wouldn't be my brother if he were not. It was this irregular passion that dictated his words. "Listen to me, madam," he cried at last; "let us live like people who understand life! It is unpleasant to be forced to say such things outright, but you have a way of bringing one down to the rudiments. I am faithless, I am heartless, I am brutal, I am everything horrible – it's understood. Take your revenge, console yourself; you are too pretty a woman to have anything to complain of. Here is a handsome young man sighing himself into a consumption for you. Listen to the poor fellow, and you will find that virtue is none the less becoming for being good-natured. You will see that it's not after all such a doleful world, and that there is even an advantage in having the most impudent of husbands."' Madame Clairin paused; Longmore had turned very pale. 'You may believe it,' she said; 'the speech took place in my presence; things were done in order. And now, Mr Longmore' – this with a smile which he was too troubled at the moment to appreciate, but which he remembered later with a kind of awe – 'we count upon you!'

'He said this to her, face to face, as you say it to me now?' Longmore asked slowly, after a silence.

'Word for word, and with the greatest politeness.'

'And Madame de Mauves – what did she say?'

Madame Clairin smiled again. 'To such a speech as that a woman says – nothing. She had been sitting with a piece of needlework, and I think she had not seen her husband since their quarrel the day before. He came in with the gravity of an ambassador, and I am sure that when he made his *demande en mariage* his manner was not more respectful. He only wanted white gloves!' said Madame Clairin. 'Euphemia sat silent a few moments, drawing her stitches, and then without a word, without a glance, she walked out of the room. It was just what she should have done!'

'Yes,' Longmore repeated, 'it was just what she should have done.'

'And I, left alone with my brother, do you know what I said?'

Longmore shook his head. '*Mauvais sujet!*' he suggested.

' "You have done me the honour," I said, "to take this step in my presence. I don't pretend to qualify it. You know what you are about, and it's your own affair. But you may confide in my discretion." Do you think he has had reason to complain of it?' She received no answer; Longmore was slowly turning away and passing his gloves mechanically round the band of his hat. 'I hope,' she cried, 'you are not going to start for Brussels!'

Plainly, Longmore was deeply disturbed, and Madame Clairin might congratulate herself on the success of her plea for old-fashioned manners. And yet there was something that left her more puzzled than satisfied in the reflective tone with which he answered, 'No, I shall remain here for the present.' The processes of his mind seemed provokingly subterranean, and she could have fancied for a moment that he was linked with her sister in some monstrous conspiracy of asceticism.

'Come this evening,' she boldly resumed. 'The rest will take care of itself. Meanwhile I shall take the liberty of telling my sister-in-law that I have repeated – in short, that I have put you *au fait*.'

Longmore started and coloured, and she hardly knew whether he were going to assent or to demur. 'Tell her what you please. Nothing you can tell her will affect her conduct.'

'Voyons! Do you mean to tell me that a woman young, pretty, sentimental, neglected – insulted, if you will –? I see you don't believe it. Believe simply in your own opportunity! But for Heaven's sake, if it is to lead anywhere, don't come back with that *visage de croquemort*. You look as if you were going to bury your heart – not to offer it to a pretty woman. You are much better when you smile – you are very nice then. Come, do yourself justice.'

'Yes,' he said, 'I must do myself justice.' And abruptly, with a bow, he took his departure.

VII

He felt, when he found himself unobserved, in the open air, that he must plunge into violent action, walk fast and far, and defer the opportunity for thought. He strode away into the forest, swinging his cane, throwing back his head, gazing away into the verdurous vistas, and following the road without a purpose. He felt immensely excited, but he could hardly have said whether his emotion was a pain or a joy. It was joyous as all increase of freedom is joyous; something seemed to have been cleared out of his path; his destiny appeared to have rounded a cape and brought him into sight of an open sea. But his freedom resolved itself somehow into the need of despising all mankind, with a single exception; and the fact of Madame de Mauves inhabiting a planet contaminated by the presence of this baser multitude kept his elation from seeming a pledge of ideal bliss.

But she was there, and circumstances now forced them to be intimate. She had ceased to have what men call a secret for him, and this fact itself brought with it a sort of rapture. He had no prevision that he should 'profit', in the vulgar sense, by the extraordinary position into which they had been thrown; it might be but a cruel trick of destiny to make hope a harsher mockery and renunciation a keener suffering. But above all this rose the conviction that she could do nothing that would not deepen his admiration.

It was this feeling that circumstance – odious as it was in itself – was to force the beauty of her character into more perfect relief that made him stride along as if he were celebrating a kind of spiritual festival. He rambled at random for a couple of hours, and found at last that he had left the forest behind him and had wandered into an unfamiliar region. It was a perfectly rural scene, and the still summer day gave it a charm for which its meagre elements but half accounted.

Longmore thought he had never seen anything so characteristically French; all the French novels seemed to have described it, all the French landscapists to have painted it. The fields and trees were of a cool metallic green; the grass looked as if it might stain your trousers, and the foliage your hands. The clear light had a sort of mild greyness; the sunbeams were of silver rather than gold. A great red-roofed, high-stacked farmhouse, with white-washed walls and a straggling yard, surveyed the high road, on one side, from behind a transparent curtain of poplars. A narrow stream, half choked with emerald rushes and edged with grey aspens, occupied the opposite quarter. The meadows rolled and sloped away gently to the low horizon, which was barely concealed by the continuous line of clipped and marshalled trees. The prospect was not rich, but it had a frank homeliness which touched the young man's fancy. It was full of light atmosphere and diffused sunshine, and if it was prosaic, it was soothing.

Longmore was disposed to walk further, and he advanced along the road beneath the poplars. In twenty minutes he came to a village which straggled away to the right, among orchards and *potagers*. On the left, at a stone's throw from the road, stood a little pink-faced inn, which reminded him that he had not breakfasted, having left home with a prevision of hospitality from Madame de Mauves. In the inn he found a brick-tiled

parlour and a hostess in sabots and a white cap, whom, over
the omelette she speedily served him – borrowing licence from
the bottle of sound red wine which accompanied it – he assured
that she was a true artist. To reward his compliment, she
invited him to smoke his cigar in her little garden behind the
house.

Here he found a *tonnelle* and a view of ripening crops,
stretching down to the stream. The *tonnelle* was rather close,
and he preferred to lounge on a bench against the pink wall, in
the sun, which was not too hot. Here, as he rested and gazed
and mused, he fell into a train of thought which, in an indefinable fashion, was a soft influence from the scene about him.
His heart, which had been beating fast for the past three hours,
gradually checked its pulses and left him looking at life with a
rather more level gaze. The homely tavern sounds coming out
through the open windows, the sunny stillness of the fields and
crops, which covered so much vigorous natural life, suggested
very little that was transcendental, had very little to say about
renunciation – nothing at all about spiritual zeal. They seemed
to utter a message from plain ripe nature, to express the un-
perverted reality of things, to say that the common lot is not
brilliantly amusing, and that the part of wisdom is to grasp
frankly at experience, lest you miss it altogether. What reason
there was for his falling a-wondering after this whether a
deeply wounded heart might be soothed and healed by such a
scene, it would be difficult to explain; certain it is that, as he
sat there, he had a waking dream of an unhappy woman strolling by the slow-flowing stream before him, and pulling down
the fruit-laden boughs in the orchards. He mused and mused,
and at last found himself feeling angry that he could not somehow think worse of Madame de Mauves – or at any rate think
otherwise. He could fairly claim that in a sentimental way he
asked very little of life – he made modest demands on passion;
why then should his only passion be born to ill-fortune? why
should his first – his last – glimpse of positive happiness be so
indissolubly linked with renunciation?

It is perhaps because, like many spirits of the same stock, he
had in his composition a lurking principle of asceticism to

whose authority he had ever paid an unquestioning respect, that he now felt all the vehemence of rebellion. To renounce – to renounce again – to renounce for ever – was this all that youth and longing and resolve were meant for? Was experience to be muffled and mutilated, like an indecent picture? Was a man to sit and deliberately condemn his future to be the blank memory of a regret, rather than the long reverberation of a joy? Sacrifice? The word was a trap for minds muddled by fear, an ignoble refuge of weakness. To insist now seemed not to dare, but simply to be, to live on possible terms.

His hostess came out to hang a cloth to dry on the hedge, and, though her guest was sitting quietly enough, she seemed to see in his kindled eyes a flattering testimony to the quality of her wine.

As she turned back into the house, she was met by a young man whom Longmore observed in spite of his pre-occupation. He was evidently a member of that jovial fraternity of artists whose very shabbiness has an affinity with the element of picturesqueness and unexpectedness in life – that element which provokes so much unformulated envy among people foredoomed to be respectable.

Longmore was struck first with his looking like a very clever man, and then with his looking like a very happy one. The combination, as it was expressed in his face, might have arrested the attention of even a less cynical philosopher. He had a slouched hat and a blond beard, a light easel under one arm, and an unfinished sketch in oils under the other.

He stopped and stood talking for some moments to the landlady, with a peculiarly good-humoured smile. They were discussing the possibilities of dinner; the hostess enumerated some very savoury ones, and he nodded briskly, assenting to everything. It couldn't be, Longmore thought, that he found such soft contentment in the prospect of lamb-chops and spinach and a *croûte aux fruits*. When the dinner had been ordered, he turned up his sketch, and the good woman fell a-wondering and looking away at the spot by the stream-side where he had made it.

Was it his work, Longmore wondered, that made him so

happy? Was a strong talent the best thing in the world? The landlady went back to her kitchen, and the young painter stood, as if he were waiting for something, beside the gate which opened upon the path across the fields. Longmore sat brooding and asking himself whether it was better to cultivate one of the arts than to cultivate one of the passions. Before he had answered the question the painter had grown tired of waiting. He picked up a pebble, tossed it lightly into an upper window, and called, 'Claudine!'

Claudine appeared; Longmore heard her at the window, bidding the young man to have patience. 'But I am losing my light,' he said; 'I must have my shadows in the same place as yesterday.'

'Go without me, then,' Claudine answered; 'I will join you in ten minutes.' Her voice was fresh and young; it seemed to say to Longmore that she was as happy as her companion.

'Don't forget the Chénier,'[34] cried the young man; and turning away, he passed out of the gate and followed the path across the fields until he disappeared among the trees by the side of the stream. Who was Claudine? Longmore vaguely wondered; and was she as pretty as her voice? Before long he had a chance to satisfy himself; she came out of the house with her hat and parasol, prepared to follow her companion. She had on a pink muslin dress and a little white hat, and she was as pretty as a Frenchwoman needs to be pleasing. She had a clear brown skin and a bright dark eye, and a step which seemed to keep time to some slow music, heard only by herself. Her hands were encumbered with various articles which she seemed to intend to carry with her. In one arm she held her parasol and a large roll of needlework, and in the other a shawl and a heavy white umbrella, such as painters use for sketching. Meanwhile she was trying to thrust into her pocket a paper-covered volume which Longmore saw to be the Poems of André Chénier; but in the effort she dropped the large umbrella, and uttered a half-smiling exclamation of disgust. Longmore stepped forward and picked up the umbrella, and as she, protesting her gratitude, put out her hand to take it, it seemed to him that she was unbecomingly overburdened.

'You have too much to carry,' he said; 'you must let me help you.'

'You are very good, monsieur,' she answered. 'My husband always forgets something. He can do nothing without his umbrella. He is *d'une étourderie*—'

'You must allow me to carry the umbrella,' Longmore said; 'it's too heavy for a lady.'

She assented, after many compliments to his politeness; and he walked by her side into the meadow. She went lightly and rapidly, picking her steps and glancing forward to catch a glimpse of her husband. She was graceful, she was charming, she had an air of decision and yet of sweetness, and it seemed to Longmore that a young artist would work none the worse for having her seated at his side reading Chénier's iambics. They were newly married, he supposed, and evidently their path of life had none of the mocking crookedness of some others. They asked little; but what need one ask more than such quiet summer days, with the creature one loves, by a shady stream, with art and books and a wide, unshadowed horizon? To spend such a morning, to stroll back to dinner in the red-tiled parlour of the inn, to ramble away again as the sun got low – all this was a vision of bliss which floated before him only to torture him with a sense of the impossible. All French-women are not coquettes, he remarked, as he kept pace with his companion. She uttered a word now and then, for polite-ness' sake, but she never looked at him, and seemed not in the least to care that he was a well-favoured young man. She cared for nothing but the young artist in the shabby coat and the slouched hat, and for discovering where he had set up his easel.

This was soon done. He was encamped under the trees, close to the stream, and, in the diffused green shade of the lit-tle wood, seemed to be in no immediate need of his umbrella. He received a vivacious rebuke, however, for forgetting it, and was informed of what he owed to Longmore's complaisance. He was duly grateful; he thanked our hero warmly, and offered him a seat on the grass. But Longmore felt like a marplot, and lingered only long enough to glance at the young man's sketch, and to see it was a very clever rendering of the silvery stream and the vivid green rushes. The young wife had spread her shawl on the grass at the base of a tree, and meant to seat herself when Longmore had gone, and murmur Chénier's verses to the music of the gurgling river. Longmore looked a while from one to the other, barely stifled a sigh, bade them good morning, and took his departure.

He knew neither where to go nor what to do; he seemed afloat on the sea of ineffectual longing. He strolled slowly back to the inn, and in the doorway met the landlady coming back from the butcher's with the lamb-chops for the dinner of her lodgers.

'Monsieur has made the acquaintance of the *dame* of our young painter,' she said with a broad smile – a smile too broad for malicious meanings. 'Monsieur has perhaps seen the young man's picture. It appears that he has a great deal of talent.'

'His picture was very pretty,' said Longmore, 'but his *dame* was prettier still.'

'She's a very nice little woman; but I pity her all the more.'

'I don't see why she's to be pitied,' said Longmore; 'they seem a very happy couple.'

The landlady gave a knowing nod.

'Don't trust to it, monsieur! Those artists – *ça n'a pas de principes!* From one day to another he can plant her there! I know them, *allez*. I have had them here very often; one year with one, another year with another.'

Longmore was puzzled for a moment. Then, 'You mean she is not his wife?' he asked.

She shrugged her shoulders. 'What shall I tell you? They are not *des hommes sérieux*, those gentlemen! They don't engage themselves for an eternity. It's none of my business, and I have no wish to speak ill of madame. She's a very nice little woman, and she loves her *jeune homme* to distraction.'

'Who is she?' asked Longmore. 'What do you know about her?'

'Nothing for certain; but it's my belief that she's better than he. I have even gone so far as to believe that she's a lady – a true lady – and that she has given up a great many things for him. I do the best I can for them, but I don't believe she has been obliged all her life to content herself with a dinner of two courses.' And she turned over her lamb-chop tenderly, as if to say that though a good cook could imagine better things, yet if you could have but one course, lamb-chops had much in their favour. 'I shall cook them with bread-crumbs. *Voilà les femmes, monsieur!*'

Longmore turned away with the feeling that women were indeed a measureless mystery, and that it was hard to say whether there was greater beauty in their strength or in their weakness. He walked back to Saint-Germain, more slowly than he had come, with less philosophic resignation to any event, and more of the urgent egotism of the passion which philosophers call the supremely selfish one. Every now and then the episode of the happy young painter and the charming woman who had given up a great many things for him rose vividly in his mind, and seemed to mock his moral unrest like some obtrusive vision of unattainable bliss.

The landlady's gossip had cast no shadow on its brightness; her voice seemed that of the vulgar chorus of the uninitiated, which stands always ready with its gross prose rendering of the inspired passages of human action. Was it possible a man could take *that* from a woman – take all that lent lightness to that other woman's footstep and intensity to her glance – and not give her the absolute certainty of a devotion as unalterable as the process of the sun? Was it possible that such a rapturous union had the seeds of trouble – that the charm of such a perfect accord could be broken by anything but death? Longmore felt an immense desire to cry out a thousand times 'No!' for it seemed to him at last that he was somehow spiritually the same as the young painter, and that the latter's companion had the soul of Euphemia.

The heat of the sun, as he walked along, became oppressive, and when he re-entered the forest he turned aside into the deepest shade he could find, and stretched himself on the mossy ground at the foot of a great beech. He lay for a while staring up into the verdurous dusk overhead, and trying to conceive Madame de Mauves hastening towards some quiet stream-side where he waited, as he had seen that trusting creature do an hour before. It would be hard to say how well he succeeded;

but the effort soothed him rather than excited him, and as he had had a good deal both of moral and physical fatigue, he sank at last into a quiet sleep.

While he slept he had a strange, vivid dream. He seemed to be in a wood, very much like the one on which his eyes had lately closed; but the wood was divided by the murmuring stream he had left an hour before. He was walking up and down, he thought restlessly and in intense expectation of some momentous event. Suddenly, at a distance, through the trees, he saw the gleam of a woman's dress, and hurried forward to meet her. As he advanced he recognized her, but he saw at the same time that she was on the opposite bank of the river. She seemed at first not to notice him, but when they were opposite each other she stopped and looked at him very gravely and pityingly. She made him no motion that he should cross the stream, but he wished greatly to stand by her side. He knew the water was deep, and it seemed to him that he knew that he should have to plunge, and that he feared that when he rose to the surface she would have disappeared. Nevertheless, he was going to plunge, when a boat turned into the current from above and came swiftly towards them, guided by an oarsman who was sitting so that they could not see his face. He brought the boat to the bank where Longmore stood; the latter stepped in, and with a few strokes they touched the opposite shore. Longmore got out, and, though he was sure he had crossed the stream, Madame de Mauves was not there. He turned with a kind of agony and saw that now she was on the other bank – the one he had left. She gave him a grave, silent glance, and walked away up the stream. The boat and the boatman resumed their course, but after going a short distance they stopped, and the boatman turned back and looked at the still divided couple. Then Longmore recognized him – just as he had recognized him a few days before at the restaurant in the Bois de Boulogne.

VIII

He must have slept some time after he ceased dreaming, for he had no immediate memory of his dream. It came back to him later, after he had roused himself and had walked nearly home. No great ingenuity was needed to make it seem a rather striking allegory, and it haunted and oppressed him for the rest of the day. He took refuge, however, in his quickened conviction that the only sound policy in life is to grasp unsparingly at happiness; and it seemed no more than one of the vigorous measures dictated by such a policy, to return that evening to Madame de Mauves. And yet when he had decided to do so, and had carefully dressed himself, he felt an irresistible nervous tremor which made it easier to linger at his open window, wondering, with a strange mixture of dread and desire, whether Madame Clairin had told her sister-in-law what she had told him. His presence now might be simply a gratuitous annoyance; and yet his absence might seem to imply that it was in the power of circumstances to make them ashamed to meet each other's eyes. He sat a long time with his head in his hands, lost in a painful confusion of hopes and questionings. He felt at moments as if he could throttle Madame Clairin, and yet he could not help asking himself whether it were not possible that she had done him a service. It was late when he left the hotel, and as he entered the gate of the other house his heart was beating so fast that he was sure his voice would show it.

The servant ushered him into the drawing-room, which was empty, with the lamp burning low. But the long windows were open, and their light curtains swaying in a soft, warm wind, so that Longmore immediately stepped out upon the terrace. There he found Madame de Mauves alone, slowly pacing up and down. She was dressed in white, very simply, and her hair was arranged, not as she usually wore it, but in a single loose coil, like that of a person unprepared for company.

She stopped when she saw Longmore, seemed slightly startled, uttered an exclamation, and stood waiting for him to speak. He looked at her, tried to say something, but found no words. He knew it was awkward, it was offensive, to stand gazing at her; but he could not say what was suitable, and he dared not say what he wished.

Her face was indistinct in the dim light, but he could see that her eyes were fixed on him, and he wondered what they expressed. Did they warn him, did they plead, or did they confess to a sense of provocation? For an instant his head swam; he felt as if it would make all things clear to stride forward and fold her in his arms. But a moment later he was still standing looking at her; he had not moved; he knew that she had spoken, but he had not understood her.

'You were here this morning,' she continued; and now, slowly, the meaning of her words came to him. 'I had a bad headache and had to shut myself up.' She spoke in her usual voice.

Longmore mastered his agitation and answered her without betraying himself. 'I hope you are better now.'

'Yes, thank you, I am better – much better.'

He was silent a moment, and she moved away to a chair and seated herself. After a pause he followed her and stood before her, leaning against the balustrade of the terrace. 'I hoped you might have been able to come out for the morning into the forest. I went alone; it was a lovely day, and I took a long walk.'

'It was a lovely day,' she said, absently, and sat with her eyes lowered, slowly opening and closing her fan. Longmore, as he watched her, felt more and more sure that her sister-in-law had seen her since her interview with him; that her attitude towards him was changed. It was this same something that chilled the ardour with which he had come, or at least converted the dozen passionate speeches that kept rising to his lips into a kind of reverential silence. No, certainly, he could not clasp her to his arms now, any more than some antique worshipper could have clasped the marble statue in his temple. But Longmore's statue spoke at last, with a full human voice, and even with a shade of human hesitation. She looked up, and it seemed to him that her eyes shone through the dusk.

'I am very glad you came this evening,' she said. 'I have a particular reason for being glad. I half expected you, and yet I thought it possible you might not come.'

'As I have been feeling all day,' Longmore answered, 'it was impossible I should not come. I have spent the day in thinking of you.'

She made no immediate reply, but continued to open and close her fan thoughtfully. At last – 'I have something to say to you,' she said abruptly. 'I want you to know to a certainty that I have a very high opinion of you.' Longmore started and shifted his position. To what was she coming? But he said nothing, and she went on –

'I take a great interest in you; there is no reason why I should not say it – I have a great friendship for you.'

He began to laugh; he hardly knew why, unless that this seemed the very mockery of coldness. But she continued without heeding him –

'You know, I suppose, that a great disappointment always implies a great confidence – a great hope?'

'I have hoped,' he said, 'hoped strongly; but doubtless never rationally enough to have a right to bemoan my disappointment.'

'You do yourself injustice. I have such confidence in your reason that I should be greatly disappointed if I were to find it wanting.'

'I really almost believe that you are amusing yourself at my expense,' cried Longmore. 'My reason? Reason is a mere word! The only reality in the world is the thing one *feels*!'

She rose to her feet and looked at him gravely. His eyes by this time were accustomed to the imperfect light, and he could see that her look was reproachful, and yet that it was beseechingly kind. She shook her head impatiently, and laid her fan upon his arm with a strong pressure.

'If that were so, it would be a weary world. I know what you feel, however, nearly enough. You needn't try to express it. It's enough that it gives me the right to ask a favour of you – to make an urgent, a solemn request.'

'Make it; I listen.'

'*Don't disappoint me*. If you don't understand me now, you will to-morrow, or very soon. When I said just now that I had a very high opinion of you, I meant it very seriously. It was not a vain compliment. I believe that there is no appeal one may make to your generosity which can remain long unanswered. If this were to happen, – if I were to find you selfish where I thought you generous, narrow where I thought you large' – and she spoke slowly, with her voice lingering with emphasis on each of these words – 'vulgar where I thought you rare – I should think worse of human nature. I should suffer – I should suffer keenly. I should say to myself in the dull days of the future, "There was one man who might have done so and so; and he, too, failed." But this shall not be. You have made too good an impression on me not to make the very best. If you wish to please me for ever, there is a way.'

She was standing close to him, with her dress touching him, her eyes fixed on his. As she went on her manner grew strangely intense, and she had the singular appearance of a woman preaching reason with a kind of passion. Longmore was confused, dazzled, almost bewildered. The intention of her words was all remonstrance, refusal, dismissal; but her presence there, so close, so urgent, so personal, seemed a distracting contradiction of it. She had never been so lovely. In her white dress, with her pale face and deeply lighted eyes, she seemed the very spirit of the summer night. When she had ceased speaking she drew a long breath; Longmore felt it on his cheek, and it stirred in his whole being a sudden rapturous conjecture. Were her words in their soft severity a mere delusive spell, meant to throw into relief her almost ghostly beauty, and was this the only truth, the only reality, the only law?

He closed his eyes and felt that she was watching him, not without pain and perplexity herself. He looked at her again, met her own eyes, and saw a tear in each of them. Then this last suggestion of his desire seemed to die away with a stifled murmur, and her beauty, more and more radiant in the darkness, rose before him as a symbol of something vague which was yet more beautiful than itself.

'I may understand you to-morrow,' he said, 'but I don't understand you now.'

'And yet I took counsel with myself to-day and asked myself how I had best speak to you. On one side I might have refused to see you at all.' Longmore made a violent movement, and she added – 'In that case I should have written to you. I might see you, I thought, and simply say to you that there were excellent reasons why we should part, and that I begged this visit should be your last. This I inclined to do; what made me decide otherwise was – simply friendship! I said to myself that I should be glad to remember in future days, not that I had dismissed you, but that you had gone away out of the fulness of your own wisdom.'

'The fulness – the fulness!' cried Longmore.

'I am prepared, if necessary,' Madame de Mauves continued after a pause, 'to fall back upon my strict right. But, as I said before, I shall be greatly disappointed if I am obliged to do that.'

'When I hear you say that,' Longmore answered, 'I feel so angry, so horribly irritated, that I wonder I don't leave you without more words.'

'If you should go away in anger, this idea of mine about our parting would be but half realized. No, I don't want to think of you as angry; I don't want even to think of you as making a serious sacrifice. I want to think of you as—'

'As a creature who never has existed – who never can exist! A creature who knew you without loving you – who left you without regretting you!'

She turned impatiently away and walked to the other end of the terrace. When she came back, he saw that her impatience had become a cold sternness. She stood before him again, looking at him from head to foot, in deep reproachfulness, almost in scorn. Beneath her glance he felt a kind of shame. He coloured; she observed it and withheld something she was about to say. She turned away again, walked to the other end of the terrace, and stood there looking away into the garden. It seemed to him that she had guessed he understood her, and slowly – slowly – half as the fruit of his vague self-reproach – he did understand her. She was giving him a chance to do gallantly what it seemed unworthy of both of them he should do meanly.

She liked him, she must have liked him greatly, to wish so to spare him, to go to the trouble of conceiving an ideal of conduct for him. With this sense of her friendship – her strong friendship she had just called it – Longmore's soul rose with a new flight, and suddenly felt itself breathing a clearer air. The words ceased to seem a mere bribe to his ardour; they were charged with ardour themselves; they were a present happiness. He moved rapidly towards her with a feeling that this was something he might immediately enjoy.

They were separated by two-thirds of the length of the terrace, and he had to pass the drawing-room window. As he did so he started with an exclamation. Madame Clairin stood posted there, watching him. Conscious, apparently, that she might be suspected of eavesdropping, she stepped forward with a smile and looked from Longmore to his hostess.

'Such a *tête-à-tête* as that,' she said, 'one owes no apology for interrupting. One ought to come in for good manners.'

Madame de Mauves turned round, but she answered nothing. She looked straight at Longmore, and her eyes had extraordinary eloquence. He was not exactly sure, indeed, what she meant them to say; but they seemed to say plainly something of this kind: 'Call it what you will, what you have to urge upon me is the thing which this woman can best conceive. What I ask of you is something she cannot!' They seemed, somehow, to beg him to suffer her to be herself, and to intimate that that self was as little as possible like Madame Clairin. He felt an immense answering desire not to do anything which would seem natural to this lady. He had laid his hat and stick on the parapet of the terrace. He took them up, offered his hand to Madame de Mauves with a simple good-night, bowed silently to Madame Clairin, and departed.

IX

He went home, and without lighting his candle flung himself on his bed. But he got no sleep till morning; he lay hour after hour tossing, thinking, wondering; his mind had never been so active. It seemed to him that Euphemia had given him in those last moments an inspiring commission, and that she had

expressed herself almost as largely as if she had listened assent-
ingly to an assurance of his love. It was neither easy nor
delightful thoroughly to understand her; but little by little her
perfect meaning sank into his mind and soothed it with a sense
of opportunity which somehow stifled his sense of loss. For,
to begin with, she meant that she could love him in no degree
or contingency, in no imaginable future. This was absolute; he
felt that he could alter it no more than he could pull down
the constellations he lay gazing at through his open window.
He wondered what it was, in the background of her life, that
she had so attached herself to. A sense of duty unquenchable
to the end? A love that no outrage could stifle? 'Good heavens!'
he thought, 'is the world so rich in the purest pearls of passion,
that such tenderness as that can be wasted for ever – poured
away without a sigh into bottomless darkness?' Had she, in
spite of the detestable present, some precious memory which
contained the germ of a shrinking hope? Was she prepared to
submit to everything and yet to believe? Was it strength, was
it weakness, was it a vulgar fear, was it conviction, conscience,
constancy?

Longmore sank back with a sigh and an oppressive feeling
that it was vain to guess at such a woman's motives. He only
felt that those of Madame de Mauves were buried deep in her
soul, and that they must be of the noblest, and contain nothing
base. He had a dim, overwhelming sense of a sort of invulner-
able constancy being the supreme law of her character – a
constancy which still found a foothold among crumbling
ruins. 'She has loved once,' he said to himself as he rose and
wandered to his window; 'that is for ever. Yes, yes – if she
loved again she would be *common*.' He stood for a long time
looking out into the starlit silence of the town and forest, and
thinking of what life would have been if his constancy had met
hers before this had happened. But life was this, now, and he
must live. It was living keenly to stand there with such a request
from such a woman still ringing in one's ears. He was not to
disappoint her, he was to justify a conception which it had
beguiled her weariness to shape. Longmore's imagination
expanded; he threw back his head and seemed to be looking

for Madame de Mauves' conception among the blinking, mocking stars. But it came to him rather on the mild night-wind, wandering in over the house-tops which covered the rest of so many heavy human hearts. What she asked, he felt that she was asking not for her own sake (she feared nothing, she needed nothing), but for that of his own happiness and his own character. He must assent to destiny. Why else was he young and strong, intelligent and resolute? He must not give it to her to reproach him with thinking that she had a moment's attention for his love – to plead, to argue, to break off in bitterness; he must see everything from above, her indifference and his own ardour; he must prove his strength, he must do the handsome thing; he must decide that the handsome thing was to submit to the inevitable, to be supremely delicate, to spare her all pain, to stifle his passion, to ask no compensation, to depart without delay and try to believe that wisdom is its own reward. All this, neither more nor less, it was a matter of friendship with Madame de Mauves to expect of him. And what should he gain by it? He should have pleased her! . . . He flung himself on his bed again, fell asleep at last, and slept till morning.

Before noon the next day he had made up his mind that he would leave Saint-Germain at once. It seemed easier to leave without seeing her, and yet if he might ask a grain of 'compensation', it would be five minutes face to face with her. He passed a restless day. Wherever he went he seemed to see her standing before him in the dusky halo of evening, and looking at him with an air of still negation more intoxicating than the most passionate self-surrender. He must certainly go, and yet it was hideously hard. He compromised and went to Paris to spend the rest of the day. He strolled along the Boulevards and looked at the shops, sat a while in the Tuileries gardens[35] and looked at the shabby unfortunates for whom this only was nature and summer; but simply felt, as a result of it all, that it was a very dusty, dreary, lonely world into which Madame de Mauves was turning him away.

In a sombre mood he made his way back to the Boulevards and sat down at a table on the great plain of hot asphalt, before a café. Night came on, the lamps were lighted, the tables near him found occupants, and Paris began to wear that peculiar evening look of hers which seems to say, in the flare of windows and theatre-doors, and the muffled rumble of swift-rolling carriages, that this is no world for you unless you have your pockets lined and your scruples drugged. Longmore, however, had neither scruples nor desires; he looked at the swarming city for the first time with an easy sense of repaying its indifference. Before long a carriage drove up to the pavement directly in front of him, and remained standing for several minutes without its occupant descending. It was one of those neat, plain coupés, drawn by a single powerful horse, in which one is apt to imagine a pale, handsome woman, buried among silk cushions, and yawning as she sees the gas-lamps glittering in the gutters. At last the door opened and out stepped M. de Mauves. He stopped and leaned on the window for some time, talking in an excited manner to a person within. At last he gave a nod and the carriage rolled away. He stood swinging his cane and looking up and down the Boulevard, with the air of a man fumbling, as one may say, with the loose change of time. He turned towards the café and was apparently, for want of anything better worth his attention, about to seat himself at one of the tables, when he perceived Longmore. He wavered an instant, and then, without a change in his nonchalant gait, strolled towards him with a bow and a vague smile.

It was the first time they had met since their encounter in the forest after Longmore's false start for Brussels. Madame Clairin's revelations, as we may call them, had not made the Baron especially present to his mind; he had another office for his emotions than disgust. But as M. de Mauves came towards him he felt deep in his heart that he abhorred him. He noticed, however, for the first time, a shadow upon the Baron's cool placidity, and his delight at finding that somewhere at last the shoe pinched *him*, mingled with his impulse to be as exasperatingly impenetrable as possible, enabled him to return the other's greeting with all his own self-possession.

M. de Mauves sat down, and the two men looked at each other across the table, exchanging formal greetings which did little to make their mutual scrutiny seem gracious. Longmore had no reason to suppose that the Baron knew of his sister's intimations. He was sure that M. de Mauves cared very little about his opinions, and yet he had a sense that there was that in his eyes which would have made the Baron change colour if keener suspicion had helped him to read it. M. de Mauves did not change colour, but he looked at Longmore with a half-defiant intentness which betrayed at once an irritating memory of the episode in the Bois de Boulogne, and such vigilant curiosity as was natural to a gentleman who had intrusted his 'honour' to another gentleman's magnanimity – or to his artlessness.

It would appear that Longmore seemed to the Baron to possess these virtues in rather scantier measure than a few days before; for the cloud deepened on his face, and he turned away and frowned as he lighted a cigar.

The person in the coupé, Longmore thought, whether or no the same person as the heroine of the episode of the Bois de Boulogne, was not a source of unalloyed delight. Longmore had dark blue eyes, of admirable lucidity – truth-telling eyes which had in his childhood always made his harshest task-masters smile at his primitive fibs. An observer watching the two men, and knowing something of their relations, would certainly have said that what he saw in those eyes must not a little have puzzled and tormented M. de Mauves. They judged him, they mocked him, they eluded him, they threatened him, they triumphed over him, they treated him as no pair of eyes had ever treated him. The Baron's scheme had been to make no one happy but himself, and here was Longmore already, if looks were to be trusted, primed for an enterprise more inspiring than the finest of his own achievements. Was this candid young barbarian but a *faux bonhomme* after all? He had puzzled the Baron before, and this was once too often.

M. de Mauves hated to seem preoccupied, and he took up the evening paper to help himself to look indifferent. As he glanced over it he uttered some cold common-place on the political situation, which gave Longmore a fair opportunity of replying by an ironical sally which made him seem for the moment aggressively at his ease. And yet our hero was far from being master of the situation. The Baron's ill-humour did him good, so far as it pointed to a want of harmony with the lady in the coupé; but it disturbed him sorely as he began to suspect that it possibly meant jealousy of himself. It passed through his mind that jealousy is a passion with a double face, and that in some of its moods it bears a plausible likeness to affection. It recurred to him painfully that the Baron might grow ashamed of his political compact with his wife, and he felt that it would be far more tolerable in the future to think of his continued turpitude than of his repentance. The two men sat for half an hour exchanging stinted small-talk, the Baron feeling a nervous need of playing the spy, and Longmore indulging a ferocious relish of his discomfort. These rigid courtesies were interrupted however by the arrival of a friend of M. de Mauves – a tall, pale, consumptive-looking dandy, who filled the air with the odour of heliotrope. He looked up and down the Boulevard wearily, examined the Baron's toilet from head to foot, then surveyed his own in the same fashion, and at last announced languidly that the Duchess was in town! M. de Mauves must come with him to call; she had abused him dreadfully a couple of evenings before – a sure sign she wanted to see him.

'I depend upon you,' said M. de Mauves' friend with an infantine drawl, 'to put her *en train.*'

M. de Mauves resisted, and protested that he was *d'une humeur massacrante*; but at last he allowed himself to be drawn to his feet, and stood looking awkwardly – awkwardly for M. de Mauves – at Longmore. 'You will excuse me,' he said drily; 'you, too, probably have occupation for the evening?'

'None but to catch my train,' Longmore answered, looking at his watch.

'Ah, you go back to Saint-Germain?'

'In half an hour.'

M. de Mauves seemed on the point of disengaging himself from his companion's arm, which was locked in his own; but on the latter uttering some persuasive murmur, he lifted his hat stiffly and turned away.

Longmore the next day wandered off to the terrace, to try and beguile the restlessness with which he waited for evening;

for he wished to see Madame de Mauves for the last time at the hour of long shadows and pale, pink, reflected lights, as he had almost always seen her. Destiny, however, took no account of this humble plea for poetic justice; it was his fortune to meet her on the terrace sitting under a tree, alone. It was an hour when the place was almost empty; the day was warm, but as he took his place beside her a light breeze stirred the leafy edges of the broad circle of shadow in which she sat. She looked at him with candid anxiety, and he immediately told her that he should leave Saint-Germain that evening – that he must bid her farewell. Her eye expanded and brightened for a moment as he spoke; but she said nothing and turned her glance away towards distant Paris, as it lay twinkling and flashing through its hot exhalations. 'I have a request to make of you,' he added; 'that you think of me as a man who has felt much and claimed little.'

She drew a long breath which almost suggested pain. 'I can't think of you as unhappy. That is impossible. You have a life to lead, you have duties, talents, and interests. I shall hear of your career. And then,' she continued after a pause and with the deepest seriousness, 'one can't be unhappy through having a better opinion of a friend, instead of a worse.'

For a moment he failed to understand her. 'Do you mean that there can be varying degrees in my opinion of you?'

She rose and pushed away her chair. 'I mean,' she said quickly, 'that it's better to have done nothing in bitterness – nothing in passion.' And she began to walk.

Longmore followed her, without answering. But he took off his hat and with his pocket-handkerchief wiped his forehead. 'Where shall you go? what shall you do?' he asked at last, abruptly.

'Do? I shall do as I have always done – except perhaps that I shall go for a while to Auvergne.'

'I shall go to America. I have done with Europe for the present.'

She glanced at him as he walked beside her after he had spoken these words, and then bent her eyes for a long time on the ground. At last, seeing that she was going far, she stopped and put out her hand. 'Good-by,' she said; 'may you have all the happiness you deserve!'

He took her hand and looked at her, but something was passing in him that made it impossible to return her hand's light pressure. Something of infinite value was floating past him, and he had taken an oath not to raise a finger to stop it. It was borne by the strong current of the world's great life and not of his own small one. Madame de Mauves disengaged her hand, gathered her shawl, and smiled at him almost as you would do at a child you should wish to encourage. Several moments later he was still standing watching her receding figure. When it had disappeared, he shook himself, walked rapidly back to his hotel, and without waiting for the evening train paid his bill and departed.

Later in the day M. de Mauves came into his wife's drawing-room, where she sat waiting to be summoned to dinner. He was dressed with a scrupulous freshness which seemed to indicate an intention of dining out. He walked up and down for some moments in silence, then rang the bell for a servant, and went out into the hall to meet him. He ordered the carriage to take him to the station, paused a moment with his hand on the knob of the door, dismissed the servant angrily as the latter lingered observing him, re-entered the drawing-room, resumed his restless walk, and at last stopped abruptly before his wife, who had taken up a book. 'May I ask the favour,' he said with evident effort, in spite of a forced smile of easy courtesy, 'of having a question answered?'

'It's a favour I never refused,' Madame de Mauves replied.

'Very true. Do you expect this evening a visit from Mr Longmore?'

'Mr Longmore,' said his wife, 'has left Saint-Germain.' M. de Mauves started and his smile expired. 'Mr Longmore,' his wife continued, 'has gone to America.'

M. de Mauves stared a moment, flushed deeply, and turned away. Then recovering himself – 'Had anything happened?' he asked. 'Had he a sudden call?'

But his question received no answer. At the same moment the servant threw open the door and announced dinner;

Madame Clairin rustled in, rubbing her white hands, Madame de Mauves passed silently into the dinning-room, and he stood frowning and wondering. Before long he went out upon the terrace and continued his uneasy walk. At the end of a quarter of an hour the servant came to inform him that the carriage was at the door. 'Send it away,' he said curtly. 'I shall not use it.' When the ladies had half finished dinner he went in and joined them, with a formal apology to his wife for his tardiness.

The dishes were brought back, but he hardly tasted them; on the other hand, he drank a great deal of wine. There was little talk; what there was, was supplied by Madame Clairin. Twice she saw her brother's eyes fixed on her own, over his wineglass, with a piercing, questioning glance. She replied by an elevation of the eyebrows which did the office of a shrug of the shoulders. M. de Mauves was left alone to finish his wine; he sat over it for more than an hour, and let the darkness gather about him. At last the servant came in with a letter and lighted a candle. The letter was a telegram, which M. de Mauves, when he had read it, burnt at the candle. After five minutes' meditation, he wrote a message on the back of a visiting-card and gave it to the servant to carry to the office. The man knew quite as much as his master suspected about the lady to whom the telegram was addressed; but its contents puzzled him; they consisted of the single word, *Impossible*.' As the evening passed without her brother reappearing in the drawing-room, Madame Clairin came to him where he sat by his solitary candle. He took no notice of her presence for some time; but he was the one person to whom she allowed this licence. At last, speaking in a peremptory tone, 'The American has gone home at an hour's notice,' he said. 'What does it mean?'

Madame Clairin now gave free play to the shrug she had been obliged to suppress at the table. 'It means that I have a sister-in-law whom I have not the honour to understand.'

He said nothing more, and silently allowed her to depart, as if it had been her duty to provide him with an explanation, and he was disgusted with her levity. When she had gone, he went into the garden and walked up and down, smoking. He saw his wife sitting alone on the terrace, but remained below strolling along the narrow paths. He remained a long time. It became late, and Madame de Mauves disappeared. Towards midnight he dropped upon a bench, tired, with a kind of angry sigh. It was sinking into his mind that he, too, did not understand Madame Clairin's sister-in-law.

Longmore was obliged to wait a week in London for a ship. It was very hot, and he went out one day to Richmond. In the garden of the hotel at which he dined he met his friend Mrs Draper, who was staying there. She made eager inquiry about Madame de Mauves; but Longmore at first, as they sat looking out at the famous view of the Thames, parried her questions and confined himself to small-talk. At last she said she was afraid he had something to conceal; whereupon, after a pause, he asked her if she remembered recommending him, in the letter she sent to him at Saint-Germain, to draw the sadness from her friend's smile. 'The last I saw of her was her smile,' said he – 'when I bade her good-bye.'

'I remember urging you to "console" her,' Mrs Draper answered, 'and I wondered afterwards whether – a model of discretion as you are – I had not given you rather foolish advice.'

'She has her consolation in herself,' he said; 'she needs none that any one else can offer her. That's for troubles for which – be it more, be it less – our own folly has to answer. Madame de Mauves has not a grain of folly left.'

'Ah, don't say that!' murmured Mrs Draper. 'Just a little folly is very graceful.'

Longmore rose to go, with a quick, nervous movement. 'Don't talk of grace,' he said, 'till you have measured her reason!'

For two years after his return to America he heard nothing of Madame de Mauves. That he thought of her intently, constantly, I need hardly say; most people wondered why such a clever young man should not 'devote' himself to something; but to himself he seemed absorbingly occupied. He never wrote to her; he believed that she preferred it. At last he heard that Mrs Draper had come home, and he immediately called on her. 'Of course,' she said after the first greetings, 'you are dying for news of Madame de Mauves. Prepare yourself for something strange. I heard from her two or three times during the year after your return. She left Saint-Germain and went to live in the country, on some old property of her husband's. She wrote me very kind little notes, but I felt somehow that – in spite of what you said about "consolation" – they were the notes of a very sad woman. The only advice I could have given her was to leave her wretch of a husband and come back to her own land and her own people. But this I didn't feel free to do, and yet it made me so miserable not to be able to help her that I preferred to let our correspondence die a natural death. I had no news of her for a year. Last summer, however, I met at Vichy a clever young Frenchman whom I accidentally learned to be a friend of Euphemia's charming sister-in-law, Madame Clairin. I lost no time in asking him what he knew about Madame de Mauves – a countrywoman of mine and an old friend. 'I congratulate you on possessing her friendship,' he answered. 'That's the charming little woman who killed her husband.' You may imagine that I promptly asked for an explanation, and he proceeded to relate to me what he called the whole story. M. de Mauves had *fait quelques folies*, which his wife had taken absurdly to heart. He had repented and asked her forgiveness, which she had inexorably refused. She was very pretty, and severity, apparently, suited her style; for whether or no her husband had been in love with her before, he fell madly in love with her now. He was the proudest man in France, but he had begged her on his knees to be re-admitted to favour. All in vain! She was stone, she was ice, she was outraged virtue. People noticed a great change in him; he gave up society, ceased to care for anything, looked shockingly. One fine day they learned that he had blown out his brains. My friend had the story, of course, from Madame Clairin.'

Longmore was strongly moved, and his first impulse after he had recovered his composure was to return immediately to Europe. But several years have passed, and he still lingers at home. The truth is, that in the midst of all the ardent tenderness of his memory of Madame de Mauves, he has become conscious of a singular feeling – a feeling for which awe would be hardly too strong a name.

FOUR MEETINGS

I saw her only four times,[1] but I remember them vividly; she made an impression upon me. I thought her very pretty and very interesting – a charming specimen of a type. I am very sorry to hear of her death; and yet, when I think of it, why should I be sorry? The last time I saw her she was certainly not—. But I will describe all our meetings in order.

I

The first one took place in the country, at a little tea-party, one snowy night. It must have been some seventeen years ago.[2] My friend Latouche, going to spend Christmas with his mother, had persuaded me to go with him, and the good lady had given in our honour the entertainment of which I speak. To me it was really entertaining; I had never been in the depths of New England at that season. It had been snowing all day and the drifts were knee-high. I wondered how the ladies had made their way to the house; but I perceived that at Grimwinter a conversazione offering the attraction of two gentlemen from New York was felt to be worth an effort.

Mrs Latouche in the course of the evening asked me if I 'didn't want to' show the photographs to some of the young ladies. The photographs were in a couple of great portfolios, and had been brought home by her son, who, like myself, was lately returned from Europe. I looked round and was struck with the fact that most of the young ladies were provided with an object of interest more absorbing than the most vivid sun-picture.³ But there was a person standing alone near the mantle-shelf, and looking round the room with a small, gentle smile which seemed at odds, somehow, with her isolation. I looked at her a moment, and then said, 'I should like to show them to that young lady.'

'Oh yes,' said Mrs Latouche, 'she is just the person. She doesn't care for flirting; I will speak to her.'

I rejoined that if she did not care for flirting, she was, perhaps, not just the person; but Mrs Latouche had already gone to propose the photographs to her.

'She's delighted,' she said, coming back. 'She is just the person, so quiet and so bright.' And then she told me the young lady was, by name, Miss Caroline Spencer, and with this she introduced me.

Miss Caroline Spencer was not exactly a beauty, but she was a charming little figure. She must have been close upon thirty, but she was made almost like a little girl, and she had the complexion of a child. She had a very pretty head, and her hair was arranged as nearly as possible like the hair of a Greek bust, though indeed it was to be doubted if she had ever seen a Greek bust. She was 'artistic', I suspected, so far as Grimwinter allowed such tendencies. She had a soft, surprised eye, and thin lips, with very pretty teeth. Round her neck she wore what ladies call, I believe, a 'ruche', fastened with a very small pin in pink coral, and in her hand she carried a fan made of plaited straw and adorned with pink ribbon. She wore a scanty black silk dress. She spoke with a kind of soft precision, showing her white teeth between her narrow but tender-looking lips, and she seemed extremely pleased, even a little fluttered, at the prospect of my demonstrations. These went forward very smoothly, after I had moved the portfolios out of their corner and placed a couple of chairs near a lamp. The photographs were usually things I knew, – large views of Switzerland, Italy and Spain, landscapes, copies of famous buildings, pictures and statues. I said what I could about them, and my companion, looking at them as I held them up, sat perfectly still, with her straw fan raised to her under-lip. Occasionally, as I laid one of the pictures down, she said very softly, 'Have you seen that place?' I usually answered that I had seen it several times (I had been a great traveller), and then I felt that she looked at me askance for a moment with her pretty eyes. I had asked her at the outset whether she had been to Europe; to this she answered, 'No, no, no,' in a little quick, confidential whisper. But after that, though she never took her eyes off the pictures, she said so little that I was afraid she was bored. Accordingly, after we had finished one portfolio, I offered, if she desired it, to desist. I felt that she was not bored, but her reticence puzzled me and I wished to make her speak. I turned round to look at her, and saw that there was a faint flush in each of her cheeks. She was waving her little fan to and fro. Instead of looking at me she fixed her eyes upon the other portfolio, which was leaning against the table.

'Won't you show me that?' she asked, with a little tremor in her voice. I could almost have believed she was agitated.

'With pleasure,' I answered, 'if you are not tired.'

'No, I am not tired,' she affirmed. 'I like it – I love it.'

And as I took up the other portfolio she laid her hand upon it, rubbing it softly.

'And have you been here too?' she asked.

On my opening the portfolio it appeared that I had been there. One of the first photographs was a large view of the Castle of Chillon,[4] on the Lake of Geneva.

'Here,' I said, 'I have been many a time. Is it not beautiful?' And I pointed to the perfect reflection of the rugged rocks and pointed towers in the clear, still water. She did not say, 'Oh, enchanting!' and push it away to see the next picture. She looked awhile, and then she asked if it was not where Bonivard, about whom Byron wrote, was confined. I assented, and tried to quote some of Byron's verses, but in this attempt I succeeded imperfectly.

She fanned herself a moment and then repeated the lines correctly, in a soft, flat, and yet agreeable voice. By the time she had finished, she was blushing. I complimented her and told her she was perfectly equipped for visiting Switzerland and Italy. She looked at me askance again, to see whether I was serious, and I added, that if she wished to recognize Byron's descriptions she must go abroad speedily; Europe was getting sadly dis-Byronized.[5]

'How soon must I go?' she asked.

'Oh, I will give you ten years.'

'I think I can go within ten years,' she answered very soberly.

'Well,' I said, 'you will enjoy it immensely; you will find it very charming.' And just then I came upon a photograph of some nook in a foreign city which I had been very fond of, and which recalled tender memories. I discoursed (as I suppose) with a certain eloquence; my companion sat listening, breathless.

'Have you been *very* long in foreign lands?' she asked, some time after I had ceased.

'Many years,' I said.

'And have you travelled everywhere?'

'I have travelled a great deal. I am very fond of it; and, happily, I have been able.'

Again she gave me her sidelong gaze. 'And do you know the foreign languages?'

'After a fashion.'

'Is it hard to speak them?'

'I don't believe you would find it hard,' I gallantly responded.

'Oh, I shouldn't want to speak – I should only want to listen,' she said. Then, after a pause, she added – 'They say the French theatre is so beautiful.'

'It is the best in the world.'

'Did you go there very often?'

'When I was first in Paris I went every night.'

'Every night!' And she opened her clear eyes very wide. 'That to me is –' and she hesitated a moment – 'is very wonderful.' A few minutes later she asked – 'Which country do you prefer?'

'There is one country I prefer to all others. I think you would do the same.'

She looked at me a moment, and then she said softly – 'Italy?'

'Italy,' I answered softly, too; and for a moment we looked at each other. She looked as pretty as if, instead of showing her photographs, I had been making love to her. To increase the analogy, she glanced away, blushing. There was a silence, which she broke at last by saying –

'That is the place, which – in particular – I thought of going to.'

'Oh, that's the place – that's the place!' I said.

She looked at two or three photographs in silence. 'They say it is not so dear.'

'As some other countries? Yes, that is not the least of its charms.'

'But it is all very dear, is it not?'

'Europe, you mean?'

'Going there and travelling. That has been the trouble. I have very little money. I give lessons,' said Miss Spencer.

'Of course one must have money,' I said, 'but one can manage with a moderate amount.'

'I think I should manage. I have laid something by, and I am always adding a little to it. It's all for that.' She paused a moment, and then went on with a kind of suppressed eagerness, as if telling me the story were a rare, but a possibly impure, satisfaction. 'But it has not been only the money; it has been everything. Everything has been against it. I have waited and waited. It has been a mere castle in the air. I am almost afraid to talk about it. Two or three times it has been a little nearer, and then I have talked about it and it has melted away. I have talked about it too much,' she said, hypocritically; for I saw that such talking was now a small tremulous ecstasy. 'There is a lady who is a great friend of mine; she doesn't want to go; I always talk to her about it. I tire her dreadfully. She told me once she didn't know what would become of me. I should go crazy if I did not go to Europe, and I should certainly go crazy if I did.'

'Well,' I said, 'you have not gone yet, and nevertheless you are not crazy.'

She looked at me a moment, and said – 'I am not so sure. I don't think of anything else. I am always thinking of it. It prevents me from thinking of things that are nearer home – things that I ought to attend to. That is a kind of craziness.'

'The cure for it is to go,' I said.

'I have a faith that I shall go. I have a cousin in Europe!' she announced.

We turned over some more photographs, and I asked her if she had always lived at Grimwinter.

'Oh, no, sir,' said Miss Spencer. 'I have spent twenty-three months in Boston.'

I answered, jocosely, that in that case foreign lands would probably prove a disappointment to her; but I quite failed to alarm her.

'I know more about them than you might think,' she said, with her shy, neat little smile. 'I mean by reading; I have read a great deal. I have not only read Byron; I have read histories and guide-books. I know I shall like it!'

'I understand your case,' I rejoined. 'You have the native American passion – the passion for the picturesque.[6] With us, I think, it is primordial – antecedent to experience. Experience comes and only shows us something we have dreamt of.'

'I think that is very true,' said Caroline Spencer. 'I have dreamt of everything; I shall know it all!'

'I am afraid you have wasted a great deal of time.'

'Oh yes, that has been my great wickedness.'

The people about us had begun to scatter; they were taking their leave. She got up and put out her hand to me, timidly, but with a peculiar brightness in her eyes.

'I am going back there,' I said, as I shook hands with her. 'I shall look out for you.'

'I will tell you,' she answered, 'if I am disappointed.'

And she went away, looking delicately agitated and moving her little straw fan.

II

A few months after this I returned to Europe, and some three years elapsed. I had been living in Paris, and, toward the end of October, I went from that city to Havre,[7] to meet my sister and her husband, who had written me that they were about to arrive there. On reaching Havre I found that the steamer was already in; I was nearly two hours late. I repaired directly to the hotel, where my relatives were already established. My sister had gone to bed, exhausted and disabled by her voyage; she was a sadly incompetent sailor, and her sufferings on this occasion had been extreme. She wished, for the moment, for undisturbed rest, and was unable to see me more than five minutes; so it was agreed that we should remain at Havre until the next day. My brother-in-law, who was anxious about his wife, was unwilling to leave her room; but she insisted upon his going out with me to take a walk and recover his land-legs. The early autumn day was warm and charming, and our stroll through the bright-coloured, busy streets of the old French sea-port was sufficiently entertaining. We walked along the sunny, noisy quays and then turned into a wide, pleasant street which lay half in sun and half in shade – a French provincial street, that looked like an old water-colour drawing: tall, grey, steep-roofed, red-gabled, many-storeyed houses; green shutters on windows and old scroll-work above them; flower-pots in balconies and white-capped women in door-ways. We walked in the shade; all this stretched away on the sunny side of the street and made a picture. We looked at it as we passed along; then, suddenly, my brother-in-law stopped – pressing my arm and staring. I followed his gaze and saw that we had paused just before coming to a café, where, under an awning, several tables and chairs were disposed upon the pavement. The windows were open behind; half-a-dozen plants in tubs were ranged beside the door; the pavement was besprinkled with clean bran. It was a nice little, quiet, old-fashioned café; inside, in the comparative dusk, I saw a stout, handsome woman, with pink ribbons in her cap, perched up with a mirror behind her back, smiling at some one who was out of sight. All this, however, I perceived afterwards; what I first observed was a lady sitting alone, outside, at one of the little marble-topped tables. My brother-in-law had stopped to look at her. There was something on the little table, but she was leaning back quietly, with her hands folded, looking down the street, away from us. I saw her only in something less than profile; nevertheless, I instantly felt that I had seen her before.

'The little lady of the steamer!' exclaimed my brother-in-law.

'Was she on your steamer?' I asked.

'From morning till night. She was never sick. She used to sit perpetually at the side of the vessel with her hands crossed that way, looking at the eastward horizon.'

'Are you going to speak to her?'

'I don't know her. I never made acquaintance with her. I was too seedy. But I used to watch her and – I don't know why – to be interested in her. She's a dear little Yankee woman. I have an idea she is a school-mistress taking a holiday – for which her scholars have made up a purse.'

She turned her face a little more into profile, looking at the steep, grey house-fronts opposite to her. Then I said – 'I shall speak to her myself.'

'I wouldn't; she is very shy,' said my brother-in-law.

'My dear fellow, I know her. I once showed her photographs at a tea-party.'

And I went up to her. She turned and looked at me, and I saw she was in fact Miss Caroline Spencer. But she was not so quick to recognize me; she looked startled. I pushed a chair to the table and sat down.

'Well,' I said, 'I hope you are not disappointed!'

She stared, blushing a little; then she gave a small jump which betrayed recognition.

'It was you who showed me the photographs – at Grimwinter!'

'Yes, it was I. This happens very charmingly, for I feel as if it were for me to give you a formal reception here – an official welcome. I talked to you so much about Europe.'

'You didn't say too much. I am so happy!' she softly exclaimed.

Very happy she looked. There was no sign of her being older; she was as gravely, decently, demurely pretty as before. If she had seemed before a thin-stemmed, mild-hued flower of Puritanism, it may be imagined whether in her present situation this delicate bloom was less apparent. Beside her an old gentleman was drinking absinthe; behind her the *dame de comptoir* in the pink ribbons was calling 'Alcibiade! Alcibiade!'

to the long-aproned waiter. I explained to Miss Spencer that my companion had lately been her ship-mate, and my brother-in-law came up and was introduced to her. But she looked at him as if she had never seen him before, and I remembered that he had told me that her eyes were always fixed upon the eastward horizon. She had evidently not noticed him, and, still timidly smiling, she made no attempt whatever to pretend that she had. I staid with her at the café door, and he went back to the hotel and to his wife. I said to Miss Spencer that this meeting of ours in the first hour of her landing was really very strange, but that I was delighted to be there and receive her first impressions.

'Oh, I can't tell you,' she said; 'I feel as if I were in a dream. I have been sitting here for an hour, and I don't want to move. Everything is so picturesque. I don't know whether the coffee has intoxicated me; it's so delicious.'

'Really,' said I, 'if you are so pleased with this poor prosaic Havre, you will have no admiration left for better things. Don't spend your admiration all the first day; remember it's your intellectual letter of credit. Remember all the beautiful places and things that are waiting for you; remember that lovely Italy!'

'I'm not afraid of running short,' she said gayly, still looking at the opposite houses. 'I could sit here all day, saying to myself that here I am at last. It's so dark, and old, and different.'

'By the way,' I inquired, 'how come you to be sitting here? Have you not gone to one of the inns?' For I was half amused, half alarmed at the good conscience with which this delicately pretty woman had stationed herself in conspicuous isolation on the edge of the sidewalk.

'My cousin brought me here,' she answered. 'You know I told you I had a cousin in Europe. He met me at the steamer this morning.'

'It was hardly worth his while to meet you if he was to desert you so soon.'

'Oh, he has only left me for half an hour,' said Miss Spencer. 'He has gone to get my money.'

'Where is your money?'

She gave a little laugh. 'It makes me feel very fine to tell you! It is in some circular notes.'[8]

'And where are your circular notes?'

'In my cousin's pocket.'

This statement was very serenely uttered, but – I can hardly say why – it gave me a sensible chill. At the moment I should have been utterly unable to give the reason of this sensation, for I knew nothing of Miss Spencer's cousin. Since he was her cousin, the presumption was in his favour. But I felt suddenly uncomfortable at the thought that, half an hour after her landing, her scanty funds should have passed into his hands.

'Is he to travel with you?' I asked.

'Only as far as Paris. He is an art-student in Paris. I wrote to him that I was coming, but I never expected him to come off to the ship. I supposed he would only just meet me at the train in Paris. It is very kind of him. But he *is* very kind – and very bright.'

I instantly became conscious of an extreme curiosity to see this bright cousin who was an art-student.

'He is gone to the banker's?' I asked.

'Yes, to the banker's. He took me to an hotel – such a queer, quaint, delicious little place, with a court in the middle, and a gallery all round, and a lovely landlady, in such a beautifully fluted cap, and such a perfectly fitting dress! After a while we came out to walk to the banker's, for I haven't got any French money. But I was very dizzy from the motion of the vessel, and I thought I had better sit down. He found this place for me here, and he went off to the banker's himself. I am to wait here till he comes back.'

It may seem very fantastic, but it passed through my mind that he would never come back. I settled myself in my chair beside Miss Spencer and determined to await the event. She was extremely observant; there was something touching in it. She noticed everything that the movement of the street brought before us – the peculiarities of costume, the shapes of vehicles, the big Norman horses, the fat priests, the shaven poodles. We talked of these things, and there was something charming in her freshness of perception and the way her book-nourished fancy recognized and welcomed everything.

'And when your cousin comes back what are you going to do?' I asked.

She hesitated a moment. 'We don't quite know.'

'When do you go to Paris? If you go by the four o'clock train I may have the pleasure of making the journey with you.'

'I don't think we shall do that. My cousin thinks I had better stay here a few days.'

'Oh!' said I; and for five minutes said nothing more. I was wondering what her cousin was, in vulgar parlance, 'up to'. I looked up and down the street, but saw nothing that looked like a bright American art-student. At last I took the liberty of observing that Havre was hardly a place to choose as one of the æsthetic stations of a European tour. It was a place of convenience,[9] nothing more; a place of transit, through which transit should be rapid. I recommended her to go to Paris by the afternoon train, and meanwhile to amuse herself by driving to the ancient fortress[10] at the mouth of the harbour – that picturesque, circular structure which bore the name of Francis the First[11] and looked like a small castle of St Angelo.[12] (It has lately been demolished.)[13]

She listened with much interest; then for a moment she looked grave.

'My cousin told me that when he returned he should have something particular to say to me, and that we could do nothing or decide nothing until I should have heard it. But I will make him tell me quickly, and then we will go to the ancient fortress. There is no hurry to get to Paris; there is plenty of time.'

She smiled with her softly severe little lips as she spoke those last words. But I, looking at her with a purpose, saw just a tiny gleam of apprehension in her eye.

'Don't tell me,' I said, 'that this wretched man is going to give you bad news!'

'I suspect it is a little bad, but I don't believe it is very bad. At any rate, I must listen to it.'

I looked at her again an instant. 'You didn't come to Europe to listen,' I said. 'You came to see!' But now I was sure her cousin would come back; since he had something disagreeable to say to her, he certainly would turn up. We sat a while longer, and I asked her about her plans of travel. She had them on her fingers' ends, and she told over the names with a kind of solemn distinctness: from Paris to Dijon and to Avignon, from Avignon to Marseilles and the Cornice road; thence to Genoa, to Spezia, to Pisa, to Florence, to Rome. It apparently had never occurred to her that there could be the least incommodity in her travelling alone; and since she was unprovided with a companion I of course scrupulously abstained from disturbing her sense of security.

At last her cousin came back. I saw him turn towards us out of a side-street, and from the moment my eyes rested upon him I felt that this was the bright American art-student. He wore a slouch hat and a rusty black velvet jacket, such as I had often encountered in the Rue Bonaparte.[14] His shirt-collar revealed a large section of a throat which, at a distance, was not strikingly statuesque. He was tall and lean; he had red hair and freckles. So much I had time to observe while he approached the café, staring at me with natural surprise from under his umbrageous coiffure. When he came up to us I immediately introduced myself to him as an old acquaintance of Miss Spencer. He looked at me hard with a pair of little red eyes, then he made me a solemn bow in the French fashion, with his sombrero.

'You were not on the ship?' he said.

'No, I was not on the ship. I have been in Europe these three years.'

He bowed once more, solemnly, and motioned me to be seated again. I sat down, but it was only for the purpose of observing him an instant – I saw it was time I should return to my sister. Miss Spencer's cousin was a queer fellow. Nature had not shaped him for a Raphaelesque or Byronic attire,[15] and his velvet doublet and naked throat were not in harmony with his facial attributes. His hair was cropped close to his head; his ears were large and ill-adjusted to the same. He had a lackadaisical carriage and a sentimental droop which were peculiarly at variance with his keen, strange-coloured eyes. Perhaps I was prejudiced, but I thought his eyes treacherous. He said nothing for some time; he leaned his hands on his cane and looked up and down the street. Then at last, slowly lifting his cane and pointing with it, 'That's a very nice bit,' he remarked, softly. He had his head on one side, and his little eyes were half closed. I followed the direction of his stick; the object it indicated was a red cloth hung out of an old window. 'Nice bit of colour,' he continued; and without moving his head he transferred his half-closed gaze to me. 'Composes well,' he pursued. 'Make a nice thing.' He spoke in a hard, vulgar voice.

'I see you have a great deal of eye,' I replied. 'Your cousin tells me you are studying art.' He looked at me in the same way without answering, and I went on with deliberate urbanity – 'I suppose you are at the studio of one of those great men.'

Still he looked at me, and then he said softly – 'Gérôme.'[16]

'Do you like it?' I asked.

'Do you understand French?' he said.

'Some kinds,' I answered.

He kept his little eyes on me; then he said – 'J'adore la peinture!'

'Oh, I understand that kind!' I rejoined. Miss Spencer laid her hand upon her cousin's arm with a little pleased and fluttered movement; it was delightful to be among people who were on such easy terms with foreign tongues. I got up to take leave, and asked Miss Spencer where, in Paris, I might have the honour of waiting upon her. To what hotel would she go?

She turned to her cousin inquiringly and he honoured me again with his little languid leer. 'Do you know the Hôtel des Princes?'

'I know where it is.'

'I shall take her there.'

'I congratulate you,' I said to Caroline Spencer. 'I believe it is the best inn in the world; and in case I should still have a moment to call upon you here, where are you lodged?'

'Oh, it's such a pretty name,' said Miss Spencer, gleefully. 'À la Belle Normande.'[17]

As I left them her cousin gave me a great flourish with his picturesque hat.

III

My sister, as it proved, was not sufficiently restored to leave Havre by the afternoon train; so that, as the autumn dusk began to fall, I found myself at liberty to call at the sign of the Fair Norman. I must confess that I had spent much of the interval in wondering what the disagreeable thing was that my charming friend's disagreeable cousin had been telling her. The 'Belle Normande' was a modest inn in a shady by-street, where it gave me satisfaction to think Miss Spencer must have encountered local colour in abundance. There was a crooked little court, where much of the hospitality of the house was carried on; there was a staircase climbing to bed-rooms on the outer side of the wall; there was a small trickling fountain with a stucco statuette in the midst of it; there was a little boy in a white cap and apron cleaning copper vessels at a conspicuous kitchen door; there was a chattering landlady, neatly laced, arranging apricots and grapes into an artistic pyramid upon a pink plate. I looked about, and on a green bench outside of an open door labelled *Salle à Manger,* I perceived Caroline Spencer. No sooner had I looked at her than I saw that something had happened since the morning. She was leaning back on her bench, her hands were clasped in her lap, and her eyes were fixed upon the landlady, at the other side of the court, manipulating her apricots.

But I saw she was not thinking of apricots. She was staring absently, thoughtfully; as I came near her I perceived that she had been crying. I sat down on the bench beside her before she saw me; then, when she had done so, she simply turned round, without surprise, and rested her sad eyes upon me. Something very bad indeed had happened; she was completely changed.

I immediately charged her with it. 'Your cousin has been giving you bad news; you are in great distress.'

For a moment she said nothing, and I supposed that she was afraid to speak, lest her tears should come back. But presently I perceived that in the short time that had elapsed since my leaving her in the morning she had shed them all, and that she was now softly stoical – intensely composed.

'My poor cousin is in distress,' she said at last. 'His news
was bad.' Then, after a brief hesitation – 'He was in terrible
want of money.'

'In want of yours, you mean?'

'Of any that he could get – honestly. Mine was the only money.'

'And he has taken yours?'

She hesitated again a moment, but her glance, meanwhile,
was pleading. 'I gave him what I had.'

I have always remembered the accent of those words as the
most angelic bit of human utterance I had ever listened to; but
then, almost with a sense of personal outrage, I jumped up.
'Good heavens!' I said, 'do you call that getting it honestly?'

I had gone too far; she blushed deeply. 'We will not speak of
it,' she said.

'We *must* speak of it,' I answered, sitting down again. 'I am
your friend; it seems to me you need one. What is the matter
with your cousin?'

'He is in debt.'

'No doubt! But what is the special fitness of your paying his
debts?'

'He has told me all his story; I am very sorry for him.'

'So am I! But I hope he will give you back your money.'

'Certainly he will; as soon as he can.'

'When will that be?'

'When he has finished his great picture.'

'My dear young lady, confound his great picture! Where is
this desperate cousin?'

She certainly hesitated now. Then – 'At his dinner,' she
answered.

I turned about and looked through the open door into the
salle à manger. There, alone at the end of a long table, I perceived the object of Miss Spencer's compassion – the bright
young art-student. He was dining too attentively to notice me
at first; but in the act of setting down a well-emptied wineglass
he caught sight of my observant attitude. He paused in his
repast, and, with his head on one side and his meagre jaws
slowly moving, fixedly returned my gaze. Then the landlady
came lightly brushing by with her pyramid of apricots.

'And that nice little plate of fruit is for him?' I exclaimed.

Miss Spencer glanced at it tenderly. 'They do that so prettily!' she murmured.

I felt helpless and irritated. 'Come now, really,' I said; 'do you approve of that long strong fellow accepting your funds?' She looked away from me; I was evidently giving her pain. The case was hopeless; the long strong fellow had 'interested' her.

'Excuse me if I speak of him so unceremoniously,' I said. 'But you are really too generous, and he is not quite delicate enough. He made his debts himself – he ought to pay them himself.'

'He has been foolish,' she answered; 'I know that. He has told me everything. We had a long talk this morning; the poor fellow threw himself upon my charity. He has signed notes to a large amount.'

'The more fool he!'

'He is in extreme distress; and it is not only himself. It is his poor wife.'

'Ah, he has a poor wife?'

'I didn't know it – but he confessed everything. He married two years since, secretly.'

'Why secretly?'

Caroline Spencer glanced about her, as if she feared listeners. Then softly, in a little impressive tone – 'She was a Countess!'

'Are you very sure of that?'

'She has written me a most beautiful letter.'

'Asking you for money, eh?'

'Asking me for confidence and sympathy,' said Miss Spencer. 'She has been disinherited by her father. My cousin told me the story and she tells it in her own way, in the letter. It is like an old romance. Her father opposed the marriage and when he discovered that she had secretly disobeyed him he cruelly cast her off. It is really most romantic. They are the oldest family in Provence.'

I looked and listened, in wonder. It really seemed that the poor woman was enjoying the 'romance' of having a discarded Countess-cousin, out of Provence, so deeply as almost to lose the sense of what the forfeiture of her money meant for her.

'My dear young lady,' I said, 'you don't want to be ruined for picturesqueness' sake?'

'I shall not be ruined. I shall come back before long to stay with them. The Countess insists upon that.'

'Come back! You are going home, then?'

She sat for a moment with her eyes lowered, then with an heroic suppression of a faint tremor of the voice – 'I have no money for travelling!' she answered.

'You gave it *all* up?'

'I have kept enough to take me home.'

I gave an angry groan, and at this juncture Miss Spencer's cousin, the fortunate possessor of her sacred savings and of the hand of the Provençal Countess, emerged from the little dining-room. He stood on the threshold for an instant, removing the stone from a plump apricot which he had brought away from the table; then he put the apricot into his mouth, and while he let it sojourn there, gratefully, stood looking at us, with his long legs apart and his hands dropped into the pockets of his velvet jacket. My companion got up, giving him a thin glance which I caught in its passage, and which expressed a strange commixture of resignation and fascination – a sort of perverted exaltation. Ugly, vulgar, pretentious, dishonest as I thought the creature, he had appealed successfully to her eager and tender imagination. I was deeply disgusted, but I had no warrant to interfere, and at any rate I felt that it would be vain.

The young man waved his hand with a pictorial gesture. 'Nice old court,' he observed. 'Nice mellow old place. Good tone in that brick. Nice crooked old staircase.'

Decidedly, I couldn't stand it; without responding I gave my hand to Caroline Spencer. She looked at me an instant with her little white face and expanded eyes, and as she showed her pretty teeth I suppose she meant to smile.

'Don't be sorry for me,' she said, 'I am very sure I shall see something of this dear old Europe yet.'

I told her that I would not bid her good-bye – I should find a moment to come back the next morning. Her cousin, who had put on his sombrero again, flourished it off at me by way of a bow – upon which I took my departure.

The next morning I came back to the inn, where I met in the court the landlady, more loosely laced than in the evening. On my asking for Miss Spencer – 'Partie, monsieur,' said the hostess. 'She went away last night at ten o'clock, with her – her – not her husband, eh? – in fine her Monsieur. They went down to the American ship.' I turned away; the poor girl had been about thirteen hours in Europe.

IV

I myself, more fortunate, was there some five years longer. During this period I lost my friend Latouche, who died of a malarious fever during a tour in the Levant. One of the first things I did on my return was to go up to Grimwinter to pay a consolatory visit to his poor mother. I found her in deep affliction, and I sat with her the whole of the morning that followed my arrival (I had come in late at night), listening to her tearful descant and singing the praises of my friend. We talked of nothing else, and our conversation terminated only with the arrival of a quick little woman who drove herself up to the door in a 'carry-all',[18] and whom I saw toss the reins upon the horse's back with the briskness of a startled sleeper throwing back the bed-clothes. She jumped out of the carry-all and she jumped into the room. She proved to be the minister's wife and the great town-gossip, and she had evidently, in the latter capacity, a choice morsel to communicate. I was as sure of this as I was that poor Mrs Latouche was not absolutely too bereaved to listen to her. It seemed to me discreet to retire; I said I believed I would go and take a walk before dinner.

'And, by the way,' I added, 'if you will tell me where my old friend Miss Spencer lives I will walk to her house.'

The minister's wife immediately responded. Miss Spencer lived in the fourth house beyond the Baptist church; the Baptist church was the one on the right, with that queer green thing over the door; they called it a portico, but it looked more like an old-fashioned bedstead.

'Yes, do go and see poor Caroline,' said Mrs Latouche. 'It will refresh her to see a strange face.'

'I should think she had had enough of strange faces!' cried the minister's wife.

'I mean, to see a visitor,' said Mrs Latouche, amending her phrase.

'I should think she had had enough of visitors!' her companion rejoined. 'But *you* don't mean to stay ten years,' she added, glancing at me.

'Has she a visitor of that sort?' I inquired, perplexed.

'You will see the sort!' said the minister's wife. 'She's easily seen; she generally sits in the front yard. Only take care what you say to her, and be very sure you are polite.'

'Ah, she is so sensitive?'

The minister's wife jumped up and dropped me a curtsey – a most ironical curtsey.

'That's what she is, if you please. She's a Countess!'

And pronouncing this word with the most scathing accent, the little woman seemed fairly to laugh in the Countess's face. I stood a moment, staring, wondering, remembering.

'Oh, I shall be very polite!' I cried; and grasping my hat and stick, I went on my way.

I found Miss Spencer's residence without difficulty. The Baptist church was easily identified, and the small dwelling near it, of a rusty white, with a large central chimney-stack and a Virginia creeper, seemed naturally and properly the abode of a frugal old maid with a taste for the picturesque. As I approached I slackened my pace, for I had heard that some one was always sitting in the front yard, and I wished to reconnoitre. I looked cautiously over the low white fence which separated the small garden-space from the unpaved street; but I descried nothing in the shape of a Countess. A small straight path led up to the crooked doorstep, and on either side of it was a little grass-plot, fringed with currant-bushes. In the middle of the grass, on either side, was a large quince-tree, full of antiquity and contortions, and beneath one of the quince-trees were placed a small table and a couple of chairs. On the table lay a piece of unfinished embroidery and two or three books in bright-coloured paper covers. I went in at the gate and paused half-way along the path, scanning the place for some farther token of its occupant, before whom – I could hardly have said why – I hesitated abruptly to present myself. Then I saw that the poor little house was very shabby. I felt a sudden doubt of my right to intrude; for curiosity had been my motive, and curiosity here seemed singularly indelicate. While I hesitated, a figure appeared in the open door-way and stood there looking at me. I immediately recognized Caroline Spencer, but she looked at me as if she had never seen me before. Gently, but gravely and timidly, I advanced to the door-step, and then I said, with an attempt at friendly badinage –

'I waited for you over there to come back, but you never came.'

'Waited where, sir?' she asked softly, and her light-coloured eyes expanded more than before.

She was much older; she looked tired and wasted.

'Well,' I said, 'I waited at Havre.'

She stared; then she recognized me. She smiled and blushed and clasped her two hands together. 'I remember you now,' she said. 'I remember that day.' But she stood there, neither coming out nor asking me to come in. She was embarrassed.

I, too, felt a little awkward. I poked my stick into the path. 'I kept looking out for you, year after year,' I said.

'You mean in Europe?' murmured Miss Spencer.

'In Europe, of course! Here, apparently, you are easy enough to find.'

She leaned her hand against the unpainted door-post, and her head fell a little to one side. She looked at me for a moment without speaking, and I thought I recognized the expression that one sees in women's eyes when tears are rising. Suddenly she stepped out upon the cracked slab of stone before the threshold and closed the door behind her. Then she began to smile intently, and I saw that her teeth were as pretty as ever. But there had been tears too.

'Have you been there ever since?' she asked, almost in a whisper.

'Until three weeks ago. And you – you never came back?'

Still looking at me with her fixed smile, she put her hand

behind her and opened the door again. 'I am not very polite,' she said. 'Won't you come in?'

'I am afraid I incommode you.'

'Oh no!' she answered, smiling more than ever. And she pushed back the door, with a sign that I should enter.

I went in, following her. She led the way to a small room on the left of the narrow hall, which I supposed to be her parlour, though it was at the back of the house, and we passed the closed door of another apartment which apparently enjoyed a view of the quince-trees. This one looked out upon a small wood-shed and two clucking hens. But I thought it very pretty, until I saw that its elegance was of the most frugal kind; after which, presently, I thought it prettier still, for I had never seen faded chintz and old mezzotint[19] engravings, framed in varnished autumn leaves, disposed in so graceful a fashion. Miss Spencer sat down on a very small portion of the sofa, with her hands tightly clasped in her lap. She looked ten years older, and it would have sounded very perverse now to speak of her as pretty. But I thought her so; or at least I thought her touching. She was peculiarly agitated. I tried to appear not to notice it; but suddenly, in the most inconsequent fashion – it was an irresistible memory of our little friendship at Havre – I said to her – 'I do incommode you. You are distressed.'

She raised her two hands to her face, and for a moment kept it buried in them. Then, taking them away – 'It's because you remind me . . .' she said.

'I remind you, you mean, of that miserable day at Havre?'

She shook her head. 'It was not miserable. It was delightful.'

'I never was so shocked as when, on going back to your inn the next morning, I found you had set sail again.'

She was silent a moment; and then she said – 'Please let us not speak of that.'

'Did you come straight back here?' I asked.

'I was back here just thirty days after I had gone away.'

'And here you have remained ever since?'

'Oh yes!' she said gently.

'When are you going to Europe again?'

This question seemed brutal; but there was something that irritated me in the softness of her resignation, and I wished to extort from her some expression of impatience.

She fixed her eyes for a moment upon a small sun-spot on the carpet; then she got up and lowered the window-blind a little, to obliterate it. Presently, in the same mild voice, answering my question, she said – 'Never!'

'I hope your cousin repaid you your money.'

'I don't care for it now,' she said, looking away from me.

'You don't care for your money?'

'For going to Europe.'

'Do you mean that you would not go if you could?'

'I can't – I can't,' said Caroline Spencer. 'It is all over; I never think of it.'

'He never repaid you, then!' I exclaimed.

'Please – please,' she began.

But she stopped; she was looking toward the door. There had been a rustling and a sound of steps in the hall.

I also looked toward the door, which was open, and now admitted another person – a lady who paused just within the threshold. Behind her came a young man. The lady looked at me with a good deal of fixedness – long enough for my glance to receive a vivid impression of herself. Then she turned to Caroline Spencer, and, with a smile and a strong foreign accent –

'Excuse my interruption!' she said. 'I knew not you had company – the gentleman came in so quietly.'

With this, she directed her eyes toward me again.

She was very strange; yet my first feeling was that I had seen her before. Then I perceived that I had only seen ladies who were very much like her. But I had seen them very far away from Grimwinter, and it was an odd sensation to be seeing her here. Whither was it the sight of her seemed to transport me? To some dusky landing before a shabby Parisian *quatrième* – to an open door revealing a greasy antechamber, and to Madame leaning over the banisters while she holds a faded dressing-gown together and bawls down to the portress to bring up her coffee. Miss Spencer's visitor was a very large woman, of middle age, with a plump, dead-white face and hair drawn back *à la chinoise*. She had a small, penetrating eye, and what is called in French an agreeable smile. She wore an old pink cashmere dressing-gown, covered with white embroideries, and, like the figure in my momentary vision, she was holding it together in front with a bare and rounded arm and a plump and deeply-dimpled hand.

'It is only to spick about my *café*,' she said to Miss Spencer with her agreeable smile. 'I should like it served in the garden under the leetle tree.'

The young man behind her had now stepped into the room, and he also stood looking at me. He was a pretty-faced little fellow, with an air of provincial foppishness – a tiny Adonis of Grimwinter. He had a small, pointed nose, a small, pointed chin, and, as I observed, the most diminutive feet. He looked at me foolishly, with his mouth open.

'You shall have your coffee,' said Miss Spencer, who had a faint red spot in each of her cheeks.

'It is well!' said the lady in the dressing-gown. 'Find your bouk,' she added, turning to the young man.

He looked vaguely round the room. 'My grammar, d'ye mean?' he asked, with a helpless intonation.

But the large lady was looking at me curiously, and gathering in her dressing-gown with her white arm.

'Find your bouk, my friend,' she repeated.

'My poetry, d'ye mean?' said the young man, also gazing at me again.

'Never mind your bouk,' said his companion. 'To-day we will talk. We will make some conversation. But we must not interrupt. Come,' and she turned away. 'Under the leetle tree,' she added, for the benefit of Miss Spencer.

Then she gave me a sort of salutation, and a 'Monsieur!' – with which she swept away again, followed by the young man.

Caroline Spencer stood there with her eyes fixed upon the ground.

'Who is that?' I asked.

'The Countess, my cousin.'

'And who is the young man?'

'Her pupil, Mr Mixter.'

This description of the relation between the two persons who had just left the room made me break into a little laugh. Miss Spencer looked at me gravely.

'She gives French lessons; she has lost her fortune.'

'I see,' I said. 'She is determined to be a burden to no one. That is very proper.'

Miss Spencer looked down on the ground again. 'I must go and get the coffee,' she said.

'Has the lady many pupils?' I asked.

'She has only Mr Mixter. She gives all her time to him.'

At this I could not laugh, though I smelt provocation. Miss Spencer was too grave. 'He pays very well,' she presently added, with simplicity. 'He is very rich. He is very kind. He takes the Countess to drive.' And she was turning away.

'You are going for the Countess's coffee?' I said.

'If you will excuse me a few moments.'

'Is there no one else to do it?'

She looked at me with the softest serenity. 'I keep no servants.'

'Can she not wait upon herself?'

'She is not used to that.'

'I see,' said I, as gently as possible. 'But before you go, tell me this: who is this lady?'

'I told you about her before – that day. She is the wife of my cousin, whom you saw.'

'The lady who was disowned by her family in consequence of her marriage?'

'Yes; they have never seen her again. They have cast her off.'

'And where is her husband?'

'He is dead.'

'And where is your money?'

The poor girl flinched; there was something too methodical in my questions. 'I don't know,' she said wearily.

But I continued a moment. 'On her husband's death this lady came over here?'

'Yes, she arrived one day.'

'How long ago?'

'Two years.'

'She has been here ever since?'

'Every moment.'

'How does she like it?'

'Not at all.'

'And how do *you* like it?'

Miss Spencer laid her face in her two hands an instant, as she had done ten minutes before. Then, quickly, she went to get the Countess's coffee.

I remained alone in the little parlour; I wanted to see more – to learn more. At the end of five minutes the young man whom Miss Spencer had described as the Countess's pupil came in. He stood looking at me for a moment with parted lips. I saw he was a very rudimentary young man.

'She wants to know if you won't come out there?' he observed at last.

'Who wants to know?'

'The Countess. That French lady.'

'She has asked you to bring me?'

'Yes, sir,' said the young man feebly, looking at my six feet of stature.

I went out with him, and we found the Countess sitting under one of the little quince-trees in front of the house. She was drawing a needle through the piece of embroidery which she had taken from the small table. She pointed graciously to the chair beside her and I seated myself. Mr Mixter glanced about him, and then sat down in the grass at her feet. He gazed upward, looking with parted lips from the Countess to me.

'I am sure you speak French,' said the Countess, fixing her brilliant little eyes upon me.

'I do, madam, after a fashion,' I answered, in the lady's own tongue.

'*Voilà!*' she cried most expressively. 'I knew it so soon as I looked at you. You have been in my poor dear country.'

'A long time.'

'You know Paris?'

'Thoroughly, madam.' And with a certain conscious purpose I let my eyes meet her own.

She presently, hereupon, moved her own and glanced down

at Mr Mixter. 'What are we talking about?' she demanded of
her attentive pupil.

He pulled his knees up, plucked at the grass with his hand,
stared, blushed a little. 'You are talking French,' said Mr
Mixter.

'*La belle découverte!*' said the Countess. 'Here are ten
months,' she explained to me, 'that I am giving him lessons.
Don't put yourself out not to say he's a fool; he won't understand you.'

'I hope your other pupils are more gratifying,' I remarked.

'I have no others. They don't know what French is in this
place; they don't want to know. You may therefore imagine the
pleasure it is to me to meet a person who speaks it like yourself.' I replied that my own pleasure was not less, and she went
on drawing her stitches through her embroidery, with her little
finger curled out. Every few moments she put her eyes close to
her work, near-sightedly. I thought her a very disagreeable person; she was coarse, affected, dishonest, and no more a
Countess than I was a caliph. 'Talk to me of Paris,' she went
on. 'The very name of it gives me an emotion! How long since
you were there?'

'Two months ago.'

'Happy man! Tell me something about it. What were they
doing? Oh, for an hour of the boulevard!'

'They were doing about what they are always doing –
amusing themselves a good deal.'

'At the theatres, eh?' sighed the Countess. 'At the
cafés-concerts – at the little tables in front of the doors? *Quelle
existence!* You know I am a Parisienne, monsieur,' she added,
'– to my finger-tips.'

'Miss Spencer was mistaken, then,' I ventured to rejoin, 'in
telling me that you are a Provençale.'

She stared a moment, then she put her nose to her embroidery, which had a dingy, desultory aspect. 'Ah, I am a
Provençale by birth; but I am a Parisienne by – inclination.'

'And by experience, I suppose?' I said.

She questioned me a moment with her hard little eyes. 'Oh,
experience! I could talk of experience if I wished. I never

expected, for example, that experience had *this* in store for me.' And she pointed with her bare elbow, and with a jerk of her head, at everything that surrounded her – at the little white house, the quince-tree, the rickety paling, even at Mr Mixter.

'You are in exile!' I said, smiling.

'You may imagine what it is! These two years that I have been here I have passed hours – hours! One gets used to things, and sometimes I think I have got used to this. But there are some things that are always beginning over again. For example, my coffee.'

'Do you always have coffee at this hour?' I inquired.

She tossed back her head and measured me.

'At what hour would you prefer me to have it? I must have my little cup after breakfast.'

'Ah, you breakfast at this hour?'

'At mid-day – *comme cela se fait*. Here they breakfast at a quarter past seven! That "quarter past" is charming!'

'But you were telling me about your coffee,' I observed, sympathetically.

'My *cousine* can't believe in it; she can't understand it. She's an excellent girl; but that little cup of black coffee, with a drop of cognac, served at this hour – they exceed her comprehension. So I have to break the ice every day, and it takes the coffee the time you see to arrive. And when it arrives, monsieur! If I don't offer you any of it you must not take it ill. It will be because I know you have drunk it on the boulevard.'

I resented extremely this scornful treatment of poor Caroline Spencer's humble hospitality; but I said nothing, in order to say nothing uncivil. I only looked on Mr Mixter, who had clasped his arms round his knees and was watching my companion's demonstrative graces in solemn fascination. She presently saw that I was observing him; she glanced at me with a little bold explanatory smile. 'You know, he adores me,' she murmured, putting her nose into her tapestry again. I expressed the promptest credence and she went on. 'He dreams of becoming my lover! Yes, it's his dream. He has read a French novel;[20] it took him six months. But ever since that he has thought himself the hero, and me the heroine!'

Mr Mixter had evidently not an idea that he was being talked about; he was too preoccupied with the ecstasy of contemplation. At this moment Caroline Spencer came out of the house, bearing a coffee-pot on a little tray. I noticed that on her way from the door to the table she gave me a single quick, vaguely appealing glance. I wondered what it signified; I felt that it signified a sort of half-frightened longing to know what, as a man of the world who had been in France, I thought of the Countess. It made me extremely uncomfortable. I could not tell her that the Countess was very possibly the runaway wife of a little hair-dresser. I tried suddenly, on the contrary, to show a high consideration for her. But I got up; I couldn't stay longer. It vexed me to see Caroline Spencer standing there like a waiting-maid.

'You expect to remain some time at Grimwinter?' I said to the Countess.

She gave a terrible shrug.

'Who knows? Perhaps for years. When one is in misery! * * * Chère belle,' she added, turning to Miss Spencer, 'you have forgotten the cognac!'

I detained Caroline Spencer as, after looking a moment in silence at the little table, she was turning away to procure this missing delicacy. I silently gave her my hand in farewell. She looked very tired, but there was a strange hint of prospective patience in her severely mild little face. I thought she was rather glad I was going. Mr Mixter had risen to his feet and was pouring out the Countess's coffee. As I went back past the Baptist church I reflected that poor Miss Spencer had been right in her presentiment that she should still see something of that dear old Europe.

DAISY MILLER

A Study

I

At the little town of Vevey,[1] in Switzerland, there is a particularly comfortable hotel. There are, indeed, many hotels; for the entertainment of tourists is the business of the place, which, as many travellers will remember, is seated upon the edge of a remarkably blue lake – a lake that it behoves every tourist to visit. The shore of the lake presents an unbroken array of establishments of this order, of every category, from the 'grand hotel' of the newest fashion, with a chalk-white front, a hundred balconies, and a dozen flags flying from its roof, to the little Swiss *pension* of an elder day, with its name inscribed in German-looking lettering upon a pink or yellow wall, and an awkward summer-house in the angle of the garden. One of the hotels at Vevey, however, is famous, even classical, being distinguished from many of its upstart neighbours by an air both of luxury and of maturity. In this region, in the month of June, American travellers are extremely numerous; it may be said, indeed, that Vevey assumes at this period some of the characteristics of an American watering-place. There are sights and sounds which evoke a vision, an echo, of Newport[2] and Saratoga.[3] There is a flitting hither and thither of 'stylish' young girls, a rustling of muslin flounces, a rattle of dance-music in the morning hours, a sound of high-pitched voices at all times. You receive an impression of these things at the excellent inn of the 'Trois Couronnes',[4] and are transported in fancy to the Ocean House[5] or to Congress Hall.[6] But at the 'Trois Couronnes', it must be added, there are other features that are much at variance with these suggestions: neat German waiters, who look like secrctaries of legation;[7] Russian princesses sitting in the garden; little Polish boys walking about, held by the hand, with their governors; a view of the snowy crest of the Dent du Midi and the picturesque towers of the Castle of Chillon.[8]

I hardly know whether it was the analogies or the differences that were uppermost in the mind of a young American, who, two or three years ago, sat in the garden of the 'Trois Couronnes', looking about him, rather idly, at some of the graceful objects I have mentioned. It was a beautiful summer morning, and in whatever fashion the young American looked at things, they must have seemed to him charming. He had come from Geneva the day before, by the little steamer, to see his aunt, who was staying at the hotel – Geneva having been for a long time his place of residence. But his aunt had a headache – his aunt had almost always a headache – and now she was shut up in her room, smelling camphor, so that he was at liberty to wander about. He was some seven-and-twenty years of age; when his friends spoke of him, they usually said that he was at Geneva, 'studying'. When his enemies spoke of him they said – but, after all, he had no enemies; he was an extremely amiable fellow, and universally liked. What I should say is, simply, that when certain persons spoke of him they affirmed that the reason of his spending so much time at Geneva was that he was extremely devoted to a lady who lived there – a foreign lady – a person older than himself. Very few Americans – indeed I think none – had ever seen this lady, about whom there were some singular stories. But Winterbourne had an old attachment for the little metropolis of Calvinism;[9] he had been put to school there as a boy, and he had afterwards gone to college there[10] – circumstances which had led to his forming a great many youthful friendships. Many of these he had kept, and they were a source of great satisfaction to him.

After knocking at his aunt's door and learning that she was indisposed, he had taken a walk about the town, and then he had come in to his breakfast. He had now finished his breakfast; but he was drinking a small cup of coffee, which had been served to him on a little table in the garden by one of the waiters who looked like an *attaché*. At last he finished his coffee and lit a cigarette. Presently a small boy came walking along the path – an urchin of nine or ten. The child, who was diminutive for his years, had an aged expression of countenance, a pale complexion, and sharp little features. He was dressed in knickerbockers,[11] with red stockings, which displayed his poor little spindleshanks; he also wore a brilliant red cravat. He carried in his hand a long alpenstock,[12] the sharp point of which he thrust into everything that he approached – the flower-beds, the garden-benches, the trains of the ladies' dresses. In front of Winterbourne he paused, looking at him with a pair of bright, penetrating little eyes.

'Will you give me a lump of sugar?' he asked, in a sharp, hard little voice – a voice immature, and yet, somehow, not young.

Winterbourne glanced at the small table near him, on which his coffee-service rested, and saw that several morsels of sugar remained. 'Yes, you may take one,' he answered; 'but I don't think sugar is good for little boys.'

This little boy stepped forward and carefully selected three of the coveted fragments, two of which he buried in the pocket of his knickerbockers, depositing the other as promptly in another place. He poked his alpenstock, lance-fashion, into Winterbourne's bench, and tried to crack the lump of sugar with his teeth.

'Oh, blazes; it's har-r-d!' he exclaimed, pronouncing the adjective in a peculiar manner.

Winterbourne had immediately perceived that he might have the honour of claiming him as a fellow-countryman.[13] 'Take care you don't hurt your teeth,' he said, paternally.

'I haven't got any teeth to hurt. They have all come out. I have only got seven teeth. My mother counted them last night, and one came out right afterwards. She said she'd slap me if any more came out. I can't help it. It's this old Europe. It's the climate that makes them come out. In America they didn't come out. It's these hotels.'

Winterbourne was much amused. 'If you eat three lumps of sugar, your mother will certainly slap you,' he said.

'She's got to give me some candy, then,' rejoined his young

interlocutor. 'I can't get any candy here – any American candy. American candy's the best candy.'

'And are American little boys the best little boys?' asked Winterbourne.

'I don't know. I'm an American boy,' said the child.

'I see you are one of the best!' laughed Winterbourne.

'Are you an American man?' pursued this vivacious infant. And then, on Winterbourne's affirmative reply – 'American men are the best,' he declared.

His companion thanked him for the compliment; and the child, who had now got astride of his alpenstock, stood looking about him, while he attacked a second lump of sugar. Winterbourne wondered if he himself had been like this in his infancy, for he had been brought to Europe at about this age.

'Here comes my sister!' cried the child, in a moment. 'She's an American girl.'

Winterbourne looked along the path and saw a beautiful young lady advancing. 'American girls are the best girls,' he said, cheerfully, to his young companion.

'My sister ain't the best!' the child declared. 'She's always blowing at me.'

'I imagine that is your fault, not hers,' said Winterbourne. The young lady meanwhile had drawn near. She was dressed in white muslin, with a hundred frills and flounces, and knots of pale-coloured ribbon. She was bare-headed; but she balanced in her hand a large parasol, with a deep border of embroidery; and she was strikingly, admirably pretty. 'How pretty they are!' thought Winterbourne, straightening himself in his seat, as if he were prepared to rise.

The young lady paused in front of his bench, near the parapet of the garden, which overlooked the lake. The little boy had now converted his alpenstock into a vaulting-pole, by the aid of which he was springing about in the gravel, and kicking it up not a little.

'Randolph,' said the young lady, 'what *are* you doing?'

'I'm going up the Alps,' replied Randolph. 'This is the way!' And he gave another little jump, scattering the pebbles about Winterbourne's ears.

'That's the way they come down,' said Winterbourne.

'He's an American man!' cried Randolph, in his little hard voice.

The young lady gave no heed to this announcement, but looked straight at her brother. 'Well, I guess you had better be quiet,' she simply observed.

It seemed to Winterbourne that he had been in a manner presented. He got up and stepped slowly towards the young girl, throwing away his cigarette. 'This little boy and I have made acquaintance,' he said, with great civility. In Geneva, as he had been perfectly aware, a young man was not at liberty to speak to a young unmarried lady except under certain rarely-occurring conditions; but here at Vevey, what conditions could be better than these? – a pretty American girl coming and standing in front of you in a garden. This pretty American girl, however, on hearing Winterbourne's observation, simply glanced at him; she then turned her head and looked over the parapet, at the lake and the opposite mountains. He wondered whether he had gone too far; but he decided that he must advance farther, rather than retreat. While he was thinking of something else to say, the young lady turned to the little boy again.

'I should like to know where you got that pole,' she said.

'I bought it!' responded Randolph.

'You don't mean to say you're going to take it to Italy.'

'Yes, I am going to take it to Italy!' the child declared.

The young girl glanced over the front of her dress, and smoothed out a knot or two of ribbon. Then she rested her eyes upon the prospect again. 'Well, I guess you had better leave it somewhere,' she said, after a moment.

'Are you going to Italy?' Winterbourne inquired, in a tone of great respect.

The young lady glanced at him again. 'Yes, sir,' she replied. And she said nothing more.

'Are you – a – going over the Simplon?'[14] Winterbourne pursued, a little embarrassed.

'I don't know,' she said. 'I suppose it's some mountain. Randolph, what mountain are we going over?'

'Going where?' the child demanded.

'To Italy,' Winterbourne explained.

'I don't know,' said Randolph. 'I don't want to go to Italy. I want to go to America.'

'Oh, Italy is a beautiful place!' rejoined the young man.

'Can you get candy there?' Randolph loudly inquired.

'I hope not,' said his sister. 'I guess you have had enough candy, and mother thinks so too.'

'I haven't had any for ever so long – for a hundred weeks!' cried the boy, still jumping about.

The young lady inspected her flounces and smoothed her ribbons again; and Winterbourne presently risked an observation upon the beauty of the view. He was ceasing to be embarrassed, for he had begun to perceive that she was not in the least embarrassed herself. There had not been the slightest alteration in her charming complexion; she was evidently neither offended nor fluttered. If she looked another way when he spoke to her, and seemed not particularly to hear him, this was simply her habit, her manner. Yet, as he talked a little more, and pointed out some of the objects of interest in the view, with which she appeared quite unacquainted, she gradually gave him more of the benefit of her glance; and then he saw that this glance was perfectly direct and unshrinking. It was not, however, what would have been called an immodest glance, for the young girl's eyes were singularly honest and fresh. They were wonderfully pretty eyes; and, indeed, Winterbourne had not seen for a long time anything prettier than his fair countrywoman's various features – her complexion, her nose, her ears, her teeth. He had a great relish for feminine beauty; he was addicted to observing and analysing it; and as regards this young lady's face he made several observations. It was not at all insipid, but it was not exactly expressive; and though it was eminently delicate Winterbourne mentally accused it – very forgivingly – of a want of finish. He thought it very possible that Master Randolph's sister was a coquette; he was sure she had a spirit of her own; but in her bright, sweet, superficial little visage there was no mockery, no irony. Before long it became obvious that she was much disposed

towards conversation. She told him that they were going to
Rome for the winter – she and her mother and Randolph. She
asked him if he was a 'real American'; she wouldn't have taken
him for one; he seemed more like a German – this was said
after a little hesitation, especially when he spoke. Winterbourne, laughing, answered that he had met Germans who
spoke like Americans; but that he had not, so far as he remembered, met an American who spoke like a German. Then he
asked her if she would not be more comfortable in sitting upon
the bench which he had just quitted. She answered that she
liked standing up and walking about; but she presently sat
down. She told him she was from New York State – 'if you
know where that is'. Winterbourne learned more about her by
catching hold of her small, slippery brother and making him
stand a few minutes by his side.

'Tell me your name, my boy,' he said.

'Randolph C. Miller,' said the boy, sharply. 'And I'll tell you
her name;' and he levelled his alpenstock at his sister.

'You had better wait till you are asked!' said this young
lady, calmly.

'I should like very much to know your name,' said Winterbourne.

'Her name is Daisy Miller!' cried the child. 'But that isn't
her real name; that isn't her name on her cards.'[15]

'It's a pity you haven't got one of my cards!' said Miss Miller.

'Her real name is Annie P. Miller,' the boy went on.

'Ask him *his* name,' said his sister, indicating Winterbourne.

But on this point Randolph seemed perfectly indifferent; he
continued to supply information with regard to his own family.
'My father's name is Ezra B. Miller,' he announced. 'My father
ain't in Europe; my father's in a better place than Europe.'

Winterbourne imagined for a moment that this was the
manner in which the child had been taught to intimate that Mr
Miller had been removed to the sphere of celestial rewards. But
Randolph immediately added, 'My father's in Schenectady.[16]
He's got a big business. My father's rich, you bet.'

'Well!' ejaculated Miss Miller, lowering her parasol and
looking at the embroidered border. Winterbourne presently

released the child, who departed, dragging his alpenstock along the path. 'He doesn't like Europe,' said the young girl. 'He wants to go back.'

'To Schenectady, you mean?'

'Yes; he wants to go right home. He hasn't got any boys here. There is one boy here, but he always goes round with a teacher; they won't let him play.'

'And your brother hasn't any teacher?' Winterbourne inquired.

'Mother thought of getting him one, to travel round with us. There was a lady told her of a very good teacher; an American lady – perhaps you know her – Mrs Sanders. I think she came from Boston. She told her of this teacher, and we thought of getting him to travel round with us. But Randolph said he didn't want a teacher travelling round with us. He said he wouldn't have lessons when he was in the cars.[17] And we *are* in the cars about half the time. There was an English lady we met in the cars – I think her name was Miss Featherstone; perhaps you know her. She wanted to know why I didn't give Randolph lessons – give him "instruction", she called it. I guess he could give me more instruction than I could give him. He's very smart.'

'Yes,' said Winterbourne; 'he seems very smart.'

'Mother's going to get a teacher for him as soon as we get to Italy. Can you get good teachers in Italy?'

'Very good, I should think,' said Winterbourne.

'Or else she's going to find some school. He ought to learn some more. He's only nine. He's going to college.' And in this way Miss Miller continued to converse upon the affairs of her family, and upon other topics. She sat there with her extremely pretty hands, ornamented with very brilliant rings, folded in her lap, and with her pretty eyes now resting upon those of Winterbourne, now wandering over the garden, the people who passed by, and the beautiful view. She talked to Winterbourne as if she had known him a long time. He found it very pleasant. It was many years since he had heard a young girl talk so much. It might have been said of this unknown young lady, who had come and sat down beside him upon a bench, that she chattered. She was very quiet, she sat in a charming tranquil attitude; but her lips and her eyes were constantly moving. She had a soft, slender, agreeable voice, and her tone was decidedly sociable. She gave Winterbourne a history of her movements and intentions, and those of her mother and brother, in Europe, and enumerated, in particular, the various hotels at which they had stopped. 'That English lady in the cars,' she said – 'Miss Featherstone – asked me if we didn't all live in hotels in America. I told her I had never been in so many hotels in my life as since I came to Europe. I have never seen so many – it's nothing but hotels.' But Miss Miller did not make this remark with a querulous accent; she appeared to be in the best humour with everything. She declared that the hotels were very good, when once you got used to their ways, and that Europe was perfectly sweet. She was not disappointed – not a bit. Perhaps it was because she had heard so much about it before. She had ever so many intimate friends that had been there ever so many times. And then she had had ever so many dresses and things from Paris. Whenever she put on a Paris dress she felt as if she were in Europe.

'It was a kind of a wishing-cap,' said Winterbourne.

'Yes,' said Miss Miller, without examining this analogy; 'it always made me wish I was here. But I needn't have done that for dresses. I am sure they send all the pretty ones to America; you see the most frightful things here. The only thing I don't like,' she proceeded, 'is the society. There isn't any society; or, if there is, I don't know where it keeps itself. Do you? I suppose there is some society somewhere, but I haven't seen anything of it. I'm very fond of society, and I have always had a great deal of it. I don't mean only in Schenectady, but in New York. I used to go to New York every winter. In New York I had lots of society. Last winter I had seventeen dinners given me; and three of them were by gentlemen,' added Daisy Miller. 'I have more friends in New York than in Schenectady – more gentle-men friends; and more young lady friends too,' she resumed in a moment. She paused again for an instant; she was looking at Winterbourne with all her prettiness in her lively eyes and in her light, slightly monotonous smile. 'I have always had,' she said, 'a great deal of gentlemen's society.'

Poor Winterbourne was amused, perplexed, and decidedly charmed. He had never yet heard a young girl express herself in just this fashion; never, at least, save in cases where to say such things seemed a kind of demonstrative evidence of a certain laxity of deportment. And yet was he to accuse Miss Daisy Miller of actual or potential *inconduite*,[18] as they said at Geneva? He felt that he had lived at Geneva so long that he had lost a good deal; he had become dishabituated to the American tone. Never, indeed, since he had grown old enough to appreciate things, had he encountered a young American girl of so pronounced a type as this. Certainly she was very charming; but how deucedly sociable! Was she simply a pretty girl from New York State – were they all like that, the pretty girls who had a good deal of gentlemen's society? Or was she also a designing, an audacious, an unscrupulous young person? Winterbourne had lost his instinct in this matter, and his reason could not help him. Miss Daisy Miller looked extremely innocent. Some people had told him that, after all, American girls were exceedingly innocent; and others had told him that, after all, they were not. He was inclined to think Miss Daisy Miller was a flirt – a pretty American flirt. He had never, as yet, had any relations with young ladies of this category. He had known, here in Europe, two or three women – persons older than Miss Daisy Miller, and provided, for respectability's sake, with husbands – who were great coquettes – dangerous, terrible women, with whom one's relations were liable to take a serious turn. But this young girl was not a coquette in that sense; she was very unsophisticated; she was only a pretty American flirt. Winterbourne was almost grateful for having found the formula that applied to Miss Daisy Miller. He leaned back in his seat; he remarked to himself that she had the most charming nose he had ever seen; he wondered what were the regular conditions and limitations of one's intercourse with a pretty American flirt. It presently became apparent that he was on the way to learn.

'Have you been to that old castle?' asked the young girl, pointing with her parasol to the far-gleaming walls of the Château de Chillon.

'Yes, formerly, more than once,'[19] said Winterbourne. 'You too, I suppose, have seen it?'

'No; we haven't been there. I want to go there dreadfully. Of course I mean to go there. I wouldn't go away from here without having seen that old castle.'

'It's a very pretty excursion,' said Winterbourne, 'and very easy to make. You can drive, you know, or you can go by the little steamer.'

'You can go in the cars,' said Miss Miller.

'Yes; you can go in the cars,' Winterbourne assented.

'Our courier[20] says they take you right up to the castle,' the young girl continued. 'We were going last week; but my mother gave out. She suffers dreadfully from dyspepsia. She said she couldn't go. Randolph wouldn't go either; he says he doesn't think much of old castles. But I guess we'll go this week, if we can get Randolph.'

'Your brother is not interested in ancient monuments?' Winterbourne inquired, smiling.

'He says he don't care much about old castles. He's only nine. He wants to stay at the hotel. Mother's afraid to leave him alone, and the courier won't stay with him; so we haven't been to many places. But it will be too bad if we don't go up there.' And Miss Miller pointed again at the Château de Chillon.

'I should think it might be arranged,' said Winterbourne. 'Couldn't you get some one to stay – for the afternoon – with Randolph?'

Miss Miller looked at him a moment; and then, very placidly – 'I wish *you* would stay with him!' she said.

Winterbourne hesitated a moment. 'I would much rather go to Chillon with you.'

'With me?' asked the young girl, with the same placidity.

She didn't rise, blushing, as a young girl at Geneva would have done; and yet Winterbourne, conscious that he had been very bold, thought it possible she was offended. 'With your mother,' he answered very respectfully.

But it seemed that both his audacity and his respect were lost upon Miss Daisy Miller. 'I guess my mother won't go, after all,' she said. 'She don't like to ride round in the afternoon. But did you really mean what you said just now; that you would like to go up there?'

'Most earnestly,' Winterbourne declared.

'Then we may arrange it. If mother will stay with Randolph, I guess Eugenio will.'

'Eugenio?' the young man inquired.

'Eugenio's our courier. He doesn't like to stay with Randolph; he's the most fastidious man I ever saw. But he's a splendid courier. I guess he'll stay at home with Randolph if mother does, and then we can go to the castle.'

Winterbourne reflected for an instant as lucidly as possible – 'we' could only mean Miss Daisy Miller and himself. This programme seemed almost too agreeable for credence; he felt as if he ought to kiss the young lady's hand. Possibly he would have done so – and quite spoiled the project; but at this moment another person – presumably Eugenio – appeared. A tall, handsome man, with superb whiskers, wearing a velvet morning-coat and a brilliant watch-chain, approached Miss Miller, looking sharply at her companion. 'Oh, Eugenio!' said Miss Miller, with the friendliest accent.

Eugenio had looked at Winterbourne from head to foot; he now bowed gravely to the young lady. 'I have the honour to inform mademoiselle that luncheon is upon the table.'

Miss Miller slowly rose. 'See here, Eugenio,' she said. 'I'm going to that old castle, any way.'

'To the Château de Chillon, mademoiselle?' the courier inquired. 'Mademoiselle has made arrangements?' he added, in a tone which struck Winterbourne as very impertinent.

Eugenio's tone apparently threw, even to Miss Miller's own apprehension, a slightly ironical light upon the young girl's situation. She turned to Winterbourne, blushing a little – a very little. 'You won't back out?' she said.

'I shall not be happy till we go!' he protested.

'And you are staying in this hotel?' she went on. 'And you are really an American?'

The courier stood looking at Winterbourne, offensively. The young man, at least, thought his manner of looking an offence to Miss Miller; it conveyed an imputation that she

'picked up' acquaintances. 'I shall have the honour of presenting to you a person who will tell you all about me,' he said
smiling, and referring to his aunt.

'Oh, well, we'll go some day,' said Miss Miller. And she
gave him a smile and turned away. She put up her parasol and
walked back to the inn beside Eugenio. Winterbourne stood
looking after her; and as she moved away, drawing her muslin
furbelows[21] over the gravel, said to himself that she had the
tournure of a princess.

II

He had, however, engaged to do more than proved feasible, in
promising to present his aunt, Mrs Costello, to Miss Daisy
Miller. As soon as the former lady had got better of her headache he waited upon her in her apartment; and, after the proper
inquiries in regard to her health, he asked her if she had
observed, in the hotel, an American family – a mamma, a
daughter, and a little boy.

'And a courier?' said Mrs Costello. 'Oh, yes, I have observed
them. Seen them – heard them – and kept out of their way.'
Mrs Costello was a widow with a fortune; a person of much
distinction, who frequently intimated that, if she were not so
dreadfully liable to sick-headaches, she would probably have
left a deeper impress upon her time. She had a long pale face, a
high nose, and a great deal of very striking white hair, which
she wore in large puffs and *rouleaux*[22] over the top of her head.
She had two sons married in New York, and another who was
now in Europe. This young man was amusing himself at Homburg,[23] and, though he was on his travels, was rarely perceived
to visit any particular city at the moment selected by his mother
for her own appearance there. Her nephew, who had come up
to Vevey expressly to see her, was therefore more attentive
than those who, as she said, were nearer to her. He had imbibed
at Geneva the idea that one must always be attentive to one's
aunt. Mrs Costello had not seen him for many years, and she
was greatly pleased with him, manifesting her approbation by

initiating him into many of the secrets of that social sway which, as she gave him to understand, she exerted in the American capital. She admitted that she was very exclusive; but, if he were acquainted with New York, he would see that one had to be. And her picture of the minutely hierarchical constitution of the society of that city, which she presented to him in many different lights, was, to Winterbourne's imagination, almost oppressively striking.

He immediately perceived, from her tone, that Miss Daisy Miller's place in the social scale was low. 'I am afraid you don't approve of them,' he said.

'They are very common,' Mrs Costello declared. 'They are the sort of Americans that one does one's duty by not – not accepting.'

'Ah, you don't accept them?' said the young man.

'I can't, my dear Frederick. I would if I could, but I can't.'

'The young girl is very pretty,' said Winterbourne, in a moment.

'Of course she's pretty. But she is very common.'

'I see what you mean, of course,' said Winterbourne, after another pause.

'She has that charming look that they all have,' his aunt resumed. 'I can't think where they pick it up; and she dresses in perfection – no, you don't know how well she dresses. I can't think where they get their taste.'

'But, my dear aunt, she is not, after all, a Comanche[24] savage.'

'She is a young lady,' said Mrs Costello, 'who has an intimacy with her mamma's courier?'

'An intimacy with the courier?' the young man demanded.

'Oh, the mother is just as bad! They treat the courier like a familiar friend – like a gentleman. I shouldn't wonder if he dines with them. Very likely they have never seen a man with such good manners, such fine clothes, so like a gentleman. He probably corresponds to the young lady's idea of a Count. He sits with them in the garden, in the evening. I think he smokes.'

Winterbourne listened with interest to these disclosures; they helped him to make up his mind about Miss Daisy.

Evidently she was rather wild. 'Well,' he said, 'I am not a courier, and yet she was very charming to me.'

'You had better have said at first,' said Mrs Costello with dignity, 'that you had made her acquaintance.'

'We simply met in the garden, and we talked a bit.'

'*Tout bonnement!* And pray what did you say?'

'I said I should take the liberty of introducing her to my admirable aunt.'

'I am much obliged to you.'

'It was to guarantee my respectability,' said Winterbourne.

'And pray who is to guarantee hers?'

'Ah, you are cruel!' said the young man. 'She's a very nice girl.'

'You don't say that as if you believed it,' Mrs Costello observed.

'She is completely uncultivated,' Winterbourne went on. 'But she is wonderfully pretty, and, in short, she is very nice. To prove that I believe it, I am going to take her to the Château de Chillon.'

'You two are going off there together? I should say it proved just the contrary. How long had you known her, may I ask, when this interesting project was formed? You haven't been twenty-four hours in the house.'

'I had known her half an hour!' said Winterbourne, smiling.

'Dear me!' cried Mrs Costello. 'What a dreadful girl!'

Her nephew was silent for some moments. 'You really think, then,' he began, earnestly, and with a desire for trustworthy information – 'you really think that—' But he paused again.

'Think what, sir?' said his aunt.

'That she is the sort of young lady who expects a man – sooner or later – to carry her off?'

'I haven't the least idea what such young ladies expect a man to do. But I really think that you had better not meddle with little American girls that are uncultivated, as you call them. You have lived too long out of the country. You will be sure to make some great mistake. You are too innocent.'

'My dear aunt, I am not so innocent,' said Winterbourne, smiling and curling his moustache.

'You are too guilty, then!'

Winterbourne continued to curl his moustache, meditatively. 'You won't let the poor girl know you then?' he asked at last.

'Is it literally true that she is going to the Château de Chillon with you?'

'I think that she fully intends it.'

'Then, my dear Frederick,' said Mrs Costello, 'I must decline the honour of her acquaintance. I am an old woman, but I am not too old – thank Heaven – to be shocked!'

'But don't they all do these things – the young girls in America?' Winterbourne inquired.

Mrs Costello stared a moment. 'I should like to see my granddaughters do them!' she declared, grimly.

This seemed to throw some light upon the matter, for Winterbourne remembered to have heard that his pretty cousins in New York were 'tremendous flirts'. If, therefore, Miss Daisy Miller exceeded the liberal licence allowed to these young ladies, it was probable that anything might be expected of her. Winterbourne was impatient to see her again, and he was vexed with himself that, by instinct, he should not appreciate her justly.

Though he was impatient to see her, he hardly knew what he should say to her about his aunt's refusal to become acquainted with her; but he discovered, promptly enough, that with Miss Daisy Miller there was no great need of walking on tiptoe. He found her that evening in the garden, wandering about in the warm starlight, like an indolent sylph, and swinging to and fro the largest fan he had ever beheld. It was ten o'clock. He had dined with his aunt, had been sitting with her since dinner, and had just taken leave of her till the morrow. Miss Daisy Miller seemed very glad to see him; she declared it was the longest evening she had ever passed.

'Have you been all alone?' he asked.

'I have been walking round with mother. But mother gets tired walking round,' she answered.

'Has she gone to bed?'

'No; she doesn't like to go to bed,' said the young girl. 'She doesn't sleep – not three hours. She says she doesn't know how she lives. She's dreadfully nervous. I guess she sleeps more than she thinks. She's gone somewhere after Randolph; she wants to try to get him to go to bed. He doesn't like to go to bed.'

'Let us hope she will persuade him,' observed Winterbourne.

'She will talk to him all she can; but he doesn't like her to talk to him,' said Miss Daisy, opening her fan. 'She's going to try to get Eugenio to talk to him. But he isn't afraid of Eugenio. Eugenio's a splendid courier, but he can't make much impression on Randolph! I don't believe he'll go to bed before eleven.' It appeared that Randolph's vigil was in fact triumphantly prolonged, for Winterbourne strolled about with the young girl for some time without meeting her mother. 'I have been looking round for that lady you want to introduce me to,' his companion resumed. 'She's your aunt.' Then, on Winterbourne's admitting the fact, and expressing some curiosity as to how she had learned it, she said she had heard all about Mrs Costello from the chambermaid. She was very quiet and very *comme il faut*; she wore white puffs; she spoke to no one, and she never dined at the *table d'hôte*.[25] Every two days she had a headache. 'I think that's a lovely description, headache and all!' said Miss Daisy, chattering along in her thin, gay voice. 'I want to know her ever so much. I know just what *your* aunt would be; I know I should like her. She would be very exclusive. I like a lady to be exclusive; I'm dying to be exclusive myself. Well, we *are* exclusive, mother and I. We don't speak to every one – or they don't speak to us. I suppose it's about the same thing. Any way, I shall be ever so glad to know your aunt.'

Winterbourne was embarrassed. 'She would be most happy,' he said; 'but I am afraid those headaches will interfere.'

The young girl looked at him through the dusk. 'But I suppose she doesn't have a headache every day,' she said, sympathetically.

Winterbourne was silent a moment. 'She tells me she does,' he answered at last – not knowing what to say.

Miss Daisy Miller stopped and stood looking at him. Her prettiness was still visible in the darkness; she was opening and closing her enormous fan. 'She doesn't want to know me!' she said, suddenly. 'Why don't you say so? You needn't be afraid. I'm not afraid!' And she gave a little laugh.

Winterbourne fancied there was a tremor in her voice; he was touched, shocked, mortified by it. 'My dear young lady,' he protested, 'she knows no one. It's her wretched health.'

The young girl walked on a few steps, laughing still. 'You needn't be afraid,' she repeated. 'Why should she want to know me?' Then she paused again; she was close to the parapet of the garden, and in front of her was the starlit lake. There was a vague sheen upon its surface, and in the distance were dimly-seen mountain forms. Daisy Miller looked out upon the mysterious prospect, and then she gave another little laugh. 'Gracious! she *is* exclusive!' she said. Winterbourne wondered whether she was seriously wounded, and for a moment almost wished that her sense of injury might be such as to make it becoming in him to attempt to reassure and comfort her. He had a pleasant sense that she would be very approachable for consolatory purposes. He felt then, for the instant, quite ready to sacrifice his aunt, conversationally; to admit that she was a proud, rude woman, and to declare that they needn't mind her. But before he had time to commit himself to this perilous mixture of gallantry and impiety, the young lady, resuming her walk, gave an exclamation in quite another tone. 'Well; here's mother! I guess she hasn't got Randolph to go to bed.' The figure of a lady appeared, at a distance, very indistinct in the darkness, and advancing with a slow and wavering movement. Suddenly it seemed to pause.

'Are you sure it is your mother? Can you distinguish her in this thick dusk?' Winterbourne asked.

'Well!' cried Miss Daisy Miller, with a laugh, 'I guess I know my own mother. And when she has got on my shawl, too! She is always wearing my things.'

The lady in question, ceasing to advance, hovered vaguely about the spot at which she had checked her steps.

'I am afraid your mother doesn't see you,' said Winterbourne. 'Or perhaps,' he added – thinking, with Miss Miller, the joke permissible – 'perhaps she feels guilty about your shawl.'

'Oh, it's a fearful old thing!' the young girl replied, serenely. 'I told her she could wear it. She won't come here, because she sees you.'

'Ah, then,' said Winterbourne, 'I had better leave you.'

'Oh no; come on!' urged Miss Daisy Miller.

'I'm afraid your mother doesn't approve of my walking with you.'

Miss Miller gave him a serious glance. 'It isn't for me; it's for you – that is, it's for *her*. Well; I don't know who it's for! But mother doesn't like any of my gentlemen friends. She's right down timid. She always makes a fuss if I introduce a gentleman. But I *do* introduce them – almost always. If I didn't introduce my gentlemen friends to mother,' the young girl added, in her little soft, flat monotone, 'I shouldn't think I was natural.'

'To introduce me,' said Winterbourne, 'you must know my name.' And he proceeded to pronounce it.

'Oh, dear; I can't say all that!' said his companion, with a laugh. But by this time they had come up to Mrs Miller, who, as they drew near, walked to the parapet of the garden and leaned upon it, looking intently at the lake and turning her back upon them. 'Mother!' said the young girl, in a tone of decision. Upon this the elder lady turned round. 'Mr Winterbourne,' said Miss Daisy Miller, introducing the young man very frankly and prettily. 'Common' she was, as Mrs Costello had pronounced her; yet it was a wonder to Winterbourne that, with her commonness, she had a singularly delicate grace.

Her mother was a small, spare, light person, with a wandering eye, a very exiguous nose, and a large forehead, decorated with a certain amount of thin, much-frizzled hair. Like her daughter, Mrs Miller was dressed with extreme elegance; she had enormous diamonds in her ears. So far as Winterbourne could observe, she gave him no greeting – she certainly was not looking at him. Daisy was near her, pulling her shawl straight. 'What are you doing, poking round here?' this young lady inquired; but by no means with that harshness of accent which her choice of words may imply.

'I don't know,' said her mother, turning towards the lake again.

'I shouldn't think you'd want that shawl!' Daisy exclaimed.

'Well – I do!' her mother answered, with a little laugh.

'Did you get Randolph to go to bed?' asked the young girl.

'No; I couldn't induce him,' said Mrs Miller, very gently. 'He wants to talk to the waiter. He likes to talk to that waiter.'

'I was telling Mr Winterbourne,' the young girl went on; and to the young man's ear her tone might have indicated that she had been uttering his name all her life.

'Oh, yes!' said Winterbourne; 'I have the pleasure of knowing your son.'

Randolph's mamma was silent; she turned her attention to the lake. But at last she spoke. 'Well, I don't see how he lives!'

'Anyhow, it isn't so bad as it was at Dover,' said Daisy Miller.

'And what occurred at Dover?' Winterbourne asked.

'He wouldn't go to bed at all. I guess he sat up all night – in the public parlour. He wasn't in bed at twelve o'clock: I know that.'

'It was half-past twelve,' declared Mrs Miller, with mild emphasis.

'Does he sleep much during the day?' Winterbourne demanded.

'I guess he doesn't sleep much,' Daisy rejoined.

'I wish he would!' said her mother. 'It seems as if he couldn't.'

'I think he's real tiresome,' Daisy pursued.

Then, for some moments, there was silence. 'Well, Daisy Miller,' said the elder lady, presently, 'I shouldn't think you'd want to talk against your own brother!'

'Well, he *is* tiresome, mother,' said Daisy, quite without the asperity of a retort.

'He's only nine,' urged Mrs Miller.

'Well, he wouldn't go to that castle,' said the young girl. 'I'm going there with Mr Winterbourne.'

To this announcement, very placidly made, Daisy's mamma offered no response. Winterbourne took for granted that she deeply disapproved of the projected excursion; but he said to himself that she was a simple, easily-managed person, and that a few deferential protestations would take the edge from her displeasure. 'Yes,' he began; 'your daughter has kindly allowed me the honour of being her guide.'

Mrs Miller's wandering eyes attached themselves, with a sort of appealing air, to Daisy, who, however, strolled a few steps farther, gently humming to herself. 'I presume you will go in the cars,' said her mother.

'Yes; or in the boat,' said Winterbourne.

'Well, of course, I don't know,' Mrs Miller rejoined. 'I have never been to that castle.'

'It is a pity you shouldn't go,' said Winterbourne, beginning to feel reassured as to her opposition. And yet he was quite prepared to find that, as a matter of course, she meant to accompany her daughter.

'We've been thinking ever so much about going,' she pursued; 'but it seems as if we couldn't. Of course Daisy – she wants to go round. But there's a lady here – I don't know her name – she says she shouldn't think we'd want to go to see castles *here*; she should think we'd want to wait till we got to Italy. It seems as if there would be so many there,' continued Mrs Miller, with an air of increasing confidence. 'Of course, we only want to see the principal ones. We visited several in England,' she presently added.

'Ah, yes! in England there are beautiful castles,' said Winterbourne. 'But Chillon, here, is very well worth seeing.'

'Well, if Daisy feels up to it—,' said Mrs Miller, in a tone impregnated with a sense of the magnitude of the enterprise. 'It seems as if there was nothing she wouldn't undertake.'

'Oh, I think she'll enjoy it!' Winterbourne declared. And he desired more and more to make it a certainty that he was to have the privilege of a *tête-à-tête* with the young lady, who was still strolling along in front of them, softly vocalizing. 'You are not disposed, madam,' he inquired, 'to undertake it yourself?'

Daisy's mother looked at him, an instant, askance, and then walked forward in silence. Then – 'I guess she had better go alone,' she said, simply.

Winterbourne observed to himself that this was a very different type of maternity from that of the vigilant matrons who massed themselves in the forefront of social intercourse in the dark old city[26] at the other end of the lake. But his meditations were interrupted by hearing his name very distinctly pronounced by Mrs Miller's unprotected daughter.

'Mr Winterbourne!' murmured Daisy.

'Mademoiselle!' said the young man.

'Don't you want to take me out in a boat?'

'At present?' he asked.

'Of course!' said Daisy.

'Well, Annie Miller!' exclaimed her mother.

'I beg you, madam, to let her go,' said Winterbourne, ardently; for he had never yet enjoyed the sensation of guiding through the summer starlight a skiff freighted with a fresh and beautiful young girl.

'I shouldn't think she'd want to,' said her mother. 'I should think she'd rather go indoors.'

'I'm sure Mr Winterbourne wants to take me,' Daisy declared. 'He's so awfully devoted!'

'I will row you over to Chillon, in the starlight.'

'I don't believe it!' said Daisy.

'Well!' ejaculated the elder lady again.

'You haven't spoken to me for half an hour,' her daughter went on.

'I have been having some very pleasant conversation with your mother,' said Winterbourne.

'Well; I want you to take me out in a boat!' Daisy repeated. They had all stopped, and she had turned round and was looking at Winterbourne. Her face wore a charming smile, her pretty eyes were gleaming, she was swinging her great fan about. No; it's impossible to be prettier than that, thought Winterbourne.

'There are half-a-dozen boats moored at that landing-place,' he said, pointing to certain steps which descended from the garden to the lake. 'If you will do me the honour to accept my arm, we will go and select one of them.'

Daisy stood there smiling; she threw back her head and gave

a little light laugh. 'I like a gentleman to be formal!' she declared.

'I assure you it's a formal offer.'

'I was bound I would make you say something,' Daisy went on.

'You see it's not very difficult,' said Winterbourne. 'But I am afraid you are chaffing me.'

'I think not, sir,' remarked Mrs Miller, very gently.

'Do, then, let me give you a row,' he said to the young girl.

'It's quite lovely, the way you say that!' cried Daisy.

'It will be still more lovely to do it.'

'Yes, it would be lovely!' said Daisy. But she made no movement to accompany him; she only stood there laughing.

'I should think you had better find out what time it is,' interposed her mother.

'It is eleven o'clock, madam,' said a voice, with a foreign accent, out of the neighbouring darkness; and Winterbourne, turning, perceived the florid personage who was in attendance upon the two ladies. He had apparently just approached.

'Oh, Eugenio,' said Daisy, 'I am going out in a boat!'

Eugenio bowed. 'At eleven o'clock, mademoiselle?'

'I am going with Mr Winterbourne. This very minute.'

'Do tell her she can't,' said Mrs Miller to the courier.

'I think you had better not go out in a boat, mademoiselle,' Eugenio declared.

Winterbourne wished to Heaven this pretty girl were not so familiar with her courier; but he said nothing.

'I suppose you don't think it's proper!' Daisy exclaimed. 'Eugenio doesn't think anything's proper.'

'I am at your service,' said Winterbourne.

'Does mademoiselle propose to go alone?' asked Eugenio of Mrs Miller.

'Oh, no; with this gentleman!' answered Daisy's mamma.

The courier looked for a moment at Winterbourne – the latter thought he was smiling – and then, solemnly, with a bow, 'As mademoiselle pleases!' he said.

'Oh, I hoped you would make a fuss!' said Daisy. 'I don't care to go now.'

'I myself shall make a fuss if you don't go,' said Winterbourne.

'That's all I want – a little fuss!' And the young girl began to laugh again.

'Mr Randolph has gone to bed!' the courier announced, frigidly.

'Oh, Daisy; now we can go!' said Mrs Miller.

Daisy turned away from Winterbourne, looking at him, smiling and fanning herself. 'Good-night,' she said; 'I hope you are disappointed, or disgusted, or something!'

He looked at her, taking the hand she offered him. 'I am puzzled,' he answered.

'Well; I hope it won't keep you awake!' she said, very smartly; and, under the escort of the privileged Eugenio, the two ladies passed towards the house.

Winterbourne stood looking after them; he was indeed puzzled. He lingered beside the lake for a quarter of an hour, turning over the mystery of the young girl's sudden familiarities and caprices. But the only very definite conclusion he came to was that he should enjoy deucedly 'going off' with her somewhere.

Two days afterwards he went off with her to the Castle of Chillon. He waited for her in the large hall of the hotel, where the couriers, the servants, the foreign tourists were lounging about and staring. It was not the place he would have chosen, but she had appointed it. She came tripping downstairs, buttoning her long gloves, squeezing her folded parasol against her pretty figure, dressed in the perfection of a soberly elegant travelling-costume. Winterbourne was a man of imagination and, as our ancestors used to say, of sensibility;[27] as he looked at her dress and, on the great staircase, her little rapid, confiding step, he felt as if there were something romantic going forward. He could have believed he was going to elope with her. He passed out with her among all the idle people that were assembled there; they were all looking at her very hard; she had begun to chatter as soon as she joined him. Winterbourne's preference had been that they should be conveyed to Chillon in a carriage; but she expressed a lively wish to go in the little steamer; she declared that she had a passion for steamboats. There was always such a lovely breeze upon the water, and you saw such lots of people. The sail was not long, but Winterbourne's companion found time to say a great many things. To the young man himself their little excursion was so much of an escapade – an adventure – that, even allowing for her habitual sense of freedom, he had some expectation of seeing her regard it in the same way. But it must be confessed that, in this particular, he was disappointed. Daisy Miller was extremely animated, she was in charming spirits; but she was apparently not at all excited; she was not fluttered; she avoided neither his eyes nor those of any one else; she blushed neither when she looked at him nor when she saw that people were looking at her. People continued to look at her a great deal, and Winterbourne took much satisfaction in his pretty companion's distinguished air. He had been a little afraid that she would talk loud, laugh overmuch, and even, perhaps, desire to move about the boat a good deal. But he quite forgot his fears; he sat smiling, with his eyes upon her face, while, without moving from her place, she delivered herself of a great number of original reflections. It was the most charming garrulity he had ever heard. He had assented to the idea that she was 'common'; but was she so, after all, or was he simply getting used to her commonness? Her conversation was chiefly of what metaphysicians term the objective cast;[28] but every now and then it took a subjective turn.

'What on *earth* are you so grave about?' she suddenly demanded, fixing her agreeable eyes upon Winterbourne's.

'Am I grave?' he asked. 'I had an idea I was grinning from ear to ear.'

'You look as if you were taking me to a funeral. If that's a grin, your ears are very near together.'

'Should you like me to dance a hornpipe on the deck?'

'Pray do, and I'll carry round your hat. It will pay the expenses of our journey.'

'I never was better pleased in my life,' murmured Winterbourne.

She looked at him a moment, and then burst into a little

laugh. 'I like to make you say those things! You're a queer mixture!'

In the castle, after they had landed, the subjective element decidedly prevailed. Daisy tripped about the vaulted chambers, rustled her skirts in the corkscrew staircases, flirted back with a pretty little cry and a shudder from the edge of the *oubliettes*,[29] and turned a singularly well-shaped ear to everything that Winterbourne told her about the place. But he saw that she cared very little for feudal antiquities, and that the dusky traditions of Chillon made but a slight impression upon her. They had the good fortune to have been able to walk about without other companionship than that of the custodian; and Winterbourne arranged with this functionary that they should not be hurried – that they should linger and pause wherever they chose. The custodian interpreted the bargain generously – Winterbourne, on his side, had been generous – and ended by leaving them quite to themselves. Miss Miller's observations were not remarkable for logical consistency; for anything she wanted to say she was sure to find a pretext. She found a great many pretexts in the rugged embrasures of Chillon for asking Winterbourne sudden questions about himself – his family, his previous history, his tastes, his habits, his intentions – and for supplying information upon corresponding points in her own personality. Of her own tastes, habits and intentions Miss Miller was prepared to give the most definite, and indeed the most favourable, account.

'Well; I hope you know enough!' she said to her companion, after he had told her the history of the unhappy Bonivard.[30] 'I never saw a man that knew so much!' The history of Bonivard had evidently, as they say, gone into one ear and out of the other. But Daisy went on to say that she wished Winterbourne would travel with them and 'go round' with them; they might know something, in that case. 'Don't you want to come and teach Randolph?' she asked. Winterbourne said that nothing could possibly please him so much; but that he had unfortunately other occupations. 'Other occupations? I don't believe it!' said Miss Daisy. 'What do you mean? You are not in business.' The young man admitted that he was not in business;

but he had engagements which, even within a day or two, would force him to go back to Geneva. 'Oh, bother!' she said. 'I don't believe it!' and she began to talk about something else. But a few moments later, when he was pointing out to her the pretty design of an antique fireplace, she broke out irrelevantly, 'You don't mean to say you are going back to Geneva?'

'It is a melancholy fact that I shall have to return to Geneva to-morrow.'

'Well, Mr Winterbourne,' said Daisy; 'I think you're horrid!'

'Oh, don't say such dreadful things!' said Winterbourne – 'just at the last.'

'The last!' cried the young girl. 'I call it the first. I have half a mind to leave you here and go straight back to the hotel alone.' And for the next ten minutes she did nothing but call him horrid. Poor Winterbourne was fairly bewildered; no young lady had as yet done him the honour to be so agitated by the announcement of his movements. His companion, after this, ceased to pay any attention to the curiosities of Chillon or the beauties of the lake; she opened fire upon the mysterious charmer in Geneva, whom she appeared to have instantly taken it for granted that he was hurrying back to see. How did Miss Daisy Miller know that there was a charmer in Geneva? Winterbourne, who denied the existence of such a person, was quite unable to discover; and he was divided between amazement at the rapidity of her induction and amusement at the frankness of her *persiflage*. She seemed to him, in all this, an extraordinary mixture of innocence and crudity. 'Does she never allow you more than three days at a time?' asked Daisy, ironically. 'Doesn't she give you a vacation in summer? There's no one so hard worked but they can get leave to go off somewhere at this season. I suppose, if you stay another day, she'll come after you in the boat. Do wait over till Friday, and I will go down to the landing to see her arrive!' Winterbourne began to think he had been wrong to feel disappointed in the temper in which the young lady had embarked. If he had missed the personal accent, the personal accent was now making its appearance. It sounded very distinctly, at last, in her telling him she would stop 'teasing' him if he would promise her solemnly to come down to Rome in the winter.

'That's not a difficult promise to make,' said Winterbourne. 'My aunt has taken an apartment in Rome for the winter, and has already asked me to come and see her.'

'I don't want you to come for your aunt,' said Daisy; 'I want you to come for me.' And this was the only allusion that the young man was ever to hear her make to his invidious kinswoman. He declared that, at any rate, he would certainly come. After this Daisy stopped teasing. Winterbourne took a carriage, and they drove back to Vevey in the dusk; the young girl was very quiet.

In the evening Winterbourne mentioned to Mrs Costello that he had spent the afternoon at Chillon, with Miss Daisy Miller.

'The Americans – of the courier?' asked this lady.

'Ah, happily,' said Winterbourne, 'the courier stayed at home.'

'She went with you all alone?'

'All alone.'

Mrs Costello sniffed a little at her smelling-bottle. 'And that,' she exclaimed, 'is the young person you wanted me to know!'

III

Winterbourne, who had returned to Geneva the day after his excursion to Chillon, went to Rome towards the end of January.[31] His aunt had been established there for several weeks, and he had received a couple of letters from her. 'Those people you were so devoted to last summer at Vevey have turned up here, courier and all,' she wrote. 'They seem to have made several acquaintances, but the courier continues to be the most *intime*. The young lady, however, is also very intimate with some third-rate Italians, with whom she rackets about in a way that makes much talk. Bring me that pretty novel of Cherbuliez's – 'Paule Méré'[32] – and don't come later than the 23rd.'

In the natural course of events, Winterbourne, on arriving in Rome, would presently have ascertained Mrs Miller's address at the American banker's[33] and have gone to pay his compliments to Miss Daisy. 'After what happened at Vevey I certainly think I may call upon them,' he said to Mrs Costello.

'If, after what happens – at Vevey and everywhere – you desire to keep up the acquaintance, you are very welcome. Of course a man may know every one. Men are welcome to the privilege!'

'Pray what is it that happens – here, for instance?' Winterbourne demanded.

'The girl goes about alone with her foreigners. As to what happens farther, you must apply elsewhere for information. She has picked up half-a-dozen of the regular Roman fortune-hunters, and she takes them about to people's houses. When she comes to a party she brings with her a gentleman with a good deal of manner and a wonderful moustache.'

'And where is the mother?'

'I haven't the least idea. They are very dreadful people.'

Winterbourne meditated a moment. 'They are very ignorant – very innocent only. Depend upon it they are not bad.'

'They are hopelessly vulgar,' said Mrs Costello. 'Whether or no being hopelessly vulgar is being "bad" is a question for the metaphysicians. They are bad enough to dislike, at any rate; and for this short life that is quite enough.'

The news that Daisy Miller was surrounded by half-a-dozen wonderful moustaches checked Winterbourne's impulse to go straightway to see her. He had perhaps not definitely flattered himself that he had made an ineffaceable impression upon her heart, but he was annoyed at hearing of a state of affairs so little in harmony with an image that had lately flitted in and out of his own meditations; the image of a very pretty girl looking out of an old Roman window and asking herself urgently when Mr Winterbourne would arrive. If, however, he determined to wait a little before reminding Miss Miller of his claims to her consideration, he went very soon to call upon two or three other friends. One of these friends was an American lady who had spent several winters at Geneva, where she had placed her children at school. She was a very accomplished woman and she lived in the Via Gregoriana.[34] Winterbourne found her in a little crimson drawing-room, on a third floor; the room was filled with southern sunshine. He had not been there ten minutes when the servant came in, announcing 'Madame Mila!' This announcement was presently followed by the entrance of little Randolph Miller, who stopped in the middle of the room and stood staring at Winterbourne. An instant later his pretty sister crossed the threshold; and then, after a considerable interval, Mrs Miller slowly advanced.

'I know you!' said Randolph.

'I'm sure you know a great many things,' exclaimed Winterbourne, taking him by the hand. 'How is your education coming on?'

Daisy was exchanging greetings very prettily with her hostess; but when she heard Winterbourne's voice she quickly turned her head. 'Well, I declare!' she said.

'I told you I should come, you know,' Winterbourne rejoined, smiling.

'Well – I didn't believe it,' said Miss Daisy.

'I am much obliged to you,' laughed the young man.

'You might have come to see me!' said Daisy.

'I arrived only yesterday.'

'I don't believe that!' the young girl declared.

Winterbourne turned with a protesting smile to her mother; but this lady evaded his glance, and seating herself, fixed her eyes upon her son. 'We've got a bigger place than this,' said Randolph. 'It's all gold on the walls.'

Mrs Miller turned uneasily in her chair. 'I told you if I were to bring you, you would say something!' she murmured.

'I told *you*!' Randolph exclaimed. 'I tell *you*, sir!' he added jocosely, giving Winterbourne a thump on the knee. 'It *is* bigger, too!'

Daisy had entered upon a lively conversation with her hostess; Winterbourne judged it becoming to address a few words to her mother. 'I hope you have been well since we parted at Vevey,' he said.

Mrs Miller now certainly looked at him – at his chin. 'Not very well, sir,' she answered.

'She's got the dyspepsia,' said Randolph. 'I've got it too. Father's got it. I've got it worst!'

This announcement, instead of embarrassing Mrs Miller, seemed to relieve her. 'I suffer from the liver,' she said. 'I think it's this climate; it's less bracing than Schenectady, especially in the winter season. I don't know whether you know we reside at Schenectady. I was saying to Daisy that I certainly hadn't found any one like Dr Davis, and I didn't believe I should. Oh, at Schenectady, he stands first; they think everything of him. He has so much to do, and yet there was nothing he wouldn't do for me. He said he never saw anything like my dyspepsia, but he was bound to cure it. I'm sure there was nothing he wouldn't try. He was just going to try something new when we came off. Mr Miller wanted Daisy to see Europe for herself. But I wrote to Mr Miller that it seems as if I couldn't get on without Dr Davis. At Schenectady he stands at the very top; and there's a great deal of sickness there, too. It affects my sleep.'

Winterbourne had a good deal of pathological gossip with Dr Davis's patient, during which Daisy chattered unremittingly to her own companion. The young man asked Mrs Miller how she was pleased with Rome. 'Well, I must say I am disappointed,' she answered. 'We had heard so much about it; I suppose we had heard too much. But we couldn't help that. We had been led to expect something different.'

'Ah, wait a little, and you will become very fond of it,' said Winterbourne.

'I hate it worse and worse every day!' cried Randolph.

'You are like the infant Hannibal,'[35] said Winterbourne.

'No, I ain't!' Randolph declared, at a venture.

'You are not much like an infant,' said his mother. 'But we have seen places,' she resumed, 'that I should put a long way before Rome.' And in reply to Winterbourne's interrogation, 'There's Zurich,' she observed; 'I think Zurich is lovely; and we hadn't heard half so much about it.'

'The best place we've seen is the City of Richmond!' said Randolph.

'He means the ship,'[36] his mother explained. 'We crossed in that ship. Randolph had a good time on the City of Richmond.'

'It's the best place I've seen,' the child repeated. 'Only it was turned the wrong way.'

'Well, we've got to turn the right way some time,' said Mrs Miller, with a little laugh. Winterbourne expressed the hope that her daughter at least found some gratification in Rome, and she declared that Daisy was quite carried away. 'It's on account of the society – the society's splendid. She goes round everywhere; she has made a great number of acquaintances. Of course she goes round more than I do. I must say they have been very sociable; they have taken her right in. And then she knows a great many gentlemen. Oh, she thinks there's nothing like Rome. Of course, it's a great deal pleasanter for a young lady if she knows plenty of gentlemen.'

By this time Daisy had turned her attention again to Winterbourne. 'I've been telling Mrs Walker how mean you were!' the young girl announced.

'And what is the evidence you have offered?' asked Winterbourne, rather annoyed at Miss Miller's want of appreciation of the zeal of an admirer who on his way down to Rome had stopped neither at Bologna nor at Florence, simply because of a certain sentimental impatience. He remembered that a cynical compatriot had once told him that American women – the pretty ones, and this gave a largeness to the axiom – were at once the most exacting in the world and the least endowed with a sense of indebtedness.

'Why, you were awfully mean at Vevey,' said Daisy. 'You wouldn't do anything. You wouldn't stay there when I asked you.'

'My dearest young lady,' cried Winterbourne, with eloquence, 'have I come all the way to Rome to encounter your reproaches?'

'Just hear him say that!' said Daisy to her hostess, giving a twist to a bow on this lady's dress. 'Did you ever hear anything so quaint?'

'So quaint, my dear?' murmured Mrs Walker, in the tone of a partisan of Winterbourne.

'Well, I don't know,' said Daisy, fingering Mrs Walker's ribbons. 'Mrs Walker, I want to tell you something.'

'Motherr,' interposed Randolph, with his rough ends to his words, 'I tell you you've got to go. Eugenio'll raise something!'

'I'm not afraid of Eugenio,' said Daisy, with a toss of her head. 'Look here, Mrs Walker,' she went on, 'you know I'm coming to your party.'

'I am delighted to hear it.'

'I've got a lovely dress.'

'I am very sure of that.'

'But I want to ask a favour – permission to bring a friend.'

'I shall be happy to see any of your friends,' said Mrs Walker, turning with a smile to Mrs Miller.

'Oh, they are not my friends,' answered Daisy's mamma, smiling shyly, in her own fashion. 'I never spoke to them!'

'It's an intimate friend of mine – Mr Giovanelli,' said Daisy, without a tremor in her clear little voice or a shadow on her brilliant little face.

Mrs Walker was silent a moment, she gave a rapid glance at Winterbourne. 'I shall be glad to see Mr Giovanelli,' she then said.

'He's an Italian,' Daisy pursued, with the prettiest serenity. 'He's a great friend of mine – he's the handsomest man in the world – except Mr Winterbourne! He knows plenty of Italians, but he wants to know some Americans. He thinks ever so much of Americans. He's tremendously clever. He's perfectly lovely!'

It was settled that this brilliant personage should be brought to Mrs Walker's party, and then Mrs Miller prepared to take her leave. 'I guess we'll go back to the hotel,' she said.

'You may go back to the hotel, mother, but I'm going to take a walk,' said Daisy.

'She's going to walk with Mr Giovanelli,' Randolph proclaimed.

'I am going to the Pincio,'[37] said Daisy, smiling.

'Alone, my dear – at this hour?' Mrs Walker asked. The afternoon was drawing to a close – it was the hour for the throng of carriages and of contemplative pedestrians. 'I don't think it's safe, my dear,' said Mrs Walker.

'Neither do I,' subjoined Mrs Miller. 'You'll get the fever[38] as sure as you live. Remember what Dr Davis told you!'

'Give her some medicine before she goes,' said Randolph.

The company had risen to its feet; Daisy, still showing her pretty teeth, bent over and kissed her hostess. 'Mrs Walker, you are too perfect,' she said. 'I'm not going alone; I am going to meet a friend.'

'Your friend won't keep you from getting the fever,' Mrs Miller observed.

'Is it Mr Giovanelli?' asked the hostess.

Winterbourne was watching the young girl; at this question his attention quickened. She stood there smiling and smoothing her bonnet-ribbons; she glanced at Winterbourne. Then, while she glanced and smiled, she answered without a shade of hesitation, 'Mr Giovanelli – the beautiful Giovanelli.'

'My dear young friend,' said Mrs Walker, taking her hand, pleadingly, 'don't walk off to the Pincio at this hour to meet a beautiful Italian.'

'Well, he speaks English,' said Mrs Miller.

'Gracious me!' Daisy exclaimed, 'I don't want to do anything improper. There's an easy way to settle it.' She continued to glance at Winterbourne. 'The Pincio is only a hundred yards distant, and if Mr Winterbourne were as polite as he pretends he would offer to walk with me!'

Winterbourne's politeness hastened to affirm itself, and the young girl gave him gracious leave to accompany her. They passed downstairs before her mother, and at the door Winterbourne perceived Mrs Miller's carriage drawn up, with the ornamental courier whose acquaintance he had made at Vevey seated within. 'Good-bye, Eugenio!' cried Daisy. 'I'm going to take a walk.' The distance from the Via Gregoriana to the beautiful garden at the other end of the Pincian Hill is, in fact, rapidly traversed. As the day was splendid, however, and the concourse of vehicles, walkers and loungers numerous, the young Americans found their progress much delayed. This fact was highly agreeable to Winterbourne, in spite of his consciousness of his singular situation. The slow-moving, idly-gazing Roman crowd bestowed much attention upon the extremely pretty young foreign lady who was passing through it upon his arm; and he wondered what on earth had been in Daisy's mind when she proposed to expose herself, unattended, to its appreciation. His own mission, to her sense, apparently, was to consign her to the hands of Mr Giovanelli; but Winterbourne, at once annoyed and gratified, resolved that he would do no such thing.

'Why haven't you been to see me?' asked Daisy. 'You can't get out of that.'

'I have had the honour of telling you that I have only just stepped out of the train.'

'You must have stayed in the train a good while after it stopped!' cried the young girl, with her little laugh. 'I suppose you were asleep. You have had time to go to see Mrs Walker.'

'I knew Mrs Walker—' Winterbourne began to explain.

'I knew where you knew her. You knew her at Geneva. She told me so. Well, you knew me at Vevey. That's just as good. So you ought to have come.' She asked him no other question than this; she began to prattle about her own affairs. 'We've got splendid rooms at the hotel; Eugenio says they're the best rooms in Rome. We are going to stay all winter – if we don't die of the fever; and I guess we'll stay then. It's a great deal nicer than I thought; I thought it would be fearfully quiet; I was sure it would be awfully poky. I was sure we should be going round all the time with one of those dreadful old men that explain about the pictures and things. But we only had about a week of that, and now I'm enjoying myself. I know ever so many people, and they are all so charming. The society's extremely select. There are all kinds – English, and Germans, and Italians. I think I like the English best. I like their style of conversation. But there are some lovely Americans. I never saw anything so hospitable. There's something or other every day. There's not much dancing; but I must say I never thought dancing was everything. I was always fond of conversation. I guess I shall have plenty at Mrs Walker's – her rooms are so small.' When they had passed the gate of the Pincian Gardens, Miss Miller began to wonder where

Mr Giovanelli might be. 'We had better go straight to that place in front,' she said, 'where you look at the view.'

'I certainly shall not help you to find him,' Winterbourne declared.

'Then I shall find him without you,' said Miss Daisy.

'You certainly won't leave me!' cried Winterbourne.

She burst into her little laugh. 'Are you afraid you'll get lost – or run over? But there's Giovanelli, leaning against that tree. He's staring at the women in the carriages: did you ever see anything so cool?'

Winterbourne perceived at some distance a little man standing with folded arms, nursing his cane. He had a handsome face, an artfully poised hat, a glass in one eye and a nosegay in his button-hole. Winterbourne looked at him a moment and then said, 'Do you mean to speak to that man?'

'Do I mean to speak to him? Why, you don't suppose I mean to communicate by signs?'

'Pray understand, then,' said Winterbourne, 'that I intend to remain with you.'

Daisy stopped and looked at him, without a sign of troubled consciousness in her face; with nothing but the presence of her charming eyes and her happy dimples. 'Well, she's a cool one!' thought the young man.

'I don't like the way you say that,' said Daisy. 'It's too imperious.'

'I beg your pardon if I say it wrong. The main point is to give you an idea of my meaning.'

The young girl looked at him more gravely, but with eyes that were prettier than ever. 'I have never allowed a gentleman to dictate to me, or to interfere with anything I do.'

'I think you have made a mistake,' said Winterbourne. 'You should sometimes listen to a gentleman – the right one?'

Daisy began to laugh again. 'I do nothing but listen to gentlemen!' she exclaimed. 'Tell me if Mr Giovanelli is the right one?'

The gentleman with the nosegay in his bosom had now perceived our two friends, and was approaching the young girl with obsequious rapidity. He bowed to Winterbourne as well as to the latter's companion; he had a brilliant smile, an intelligent eye; Winterbourne thought him not a bad-looking fellow. But he nevertheless said to Daisy – 'No, he's not the right one.'

Daisy evidently had a natural talent for performing introductions; she mentioned the name of each of her companions to the other. She strolled along with one of them on each side of her; Mr Giovanelli, who spoke English very cleverly – Winterbourne afterwards learned that he had practised the idiom upon a great many American heiresses – addressed her a great deal of very polite nonsense; he was extremely urbane, and the young American, who said nothing, reflected upon that profundity of Italian cleverness which enables people to appear more gracious in proportion as they are more acutely disappointed. Giovanelli, of course, had counted upon something more intimate; he had not bargained for a party of three. But he kept his temper in a manner which suggested far-stretching intentions. Winterbourne flattered himself that he had taken his measure. 'He is not a gentleman,' said the young American; 'he is only a clever imitation of one. He is a music-master, or a penny-a-liner,[39] or a third-rate artist. Damn his good looks!' Mr Giovanelli had certainly a very pretty face; but Winterbourne felt a superior indignation at his own lovely fellow-countrywoman's not knowing the difference between a spurious gentleman and a real one. Giovanelli chattered and jested and made himself wonderfully agreeable. It was true that if he was an imitation the imitation was very skilful. 'Nevertheless,' Winterbourne said to himself, 'a nice girl ought to know!' And then he came back to the question whether this was in fact a nice girl. Would a nice girl – even allowing for her being a little American flirt – make a rendezvous with a presumably low-lived foreigner? The rendezvous in this case, indeed, had been in broad daylight, and in the most crowded corner of Rome; but was it not impossible to regard the choice of these circumstances as a proof of extreme cynicism? Singular though it may seem, Winterbourne was vexed that the young girl, in joining her *amoroso*, should not appear more impatient of his own company, and he was vexed because of his inclination. It was impossible to regard her as a perfectly well-conducted young lady; she was wanting in a certain indispensable delicacy. It would therefore simplify matters greatly to be able to treat her as the object of one of those sentiments which are called by romancers 'lawless passions'. That she should seem to wish to get rid of him would help him to think more lightly of her, and to be able to think more lightly of her would make her much less perplexing. But Daisy, on this occasion, continued to present herself as an inscrutable combination of audacity and innocence.

She had been walking some quarter of an hour, attended by her two cavaliers,[40] and responding in a tone of very childish gaiety, as it seemed to Winterbourne, to the pretty speeches of Mr Giovanelli, when a carriage that had detached itself from the revolving train drew up beside the path. At the same moment Winterbourne perceived that his friend Mrs Walker – the lady whose house he had lately left – was seated in the vehicle and was beckoning to him. Leaving Miss Miller's side, he hastened to obey her summons. Mrs Walker was flushed; she wore an excited air. 'It is really too dreadful,' she said. 'That girl must not do this sort of thing. She must not walk here with you two men. Fifty people have noticed her.'

Winterbourne raised his eyebrows. 'I think it's a pity to make too much fuss about it.'

'It's a pity to let the girl ruin herself!'

'She is very innocent,' said Winterbourne.

'She's very crazy!' cried Mrs Walker. 'Did you ever see anything so imbecile as her mother? After you had all left me, just now, I could not sit still for thinking of it. It seemed too pitiful, not even to attempt to save her. I ordered the carriage and put on my bonnet, and came here as quickly as possible. Thank Heaven I have found you!'

'What do you propose to do with us?' asked Winterbourne, smiling.

'To ask her to get in, to drive her about here for half an hour, so that the world may see she is not running absolutely wild, and then to take her safely home.'

'I don't think it's a very happy thought,' said Winterbourne; 'but you can try.'

Mrs Walker tried. The young man went in pursuit of Miss Miller, who had simply nodded and smiled at his interlocutrix in the carriage and had gone her way with her own companion. Daisy, on learning that Mrs Walker wished to speak to her, retraced her steps with a perfect good grace and with Mr Giovanelli at her side. She declared that she was delighted to have a chance to present this gentleman to Mrs Walker. She immediately achieved the introduction, and declared that she had never in her life seen anything so lovely as Mrs Walker's carriage-rug.

'I am glad you admire it,' said this lady, smiling sweetly. 'Will you get in and let me put it over you?'

'Oh, no, thank you,' said Daisy. 'I shall admire it much more as I see you driving round with it.'

'Do get in and drive with me,' said Mrs Walker.

'That would be charming, but it's so enchanting just as I am!' and Daisy gave a brilliant glance at the gentlemen on either side of her.

'It may be enchanting, dear child, but it is not the custom here,' urged Mrs Walker, leaning forward in her victoria[41] with her hands devoutly clasped.

'Well, it ought to be, then!' said Daisy. 'If I didn't walk I should expire.'

'You should walk with your mother, dear,' cried the lady from Geneva, losing patience.

'With my mother dear!' exclaimed the young girl. Winterbourne saw that she scented interference. 'My mother never walked ten steps in her life. And then, you know,' she added with a laugh, 'I am more than five years old.'

'You are old enough to be more reasonable. You are old enough, dear Miss Miller, to be talked about.'

Daisy looked at Mrs Walker, smiling intensely. 'Talked about? What do you mean?'

'Come into my carriage and I will tell you.'

Daisy turned her quickened glance again from one of the gentlemen beside her to the other. Mr Giovanelli was bowing

to and fro, rubbing down his gloves and laughing very agreeably; Winterbourne thought it a most unpleasant scene. 'I don't
think I want to know what you mean,' said Daisy presently. 'I
don't think I should like it.'

Winterbourne wished that Mrs Walker would tuck in her
carriage-rug and drive away; but this lady did not enjoy being
defied, as she afterwards told him. 'Should you prefer being
thought a very reckless girl?' she demanded.

'Gracious me!' exclaimed Daisy. She looked again at Mr
Giovanelli, then she turned to Winterbourne. There was a little
pink flush in her cheek; she was tremendously pretty. 'Does Mr
Winterbourne think,' she asked slowly, smiling, throwing back
her head and glancing at him from head to foot, 'that – to save
my reputation – I ought to get into the carriage?'

Winterbourne coloured; for an instant he hesitated greatly.
It seemed so strange to hear her speak that way of her 'reputation'. But he himself, in fact, must speak in accordance with
gallantry. The finest gallantry, here, was simply to tell her the
truth; and the truth, for Winterbourne, as the few indications
I have been able to give have made him known to the reader,
was that Daisy Miller should take Mrs Walker's advice. He
looked at her exquisite prettiness; and then he said very gently,
'I think you should get into the carriage.'

Daisy gave a violent laugh. 'I never heard anything so stiff!
If this is improper, Mrs Walker,' she pursued, 'then I am all
improper, and you must give me up. Good-bye; I hope you'll
have a lovely ride!' and, with Mr Giovanelli, who made a triumphantly obsequious salute, she turned away.

Mrs Walker sat looking after her, and there were tears in Mrs
Walker's eyes. 'Get in here, sir,' she said to Winterbourne, indicating the place beside her. The young man answered that he felt
bound to accompany Miss Miller; whereupon Mrs Walker
declared that if he refused her this favour she would never speak
to him again. She was evidently in earnest. Winterbourne overtook Daisy and her companion and, offering the young girl his
hand, told her that Mrs Walker had made an imperious claim
upon his society. He expected that in answer she would say
something rather free, something to commit herself still farther

to that 'recklessness' from which Mrs Walker had so charitably endeavoured to dissuade her. But she only shook his hand, hardly looking at him, while Mr Giovanelli bade him farewell with a too emphatic flourish of the hat.

Winterbourne was not in the best possible humour as he took his seat in Mrs Walker's victoria. 'That was not clever of you,' he said candidly, while the vehicle mingled again with the throng of carriages.

'In such a case,' his companion answered, 'I don't wish to be clever, I wish to be *earnest*!'

'Well, your earnestness has only offended her and put her off.'

'It has happened very well,' said Mrs Walker. 'If she is so perfectly determined to compromise herself, the sooner one knows it the better; one can act accordingly.'

'I suspect she meant no harm,' Winterbourne rejoined.

'So I thought a month ago. But she has been going too far.'

'What has she been doing?'

'Everything that is not done here. Flirting with any man she could pick up; sitting in corners with mysterious Italians; dancing all the evening with the same partners; receiving visits at eleven o'clock at night. Her mother goes away when visitors come.'

'But her brother,' said Winterbourne, laughing, 'sits up till midnight.'

'He must be edified by what he sees. I'm told that at their hotel every one is talking about her, and that a smile goes round among the servants when a gentleman comes and asks for Miss Miller.'

'The servants be hanged!' said Winterbourne angrily. 'The poor girl's only fault,' he presently added, 'is that she is very uncultivated.'

'She is naturally indelicate,' Mrs Walker declared. 'Take that example this morning. How long had you known her at Vevey?'

'A couple of days.'

'Fancy, then, her making it a personal matter that you should have left the place!'

Winterbourne was silent for some moments; then he said, 'I suspect, Mrs Walker, that you and I have lived too long at Geneva!' And he added a request that she should inform him with what particular design she had made him enter her carriage.

'I wished to beg you to cease your relations with Miss Miller – not to flirt with her – to give her no farther opportunity to expose herself – to let her alone, in short.'

'I'm afraid I can't do that,' said Winterbourne. 'I like her extremely.'

'All the more reason that you shouldn't help her to make a scandal.'

'There shall be nothing scandalous in my attentions to her.'

'There certainly will be in the way she takes them. But I have said what I had on my conscience,' Mrs Walker pursued. 'If you wish to rejoin the young lady I will put you down. Here, by the way, you have a chance.'

The carriage was traversing that part of the Pincian Garden which overhangs the wall of Rome[42] and overlooks the beautiful Villa Borghese.[43] It is bordered by a large parapet, near which there are several seats. One of the seats, at a distance, was occupied by a gentleman and a lady, towards whom Mrs Walker gave a toss of her head. At the same moment these persons rose and walked towards the parapet. Winterbourne had asked the coachman to stop; he now descended from the carriage. His companion looked at him a moment in silence; then, while he raised his hat, she drove majestically away. Winterbourne stood there; he had turned his eyes towards Daisy and her cavalier. They evidently saw no one; they were too deeply occupied with each other. When they reached the low garden-wall they stood a moment looking off at the great flat-topped pine-clusters of the Villa Borghese; then Giovanelli seated himself familiarly upon the broad ledge of the wall. The western sun in the opposite sky sent out a brilliant shaft through a couple of cloud-bars; whereupon Daisy's companion took her parasol out of her hands and opened it. She came a little nearer and he held the parasol over her; then, still holding it, he let it rest upon her shoulder, so that both of their heads

were hidden from Winterbourne. This young man lingered a
moment, then he began to walk. But he walked – not towards
the couple with the parasol; towards the residence of his aunt,
Mrs Costello.

IV

He flattered himself on the following day that there was no
smiling among the servants when he, at least, asked for Mrs
Miller at her hotel. This lady and her daughter, however, were
not at home; and on the next day after, repeating his visit,
Winterbourne again had the misfortune not to find them. Mrs
Walker's party took place on the evening of the third day, and
in spite of the frigidity of his last interview with the hostess
Winterbourne was among the guests. Mrs Walker was one of
those American ladies who, while residing abroad, make a
point, in their own phrase, of studying European society; and
she had on this occasion collected several specimens of her
diversely-born fellow-mortals to serve, as it were, as text-books.
When Winterbourne arrived Daisy Miller was not there; but in
a few moments he saw her mother come in alone, very shyly
and ruefully. Mrs Miller's hair, above her exposed-looking
temples, was more frizzled than ever. As she approached Mrs
Walker, Winterbourne also drew near.

'You see I've come all alone,' said poor Mrs Miller. 'I'm so
frightened; I don't know what to do; it's the first time I've ever
been to a party alone – especially in this country. I wanted to
bring Randolph or Eugenio, or some one, but Daisy just pushed
me off by myself. I ain't used to going round alone.'

'And does not your daughter intend to favour us with her
society?' demanded Mrs Walker, impressively.

'Well, Daisy's all dressed,' said Mrs Miller, with that accent
of the dispassionate, if not of the philosophic, historian with
which she always recorded the current incidents of her daughter's career. 'She got dressed on purpose before dinner. But
she's got a friend of hers there; that gentleman – the Italian –
that she wanted to bring. They've got going at the piano; it

seems as if they couldn't leave off. Mr Giovanelli sings splendidly. But I guess they'll come before very long,' concluded Mrs Miller hopefully.

'I'm sorry she should come – in that way,' said Mrs Walker.

'Well, I told her that there was no use in her getting dressed before dinner if she was going to wait three hours,' responded Daisy's mamma. 'I didn't see the use of her putting on such a dress as that to sit round with Mr Giovanelli.'

'This is most horrible!' said Mrs Walker, turning away and addressing herself to Winterbourne. '*Elle s'affiche.* It's her revenge for my having ventured to remonstrate with her. When she comes I shall not speak to her.'

Daisy came after eleven o'clock, but she was not, on such an occasion, a young lady to wait to be spoken to. She rustled forward in radiant loveliness, smiling and chattering, carrying a large bouquet and attended by Mr Giovanelli. Every one stopped talking, and turned and looked at her. She came straight to Mrs Walker. 'I'm afraid you thought I never was coming, so I sent mother off to tell you. I wanted to make Mr Giovanelli practise some things before he came; you know he sings beautifully, and I want you to ask him to sing. This is Mr Giovanelli; you know I introduced him to you; he's got the most lovely voice and he knows the most charming set of songs. I made him go over them this evening, on purpose; we had the greatest time at the hotel.' Of all this Daisy delivered herself with the sweetest, brightest audibleness, looking now at her hostess and now round the room, while she gave a series of little pats, round her shoulders, to the edges of her dress. 'Is there any one I know?' she asked.

'I think every one knows you!' said Mrs Walker pregnantly, and she gave a very cursory greeting to Mr Giovanelli. This gentleman bore himself gallantly. He smiled and bowed and showed his white teeth, he curled his moustaches and rolled his eyes, and performed all the proper functions of a handsome Italian at an evening party. He sang, very prettily, half-a-dozen songs, though Mrs Walker afterwards declared that she had been quite unable to find out who asked him. It was apparently not Daisy who had given him his orders. Daisy sat at a distance from the piano, and though she had publicly, as it were, professed a high admiration for his singing, talked, not inaudibly, while it was going on.

'It's a pity these rooms are so small; we can't dance,' she said to Winterbourne, as if she had seen him five minutes before.

'I am not sorry we can't dance,' Winterbourne answered; 'I don't dance.'

'Of course you don't dance; you're too stiff,' said Miss Daisy. 'I hope you enjoyed your drive with Mrs Walker.'

'No, I didn't enjoy it; I preferred walking with you.'

'We paired off, that was much better,' said Daisy. 'But did you ever hear anything so cool as Mrs Walker's wanting me to get into her carriage and drop poor Mr Giovanelli; and under the pretext that it was proper? People have different ideas! It would have been most unkind; he had been talking about that walk for ten days.'

'He should not have talked about it at all,' said Winterbourne; 'he would never have proposed to a young lady of this country to walk about the streets with him.'

'About the streets?' cried Daisy, with her pretty stare. 'Where then would he have proposed to her to walk? The Pincio is not the streets, either; and I, thank goodness, am not a young lady of this country. The young ladies of this country have a dreadfully poky time of it, so far as I can learn; I don't see why I should change my habits for *them*.'

'I am afraid your habits are those of a flirt,' said Winterbourne gravely.

'Of course they are,' she cried, giving him her little smiling stare again. 'I'm a fearful, frightful flirt! Did you ever hear of a nice girl that was not? But I suppose you will tell me now that I am not a nice girl.'

'You're a very nice girl, but I wish you would flirt with me, and me only,' said Winterbourne.

'Ah! thank you, thank you very much; you are the last man I should think of flirting with. As I have had the pleasure of informing you, you are too stiff.'

'You say that too often,' said Winterbourne.

Daisy gave a delighted laugh. 'If I could have the sweet hope of making you angry, I would say it again.'

'Don't do that; when I am angry I'm stiffer than ever. But if you won't flirt with me, do cease at least to flirt with your friend at the piano; they don't understand that sort of thing here.'

'I thought they understood nothing else!' exclaimed Daisy.

'Not in young unmarried women.'

'It seems to me much more proper in young unmarried women than in old married ones,' Daisy declared.

'Well,' said Winterbourne, 'when you deal with natives you must go by the custom of the place. Flirting is a purely American custom; it doesn't exist here. So when you show yourself in public with Mr Giovanelli and without your mother—'

'Gracious! poor mother!' interposed Daisy.

'Though you may be flirting, Mr Giovanelli is not; he means something else.'

'He isn't preaching, at any rate,' said Daisy with vivacity. 'And if you want very much to know, we are neither of us flirting; we are too good friends for that; we are very intimate friends.'

'Ah!' rejoined Winterbourne, 'if you are in love with each other it is another affair.'

She had allowed him up to this point to talk so frankly that he had no expectation of shocking her by this ejaculation; but she immediately got up, blushing visibly, and leaving him to exclaim mentally that little American flirts were the queerest creatures in the world. 'Mr Giovanelli, at least,' she said, giving her interlocutor a single glance, 'never says such very disagreeable things to me.'

Winterbourne was bewildered; he stood staring. Mr Giovanelli had finished singing; he left the piano and came over to Daisy. 'Won't you come into the other room and have some tea?' he asked, bending before her with his decorative smile.

Daisy turned to Winterbourne, beginning to smile again. He was still more perplexed, for this inconsequent smile made nothing clear, though it seemed to prove, indeed, that she had a sweetness and softness that reverted instinctively to the pardon of offences. 'It has never occurred to Mr Winterbourne to offer me any tea,' she said, with her little tormenting manner.

'I have offered you advice,' Winterbourne rejoined.

'I prefer weak tea!' cried Daisy, and she went off with the brilliant Giovanelli. She sat with him in the adjoining room, in the embrasure of the window, for the rest of the evening. There was an interesting performance at the piano, but neither of these young people gave heed to it. When Daisy came to take leave of Mrs Walker, this lady conscientiously repaired the weakness of which she had been guilty at the moment of the young girl's arrival. She turned her back straight upon Miss Miller and left her to depart with what grace she might. Winterbourne was standing near the door; he saw it all. Daisy turned very pale and looked at her mother, but Mrs Miller was humbly unconscious of any violation of the usual social forms. She appeared, indeed, to have felt an incongruous impulse to draw attention to her own striking observance of them. 'Good-night, Mrs Walker,' she said; 'we've had a beautiful evening. You see if I let Daisy come to parties without me, I don't want her to go away without me.' Daisy turned away, looking with a pale, grave face at the circle near the door; Winterbourne saw that, for the first moment, she was too much shocked and puzzled even for indignation. He on his side was greatly touched.

'That was very cruel,' he said to Mrs Walker.

'She never enters my drawing-room again,' replied his hostess.

Since Winterbourne was not to meet her in Mrs Walker's drawing-room, he went as often as possible to Mrs Miller's hotel. The ladies were rarely at home, but when he found them the devoted Giovanelli was always present. Very often the polished little Roman was in the drawing-room with Daisy alone, Mrs Miller being apparently constantly of the opinion that discretion is the better part of surveillance. Winterbourne noted, at first with surprise, that Daisy on these occasions was never embarrassed or annoyed by his own entrance; but he very presently began to feel that she had no more surprises for him; the unexpected in her behaviour was the only thing to expect. She showed no displeasure at her *tête-à-tête* with Giovanelli being interrupted; she could chatter as freshly and freely with two gentlemen as with one; there was always in her conversation, the same odd mixture of audacity and puerility. Winterbourne remarked to himself that if she was seriously interested in Giovanelli it was very singular that she should not take more trouble to preserve the sanctity of their interviews, and he liked her the more for her innocent-looking indifference and her apparently inexhaustible good humour. He could hardly have said why, but she seemed to him a girl who would never be jealous. At the risk of exciting a somewhat derisive smile on the reader's part, I may affirm that with regard to the women who had hitherto interested him it very often seemed to Winterbourne among the possibilities that, given certain contingencies, he should be afraid – literally afraid – of these ladies. He had a pleasant sense that he should never be afraid of Daisy Miller. It must be added that this sentiment was not altogether flattering to Daisy; it was part of his conviction, or rather of his apprehension, that she would prove a very light young person.

But she was evidently very much interested in Giovanelli. She looked at him whenever he spoke; she was perpetually telling him to do this and to do that; she was constantly 'chaffing' and abusing him. She appeared completely to have forgotten that Winterbourne had said anything to displease her at Mrs Walker's little party. One Sunday afternoon, having gone to St Peter's with his aunt, Winterbourne perceived Daisy strolling about the great church in company with the inevitable Giovanelli. Presently he pointed out the young girl and her cavalier to Mrs Costello. This lady looked at them a moment through her eye-glass, and then she said:

'That's what makes you so pensive in these days, eh?'

'I had not the least idea I was pensive,' said the young man.

'You are very much pre-occupied, you are thinking of something.'

'And what is it,' he asked, 'that you accuse me of thinking of?'

'Of that young lady's – Miss Baker's, Miss Chandler's – what's her name? – Miss Miller's intrigue with that little barber's block.'[44]

'Do you call it an intrigue,' Winterbourne asked – 'an affair that goes on with such peculiar publicity?'

'That's their folly,' said Mrs Costello, 'it's not their merit.'

'No,' rejoined Winterbourne, with something of that pensiveness to which his aunt had alluded. 'I don't believe that there is anything to be called an intrigue.'

'I have heard a dozen people speak of it; they say she is quite carried away by him.'

'They are certainly very intimate,' said Winterbourne.

Mrs Costello inspected the young couple again with her optical instrument. 'He is very handsome. One easily sees how it is. She thinks him the most elegant man in the world, the finest gentleman. She has never seen anything like him; he is better even than the courier. It was the courier probably who introduced him, and if he succeeds in marrying the young lady, the courier will come in for a magnificent commission.'

'I don't believe she thinks of marrying him,' said Winterbourne, 'and I don't believe he hopes to marry her.'

'You may be very sure she thinks of nothing. She goes on from day to day, from hour to hour, as they did in the Golden Age.[45] I can imagine nothing more vulgar. And at the same time,' added Mrs Costello, 'depend upon it that she may tell you any moment that she is "engaged".'

'I think that is more than Giovanelli expects,' said Winterbourne.

'Who is Giovanelli?'

'The little Italian. I have asked questions about him and learned something. He is apparently a perfectly respectable little man. I believe he is in a small way a *cavaliere avvocato*. But he doesn't move in what are called the first circles. I think it is really not absolutely impossible that the courier introduced him. He is evidently immensely charmed with Miss Miller. If she thinks him the finest gentleman in the world, he, on his side, has never found himself in personal contact with such splendour, such opulence, such expensiveness, as this young lady's. And then she must seem to him wonderfully pretty and interesting. I rather doubt whether he dreams of marrying her. That must appear to him too impossible a piece of luck. He has nothing but his handsome face to offer, and there is a substantial Mr Miller in that mysterious land of dollars. Giovanelli knows that he hasn't a title to offer. If he were only a count or a *marchese*![46] He must wonder at his luck at the way they have taken him up.'

'He accounts for it by his handsome face, and thinks Miss Miller a young lady *qui se passe ses fantaisies*!' said Mrs Costello.

'It is very true,' Winterbourne pursued, 'that Daisy and her mamma have not yet risen to that stage of – what shall I call it? – of culture, at which the idea of catching a count or a *marchese* begins. I believe that they are intellectually incapable of that conception.'

'Ah! but the *cavaliere* can't believe it,' said Mrs Costello.

Of the observation excited by Daisy's 'intrigue', Winterbourne gathered that day at St Peter's sufficient evidence. A dozen of the American colonists in Rome came to talk with Mrs Costello, who sat on a little portable stool at the base of one of the great pilasters. The vesper-service was going forward in splendid chants and organ-tones in the adjacent choir, and meanwhile, between Mrs Costello and her friends, there was a great deal said about poor little Miss Miller's going really 'too far'. Winterbourne was not pleased with what he heard; but when, coming out upon the great steps of the church, he saw Daisy, who had emerged before him, get into an open cab with her accomplice and roll away through the cynical streets of Rome, he could not deny to himself that she was going very far indeed. He felt very sorry for her – not exactly that he believed that she had completely lost her head, but because it was painful to hear so much that was pretty and undefended and natural assigned to a vulgar place among the categories of disorder. He made an attempt after this to give a hint to Mrs Miller. He met one day in the Corso[47] a friend – a tourist like himself – who had just come out of the Doria Palace,[48] where he had been walking through the beautiful gallery.

His friend talked for a moment about the superb portrait of Innocent X. by Velasquez, which hangs in one of the cabinets of the palace, and then said, 'And in the same cabinet, by the way, I had the pleasure of contemplating a picture of a different kind[49] – that pretty American girl whom you pointed out to me last week.' In answer to Winterbourne's inquiries, his friend narrated that the pretty American girl – prettier than ever – was seated with a companion in the secluded nook in which the great papal portrait is enshrined.

'Who was her companion?' asked Winterbourne.

'A little Italian with a bouquet in his button-hole. The girl is delightfully pretty, but I thought I understood from you the other day that she was a young lady *du meilleur monde*.'

'So she is!' answered Winterbourne; and having assured himself that his informant had seen Daisy and her companion but five minutes before, he jumped into a cab and went to call on Mrs Miller. She was at home; but she apologized to him for receiving him in Daisy's absence.

'She's gone out somewhere with Mr Giovanelli,' said Mrs Miller. 'She's always going round with Mr Giovanelli.'

'I have noticed that they are very intimate,' Winterbourne observed.

'Oh! it seems as if they couldn't live without each other!' said Mrs Miller. 'Well, he's a real gentleman, anyhow. I keep telling Daisy she's engaged!'

'And what does Daisy say?'

'Oh, she says she isn't engaged. But she might as well be!' this impartial parent resumed. 'She goes on as if she was. But I've made Mr Giovanelli promise to tell me, if *she* doesn't. I should want to write to Mr Miller about it – shouldn't you?'

Winterbourne replied that he certainly should; and the state of mind of Daisy's mamma struck him as so unprecedented in the annals of parental vigilance that he gave up as utterly irrelevant the attempt to place her upon her guard.

After this Daisy was never at home, and Winterbourne ceased to meet her at the houses of their common acquaintance, because, as he perceived, these shrewd people had quite made up their minds that she was going too far. They ceased to invite her, and they intimated that they desired to express to observant Europeans the great truth that, though Miss Daisy Miller was a young American lady, her behaviour was not representative – was regarded by her compatriots as abnormal. Winterbourne wondered how she felt about all the cold shoulders that were turned towards her, and sometimes it annoyed him to suspect that she did not feel at all. He said to himself that she was too light and childish, too uncultivated and unreasoning, too provincial, to have reflected upon her ostracism or even to have perceived it. Then at other moments he believed that she carried about in her elegant and irresponsible little organism a defiant, passionate, perfectly observant consciousness of the impression she produced. He asked himself whether Daisy's defiance came from the consciousness of innocence or from her being, essentially, a young person of the reckless class. It must be admitted that holding oneself to a belief in Daisy's 'innocence' came to seem to Winterbourne more and more a matter of fine-spun gallantry. As I have already had occasion to relate, he was angry at finding himself reduced to chopping logic about this young lady; he was vexed at his want of instinctive certitude as to how far her eccentricities were generic, national, and how far they were personal. From either view of them he had somehow missed her, and now it was too late. She was 'carried away' by Mr Giovanelli.

A few days after his brief interview with her mother, he encountered her in that beautiful abode of flowering desolation known as the Palace of the Cæsars. The early Roman spring had filled the air with bloom and perfume, and the rugged surface of the Palatine[50] was muffled with tender verdure. Daisy was strolling along the top of one of those great mounds of ruin that are embanked with mossy marble and paved with monumental inscriptions. It seemed to him that Rome had never been so lovely as just then. He stood looking off at the enchanting harmony of line and colour that remotely encircles the city, inhaling the softly humid odours and feeling the freshness of the year and the antiquity of the place reaffirm themselves in mysterious interfusion. It seemed to him also that Daisy had never looked so pretty; but this had been an observation of his whenever he met her. Giovanelli was at her side, and Giovanelli, too, wore an aspect of even unwonted brilliancy.

'Well,' said Daisy, 'I should think you would be lonesome!'

'Lonesome?' asked Winterbourne.

'You are always going round by yourself. Can't you get any one to walk with you?'

'I am not so fortunate,' said Winterbourne, 'as your companion.'

Giovanelli, from the first, had treated Winterbourne with distinguished politeness; he listened with a deferential air to his remarks; he laughed, punctiliously, at his pleasantries; he seemed disposed to testify to his belief that Winterbourne was a superior young man. He carried himself in no degree like a jealous wooer; he had obviously a great deal of tact; he had no objection to your expecting a little humility of him. It even seemed to Winterbourne at times that Giovanelli would find a certain mental relief in being able to have a private understanding with him – to say to him, as an intelligent man, that, bless you, *he* knew how extraordinary was this young lady, and didn't flatter himself with delusive – or at least *too* delusive – hopes of matrimony and dollars. On this occasion he strolled away from his companion to pluck a sprig of almond blossom, which he carefully arranged in his button-hole.

'I know why you say that,' said Daisy, watching Giovanelli. 'Because you think I go round too much with *him*!' And she nodded at her attendant.

'Every one thinks so – if you care to know,' said Winterbourne.

'Of course I care to know!' Daisy exclaimed seriously. 'But I don't believe it. They are only pretending to be shocked. They don't really care a straw what I do. Besides, I don't go round so much.'

'I think you will find they do care. They will show it – disagreeably.'

Daisy looked at him a moment. 'How – disagreeably?'

'Haven't you noticed anything?' Winterbourne asked.

'I have noticed you. But I noticed you were as stiff as an umbrella the first time I saw you.'

'You will find I am not so stiff as several others,' said Winterbourne, smiling.

'How shall I find it?'

'By going to see the others.'

'What will they do to me?'

'They will give you the cold shoulder. Do you know what that means?'

Daisy was looking at him intently; she began to colour. 'Do you mean as Mrs Walker did the other night?'

'Exactly!' said Winterbourne.

She looked away at Giovanelli, who was decorating himself with his almond-blossom. Then looking back at Winterbourne – 'I shouldn't think you would let people be so unkind!' she said.

'How can I help it?' he asked.

'I should think you would say something.'

'I do say something;' and he paused a moment. 'I say that your mother tells me that she believes you are engaged.'

'Well, she does,' said Daisy very simply.

Winterbourne began to laugh. 'And does Randolph believe it?' he asked.

'I guess Randolph doesn't believe anything,' said Daisy. Randolph's scepticism excited Winterbourne to farther hilarity, and he observed that Giovanelli was coming back to them. Daisy, observing it too, addressed herself again to her countryman. 'Since you have mentioned it,' she said, 'I *am* engaged.' . . . Winterbourne looked at her; he had stopped laughing. 'You don't believe it!' she added.

He was silent a moment; and then, 'Yes, I believe it!' he said.

'Oh, no, you don't,' she answered. 'Well, then – I am not!'

The young girl and her cicerone were on their way to the gate of the enclosure, so that Winterbourne, who had but lately entered, presently took leave of them. A week afterwards he went to dine at a beautiful villa on the Cælian Hill,[51] and, on arriving, dismissed his hired vehicle. The evening was charming, and he promised himself the satisfaction of walking home beneath the Arch of Constantine[52] and past the vaguely-lighted monuments of the Forum. There was a waning moon in the sky, and her radiance was not brilliant, but she was veiled in a thin cloud-curtain which seemed to diffuse and equalize it. When, on his return from the villa (it was eleven o'clock), Winterbourne approached the dusky circle of the Colosseum,[53] it occurred to him, as a lover of the picturesque,[54] that the interior, in the pale moonshine, would be well worth a glance. He turned aside and walked to one of the empty arches, near which, as he observed, an open carriage – one of the little Roman street-cabs – was stationed. Then he passed in among the cavernous shadows of the great structure, and emerged upon the clear and silent arena. The place had never seemed to him more impressive. One-half of the gigantic circus was in deep shade; the other was sleeping in the luminous dusk. As he stood there he began to murmur Byron's famous lines,[55] out of 'Manfred'; but before he had finished his quotation he remembered that if nocturnal meditations in the Colosseum are recommended by the poets, they are deprecated by the doctors. The historic atmosphere was there, certainly; but the historic atmosphere, scientifically considered was no better than a villanous miasma.[56] Winterbourne walked to the middle of the arena, to take a more general glance, intending thereafter to make a hasty retreat. The great cross[57] in the centre was covered with shadow; it was only as he drew near it that he made it out distinctly. Then he saw that two persons were stationed upon the low steps which formed its base. One of these was a woman, seated; her companion was standing in front of her.

Presently the sound of the woman's voice came to him distinctly in the warm night-air. 'Well, he looks at us as one of the old lions or tigers may have looked at the Christian martyrs!' These were the words he heard, in the familiar accent of Miss Daisy Miller.

'Let us hope he is not very hungry,' responded the ingenious Giovanelli. 'He will have to take me first; you will serve for dessert!'

Winterbourne stopped, with a sort of horror; and, it must

be added, with a sort of relief. It was as if a sudden illumination had been flashed upon the ambiguity of Daisy's behaviour
and the riddle had become easy to read. She was a young lady
whom a gentleman need no longer be at pains to respect. He
stood there looking at her – looking at her companion, and not
reflecting that though he saw them vaguely, he himself must
have been more brightly visible. He felt angry with himself
that he had bothered so much about the right way of regarding
Miss Daisy Miller. Then, as he was going to advance again, he
checked himself; not from the fear that he was doing her injustice, but from a sense of the danger of appearing unbecomingly
exhilarated by this sudden revulsion from cautious criticism.
He turned away towards the entrance of the place; but as he
did so he heard Daisy speak again.

'Why, it was Mr Winterbourne! He saw me – and he
cuts me!'

What a clever little reprobate she was, and how smartly she
played an injured innocence! But he wouldn't cut her. Winterbourne came forward again, and went towards the great cross.
Daisy had got up; Giovanelli lifted his hat. Winterbourne had
now begun to think simply of the craziness, from a sanitary
point of view, of a delicate young girl lounging away the evening in this nest of malaria. What if she *were* a clever little
reprobate? that was no reason for her dying of the *perniciosa*.
'How long have you been here?' he asked, almost brutally.

Daisy, lovely in the flattering moonlight, looked at him a
moment. Then – 'All the evening,' she answered gently . . . 'I
never saw anything so pretty.'

'I am afraid,' said Winterbourne, 'that you will not think
Roman fever very pretty. This is the way people catch it. I won-
der,' he added, turning to Giovanelli, 'that you, a native
Roman, should countenance such a terrible indiscretion.'

'Ah,' said the handsome native, 'for myself, I am not afraid.'

'Neither am I – for you! I am speaking for this young lady.'

Giovanelli lifted his well-shaped eyebrows and showed his
brilliant teeth. But he took Winterbourne's rebuke with docility. 'I told the Signorina it was a grave indiscretion; but when
was the Signorina ever prudent?'

'I never was sick, and I don't mean to be!' the Signorina declared. 'I don't look like much, but I'm healthy! I was bound to see the Colosseum by moonlight; I shouldn't have wanted to go home without that; and we have had the most beautiful time, haven't we, Mr Giovanelli? If there has been any danger, Eugenio can give me some pills. He has got some splendid pills.'[58]

'I should advise you,' said Winterbourne, 'to drive home as fast as possible and take one!'

'What you say is very wise,' Giovanelli rejoined. 'I will go and make sure the carriage is at hand.' And he went forward rapidly.

Daisy followed with Winterbourne. He kept looking at her; she seemed not in the least embarrassed. Winterbourne said nothing; Daisy chattered about the beauty of the place. 'Well, I *have* seen the Colosseum by moonlight!' she exclaimed. 'That's one good thing.' Then, noticing Winterbourne's silence, she asked him why he didn't speak. He made no answer; he only began to laugh. They passed under one of the dark archways; Giovanelli was in front with the carriage. Here Daisy stopped a moment, looking at the young American. '*Did* you believe I was engaged the other day?' she asked.

'It doesn't matter what I believed the other day,' said Winterbourne, still laughing.

'Well, what do you believe now?'

'I believe that it makes very little difference whether you are engaged or not!'

He felt the young girl's pretty eyes fixed upon him through the thick gloom of the archway; she was apparently going to answer. But Giovanelli hurried her forward. 'Quick, quick,' he said; 'if we get in by midnight we are quite safe.'

Daisy took her seat in the carriage, and the fortunate Italian placed himself beside her. 'Don't forget Eugenio's pills!' said Winterbourne, as he lifted his hat.

'I don't care,' said Daisy, in a little strange tone, 'whether I have Roman fever or not!' Upon this the cab-driver cracked his whip, and they rolled away over the desultory patches of the antique pavement.

Winterbourne – to do him justice, as it were – mentioned to no one that he had encountered Miss Miller, at midnight, in the Colosseum with a gentleman; but nevertheless, a couple of days later, the fact of her having been there under these circumstances was known to every member of the little American circle, and commented accordingly. Winterbourne reflected that they had of course known it at the hotel, and that, after Daisy's return, there had been an exchange of jokes between the porter and the cab-driver. But the young man was conscious at the same moment that it had ceased to be a matter of serious regret to him that the little American flirt should be 'talked about' by low-minded menials. These people, a day or two later, had serious information to give: the little American flirt was alarmingly ill. Winterbourne, when the rumour came to him, immediately went to the hotel for more news. He found that two or three charitable friends had preceded him, and that they were being entertained in Mrs Miller's salon by Randolph.

'It's going round at night,' said Randolph – 'that's what made her sick. She's always going round at night. I shouldn't think she'd want to – it's so plaguey dark. You can't see anything here at night, except when there's a moon. In America there's always a moon!' Mrs Miller was invisible; she was now, at least, giving her daughter the advantage of her society. It was evident that Daisy was dangerously ill.

Winterbourne went often to ask for news of her, and once he saw Mrs Miller, who, though deeply alarmed, was – rather to his surprise – perfectly composed, and, as it appeared, a most efficient and judicious nurse. She talked a good deal about Dr Davis, but Winterbourne paid her the compliment of saying to himself that she was not, after all, such a monstrous goose. 'Daisy spoke of you the other day,' she said to him. 'Half the time she doesn't know what she's saying, but that time I think she did. She gave me a message; she told me to tell you. She told me to tell you that she never was engaged to that handsome Italian. I am sure I am very glad; Mr Giovanelli hasn't been near us since she was taken ill. I thought he was so much of a gentleman; but I don't call that very polite! A lady told me that he was afraid I was angry with him for taking

Daisy round at night. Well, so I am; but I suppose he knows I'm a lady. I would scorn to scold him. Any way, she says she's not engaged. I don't know why she wanted you to know; but she said to me three times – "Mind you tell Mr Winterbourne." And then she told me to ask if you remembered the time you went to that castle, in Switzerland. But I said I wouldn't give any such messages as that. Only, if she is not engaged, I'm sure I'm glad to know it.'

But, as Winterbourne had said, it mattered very little. A week after this the poor girl died; it had been a terrible case of the fever. Daisy's grave was in the little Protestant cemetery,[59] in an angle of the wall of imperial Rome, beneath the cypresses and the thick spring-flowers. Winterbourne stood there beside it, with a number of other mourners; a number larger than the scandal excited by the young lady's career would have led you to expect. Near him stood Giovanelli, who came nearer still before Winterbourne turned away. Giovanelli was very pale; on this occasion he had no flower in his button-hole; he seemed to wish to say something. At last he said, 'She was the most beautiful young lady I ever saw, and the most amiable.' And then he added in a moment, 'And she was the most innocent.'

Winterbourne looked at him, and presently repeated his words, 'And the most innocent?'

'The most innocent!'

Winterbourne felt sore and angry. 'Why the devil,' he asked, 'did you take her to that fatal place?'

Mr Giovanelli's urbanity was apparently imperturbable. He looked on the ground a moment, and then he said, 'For myself, I had no fear; and she wanted to go.'

'That was no reason!' Winterbourne declared.

The subtle Roman again dropped his eyes. 'If she had lived, I should have got nothing. She would never have married me, I am sure.'

'She would never have married you?'

'For a moment I hoped so. But no. I am sure.'

Winterbourne listened to him; he stood staring at the raw protuberance among the April daisies. When he turned away again Mr Giovanelli, with his light slow step, had retired.

Winterbourne almost immediately left Rome; but the following summer he again met his aunt, Mrs Costello, at Vevey. Mrs Costello was fond of Vevey. In the interval Winterbourne had often thought of Daisy Miller and her mystifying manners. One day he spoke of her to his aunt – said it was on his conscience that he had done her injustice.

'I am sure I don't know,' said Mrs Costello. 'How did your injustice affect her?'

'She sent me a message before her death which I didn't understand at the time. But I have understood it since. She would have appreciated one's esteem.'

'Is that a modest way,' asked Mrs Costello, 'of saying that she would have reciprocated one's affection?'

Winterbourne offered no answer to this question; but he presently said, 'You were right in that remark that you made last summer. I was booked to make a mistake. I have lived too long in foreign parts.'

Nevertheless, he went back to live at Geneva, whence there continue to come the most contradictory accounts of his motives of sojourn: a report that he is 'studying' hard – an intimation that he is much interested in a very clever foreign lady.

AN INTERNATIONAL
EPISODE

I

Four years ago – in 1874 – two young Englishmen had occasion to go to the United States. They crossed the ocean at midsummer, and, arriving in New York on the first day of August, were much struck with the fervid temperature of that city. Disembarking upon the wharf, they climbed into one of those huge high-hung coaches which convey passengers to the hotels, and with a great deal of bouncing and bumping, took their course through Broadway.[1] The midsummer aspect of New York is not perhaps the most favourable one; still, it is not without its picturesque and even brilliant side. Nothing could well resemble less a typical English street than the interminable avenue, rich in incongruities, through which our two travellers advanced – looking out on each side of them at the comfortable animation of the sidewalks, the high-coloured, heterogeneous architecture, the huge white marble façades, glittering in the strong, crude light and bedizened with gilded lettering, the multifarious awnings, banners and streamers, the extraordinary number of omnibuses, horse-cars and other democratic vehicles,[2] the vendors of cooling fluids, the white trousers and big straw-hats of the policemen, the tripping gait of the modish young persons on the pavement, the general brightness, newness, juvenility, both of people and things. The young men had exchanged few observations; but in crossing Union Square,[3] in front of the monument to Washington[4] – in the very shadow, indeed, projected by the image of the *pater patriæ*[5] – one of them remarked to the other, 'It seems a rum-looking place.'

'Ah, very odd, very odd,' said the other, who was the clever man of the two.

'Pity it's so beastly hot,' resumed the first speaker, after a pause.

'You know we are in a low latitude,'[6] said his friend.

'I dare say,' remarked the other.

'I wonder,' said the second speaker, presently, 'if they can give one a bath.'

'I dare say not,' rejoined the other.

'Oh, I say!' cried his comrade.

This animated discussion was checked by their arrival at the hotel, which had been recommended to them by an American gentleman whose acquaintance they made – with whom, indeed, they became very intimate – on the steamer, and who had proposed to accompany them to the inn and introduce them, in a friendly way, to the proprietor. This plan, however, had been defeated by their friend's finding that his 'partner' was awaiting him on the wharf, and that his commercial associate desired him instantly to come and give his attention to certain telegrams received from St Louis. But the two Englishmen, with nothing but their national prestige and personal graces to recommend them, were very well received at the hotel, which had an air of capacious hospitality. They found that a bath was not unattainable, and were indeed struck with the facilities for prolonged and reiterated immersion with which their apartment was supplied. After bathing a good deal – more indeed than they had ever done before on a single occasion – they made their way into the dining-room of the hotel, which was a spacious restaurant, with a fountain in the middle, a great many tall plants in ornamental tubs, and an array of French waiters. The first dinner on land, after a sea-voyage, is under any circumstances a delightful occasion, and there was something particularly agreeable in the circumstances in which our young Englishmen found themselves. They were extremely good-natured young men; they were more observant than they appeared; in a sort of inarticulate, accidentally dissimulative fashion, they were highly appreciative. This was perhaps especially the case with the elder, who was also, as I have said, the man of talent. They sat down at a little table which was a very different affair from the great clattering see-saw in the saloon of the steamer. The wide doors and windows of the restaurant stood open, beneath large awnings, to a wide pavement, where there were other plants in tubs, and rows of spreading trees, and beyond which there was a large shady square, without any palings[7] and with marble-paved walks. And above the vivid verdure rose other façades of white marble and of pale chocolate-coloured stone, squaring themselves against the deep blue sky. Here, outside, in the light and the shade and the heat, there was a great tinkling of the bells of innumerable street-cars,[8] and a constant strolling and shuffling and rustling of many pedestrians, a large proportion of whom were young women in Pompadour-looking dresses.[9] Within, the place was cool and vaguely-lighted; with the plash of water, the odour of flowers and the flitting of French waiters, as I have said, upon soundless carpets.

'It's rather like Paris, you know,' said the younger of our two travellers.

'It's like Paris – only more so,' his companion rejoined.

'I suppose it's the French waiters,' said the first speaker. 'Why don't they have French waiters in London?'

'Fancy a French waiter at a club,' said his friend.

The young Englishman stared a little, as if he could not fancy it. 'In Paris I'm very apt to dine at a place where there's an English waiter. Don't you know, what's-his-name's, close to the thingumbob?[10] They always set an English waiter at me. I suppose they think I can't speak French.'

'No, more you can.' And the elder of the young Englishmen unfolded his napkin.

His companion took no notice whatever of this declaration. 'I say,' he resumed, in a moment, 'I suppose we must learn to speak American. I suppose we must take lessons.'

'I can't understand them,' said the clever man.

'What the deuce is *he* saying?' asked his comrade, appealing from the French waiter.

'He is recommending some soft-shell crabs,' said the clever man.

And so, in desultory observation of the idiosyncrasies of the new society in which they found themselves, the young Englishmen proceeded to dine – going in largely, as the phrase is, for cooling draughts and dishes, of which their attendant offered them a very long list. After dinner they went out and slowly walked about the neighbouring streets. The early dusk of waning summer was coming on, but the heat was still very great. The pavements were hot even to the stout boot-soles of the British travellers, and the trees along the kerb-stone emitted strange exotic odours. The young men wandered through the adjoining square – that queer place without palings, and with marble walks arranged in black and white lozenges. There were a great many benches, crowded with shabby-looking people, and the travellers remarked, very justly, that it was not much like Belgrave Square.[11] On one side was an enormous hotel, lifting up into the hot darkness an immense array of open, brightly-lighted windows. At the base of this populous structure was an eternal jangle of horse-cars, and all round it, in the upper dusk, was a sinister hum of mosquitoes. The ground-floor of the hotel seemed to be a huge transparent cage, flinging a wide glare of gaslight into the street, of which it formed a sort of public adjunct, absorbing and emitting the passers-by promiscuously.[12] The young Englishmen went in with every one else, from curiosity, and saw a couple of hundred men sitting on divans along a great marble-paved corridor, with their legs stretched out, together with several dozen more standing in a *queue*, as at the ticket-office of a railway station, before a brilliantly-illuminated counter, of vast extent. These latter persons, who carried portmanteaux[13] in their hands, had a dejected, exhausted look; their garments were not very fresh, and they seemed to be rendering some mysterious tribute to a magnificent young man with a waxed moustache and a shirt front adorned with diamond buttons, who every now and then dropped an absent glance over their multitudinous patience. They were American citizens[14] doing homage to an hotel-clerk.

'I'm glad he didn't tell us to go there,' said one of our Englishmen, alluding to their friend on the steamer, who had told them so many things. They walked up the Fifth Avenue,[15] where, for instance, he had told them that all the first families lived. But the first families were out of town, and our young travellers had only the satisfaction of seeing some of the second – or perhaps even the third – taking the evening air upon balconies and high flights of doorsteps, in the streets which radiate from the more ornamental thoroughfare. They went a little way down one of these side-streets, and they saw young ladies in white dresses – charming-looking persons – seated in graceful attitudes on the chocolate-coloured steps. In one or two places these young ladies were conversing across the street with other young ladies seated in similar postures and costumes in front of the opposite houses, and in the warm night air their colloquial tones sounded strange in the ears of the young Englishmen. One of our friends, nevertheless – the younger one – intimated that he felt a disposition to intercept a few of these soft familiarities; but his companion observed, pertinently enough, that he had better be careful. 'We must not begin with making mistakes,' said his companion.

'But he told us, you know – he told us,' urged the young man, alluding again to the friend on the steamer.

'Never mind what he told us!' answered his comrade, who, if he had greater talents, was also apparently more of a moralist.

By bed-time – in their impatience to taste of a terrestrial couch again our seafarers went to bed early – it was still insufferably hot, and the buzz of the mosquitoes at the open windows might have passed for an audible crepitation of the temperature. 'We can't stand this, you know,' the young Englishmen said to each other; and they tossed about all night more boisterously than they had tossed upon the Atlantic billows. On the morrow, their first thought was that they would re-embark that day for England; and then it occurred to them that they might find an asylum nearer at hand. The cave of Æolus[16] became their ideal of comfort, and they wondered where the Americans went when they wished to cool off. They had not the least idea, and they determined to apply for information to Mr J. L. Westgate. This was the name inscribed in a bold hand on the back of a letter carefully preserved in the pocket-book of our junior traveller. Beneath the address, in the left-hand corner of the envelope, were the words, 'Introducing Lord Lambeth and Percy Beaumont, Esq.' The letter had been given to the two Englishmen by a good friend of theirs in London, who had been in America two years previously and had singled out Mr J. L. Westgate from the many friends he had left there as the consignee, as it were, of his compatriots. 'He is a capital fellow,' the Englishman in London had said, 'and he has got an awfully pretty wife. He's tremendously hospitable – he will do everything in the world for you; and as he knows every one over there, it is quite needless I should give you any other introduction. He will make you see every one; trust to him for putting you into circulation. He has got a tremendously pretty wife.' It was natural that in the hour of tribulation Lord Lambeth and Mr Percy Beaumont should have bethought themselves of a gentleman whose attractions had been thus vividly depicted; all the more so that he lived in the Fifth Avenue and that the Fifth Avenue, as they had ascertained the night before, was contiguous to their hotel. 'Ten to one he'll be out of town,' said Percy Beaumont; 'but we can at least find out where he has gone, and we can immediately start in pursuit. He can't possibly have gone to a hotter place, you know.'

'Oh, there's only one hotter place,' said Lord Lambeth, 'and I hope he hasn't gone there.'

They strolled along the shady side of the street to the number indicated upon the precious letter. The house presented an imposing chocolate-coloured expanse, relieved by facings and window-cornices of florid sculpture, and by a couple of dusty rose-trees, which clambered over the balconies and the portico. This last-mentioned feature was approached by a monumental flight of steps.

'Rather better than a London house,' said Lord Lambeth, looking down from this altitude, after they had rung the bell.

'It depends upon what London house you mean,' replied his

companion. 'You have a tremendous chance to get wet between the house-door and your carriage.'

'Well,' said Lord Lambeth, glancing at the burning heavens, 'I "guess" it doesn't rain so much here!'

The door was opened by a long negro in a white jacket, who grinned familiarly when Lord Lambeth asked for Mr Westgate.

'He ain't at home, sir; he's down town at his o'fice.'

'Oh, at his office?' said the visitors. 'And when will he be at home?'

'Well, sir, when he goes out dis way in de mo'ning, he ain't liable to come home all day.'

This was discouraging; but the address of Mr Westgate's office was freely imparted by the intelligent black, and was taken down by Percy Beaumont in his pocket-book. The two gentlemen then returned, languidly, to their hotel, and sent for a hackney-coach;[17] and in this commodious vehicle they rolled comfortably down town. They measured the whole length of Broadway again, and found it a path of fire; and then, deflecting to the left, they were deposited by their conductor before a fresh, light, ornamental structure, ten storeys high, in a street crowded with keen-faced, light-limbed young men, who were running about very quickly and stopping each other eagerly at corners and in doorways. Passing into this brilliant building, they were introduced by one of the keen-faced young men – he was a charming fellow, in wonderful cream-coloured garments and a hat with a blue ribbon, who had evidently perceived them to be aliens and helpless – to a very snug hydraulic elevator,[18] in which they took their place with many other persons, and which, shooting upward in its vertical socket, presently projected them into the seventh horizontal compartment of the edifice. Here, after brief delay, they found themselves face to face with the friend of their friend in London. His office was composed of several different rooms, and they waited very silently in one of these after they had sent in their letter and their cards. The letter was not one which it would take Mr Westgate very long to read, but he came out to speak to them more instantly than they could have expected; he had evidently jumped up from his work. He was a tall, lean personage, and was dressed all in fresh white linen; he had a thin, sharp, familiar face, with an expression that was at one and the same time sociable and business-like, a quick, intelligent eye, and a large brown moustache, which concealed his mouth and made his chin, beneath it, look small. Lord Lambeth thought he looked tremendously clever.

'How do you do, Lord Lambeth – how do you do, sir?' he said, holding the open letter in his hand. 'I'm very glad to see you – I hope you're very well. You had better come in here – I think it's cooler;' and he led the way into another room, where there were law-books and papers, and windows wide open beneath striped awnings. Just opposite one of the windows, on a line with his eyes, Lord Lambeth observed the weather-vane of a church steeple. The uproar of the street sounded infinitely far below, and Lord Lambeth felt very high in the air. 'I say it's cooler,' pursued their host, 'but everything is relative. How do you stand the heat?'

'I can't say we like it,' said Lord Lambeth; 'but Beaumont likes it better than I.'

'Well, it won't last,' Mr Westgate very cheerfully declared; 'nothing unpleasant lasts over here. It was very hot when Captain Littledale was here; he did nothing but drink sherry-cobblers.[19] He expresses some doubt in his letter whether I shall remember him – as if I didn't remember making six sherry-cobblers for him one day, in about twenty minutes. I hope you left him well; two years having elapsed since then.'

'Oh, yes, he's all right,' said Lord Lambeth.

'I am always very glad to see your countrymen,' Mr Westgate pursued. 'I thought it would be time some of you should be coming along. A friend of mine was saying to me only a day or two ago, "It's time for the water-melons and the Englishmen."'

'The Englishmen and the water-melons just now are about the same thing,' Percy Beaumont observed, wiping his dripping forehead.

'Ah, well, we'll put you on ice, as we do the melons. You must go down to Newport.'[20]

'We'll go anywhere!' said Lord Lambeth.

'Yes, you want to go to Newport – that's what you want to do,' Mr Westgate affirmed. 'But let's see – when did you get here?'

'Only yesterday,' said Percy Beaumont.

'Ah, yes, by the "Russia".²¹ Where are you staying?'

'At the "Hanover", I think they call it.'

'Pretty comfortable?' inquired Mr Westgate.

'It seems a capital place, but I can't say we like the gnats,'²² said Lord Lambeth.

Mr Westgate stared and laughed. 'Oh, no, of course you don't like the gnats. We shall expect you to like a good many things over here, but we shan't insist upon your liking the gnats; though certainly you'll admit that, as gnats, they are fine, eh? But you oughtn't to remain in the city.'

'So we think,' said Lord Lambeth. 'If you would kindly suggest something—'

'Suggest something, my dear sir?' – and Mr Westgate looked at him, narrowing his eyelids. 'Open your mouth and shut your eyes! Leave it to me, and I'll put you through. It's a matter of national pride with me that all Englishmen should have a good time; and, as I have had considerable practice, I have learned to minister to their wants. I find they generally want the right thing. So just please to consider yourselves my property; and if any one should try to appropriate you, please to say, "Hands off; too late for the market." But let's see,' continued the American, in his slow, humorous voice, with a distinctness of utterance which appeared to his visitors to be part of a facetious intention – a strangely leisurely, speculative voice for a man evidently so busy and, as they felt, so professional – 'let's see; are you going to make something of a stay, Lord Lambeth?'

'Oh dear no,' said the young Englishman; 'my cousin was coming over on some business, so I just came across, at an hour's notice, for the lark.'

'Is it your first visit to the United States?'

'Oh dear, yes.'

'I was obliged to come on some business,' said Percy Beaumont, 'and I brought Lambeth with me.'

'And *you* have been here before, sir?'

'Never – never.'

'I thought, from your referring to business—' said Mr Westgate.

'Oh, you see I'm by way of being a barrister,' Percy Beaumont answered. 'I know some people that think of bringing a suit against one of your railways, and they asked me to come over and take measures accordingly.'

Mr Westgate gave one of his slow, keen looks again. 'What's your railroad?' he asked.

'The Tennessee Central.'[23]

The American tilted back his chair a little, and poised it an instant. 'Well, I'm sorry you want to attack one of our institutions,' he said, smiling. 'But I guess you had better enjoy yourself *first*!'

'I'm certainly rather afraid I can't work in this weather,' the young barrister confessed.

'Leave that to the natives,' said Mr Westgate. 'Leave the Tennessee Central to me, Mr Beaumont. Some day we'll talk it over, and I guess I can make it square. But I didn't know you Englishmen ever did any work, in the upper classes.'

'Oh, we do a lot of work; don't we, Lambeth?' asked Percy Beaumont.

'I must certainly be at home by the 19th of September,' said the younger Englishman, irrelevantly, but gently.

'For the shooting, eh? or is it the hunting – or the fishing?' inquired his entertainer.

'Oh, I must be in Scotland,' said Lord Lambeth, blushing a little.

'Well then,' rejoined Mr Westgate, 'you had better amuse yourself first, also. You must go down and see Mrs Westgate.'

'We should be so happy – if you would kindly tell us the train,' said Percy Beaumont.

'It isn't a train – it's a boat.'

'Oh, I see. And what is the name of – a – the – a – town?'

'It isn't a town,' said Mr Westgate, laughing. 'It's a – well, what shall I call it? It's a watering-place. In short, it's Newport. You'll see what it is. It's cool; that's the principal thing.

You will greatly oblige me by going down there and putting yourself into the hands of Mrs Westgate. It isn't perhaps for me to say it; but you couldn't be in better hands. Also in those of her sister, who is staying with her. She is very fond of Englishmen. She thinks there is nothing like them.'

'Mrs Westgate or – a – her sister?' asked Percy Beaumont, modestly, yet in the tone of an inquiring traveller.

'Oh, I mean my wife,' said Mr Westgate. 'I don't suppose my sister-in-law knows much about them. She has always led a very quiet life; she has lived in Boston.'

Percy Beaumont listened with interest. 'That, I believe,' he said, 'is the most – a – intellectual town?'[24]

'I believe it is very intellectual. I don't go there much,' responded his host.

'I say, we ought to go there,' said Lord Lambeth to his companion.

'Oh, Lord Lambeth, wait till the great heat is over!' Mr Westgate interposed. 'Boston in this weather would be very trying; it's not the temperature for intellectual exertion. At Boston, you know, you have to pass an examination at the city limits; and when you come away they give you a kind of degree.'

Lord Lambeth stared, blushing a little; and Percy Beaumont stared a little also – but only with his fine natural complexion; glancing aside after a moment to see that his companion was not looking too credulous, for he had heard a great deal about American humour. 'I dare say it is very jolly,' said the younger gentleman.

'I dare say it is,' said Mr Westgate. 'Only I must impress upon you that at present – to-morrow morning, at an early hour – you will be expected at Newport. We have a house there; half the people in New York go there for the summer. I am not sure that at this very moment my wife can take you in; she has got a lot of people staying with her; I don't know who they all are; only she may have no room. But you can begin with the hotel, and meanwhile you can live at my house. In that way – simply sleeping at the hotel – you will find it tolerable. For the rest, you must make yourself at home at my place. You mustn't be shy, you know; if you are only here for a month that will be a great waste of time. Mrs Westgate won't neglect you, and you had better not try to resist her. I know something about that. I expect you'll find some pretty girls on the premises. I shall write to my wife by this afternoon's mail, and to-morrow she and Miss Alden[25] will look out for you. Just walk right in and make yourself comfortable. Your steamer leaves from this part of the city, and I will immediately send out and get you a cabin. Then, at half-past four o'clock, just call for me here, and I will go with you and put you on board. It's a big boat; you might get lost. A few days hence, at the end of the week, I will come down to Newport and see how you are getting on.'

The two young Englishmen inaugurated the policy of not resisting Mrs Westgate by submitting, with great docility and thankfulness, to her husband. He was evidently a very good fellow, and he made an impression upon his visitors; his hospitality seemed to recommend itself, consciously – with a friendly wink, as it were – as if it hinted, judicially, that you could not possibly make a better bargain. Lord Lambeth and his cousin left their entertainer to his labours and returned to their hotel, where they spent three or four hours in their respective shower-baths. Percy Beaumont had suggested that they ought to see something of the town; but 'Oh, damn the town!' his noble kinsman had rejoined. They returned to Mr Westgate's office in a carriage, with their luggage, very punctually; but it must be reluctantly recorded that, this time, he kept them waiting so long that they felt themselves missing the steamer and were deterred only by an amiable modesty from dispensing with his attendance and starting on a hasty scramble to the wharf. But when at last he appeared, and the carriage plunged into the purlieus of Broadway, they jolted and jostled to such good purpose that they reached the huge white vessel while the bell for departure was still ringing and the absorption of passengers still active. It was indeed, as Mr Westgate had said, a big boat, and his leadership in the innumerable and interminable corridors and cabins, with which he seemed perfectly acquainted, and of which any one and every one appeared to have the *entrée*, was very grateful to the slightly bewildered voyagers. He showed them their state-room – a spacious apartment, embellished with gas-lamps, mirrors *en pied* and sculptured furniture – and then, long after they had been intimately convinced that the steamer was in motion and launched upon the unknown stream that they were about to navigate, he bade them a sociable farewell.

'Well, good-bye, Lord Lambeth,' he said. 'Good-bye, Mr Percy Beaumont; I hope you'll have a good time. Just let them do what they want with you. I'll come down by-and-by and look after you.'

II

The young Englishmen emerged from their cabin and amused themselves with wandering about the immense labyrinthine steamer, which struck them as an extraordinary mixture of a ship and an hotel. It was densely crowded with passengers, the larger number of whom appeared to be ladies and very young children;[26] and in the big saloons, ornamented in white and gold, which followed each other in surprising succession, beneath the swinging gas-lights and among the small side-passages where the negro domestics of both sexes assembled with an air of philosophic leisure, every one was moving to and fro and exchanging loud and familiar observations. Eventually, at the instance of a discriminating black, our young men went and had some 'supper', in a wonderful place arranged like a theatre, where, in a gilded gallery upon which little boxes appeared to open, a large orchestra was playing operatic selections, and, below, people were handing about bills of fare, as if they had been programmes. All this was sufficiently curious; but the agreeable thing, later, was to sit out on one of the great white decks of the steamer, in the warm, breezy darkness, and, in the vague starlight, to make out the line of low, mysterious coast. The young Englishmen tried American cigars – those of Mr Westgate – and talked together as they usually talked, with many odd silences, lapses of logic and incongruities of transition; like people who have grown old together and learned to supply each other's missing phrases; or, more especially, like people thoroughly conscious of a common point of view, so that a style of conversation superficially lacking in finish might suffice for a reference to a fund of associations in the light of which everything was all right.

'We really seem to be going out to sea,' Percy Beaumont observed. 'Upon my word, we are going back to England. He has shipped us off again. I call that "real mean".'[27]

'I suppose it's all right,' said Lord Lambeth. 'I want to see those pretty girls at Newport. You know he told us the place was an island; and aren't all islands in the sea?'

'Well,' resumed the elder traveller after a while, 'if his house is as good as his cigars, we shall do very well.'

'He seems a very good fellow,' said Lord Lambeth, as if this idea had just occurred to him.

'I say, we had better remain at the inn,' rejoined his companion, presently. 'I don't think I like the way he spoke of his house. I don't like stopping in the house with such a tremendous lot of women.'

'Oh, I don't mind,' said Lord Lambeth. And then they smoked awhile in silence. 'Fancy his thinking we do no work in England!' the young man resumed.

'I dare say he didn't really think so,' said Percy Beaumont.

'Well, I guess they don't know much about England over here!' declared Lord Lambeth, humorously. And then there was another long pause. 'He was devilish civil,' observed the young nobleman.

'Nothing, certainly, could have been more civil,' rejoined his companion.

'Littledale said his wife was great fun,' said Lord Lambeth.

'Whose wife – Littledale's?'

'This American's – Mrs Westgate. What's his name? J. L.'

Beaumont was silent a moment. 'What was fun to Littledale,' he said at last, rather sententiously, 'may be death to us.'

'What do you mean by that?' asked his kinsman. 'I am as good a man as Littledale.'

'My dear boy, I hope you won't begin to flirt,' said Percy
Beaumont.

'I don't care. I dare say I shan't begin.'

'With a married woman, if she's bent upon it, it's all very
well,' Beaumont expounded. 'But our friend mentioned a
young lady – a sister, a sister-in-law. For God's sake, don't get
entangled with her.'

'How do you mean, entangled?'

'Depend upon it she will try to hook you.'

'Oh, bother!' said Lord Lambeth.

'American girls are very clever,' urged his companion.

'So much the better,' the young man declared.

'I fancy they are always up to some game of that sort,' Beaumont continued.

'They can't be worse than they are in England,' said Lord
Lambeth, judicially.

'Ah, but in England,' replied Beaumont, 'you have got your
natural protectors. You have got your mother and sisters.'

'My mother and sisters—' began the young nobleman, with
a certain energy. But he stopped in time, puffing at his cigar.

'Your mother spoke to me about it, with tears in her eyes,'
said Percy Beaumont. 'She said she felt very nervous. I promised to keep you out of mischief.'

'You had better take care of yourself,' said the object of
maternal and ducal solicitude.

'Ah,' rejoined the young barrister, 'I haven't the expectation
of a hundred thousand a year – not to mention other
attractions.'

'Well,' said Lord Lambeth, 'don't cry out before you're
hurt!'

It was certainly very much cooler at Newport, where our
travellers found themselves assigned to a couple of diminutive
bed-rooms in a far-away angle of an immense hotel. They had
gone ashore in the early summer twilight, and had very
promptly put themselves to bed; thanks to which circumstance
and to their having, during the previous hours, in their commodious cabin, slept the sleep of youth and health, they began
to feel, towards eleven o'clock, very alert and inquisitive. They

looked out of their windows across a row of small green fields, bordered with low stone dykes, of rude construction, and saw a deep blue ocean lying beneath a deep blue sky and flecked now and then with scintillating patches of foam. A strong, fresh breeze came in through the curtainless casements and prompted our young men to observe, generously, that it didn't seem half a bad climate. They made other observations after they had emerged from their rooms in pursuit of breakfast – a meal of which they partook in a huge bare hall, where a hundred negroes, in white jackets, were shuffling about upon an uncarpeted floor; where the flies were superabundant and the tables and dishes covered over with a strange, voluminous integument of coarse blue gauze; and where several little boys and girls, who had risen late, were seated in fastidious solitude at the morning repast. These young persons had not the morning paper before them, but they were engaged in languid perusal of the bill of fare.

This latter document was a great puzzle to our friends, who, on reflecting that its bewildering categories had relation to breakfast alone, had an uneasy prevision of an encyclopædic dinner-list. They found a great deal of entertainment at the hotel, an enormous wooden structure, for the erection of which it seemed to them that the virgin forests of the West must have been terribly deflowered. It was perforated from end to end with immense bare corridors, through which a strong draught was blowing – bearing along wonderful figures of ladies in white morning-dresses and clouds of Valenciennes lace,[28] who seemed to float down the long vistas with expanded furbelows, like angels spreading their wings. In front was a gigantic verandah, upon which an army might have encamped – a vast wooden terrace, with a roof as lofty as the nave of a cathedral. Here our young Englishmen enjoyed, as they supposed, a glimpse of American society, which was distributed over the measureless expanse in a variety of sedentary attitudes, and appeared to consist largely of pretty young girls, dressed as if for a *fête champêtre*[29] swaying to and fro in rocking-chairs, fanning themselves with large straw fans, and enjoying an enviable exemption from social cares. Lord

Lambeth had a theory, which it might be interesting to trace to
its origin, that it would be not only agreeable, but easily possible, to enter into relations with one of these young ladies; and
his companion found occasion to check the young nobleman's
colloquial impulses.

'You had better take care,' said Percy Beaumont, 'or you
will have an offended father or brother pulling out a
bowieknife.'[30]

'I assure you it is all right,' Lord Lambeth replied. 'You know
the Americans come to these big hotels to make acquaintances.'

'I know nothing about it, and neither do you,' said his kinsman, who, like a clever man, had begun to perceive that the
observation of American society demanded a readjustment of
one's standard.

'Hang it, then, let's find out!' cried Lord Lambeth with
some impatience. 'You know, I don't want to miss anything.'

'We will find out,' said Percy Beaumont, very reasonably.
'We will go and see Mrs Westgate and make all the proper
inquiries.'

And so the two inquiring Englishmen, who had this lady's
address inscribed in her husband's hand upon a card, descended
from the verandah of the big hotel and took their way, according to direction, along a large straight road, past a series of
fresh-looking villas, embosomed in shrubs and flowers and
enclosed in an ingenious variety of wooden palings. The morning was brilliant and cool, the villas were smart and snug, and
the walk of the young travellers was very entertaining. Everything looked as if it had received a coat of fresh paint the day
before – the red roofs, the green shutters, the clean, bright
browns and buffs of the house-fronts. The flower-beds on the
little lawns seemed to sparkle in the radiant air, and the gravel
in the short carriage-sweeps to flash and twinkle. Along the
road came a hundred little basket-phaetons,[31] in which, almost
always, a couple of ladies were sitting – ladies in white dresses
and long white gloves, holding the reins and looking at the two
Englishmen, whose nationality was not elusive, through thick
blue veils, tied tightly about their faces as if to guard their com-
plexions. At last the young men came within sight of the sea

again, and then, having interrogated a gardener over the paling of a villa, they turned into an open gate. Here they found themselves face to face with the ocean and with a very picturesque structure, resembling a magnified *chalet*[32] which was perched upon a green embankment just above it. The house had a verandah of extraordinary width all around it, and a great many doors and windows standing open to the verandah. These various apertures had, in common, such an accessible, hospitable air, such a breezy flutter, within, of light curtains, such expansive thresholds and reassuring interiors, that our friends hardly knew which was the regular entrance, and, after hesitating a moment, presented themselves at one of the windows. The room within was dark, but in a moment a graceful figure vaguely shaped itself in the rich-looking gloom, and a lady came to meet them. Then they saw that she had been seated at a table, writing, and that she had heard them and had got up. She stepped out into the light; she wore a frank, charming smile, with which she held out her hand to Percy Beaumont.

'Oh, you must be Lord Lambeth and Mr Beaumont,' she said. 'I have heard from my husband that you would come. I am extremely glad to see you.' And she shook hands with each of her visitors. Her visitors were a little shy, but they had very good manners; they responded with smiles and exclamations, and they apologized for not knowing the front door. The lady rejoined, with vivacity, that when she wanted to see people very much she did not insist upon those distinctions, and that Mr Westgate had written to her of his English friends in terms that made her really anxious. 'He said you were so terribly prostrated,' said Mrs Westgate.

'Oh, you mean by the heat?' replied Percy Beaumont. 'We were rather knocked up[33] but we feel wonderfully better. We had such a jolly – a – voyage down here. It's so very good of you to mind.'

'Yes, it's so very kind of you,' murmured Lord Lambeth.

Mrs Westgate stood smiling; she was extremely pretty. 'Well, I did mind,' she said; 'and I thought of sending for you this morning, to the Ocean House.[34] I am very glad you are better, and I am charmed you have arrived. You must come round to the other side of the piazza.'³⁵ And she led the way, with a light, smooth step, looking back at the young men and smiling.

The other side of the piazza was, as Lord Lambeth presently remarked, a very jolly place. It was of the most liberal proportions, and with its awnings, its fanciful chairs, its cushions and rugs, its view of the ocean, close at hand, tumbling along the base of the low cliffs whose level tops intervened in lawnlike smoothness, it formed a charming complement to the drawing-room. As such it was in course of use at the present moment; it was occupied by a social circle. There were several ladies and two or three gentlemen, to whom Mrs Westgate proceeded to introduce the distinguished strangers. She mentioned a great many names, very freely and distinctly; the young Englishmen, shuffling about and bowing, were rather bewildered. But at last they were provided with chairs – low wicker chairs, gilded and tied with a great many ribbons – and one of the ladies (a very young person, with a little snub nose and several dimples) offered Percy Beaumont a fan. The fan was also adorned with pink love-knots; but Percy Beaumont declined it, although he was very hot. Presently, however, it became cooler; the breeze from the sea was delicious, the view was charming, and the people sitting there looked exceedingly fresh and comfortable. Several of the ladies seemed to be young girls, and the gentlemen were slim, fair youths, such as our friends had seen the day before in New York. The ladies were working upon bands of tapestry, and one of the young men had an open book in his lap. Beaumont afterwards learned from one of the ladies that this young man had been reading aloud – that he was from Boston and was very fond of reading aloud. Beaumont said it was a great pity that they had interrupted him; he should like so much (from all he had heard) to hear a Bostonian read. Couldn't the young man be induced to go on?

'Oh no,' said his informant, very freely; 'he wouldn't be able to get the young ladies to attend to him now.'

There was something very friendly, Beaumont perceived, in

the attitude of the company; they looked at the young Englishmen with an air of animated sympathy and interest; they smiled, brightly and unanimously, at everything either of the visitors said. Lord Lambeth and his companion felt that they were being made very welcome. Mrs Westgate seated herself between them, and, talking a great deal to each, they had occasion to observe that she was as pretty as their friend Littledale had promised. She was thirty years old, with the eyes and the smile of a girl of seventeen, and she was extremely light and graceful, elegant, exquisite. Mrs Westgate was extremely spontaneous. She was very frank and demonstrative, and appeared always – while she looked at you delightedly with her beautiful young eyes – to be making sudden confessions and concessions, after momentary hesitations.

'We shall expect to see a great deal of you,' she said to Lord Lambeth, with a kind of joyous earnestness. 'We are very fond of Englishmen here; that is, there are a great many we have been fond of. After a day or two you must come and stay with us; we hope you will stay a long time. Newport's a very nice place when you come really to know it, when you know plenty of people. Of course, you and Mr Beaumont will have no difficulty about that. Englishmen are very well received here; there are almost always two or three of them about. I think they always like it, and I must say I should think they would. They receive ever so much attention. I must say I think they sometimes get spoiled; but I am sure you and Mr Beaumont are proof against that. My husband tells me you are a friend of Captain Littledale; he was such a charming man. He made himself most agreeable here, and I am sure I wonder he didn't stay. It couldn't have been pleasanter for him in his own country. Though I suppose it is very pleasant in England, for English people. I don't know myself; I have been there very little. I have been a great deal abroad, but I am always on the Continent. I must say I'm extremely fond of Paris; you know we Americans always are; we go there when we die. Did you ever hear that before? that was said by a great wit.[36] I mean the good Americans; but we are all good; you'll see that for yourself. All I know of England is London, and all I know of London is that place – on that little corner, you know, where you buy jackets – jackets with that coarse braid and those big buttons. They make very good jackets in London, I will do you the justice to say that. And some people like the hats; but about the hats I was always a heretic; I always got my hats in Paris. You can't wear an English hat – at least, I never could – unless you dress your hair à l'Anglaise; and I must say that is a talent I never possessed. In Paris they will make things to suit your peculiarities; but in England I think you like much more to have – how shall I say it? – one thing for everybody. I mean as regards dress. I don't know about other things; but I have always supposed that in other things everything was different. I mean according to the people – according to the classes, and all that. I am afraid you will think that I don't take a very favourable view; but you know you can't take a very favourable view in Dover Street, in the month of November. That has always been my fate. Do you know Jones's Hotel, in Dover Street?[37] That's all I know of England. Of course, every one admits that the English hotels are your weak point. There was always the most frightful fog; I couldn't see to try my things on. When I got over to America – into the light – I usually found they were twice too big. The next time I mean to go in the season; I think I shall go next year. I want very much to take my sister; she has never been to England. I don't know whether you know what I mean by saying that the Englishmen who come here sometimes get spoiled. I mean that they take things as a matter of course – things that are done for them. Now, naturally, they are only a matter of course when the Englishmen are very nice. But, of course, they are almost always very nice. Of course, this isn't nearly such an interesting country as England; there are not nearly so many things to see, and we haven't your country life. I have never seen anything of your country life; when I am in Europe I am always on the Continent. But I have heard a great deal about it; I know that when you are among yourselves in the country you have the most beautiful time. Of course, we have nothing of that sort, we have nothing on that scale. I don't apologize, Lord Lambeth; some Americans are always apologizing; you must have noticed that. We have the reputation of always boasting and bragging and waving the American flag; but I must say that what strikes me is that we are perpetually making excuses and trying to smooth things over. The American flag has quite gone out of fashion; it's very carefully folded up, like an old tablecloth. Why should we apologize? The English never apologize – do they? No, I must say I never apologize. You must take us as we come – with all our imperfections on our heads.[38] Of course we haven't your country life, and your old ruins, and your great estates,[39] and your leisure-class, and all that. But if we haven't, I should think you might find it a pleasant change – I think any country is pleasant where they have pleasant manners. Captain Littledale told me he had never seen such pleasant manners as at Newport; and he had been a great deal in European society. Hadn't he been in the diplomatic service? He told me the dream of his life was to get appointed to a diplomatic post in Washington. But he doesn't seem to have succeeded. I suppose that in England promotion – and all that sort of thing – is fearfully slow. With us, you know, it's a great deal too fast. You see I admit our drawbacks. But I must confess I think Newport is an ideal place. I don't know anything like it anywhere. Captain Littledale told me he didn't know anything like it anywhere. It's entirely different from most watering-places; it's a most charming life. I must say I think that when one goes to a foreign country, one ought to enjoy the differences. Of course there are differences; otherwise what did one come abroad for? Look for your pleasure in the differences, Lord Lambeth; that's the way to do it; and then I am sure you will find American society – at least Newport society – most charming and most interesting. I wish very much my husband were here; but he's dreadfully confined to New York. I suppose you think that is very strange – for a gentleman. But you see we haven't any leisure-class.'

Mrs Westgate's discourse, delivered in a soft, sweet voice, flowed on like a miniature torrent and was interrupted by a hundred little smiles, glances and gestures, which might have figured the irregularities and obstructions of such a stream. Lord Lambeth listened to her with, it must be confessed, a rather ineffectual attention, although he indulged in a good many little murmurs and ejaculations of assent and deprecation. He had no great faculty for apprehending generalizations. There were some three or four indeed which, in the play of his own intelligence, he had originated, and which had seemed convenient at the moment; but at the present time he could hardly have been said to follow Mrs Westgate as she darted gracefully about in the sea of speculation. Fortunately she asked for no especial rejoinder, for she looked about at the rest of the company as well, and smiled at Percy Beaumont, on the other side of her, as if he too must understand her and agree with her. He was rather more successful than his companion; for besides being, as we know, cleverer, his attention was not vaguely distracted by close vicinity to a remarkably interesting young girl, with dark hair and blue eyes. This was the case with Lord Lambeth, to whom it occurred after a while that the young girl with blue eyes and dark hair was the pretty sister of whom Mrs Westgate had spoken. She presently turned to him with a remark which established her identity.

'It's a great pity you couldn't have brought my brother-in-law with you. It's a great shame he should be in New York in these days.'

'Oh yes; it's so very hot,' said Lord Lambeth.

'It must be dreadful,' said the young girl.

'I dare say he is very busy,' Lord Lambeth observed.

'The gentlemen in America work too much,' the young girl went on.

'Oh, do they? I dare say they like it,' said her interlocutor.

'I don't like it. One never sees them.'

'Don't you, really?' asked Lord Lambeth. 'I shouldn't have fancied that.'

'Have you come to study American manners?' asked the young girl.

'Oh, I don't know. I just came over for a lark. I haven't got long.' Here there was a pause, and Lord Lambeth began again. 'But Mr Westgate will come down here, will not he?'

'I certainly hope he will. He must help to entertain you and Mr Beaumont.'

Lord Lambeth looked at her a little with his handsome brown eyes. 'Do you suppose he would have come down with us, if we had urged him?'

Mr Westgate's sister-in-law was silent a moment, and then – 'I dare say he would,' she answered.

'Really!' said the young Englishman. 'He was immensely civil to Beaumont and me,' he added.

'He is a dear good fellow,' the young lady rejoined. 'And he is a perfect husband. But all Americans are that,' she continued, smiling.

'Really!' Lord Lambeth exclaimed again; and wondered whether all American ladies had such a passion for generalizing as these two.

III

He sat there a good while: there was a great deal of talk; it was all very friendly and lively and jolly. Every one present, sooner or later, said something to him, and seemed to make a particular point of addressing him by name. Two or three other persons came in, and there was a shifting of seats and changing of places; the gentlemen all entered into intimate conversation with the two Englishmen, made them urgent offers of hospitality and hoped they might frequently be of service to them. They were afraid Lord Lambeth and Mr Beaumont were not very comfortable at their hotel – that it was not, as one of them said, 'so private as those dear little English inns of yours'. This last gentleman went on to say that unfortunately, as yet, perhaps, privacy was not quite so easily obtained in America as might be desired; still, he continued, you could generally get it by paying for it; in fact you could get everything in America nowadays by paying for it. American life was certainly growing a great deal more private; it was growing very much like England. Everything at Newport, for instance, was thoroughly private; Lord Lambeth would probably be struck with that. It was also represented to the strangers that it mattered very little whether their hotel was agreeable, as every one would want them to make visits; they would stay with other people, and, in any case, they would be a great deal at Mrs Westgate's. They would find that very charming; it was the pleasantest house in Newport. It was a pity Mr Westgate was always away; he was a man of the highest ability – very acute. He worked like a horse and he left his wife – well, to do about as she liked. He liked her to enjoy herself, and she seemed to know how. She was extremely brilliant, and a splendid talker. Some people preferred her sister; but Miss Alden was very different; she was in a different style altogether. Some people even thought her prettier, and, certainly, she was not so sharp. She was more in the Boston style; she had lived a great deal in Boston and she was very highly educated. Boston girls, it was intimated, were more like English young ladies.

Lord Lambeth had presently a chance to test the truth of this proposition; for on the company rising in compliance with a suggestion from their hostess that they should walk down to the rocks and look at the sea, the young Englishman again found himself, as they strolled across the grass, in proximity to Mrs Westgate's sister. Though she was but a girl of twenty, she appeared to feel the obligation to exert an active hospitality; and this was perhaps the more to be noticed as she seemed by nature a reserved and retiring person, and had little of her sister's fraternizing quality. She was perhaps rather too thin, and she was a little pale; but as she moved slowly over the grass, with her arms hanging at her sides, looking gravely for a moment at the sea and then brightly, for all her gravity, at him, Lord Lambeth thought her at least as pretty as Mrs Westgate, and reflected that if this was the Boston style the Boston style was very charming. He thought she looked very clever; he could imagine that she was highly educated; but at the same time she seemed gentle and graceful. For all her cleverness, however, he felt that she had to think a little what to say; she didn't say the first thing that came into her head; he had come from a different part of the world and from a different society, and she was trying to adapt her conversation. The others were scattering themselves near the rocks; Mrs Westgate had charge of Percy Beaumont.

'Very jolly place, isn't it?' said Lord Lambeth. 'It's a very jolly place to sit.'

'Very charming,' said the young girl; 'I often sit here; there are all kinds of cosy corners – as if they had been made on purpose.'

'Ah! I suppose you have had some of them made,' said the young man.

Miss Alden looked at him a moment. 'Oh no, we have had nothing made. It's pure nature.'

'I should think you would have a few little benches – rustic seats and that sort of thing. It might be so jolly to sit here, you know,' Lord Lambeth went on.

'I am afraid we haven't so many of those things as you,' said the young girl, thoughtfully.

'I dare say you go in for pure nature as you were saying. Nature, over here, must be so grand, you know.' And Lord Lambeth looked about him.

The little coast-line hereabouts was very pretty, but it was not at all grand; and Miss Alden appeared to rise to a perception of this fact. 'I am afraid it seems to you very rough,' she said. 'It's not like the coast scenery in Kingsley's novels.'[40]

'Ah, the novels always overdo it, you know,' Lord Lambeth rejoined. 'You must not go by the novels.'

They were wandering about a little on the rocks, and they stopped and looked down into a narrow chasm where the rising tide made a curious bellowing sound. It was loud enough to prevent their hearing each other, and they stood there for some moments in silence. The young girl looked at her companion, observing him attentively but covertly, as women, even when very young, know how to do. Lord Lambeth repaid observation; tall, straight and strong, he was handsome as certain young Englishmen, and certain young Englishmen almost alone, are handsome; with a perfect finish of feature and a look of intellectual repose and gentle good temper which seemed somehow to be consequent upon his well-cut nose and chin. And to speak of Lord Lambeth's expression of intellectual repose is not simply a civil way of saying that he looked stupid. He was evidently not a young man of an irritable imagination; he was not, as he would himself have said, tremendously clever; but, though there was a kind of appealing dulness in his eye, he looked thoroughly reasonable and competent, and his appearance proclaimed that to be a nobleman, an athlete, and an excellent fellow, was a sufficiently brilliant combination of qualities. The young girl beside him, it may be attested without farther delay, thought him the handsomest young man she had ever seen; and Bessie Alden's imagination, unlike that of her companion, was irritable. He, however, was also making up his mind that she was uncommonly pretty.

'I dare say it's very gay here – that you have lots of balls and parties,' he said; for, if he was not tremendously clever, he rather prided himself on having, with women, a sufficiency of conversation.

'Oh yes, there is a great deal going on,' Bessie Alden replied. 'There are not so many balls, but there are a good many other things. You will see for yourself; we live rather in the midst of it.'

'It's very kind of you to say that. But I thought you Americans were always dancing.'

'I suppose we dance a good deal; but I have never seen much of it. We don't do it much, at any rate, in summer. And I am sure,' said Bessie Alden, 'that we don't have so many balls as you have in England.'

'Really!' exclaimed Lord Lambeth. 'Ah, in England it all depends, you know.'

'You will not think much of our gaieties,' said the young girl, looking at him with a little mixture of interrogation and decision which was peculiar to her. The interrogation seemed earnest and the decision seemed arch; but the mixture, at any rate, was charming. 'Those things, with us, are much less splendid than in England.'

'I fancy you don't mean that,' said Lord Lambeth, laughing.

'I assure you I mean everything I say,' the young girl declared. 'Certainly, from what I have read about English society, it is very different.'

'Ah, well, you know,' said her companion, 'those things are often described by fellows who know nothing about them. You mustn't mind what you read.'

'Oh, I *shall* mind what I read!' Bessie Alden rejoined. 'When I read Thackeray and George Eliot,[41] how can I help minding them?'

'Ah, well, Thackeray – and George Eliot,' said the young nobleman; 'I haven't read much of them.'

'Don't you suppose they know about society?' asked Bessie Alden.

'Oh, I dare say they know; they were so very clever. But those fashionable novels,' said Lord Lambeth, 'they are awful rot, you know.'

His companion looked at him a moment with her dark blue eyes, and then she looked down into the chasm where the water was tumbling about. 'Do you mean Mrs Gore,[42] for instance?' she said presently, raising her eyes.

'I am afraid I haven't read that either,' was the young man's rejoinder, laughing a little and blushing. 'I am afraid you'll think I am not very intellectual.'

'Reading Mrs Gore is no proof of intellect. But I like reading everything about English life – even poor books. I am so curious about it.'

'Aren't ladies always curious?' asked the young man, jestingly.

But Bessie Alden appeared to desire to answer his question seriously. 'I don't think so – I don't think we are enough so – that we care about many things. So it's all the more of a compliment,' she added, 'that I should want to know so much about England.'

The logic here seemed a little close; but Lord Lambeth, conscious of a compliment, found his natural modesty just at hand. 'I am sure you know a great deal more than I do.'

'I really think I know a great deal – for a person who has never been there.'

'Have you really never been there?' cried Lord Lambeth. 'Fancy!'

'Never – except in imagination,' said the young girl.

'Fancy!' repeated her companion. 'But I dare say you'll go soon, won't you?'

'It's the dream of my life!' declared Bessie Alden, smiling.

'But your sister seems to know a tremendous lot about London,' Lord Lambeth went on.

The young girl was silent a moment. 'My sister and I are two very different persons,' she presently said. 'She has been a great deal in Europe. She has been in England several times. She has known a great many English people.'

'But you must have known some, too,' said Lord Lambeth.

'I don't think that I have ever spoken to one before. You are the first Englishman that – to my knowledge – I have ever talked with.'

Bessie Alden made this statement with a certain gravity – almost, as it seemed to Lord Lambeth, an impressiveness. Attempts at impressiveness always made him feel awkward, and he now began to laugh and swing his stick. 'Ah, you would have been the first to know!' he said. And then he added, after an instant – 'I'm sorry I am not a better specimen.'

The young girl looked away; but she smiled, laying aside her impressiveness. 'You must remember that you are only a beginning,' she said. Then she retraced her steps, leading the way back to the lawn, where they saw Mrs Westgate come towards them with Percy Beaumont still at her side. 'Perhaps I shall go to England next year,' Miss Alden continued; 'I want to, immensely. My sister is going to Europe, and she has asked me to go with her. If we go, I shall make her stay as long as possible in London.'

'Ah, you must come in July,' said Lord Lambeth. 'That's the time when there is most going on.'

'I don't think I can wait till July,' the young girl rejoined. 'By the first of May I shall be very impatient.' They had gone farther, and Mrs Westgate and her companion were near them. 'Kitty,' said Miss Alden, 'I have given out that we are going to London next May. So please to conduct yourself accordingly.'

Percy Beaumont wore a somewhat animated – even a slightly irritated – air. He was by no means so handsome a man as his cousin, although in his cousin's absence he might have passed for a striking specimen of the tall, muscular, fair-bearded, clear-eyed Englishman. Just now Beaumont's clear eyes which were small and of a pale grey colour, had a rather troubled light, and, after glancing at Bessie Alden while she spoke he rested them upon his kinsman. Mrs Westgate meanwhile, with her superfluously pretty gaze, looked at every one alike.

'You had better wait till the time comes,' she said to her sister. 'Perhaps next May you won't care so much about London. Mr Beaumont and I,' she went on, smiling at her companion, 'have had a tremendous discussion. We don't agree about anything. It's perfectly delightful.'

'Oh, I say, Percy!' exclaimed Lord Lambeth.

'I disagree,' said Beaumont, stroking down his black hair, 'even to the point of not thinking it delightful.'

'Oh, I say!' cried Lord Lambeth again.

'I don't see anything delightful in my disagreeing with Mrs Westgate,' said Percy Beaumont.

'Well, I do!' Mrs Westgate declared; and she turned to her sister. 'You know you have to go to town. The phaeton is there. You had better take Lord Lambeth.'

At this point Percy Beaumont certainly looked straight at his kinsman; he tried to catch his eye. But Lord Lambeth would not look at him; his own eyes were better occupied. 'I shall be very happy,' cried Bessie Alden. 'I am only going to some shops. But I will drive you about and show you the place.'

'An American woman who respects herself,' said Mrs Westgate, turning to Beaumont with her bright expository air, 'must buy something every day of her life. If she cannot do it herself, she must send out some member of her family for the purpose. So Bessie goes forth to fulfil my mission.'

The young girl had walked away, with Lord Lambeth by her side, to whom she was talking still; and Percy Beaumont watched them as they passed towards the house. 'She fulfils her own mission,' he presently said; 'that of being a very attractive young lady.'

'I don't know that I should say very attractive,' Mrs Westgate rejoined. 'She is not so much that as she is charming when you really know her. She is very shy.'

'Oh indeed?' said Percy Beaumont.

'Extremely shy,' Mrs Westgate repeated. 'But she is a dear good girl; she is a charming species of girl. She is not in the least a flirt; that isn't at all her line; she doesn't know the alphabet of that sort of thing. She is very simple – very serious. She has lived a great deal in Boston, with another sister of mine – the eldest of us – who married a Bostonian. She is very cultivated, not at all like me – I am not in the least cultivated. She has studied immensely and read everything; she is what they call in Boston "thoughtful".'

'A rum sort of girl for Lambeth to get hold of!' his lordship's kinsman privately reflected.

'I really believe,' Mrs Westgate continued, 'that the most charming girl in the world is a Boston superstructure upon a New York *fonds*; or perhaps a New York superstructure upon a Boston *fonds*. At any rate it's the mixture,' said Mrs Westgate, who continued to give Percy Beaumont a great deal of information.

Lord Lambeth got into a little basket-phaeton with Bessie Alden, and she drove the long avenue,[43] whose extent he had measured on foot a couple of hours before, into the ancient town, as it was called in that part of the world, of Newport. The ancient town was a curious affair – a collection of fresh-looking little wooden houses, painted white, scattered over a hill-side and clustered about a long, straight street, paved with enormous cobble-stones. There were plenty of shops – a large proportion of which appeared to be those of fruit-vendors, with piles of huge water-melons and pumpkins stacked in front of them; and, drawn up before the shops, or bumping about on the cobble-stones, were innumerable other basket-phaetons freighted with ladies of high fashion, who greeted each other from vehicle to vehicle and conversed on the edge of the pavement in a manner that struck Lord Lambeth as demonstrative – with a great many 'Oh, my dears', and little quick exclamations and caresses. His companion went into seventeen shops – he amused himself with counting them – and accumulated, at the bottom of the phaeton, a pile of bundles that hardly left the young Englishman a place for his feet. As she had no groom nor footman, he sat in the phaeton to hold the ponies; where, although he was not a particularly acute observer, he saw much to entertain him – especially the ladies just mentioned, who wandered up and down with the appearance of a kind of aimless intentness, as if they were looking for something to buy, and if they were tripping in and out of their vehicles, displayed remarkably pretty feet. It all seemed to Lord Lambeth very odd, and bright, and gay. Of course, before they got back to the villa, he had had a great deal of desultory conversation with Bessie Alden.

The young Englishmen spent the whole of that day and the whole of many successive days in what the French call the *intimité* of their new friends. They agreed that it was extremely jolly – that they had never known anything more agreeable. It is not proposed to narrate minutely the incidents of their sojourn on this charming shore; though if it were convenient I might present a record of impressions none the less delectable that they were not exhaustively analysed. Many of them still linger in the minds of our travellers, attended by a train of harmonious images – images of brilliant mornings on lawns and piazzas that overlooked the sea; of innumerable pretty girls; of infinite lounging and talking and laughing and flirting and lunching and dining; of universal friendliness and frankness; of occasions on which they knew every one and everything and had an extraordinary sense of ease; of drives and rides in the late afternoon, over gleaming beaches, on long sea-roads, beneath a sky lighted up by marvellous sunsets; of tea-tables, on the return, informal, irregular, agreeable; of evenings at open windows or on the perpetual verandahs, in the summer starlight, above the warm Atlantic. The young Englishmen were introduced to everybody, entertained by everybody, intimate with everybody. At the end of three days they had removed their luggage from the hotel, and had gone to stay with Mrs Westgate – a step to which Percy Beaumont at first offered some conscientious opposition. I call his opposition conscientious because it was founded upon some talk that he had had, on the second day, with Bessie Alden. He had indeed had a good deal of talk with her, for she was not literally always in conversation with Lord Lambeth. He had meditated upon Mrs Westgate's account of her sister and he discovered, for himself, that the young lady was clever and appeared to have read a great deal. She seemed very nice, though he could not make out that, as Mrs Westgate had said, she was shy. If she was shy she carried it off very well.

'Mr Beaumont,' she had said, 'please tell me something about Lord Lambeth's family. How would you say it in England? – his position.'

'His position?' Percy Beaumont repeated.

'His rank – or whatever you call it. Unfortunately we haven't got a "Peerage", like the people in Thackeray.'[44]

'That's a great pity,' said Beaumont. 'You would find it all set forth there so much better than I can do it.'

'He is a great noble, then?'

'Oh yes, he is a great noble.'

'Is he a peer?'[45]

'Almost.'

'And has he any other title than Lord Lambeth?'

'His title is the Marquis of Lambeth,' said Beaumont; and then he was silent; Bessie Alden appeared to be looking at him with interest. 'He is the son of the Duke of Bayswater,' he added, presently.

'The eldest son?'

'The only son.'

'And are his parents living?'

'Oh yes; if his father were not living he would be a duke.'

'So that when his father dies,' pursued Bessie Alden, with more simplicity than might have been expected in a clever girl, 'he will become Duke of Bayswater?'

'Of course,' said Percy Beaumont. 'But his father is in excellent health.'

'And his mother?'

Beaumont smiled a little. 'The Duchess is uncommonly robust.'

'And has he any sisters?'

'Yes, there are two.'

'And what are they called?'

'One of them is married. She is the Countess of Pimlico.'[46]

'And the other?'

'The other is unmarried; she is plain Lady Julia.'

Bessie Alden looked at him a moment. 'Is she very plain?'

Beaumont began to laugh again. 'You would not find her so handsome as her brother,' he said; and it was after this that he attempted to dissuade the heir of the Duke of Bayswater from accepting Mrs Westgate's invitation. 'Depend upon it,' he said, 'that girl means to try for you.'

'It seems to me you are doing your best to make a fool of me,' the modest young nobleman answered.

'She has been asking me,' said Beaumont, 'all about your people and your possessions.'

'I am sure it is very good of her!' Lord Lambeth rejoined.

'Well, then,' observed his companion, 'if you go, you go with your eyes open.'

'Damn my eyes!' exclaimed Lord Lambeth. 'If one is to be a dozen times a day in the house, it is a great deal more convenient to sleep there. I am sick of travelling up and down this beastly Avenue.'

Since he had determined to go, Percy Beaumont would of course have been very sorry to allow him to go alone; he was a man of conscience, and he remembered his promise to the Duchess. It was obviously the memory of this promise that made him say to his companion a couple of days later that he rather wondered he should be so fond of that girl.

'In the first place, how do you know how fond I am of her?' asked Lord Lambeth. 'And in the second place, why shouldn't I be fond of her?'

'I shouldn't think she would be in your line.'

'What do you call my "line"? You don't set her down as "fast"?'

'Exactly so. Mrs Westgate tells me that there is no such thing as the "fast girl"[47] in America; that it's an English invention and that the term has no meaning here.'

'All the better. It's an animal I detest.'

'You prefer a blue-stocking.'[48]

'Is that what you call Miss Alden?'

'Her sister tells me,' said Percy Beaumont, 'that she is tremendously literary.'

'I don't know anything about that. She is certainly very clever.'

'Well,' said Beaumont, 'I should have supposed you would have found that sort of thing awfully slow.'

'In point of fact,' Lord Lambeth rejoined, 'I find it uncommonly lively.'

After this, Percy Beaumont held his tongue; but on August 10th he wrote to the Duchess of Bayswater. He was, as I have said, a man of conscience, and he had a strong, incorruptible sense of the proprieties of life. His kinsman, meanwhile, was having a great deal of talk with Bessie Alden – on the red sea-rocks beyond the lawn; in the course of long island rides, with a slow return in the glowing twilight; on the deep verandah, late in the evening. Lord Lambeth, who had stayed at many houses, had never stayed at a house in which it was possible for a young man to converse so frequently with a young lady. This young lady no longer applied to Percy Beaumont for information concerning his lordship. She addressed herself directly to the young nobleman. She asked him a great many questions, some of which bored him a little; for he took no pleasure in talking about himself.

'Lord Lambeth,' said Bessie Alden, 'are you an hereditary legislator?'

'Oh, I say,' cried Lord Lambeth, 'don't make me call myself such names as that.'

'But you are a member of Parliament,' said the young girl.

'I don't like the sound of that either.'

'Doesn't your father sit in the House of Lords?' Bessie Alden went on.

'Very seldom,' said Lord Lambeth.

'Is it an important position?' she asked.

'Oh dear no,' said Lord Lambeth.

'I should think it would be very grand,' said Bessie Alden, 'to possess simply by an accident of birth the right to make laws for a great nation.'

'Ah, but one doesn't make laws. It's a great humbug.'

'I don't believe that,' the young girl declared. 'It must be a great privilege, and I should think that if one thought of it in the right way – from a high point of view – it would be very inspiring.'

'The less one thinks of it the better,' Lord Lambeth affirmed.

'I think it's tremendous,' said Bessie Alden; and on another occasion she asked him if he had any tenantry. Hereupon it was that, as I have said, he was a little bored.

'Do you want to buy up their leases?' he asked.

'Well – have you got any livings?'⁴⁹ she demanded.

'Oh, I say!' he cried. 'Have you got a clergyman that is looking out?' But she made him tell her that he had a Castle; he confessed to but one. It was the place in which he had been born and brought up, and, as he had an old-time liking for it, he was beguiled into describing it a little and saying it was really very jolly. Bessie Alden listened with great interest, and declared that she would give the world to see such a place. Whereupon – 'It would be awfully kind of you to come and stay there,' said Lord Lambeth. He took a vague satisfaction in the circumstance that Percy Beaumont had not heard him make the remark I have just recorded.

Mr Westgate, all this time, had not, as they said at Newport, 'come on'. His wife more than once announced that she expected him on the morrow; but on the morrow she wandered about a little, with a telegram in her jewelled fingers, declaring it was very tiresome that his business detained him in New York; that he could only hope the Englishmen were having a good time. 'I must say,' said Mrs Westgate, 'that it is no thanks to him if you are!' And she went on to explain, while she continued that slow-paced promenade which enabled her well-adjusted skirts to display themselves so advantageously, that unfortunately in America there was no leisure-class. It was Lord Lambeth's theory, freely propounded when the young men were together, that Percy Beaumont was having a very good time with Mrs Westgate, and that under the pretext of meeting for the purpose of animated discussion, they were indulging in practices that imparted a shade of hypocrisy to the lady's regret for her husband's absence.

'I assure you we are always discussing and differing,' said Percy Beaumont. 'She is awfully argumentative. American ladies certainly don't mind contradicting you. Upon my word I don't think I was ever treated so by a woman before. She's so devilish positive.'

Mrs Westgate's positive quality, however, evidently had its attractions; for Beaumont was constantly at his hostess's side. He detached himself one day to the extent of going to New York to talk over the Tennessee Central with Mr Westgate; but he was absent only forty-eight hours, during which, with Mr Westgate's assistance, he completely settled this piece of business. 'They certainly do things quickly in New York,' he observed to his cousin; and he added that Mr Westgate had seemed very uneasy lest his wife should miss her visitor – he had been in such an awful hurry to send him back to her. 'I'm afraid you'll never come up to an American husband – if that's what the wives expect,' he said to Lord Lambeth.

Mrs Westgate, however, was not to enjoy much longer the entertainment with which an indulgent husband had desired to keep her provided. On August 21st Lord Lambeth received a telegram from his mother, requesting him to return immediately to England; his father had been taken ill, and it was his filial duty to come to him.

The young Englishman was visibly annoyed. 'What the deuce does it mean?' he asked of his kinsman. 'What am I to do?'

Percy Beaumont was annoyed as well; he had deemed it his duty, as I have narrated, to write to the Duchess, but he had not expected that this distinguished woman would act so promptly upon his hint. 'It means,' he said, 'that your father is laid up. I don't suppose it's anything serious; but you have no option. Take the first steamer; but don't be alarmed.'

Lord Lambeth made his farewells; but the few last words that he exchanged with Bessie Alden are the only ones that have a place in our record. 'Of course I needn't assure you,' he said, 'that if you should come to England next year, I expect to be the first person that you inform of it.'

Bessie Alden looked at him a little and she smiled. 'Oh, if we come to London,' she answered, 'I should think you would hear of it.'

Percy Beaumont returned with his cousin, and his sense of duty compelled him, one windless afternoon, in mid-Atlantic, to say to Lord Lambeth that he suspected that the Duchess's telegram was in part the result of something he himself had written to her. 'I wrote to her – as I explicitly notified you I had promised to do – that you were extremely interested in a little American girl.'

Lord Lambeth was extremely angry, and he indulged for some moments in the simple language of resentment. But I have said that he was a reasonable young man, and I can give no better proof of it than the fact that he remarked to his companion at the end of half an hour – 'You were quite right after all. I am very much interested in her. Only, to be fair,' he added, 'you should have told my mother also that she is not – seriously – interested in me.'

Percy Beaumont gave a little laugh. 'There is nothing so charming as modesty in a young man in your position. That speech is a capital proof that you are sweet on her.'

'She is not interested – she is not!' Lord Lambeth repeated.

'My dear fellow,' said his companion, 'you are very far gone.'

IV

In point of fact, as Percy Beaumont would have said, Mrs Westgate disembarked on the 18th of May on the British coast. She was accompanied by her sister, but she was not attended by any other member of her family. To the deprivation of her husband's society Mrs Westgate was, however, habituated; she had made half-a-dozen journeys to Europe without him, and she now accounted for his absence, to interrogative friends on this side of the Atlantic, by allusion to the regrettable but conspicuous fact that in America there was no leisure-class. The two ladies came up to London and alighted at Jones's Hotel, where Mrs Westgate, who had made on former occasions the most agreeable impression at this establishment, received an obsequious greeting. Bessie Alden had felt much excited about coming to England; she had expected the 'associations'[50] would be very charming, that it would be an infinite pleasure to rest her eyes upon the things she had read about in the poets and historians. She was very fond of the poets and historians, of the picturesque,[51] of the past, of retrospect, of mementoes and reverberations of greatness; so that on coming into the great English world, where strangeness and familiarity would go hand in hand, she was prepared for a multitude of fresh emotions. They began very promptly – these tender, fluttering sensations; they began with the sight of the beautiful English landscape, whose dark richness was quickened and brightened by the season; with the carpeted fields and flowering hedge-rows, as she looked at them from the window of the train; with the spires of the rural churches, peeping above the rook-haunted tree-tops; with the oak-studded parks, the ancient homes, the cloudy light, the speech, the manners, the thousand differences. Mrs Westgate's impressions had of course much less novelty and keenness, and she gave but a wandering attention to her sister's ejaculations and rhapsodies.

'You know my enjoyment of England is not so intellectual as Bessie's,' she said to several of her friends in the course of her visit to this country. 'And yet if it is not intellectual, I can't say it is physical. I don't think I can quite say what it is, my enjoyment of England.' When once it was settled that the two ladies should come abroad and should spend a few weeks in England on their way to the Continent, they of course exchanged a good many allusions to their London acquaintance.

'It will certainly be much nicer having friends there,' Bessie Alden had said one day, as she sat on the sunny deck of the steamer, at her sister's feet, on a large blue rug.

'Whom do you mean by friends?' Mrs Westgate asked.

'All those English gentlemen whom you have known and entertained. Captain Littledale, for instance. And Lord Lambeth and Mr Beaumont,' added Bessie Alden.

'Do you expect them to give us a very grand reception?'

Bessie reflected a moment; she was addicted, as we know, to reflection. 'Well, yes.'

'My poor sweet child!' murmured her sister.

'What have I said that is so silly?' asked Bessie.

'You are a little too simple; just a little. It is very becoming, but it pleases people at your expense.'

'I am certainly too simple to understand you,' said Bessie.

'Shall I tell you a story?' asked her sister.

'If you would be so good. That is what they do to amuse simple people.'

Mrs Westgate consulted her memory, while her companion sat gazing at the shining sea. 'Did you ever hear of the Duke of Green-Erin?'[52]

'I think not,' said Bessie.

'Well, it's no matter,' her sister went on.

'It's a proof of my simplicity.'

'My story is meant to illustrate that of some other people,' said Mrs Westgate. 'The Duke of Green-Erin is what they call in England a great swell; and some five years ago he came to America. He spent most of his time in New York, and in New York he spent his days and his nights at the Butterworths'. You have heard at least of the Butterworths. *Bien*. They did everything in the world for him – they turned themselves inside out. They gave him a dozen dinner-parties and balls, and were the means of his being invited to fifty more. At first he used to come into Mrs Butterworth's box at the opera in a tweed travelling-suit; but some one stopped that. At any rate, he had a beautiful time, and they parted the best friends in the world. Two years elapse, and the Butterworths come abroad and go to London. The first thing they see in all the papers – in England those things are in the most prominent place – is that the Duke of Green-Erin has arrived in town for the Season.[53] They wait a little, and then Mr Butterworth – as polite as ever – goes and leaves a card. They wait a little more; the visit is not returned; they wait three weeks – *silence de mort* – the Duke gives no sign. The Butterworths see a lot of other people, put down the Duke of Green-Erin as a rude, ungrateful man, and forget all about him. One fine day they go to Ascot Races,[54] and there they meet him face to face. He stares a moment and then comes up to Mr Butterworth, taking something from his pocket-book – something which proves to be a bank-note. 'I'm glad to see you, Mr Butterworth,' he says, 'so that I can pay you that ten pounds I lost to you in New York. I saw the other day you remembered our bet; here are the ten pounds, Mr Butterworth. Good-bye, Mr Butterworth.' And off he goes, and that's the last they see of the Duke of Green-Erin.'

'Is that your story?' asked Bessie Alden.

'Don't you think it's interesting?' her sister replied.

'I don't believe it,' said the young girl.

'Ah!' cried Mrs Westgate, 'you are not so simple after all. Believe it or not as you please; there is no smoke without fire.'

'Is that the way,' asked Bessie after a moment, 'that you expect your friends to treat you?'

'I defy them to treat me very ill, because I shall not give them the opportunity. With the best will in the world, in that case, they can't be very disobliging.'

Bessie Alden was silent a moment. 'I don't see what makes you talk that way,' she said. 'The English are a great people.'

'Exactly; and that is just the way they have grown great – by dropping you when you have ceased to be useful. People say they are not clever; but I think they are very clever.'

'You know you have liked them – all the Englishmen you have seen,' said Bessie.

'They have liked me,' her sister rejoined; 'it would be more correct to say that. And of course one likes that.'

Bessie Alden resumed for some moments her studies in sea-green. 'Well,' she said, 'whether they like me or not, I mean to like them. And happily,' she added, 'Lord Lambeth does not owe me ten pounds.'

During the first few days after their arrival at Jones's Hotel our charming Americans were much occupied with what they would have called looking about them. They found occasion to make a large number of purchases, and their opportunities for conversation were such only as were offered by the deferential London shopmen. Bessie Alden, even in driving from the station, took an immense fancy to the British metropolis, and, at the risk of exhibiting her as a young woman of vulgar tastes, it must be recorded that for a considerable period she desired no higher pleasure than to drive about the crowded streets in a

Hansom cab.[55] To her attentive eyes they were full of a strange picturesque life, and it is at least beneath the dignity of our historic muse to enumerate the trivial objects and incidents which this simple young lady from Boston found so entertaining. It may be freely mentioned, however, that whenever, after a round of visits in Bond Street and Regent Street,[56] she was about to return with her sister to Jones's Hotel, she made an earnest request that they should be driven home by way of Westminster Abbey.[57] She had begun by asking whether it would not be possible to take the Tower[58] on the way to their lodgings; but it happened that at a more primitive stage of her culture Mrs Westgate had paid a visit to this venerable monument, which she spoke of ever afterwards, vaguely, as a dreadful disappointment; so that she expressed the liveliest disapproval of any attempt to combine historical researches with the purchase of hair-brushes and note-paper. The most she would consent to do in this line was to spend half an hour at Madame Tussaud's,[59] where she saw several dusty wax effigies of members of the Royal Family. She told Bessie that if she wished to go to the Tower she must get some one else to take her. Bessie expressed hereupon an earnest disposition to go alone; but upon this proposal as well Mrs Westgate sprinkled cold water.

'Remember,' she said, 'that you are not in your innocent little Boston. It is not a question of walking up and down Beacon Street.'[60] Then she went on to explain that there were two classes of American girls in Europe – those that walked about alone and those that did not. 'You happen to belong, my dear,' she said to her sister, 'to the class that does not.'

'It is only,' answered Bessie, laughing, 'because you happen to prevent me.' And she devoted much private meditation to this question of effecting a visit to the Tower of London.

Suddenly it seemed as if the problem might be solved; the two ladies at Jones's Hotel received a visit from Willie Woodley. Such was the social appellation of a young American who had sailed from New York a few days after their own departure, and who, having the privilege of intimacy with them in that city, had lost no time, on his arrival in London, in coming to pay them his respects. He had, in fact, gone to see them directly after going to see his tailor; than which there can be no greater exhibition of promptitude on the part of a young American who has just alighted at the Charing Cross Hotel.[61] He was a slim, pale youth, of the most amiable disposition, famous for the skill with which he led the 'German'[62] in New York. Indeed, by the young ladies who habitually figured in this fashionable frolic he was believed to be 'the best dancer in the world'; it was in these terms that he was always spoken of, and that his identity was indicated. He was the gentlest, softest young man it was possible to meet; he was beautifully dressed – 'in the English style'[63] – and he knew an immense deal about London. He had been at Newport during the previous summer, at the time of our young Englishmen's visit, and he took extreme pleasure in the society of Bessie Alden, whom he always addressed as 'Miss Bessie'. She immediately arranged with him, in the presence of her sister, that he should conduct her to the scene of Lady Jane Grey's execution.[64]

'You may do as you please,' said Mrs Westgate. 'Only – if you desire the information – it is not the custom here for young ladies to knock about London with young men.'

'Miss Bessie has waltzed with me so often,' observed Willie Woodley; 'she can surely go out with me in a Hansom.'

'I consider waltzing,' said Mrs Westgate, 'the most innocent pleasure of our time.'

'It's a compliment to our time!' exclaimed the young man, with a little laugh, in spite of himself.

'I don't see why I should regard what is done here,' said Bessie Alden. 'Why should I suffer the restrictions of a society of which I enjoy none of the privileges?'

'That's very good – very good,' murmured Willie Woodley.

'Oh, go to the Tower, and feel the axe, if you like!' said Mrs Westgate. 'I consent to your going with Mr Woodley; but I should not let you go with an Englishman.'

'Miss Bessie wouldn't care to go with an Englishman!' Mr Woodley declared, with a faint asperity that was, perhaps, not unnatural in a young man who, dressing in the manner that I have indicated, and knowing a great deal, as I have said, about

London, saw no reason for drawing these sharp distinctions. He agreed upon a day with Miss Bessie – a day of that same week.

An ingenious mind might, perhaps, trace a connection between the young girl's allusion to her destitution of social privileges and a question she asked on the morrow as she sat with her sister at lunch.

'Don't you mean to write to – to any one?' said Bessie.

'I wrote this morning to Captain Littledale,' Mrs Westgate replied.

'But Mr Woodley said that Captain Littledale had gone to India.'

'He said he thought he had heard so; he knew nothing about it.'

For a moment Bessie Alden said nothing more; then, at last, 'And don't you intend to write to – to Mr Beaumont?' she inquired.

'You mean to Lord Lambeth,' said her sister.

'I said Mr Beaumont because he was so good a friend of yours.'

Mrs Westgate looked at the young girl with sisterly candour. 'I don't care two straws for Mr Beaumont.'

'You were certainly very nice to him.'

'I am nice to every one,' said Mrs Westgate, simply.

'To every one but me,' rejoined Bessie, smiling.

Her sister continued to look at her; then, at last, 'Are you in love with Lord Lambeth?' she asked.

The young girl stared a moment, and the question was apparently too humorous even to make her blush. 'Not that I know of,' she answered.

'Because if you are,' Mrs Westgate went on, 'I shall certainly not send for him.'

'That proves what I said,' declared Bessie, smiling – 'that you are not nice to me.'

'It would be a poor service, my dear child,' said her sister.

'In what sense? There is nothing against Lord Lambeth, that I know of.'

Mrs Westgate was silent a moment. 'You *are* in love with him, then?'

Bessie stared again; but this time she blushed a little. 'Ah! if you won't be serious,' she answered, 'we will not mention him again.'

For some moments Lord Lambeth was not mentioned again, and it was Mrs Westgate who, at the end of this period, reverted to him. 'Of course I will let him know we are here; because I think he would be hurt – justly enough – if we should go away without seeing him. It is fair to give him a chance to come and thank me for the kindness we showed him. But I don't want to seem eager.'

'Neither do I,' said Bessie, with a little laugh.

'Though I confess,' added her sister, 'that I am curious to see how he will behave.'

'He behaved very well at Newport.'

'Newport is not London. At Newport he could do as he liked; but here, it is another affair. He has to have an eye to consequences.'

'If he had more freedom, then, at Newport,' argued Bessie, 'it is the more to his credit that he behaved well; and if he has to be so careful here, it is possible he will behave even better.'

'Better – better,' repeated her sister. 'My dear child, what is your point of view?'

'How do you mean – my point of view?'

'Don't you care for Lord Lambeth – a little?'

This time Bessie Alden was displeased; she slowly got up from table, turning her face away from her sister. 'You will oblige me by not talking so,' she said.

Mrs Westgate sat watching her for some moments as she moved slowly about the room and went and stood at the window. 'I will write to him this afternoon,' she said at last.

'Do as you please!' Bessie answered; and presently she turned round. 'I am not afraid to say that I like Lord Lambeth. I like him very much.'

'He is not clever,' Mrs Westgate declared.

'Well, there have been clever people whom I have disliked,' said Bessie Alden; 'so that I suppose I may like a stupid one. Besides, Lord Lambeth is not stupid.'

'Not so stupid as he looks!' exclaimed her sister, smiling.

'If I were in love with Lord Lambeth, as you said just now, it would be bad policy on your part to abuse him.'

'My dear child, don't give me lessons in policy!' cried Mrs Westgate. 'The policy I mean to follow is very deep.'

The young girl began to walk about the room again; then she stopped before her sister. 'I have never heard in the course of five minutes,' she said, 'so many hints and innuendoes. I wish you would tell me in plain English what you mean.'

'I mean that you may be much annoyed.'

'That is still only a hint,' said Bessie.

Her sister looked at her, hesitating an instant. 'It will be said of you that you have come after Lord Lambeth – that you followed him.'

Bessie Alden threw back her pretty head like a startled hind, and a look flashed into her face that made Mrs Westgate rise from her chair. 'Who says such things as that?' she demanded.

'People here.'

'I don't believe it,' said Bessie.

'You have a very convenient faculty of doubt. But my policy will be, as I say, very deep. I shall leave you to find out this kind of thing for yourself.'

Bessie fixed her eyes upon her sister, and Mrs Westgate thought for a moment there were tears in them. 'Do they talk that way here?' she asked.

'You will see. I shall leave you alone.'

'Don't leave me alone,' said Bessie Alden. 'Take me away.'

'No; I want to see what you make of it,' her sister continued.

'I don't understand.'

'You will understand after Lord Lambeth has come,' said Mrs Westgate, with a little laugh.

The two ladies had arranged that on this afternoon Willie Woodley should go with them to Hyde Park, where Bessie Alden expected to derive much entertainment from sitting on a little green chair, under the great trees, beside Rotten Row.[65] The want of a suitable escort had hitherto rendered this pleasure inaccessible; but no escort, now, for such an expedition, could have been more suitable than their devoted young countryman, whose mission in life, it might almost be said, was to find chairs for ladies, and who appeared on the stroke of half-past five with a white camellia in his button-hole.

'I have written to Lord Lambeth, my dear,' said Mrs Westgate to her sister, on coming into the room where Bessie Alden, drawing on her long grey gloves, was entertaining their visitor.

Bessie said nothing, but Willie Woodley exclaimed that his lordship was in town; he had seen his name in the *Morning Post*.[66]

'Do you read the *Morning Post?*' asked Mrs Westgate.

'Oh yes; it's great fun,' Willie Woodley affirmed.

'I want so to see it,' said Bessie, 'there is so much about it in Thackeray.'[67]

'I will send it to you every morning,' said Willie Woodley.

He found them what Bessie Alden thought excellent places, under the great trees, beside the famous avenue whose humours had been made familiar to the young girl's childhood by the pictures in *Punch*.[68] The day was bright and warm, and the crowd of riders and spectators and the great procession of carriages were proportionately dense and brilliant. The scene bore the stamp of the London Season at its height, and Bessie Alden found more entertainment in it than she was able to express to her companions. She sat silent, under her parasol, and her imagination, according to its wont, let itself loose into the great changing assemblage of striking and suggestive figures. They stirred up a host of old impressions and preconceptions, and she found herself fitting a history to this person and a theory to that, and making a place for them all in her little private museum of types. But if she said little, her sister on one side and Willie Woodley on the other expressed themselves in lively alternation.

'Look at that green dress with blue flounces,' said Mrs Westgate. '*Quelle toilette!*'

'That's the Marquis of Blackborough,' said the young man – 'the one in the white coat. I heard him speak the other night in the House of Lords; it was something about ramrods; he called them *wamwods*. He's an awful swell.'

'Did you ever see anything like the way they are pinned back?'[69] Mrs Westgate resumed. 'They never know where to stop.'

'They do nothing but stop,' said Willie Woodley. 'It prevents them from walking. Here comes a great celebrity – Lady Beatrice Bellevue. She's awfully fast; see what little steps she takes.'

'Well, my dear,' Mrs Westgate pursued, 'I hope you are getting some ideas for your *couturière*?'

'I am getting plenty of ideas,' said Bessie, 'but I don't know that my *couturière* would appreciate them.'

Willie Woodley presently perceived a friend on horseback, who drove up beside the barrier of the Row and beckoned to him. He went forward and the crowd of pedestrians closed about him, so that for some ten minutes he was hidden from sight. At last he reappeared, bringing a gentleman with him – a gentleman whom Bessie at first supposed to be his friend dismounted. But at a second glance she found herself looking at Lord Lambeth, who was shaking hands with her sister.

'I found him over there,' said Willie Woodley, 'and I told him you were here.'

And then Lord Lambeth, touching his hat a little, shook hands with Bessie. 'Fancy your being here!' he said. He was blushing and smiling; he looked very handsome, and he had a kind of splendour that he had not had in America. Bessie Alden's imagination, as we know, was just then in exercise; so that the tall young Englishman, as he stood there looking down at her, had the benefit of it. 'He is handsomer and more splendid than anything I have ever seen,' she said to herself. And then she remembered that he was a Marquis, and she thought he looked like a Marquis.

'Really, you know,' he cried, 'you ought to have let a man know you were here!'

'I wrote to you an hour ago,'[70] said Mrs Westgate.

'Doesn't all the world know it?' asked Bessie, smiling.

'I assure you I didn't know it!' cried Lord Lambeth. 'Upon my honour I hadn't heard of it. Ask Woodley now; had I, Woodley?'

'Well, I think you are rather a humbug,' said Willie Woodley.

'You don't believe that – do you, Miss Alden?' asked his lordship. 'You don't believe I'm a humbug, eh?'

'No,' said Bessie, 'I don't.'

'You are too tall to stand up, Lord Lambeth,' Mrs Westgate observed. 'You are only tolerable when you sit down. Be so good as to get a chair.'

He found a chair and placed it sidewise, close to the two ladies. 'If I hadn't met Woodley I should never have found you,' he went on. 'Should I, Woodley?'

'Well, I guess not,' said the young American.

'Not even with my letter?' asked Mrs Westgate.

'Ah, well, I haven't got your letter yet; I suppose I shall get it this evening. It was awfully kind of you to write.'

'So I said to Bessie,' observed Mrs Westgate.

'Did she say so, Miss Alden?' Lord Lambeth inquired. 'I dare say you have been here a month.'

'We have been here three,' said Mrs Westgate.

'Have you been here three months?' the young man asked again of Bessie.

'It seems a long time,' Bessie answered.

'I say, after that you had better not call me a humbug!' cried Lord Lambeth. 'I have only been in town three weeks; but you must have been hiding away. I haven't seen you anywhere.'

'Where should you have seen us – where should we have gone?' asked Mrs Westgate.

'You should have gone to Hurlingham,'[71] said Willie Woodley.

'No, let Lord Lambeth tell us,' Mrs Westgate insisted.

'There are plenty of places to go to,' said Lord Lambeth – 'each one stupider than the other. I mean people's houses; they send you cards.'

'No one has sent us cards,' said Bessie.

'We are very quiet,' her sister declared. 'We are here as travellers.'

'We have been to Madame Tussaud's,' Bessie pursued.

'Oh, I say!' cried Lord Lambeth.

'We thought we should find your image there,' said Mrs Westgate – 'yours and Mr Beaumont's.'

'In the Chamber of Horrors?' laughed the young man.

'It did duty very well for a party,' said Mrs Westgate. 'All the women were *décolletées*, and many of the figures looked as if they could speak if they tried.'

'Upon my word,' Lord Lambeth rejoined, 'you see people at London parties that look as if they couldn't speak if they tried.'

'Do you think Mr Woodley could find us Mr Beaumont?' asked Mrs Westgate.

Lord Lambeth stared and looked round him. 'I dare say he could. Beaumont often comes here. Don't you think you could find him, Woodley? Make a dive into the crowd.'

'Thank you; I have had enough diving,' said Willie Woodley. 'I will wait till Mr Beaumont comes to the surface.'

'I will bring him to see you,' said Lord Lambeth; 'where are you staying?'

'You will find the address in my letter – Jones's Hotel.'

'Oh, one of those places just out of Piccadilly?[72] Beastly hole, isn't it?' Lord Lambeth inquired.

'I believe it's the best hotel in London,' said Mrs Westgate.

'But they give you awful rubbish to eat, don't they?' his lordship went on.

'Yes,' said Mrs Westgate.

'I always feel so sorry for the people that come up to town and go to live in those places,' continued the young man. 'They eat nothing but poison.'

'Oh, I say!' cried Willie Woodley.

'Well, how do you like London, Miss Alden?' Lord Lambeth asked, unperturbed by this ejaculation.

'I think it's grand,' said Bessie Alden.

'My sister likes it, in spite of the "poison"!' Mrs Westgate exclaimed.

'I hope you are going to stay a long time.'

'As long as I can,' said Bessie.

'And where is Mr Westgate?' asked Lord Lambeth of this gentleman's wife.

'He's where he always is – in that tiresome New York.'

'He must be tremendously clever,' said the young man.

'I suppose he is,' said Mrs Westgate.

Lord Lambeth sat for nearly an hour with his American friends; but it is not our purpose to relate their conversation in full. He addressed a great many remarks to Bessie Alden, and finally turned towards her altogether, while Willie Woodley entertained Mrs Westgate. Bessie herself said very little; she was on her guard, thinking of what her sister had said to her at lunch. Little by little, however, she interested herself in Lord Lambeth again, as she had done at Newport; only it seemed to her that here he might become more interesting. He would be an unconscious part of the antiquity, the impressiveness, the picturesqueness of England; and poor Bessie Alden, like many a Yankee maiden, was terribly at the mercy of picturesqueness.

'I have often wished I were at Newport again,' said the young man. 'Those days I spent at your sister's were awfully jolly.'

'We enjoyed them very much; I hope your father is better.'

'Oh dear, yes. When I got to England, he was out grouse-shooting. It was what you call in America a gigantic fraud. My mother had got nervous. My three weeks at Newport seemed like a happy dream.'

'America certainly is very different from England,' said Bessie.

'I hope you like England better, eh?' Lord Lambeth rejoined, almost persuasively.

'No Englishman can ask that seriously of a person of another country.'

Her companion looked at her for a moment. 'You mean it's a matter of course?'

'If I were English,' said Bessie, 'it would certainly seem to me a matter of course that every one should be a good patriot.'

'Oh dear, yes; patriotism is everything,' said Lord Lambeth, not quite following, but very contented. 'Now, what are you going to do here?'

'On Thursday I am going to the Tower.'

'The Tower?'

'The Tower of London. Did you never hear of it?'

'Oh yes, I have been there,' said Lord Lambeth. 'I was taken there by my governess, when I was six years old. It's a rum idea, your going there.'

'Do give me a few more rum ideas,' said Bessie. 'I want to

see everything of that sort. I am going to Hampton Court[73] and to Windsor,[74] and to the Dulwich Gallery.'[75]

Lord Lambeth seemed greatly amused. 'I wonder you don't go to the Rosherville Gardens.'[76]

'Are they interesting?' asked Bessie.

'Oh, wonderful!'

'Are they very old? That's all I care for,' said Bessie.

'They are tremendously old; they are all falling to ruins.'

'I think there is nothing so charming as an old ruinous garden,' said the young girl. 'We must certainly go there.'

Lord Lambeth broke out into merriment. 'I say, Woodley,' he cried, 'here's Miss Alden wants to go to the Rosherville Gardens!'

Willie Woodley looked a little blank; he was caught in the fact of ignorance of an apparently conspicuous feature of London life. But in a moment he turned it off. 'Very well,' he said, 'I'll write for a permit.'

Lord Lambeth's exhilaration increased. 'Gad, I believe you Americans would go anywhere!' he cried.

'We wish to go to Parliament,' said Bessie. 'That's one of the first things.'

'Oh, it would bore you to death!' cried the young man.

'We wish to hear you speak.'

'I never speak[77] – except to young ladies,' said Lord Lambeth, smiling.

Bessie Alden looked at him awhile; smiling, too, in the shadow of her parasol. 'You are very strange,' she murmured. 'I don't think I approve of you.'

'Ah, now, don't be severe, Miss Alden!' said Lord Lambeth, smiling still more. 'Please don't be severe. I want you to like me – awfully.'

'To like you awfully? You must not laugh at me, then, when I make mistakes. I consider it my right – as a free-born American – to make as many mistakes as I choose.'

'Upon my word, I didn't laugh at you,' said Lord Lambeth.

'And not only that,' Bessie went on; 'but I hold that all my mistakes shall be set down to my credit. You must think the better of me for them.'

'I can't think better of you than I do,' the young man declared.

Bessie Alden looked at him a moment again. 'You certainly speak very well to young ladies. But why don't you address the House? – isn't that what they call it?'

'Because I have nothing to say,' said Lord Lambeth.

'Haven't you a great position?' asked Bessie Alden.

He looked a moment at the back of his glove. 'I'll set that down,' he said, 'as one of your mistakes – to your credit.' And, as if he disliked talking about his position, he changed the subject. 'I wish you would let me go with you to the Tower, and to Hampton Court, and to all those other places.'

'We shall be most happy,' said Bessie.

'And of course I shall be delighted to show you the Houses of Parliament – some day that suits you. There are a lot of things I want to do for you. I want you to have a good time. And I should like very much to present some of my friends to you, if it wouldn't bore you. Then it would be awfully kind of you to come down to Branches.'

'We are much obliged to you, Lord Lambeth,' said Bessie. 'What is Branches?'

'It's a house in the country. I think you might like it.'

Willie Woodley and Mrs Westgate, at this moment, were sitting in silence, and the young man's ear caught these last words of Lord Lambeth's. 'He's inviting Miss Bessie to one of his castles,' he murmured to his companion.

Mrs Westgate, foreseeing what she mentally called 'complications', immediately got up; and the two ladies, taking leave of Lord Lambeth, returned, under Mr Woodley's conduct, to Jones's Hotel.

V

Lord Lambeth came to see them on the morrow, bringing Percy Beaumont with him – the latter having instantly declared his intention of neglecting none of the usual offices of civility. This declaration, however, when his kinsman informed him of the advent of their American friends, had been preceded by another remark.

'Here they are, then, and you are in for it.'

'What am I in for?' demanded Lord Lambeth.

'I will let your mother give it a name. With all respect to whom,' added Percy Beaumont, 'I must decline on this occasion to do any more police duty. Her Grace must look after you herself.'

'I will give her a chance,' said her Grace's son, a trifle grimly. 'I shall make her go and see them.'

'She won't do it, my boy.'

'We'll see if she doesn't,' said Lord Lambeth.

But if Percy Beaumont took a sombre view of the arrival of the two ladies at Jones's Hotel, he was sufficiently a man of the world to offer them a smiling countenance. He fell into animated conversation – conversation, at least, that was animated on her side – with Mrs Westgate, while his companion made himself agreeable to the younger lady. Mrs Westgate began confessing and protesting, declaring and expounding.

'I must say London is a great deal brighter and prettier just now than it was when I was here last – in the month of November. There is evidently a great deal going on, and you seem to have a good many flowers. I have no doubt it is very charming for all you people, and that you amuse yourselves immensely. It is very good of you to let Bessie and me come and sit and look at you. I suppose you will think I am very satirical, but I must confess that that's the feeling I have in London.'

'I am afraid I don't quite understand to what feeling you allude,' said Percy Beaumont.

'The feeling that it's all very well for you English people. Everything is beautifully arranged for you.'

'It seems to me it is very well for some Americans, sometimes,' rejoined Beaumont.

'For some of them, yes – if they like to be patronized. But I must say I don't like to be patronized. I may be very eccentric and undisciplined and unreasonable; but I confess I never was fond of patronage. I like to associate with people on the same terms as I do in my own country; that's a peculiar taste that I have. But here people seem to expect something else – Heaven knows what! I am afraid you will think I am very ungrateful, for I certainly have received a great deal of attention. The last time I was here, a lady sent me a message that I was at liberty to come and see her.'

'Dear me, I hope you didn't go,' observed Percy Beaumont.

'You are deliciously *naïf*, I must say that for you!' Mrs Westgate exclaimed. 'It must be a great advantage to you here in London. I suppose that if I myself had a little more *naïveté*, I should enjoy it more. I should be content to sit on a chair in the Park, and see the people pass, and be told that this is the Duchess of Suffolk, and that is the Lord Chamberlain,[78] and that I must be thankful for the privilege of beholding them. I dare say it is very wicked and critical of me to ask for anything else. But I was always critical, and I freely confess to the sin of being fastidious. I am told there is some remarkably superior second-rate society provided here for strangers. *Merci!* I don't want any superior second-rate society. I want the society that I have been accustomed to.'

'I hope you don't call Lambeth and me second-rate,' Beaumont interposed.

'Oh, I am accustomed to you!' said Mrs Westgate. 'Do you know that you English sometimes make the most wonderful speeches? The first time I came to London, I went out to dine – as I told you, I have received a great deal of attention. After dinner, in the drawing-room, I had some conversation with an old lady; I assure you I had. I forget what we talked about; but she presently said, in allusion to something we were discussing, "Oh, you know, the aristocracy do so-and-so; but in one's own class of life it is very different." In one's own class of life! What is a poor unprotected American woman to do in a country where she is liable to have that sort of thing said to her?'

'You seem to get hold of some very queer old ladies; I compliment you on your acquaintance!' Percy Beaumont exclaimed. 'If you are trying to bring me to admit that London is an odious place, you'll not succeed. I'm extremely fond of it, and I think it the jolliest place in the world.'

'*Pour vous autres*. I never said the contrary,' Mrs Westgate retorted. I make use of this expression because both interlocutors had begun to raise their voices. Percy Beaumont naturally did not like to hear his country abused, and Mrs Westgate, no less naturally, did not like a stubborn debater.

'Hallo!' said Lord Lambeth; 'what are they up to now?' And he came away from the window, where he had been standing with Bessie Alden.

'I quite agree with a very clever countrywoman of mine,' Mrs Westgate continued, with charming ardour, though with imperfect relevancy. She smiled at the two gentlemen for a moment with terrible brightness, as if to toss at their feet – upon their native heath – the gauntlet of defiance. 'For me, there are only two social positions worth speaking of – that of an American lady and that of the Emperor of Russia.'[79]

'And what do you do with the American gentlemen?' asked Lord Lambeth.

'She leaves them in America!' said Percy Beaumont.

On the departure of their visitors, Bessie Alden told her sister that Lord Lambeth would come the next day, to go with them to the Tower, and that he had kindly offered to bring his 'trap',[80] and drive them thither. Mrs Westgate listened in silence to this communication, and for some time afterwards she said nothing. But at last, 'If you had not requested me the other day not to mention it,' she began, 'there is something I should venture to ask you.' Bessie frowned a little; her dark blue eyes were more dark than blue. But her sister went on. 'As it is, I will take the risk. You are not in love with Lord Lambeth: I believe it, perfectly. Very good. But is there, by chance, any danger of your becoming so? It's a very simple question; don't take offence. I have a particular reason,' said Mrs Westgate, 'for wanting to know.'

Bessie Alden for some moments said nothing; she only looked displeased. 'No; there is no danger,' she answered at last, curtly.

'Then I should like to frighten them,' declared Mrs Westgate, clasping her jewelled hands.

'To frighten whom?'

'All these people; Lord Lambeth's family and friends.'

'How should you frighten them?' asked the young girl.

'It wouldn't be I – it would be you. It would frighten them to think that you should absorb his lordship's young affections.'

Bessie Alden, with her clear eyes still overshadowed by her dark brows, continued to interrogate. 'Why should that frighten them?'

Mrs Westgate poised her answer with a smile before delivering it. 'Because they think you are not good enough. You are a charming girl, beautiful and amiable, intelligent and clever, and as *bien-élevée* as it is possible to be; but you are not a fit match for Lord Lambeth.'

Bessie Alden was immensely disgusted. 'Where do you get such extraordinary ideas?' she asked. 'You have said some such strange things lately. My dear Kitty, where do you collect them?'

Kitty was evidently enamoured of her idea. 'Yes, it would put them on pins and needles, and it wouldn't hurt you. Mr Beaumont is already most uneasy; I could soon see that.'

The young girl meditated a moment. 'Do you mean that they spy upon him – that they interfere with him?'

'I don't know what power they have to interfere, but I know that a British mamma may worry her son's life out.'

It has been intimated that, as regards certain disagreeable things, Bessie Alden had a fund of scepticism. She abstained on the present occasion from expressing disbelief, for she wished not to irritate her sister. But she said to herself that Kitty had been misinformed – that this was a traveller's tale. Though she was a girl of a lively imagination, there could in the nature of things be, to her sense, no reality in the idea of her belonging to a vulgar category. What she said aloud was – 'I must say that in that case I am very sorry for Lord Lambeth.'

Mrs Westgate, more and more exhilarated by her scheme, was smiling at her again. 'If I could only believe it was safe!' she exclaimed. 'When you begin to pity him, I, on my side, am afraid.'

'Afraid of what?'

'Of your pitying him too much.'

Bessie Alden turned away impatiently; but at the end of a minute she turned back. 'What if I should pity him too much?' she asked.

Mrs Westgate hereupon turned away, but after a moment's reflection she also faced her sister again. 'It would come, after all, to the same thing,' she said.

Lord Lambeth came the next day with his trap, and the two ladies, attended by Willie Woodley, placed themselves under his guidance and were conveyed eastward, through some of the duskier portions of the metropolis, to the great turreted donjon[81] which overlooks the London shipping. They all descended from their vehicle and entered the famous enclosure; and they secured the services of a venerable beefeater,[82] who, though there were many other claimants for legendary information, made a fine exclusive party of them and marched them through courts and corridors, through armouries and prisons. He delivered his usual peripatetic discourse, and they stopped and stared, and peeped and stooped, according to the official admonitions. Bessie Alden asked the old man in the crimson doublet[83] a great many questions; she thought it a most fascinating place. Lord Lambeth was in high good-humour; he was constantly laughing; he enjoyed what he would have called the lark. Willie Woodley kept looking at the ceilings and tapping the walls with the knuckle of a pearl-grey glove; and Mrs Westgate, asking at frequent intervals to be allowed to sit down and wait till they came back, was as frequently informed that they would never come back. To a great many of Bessie's questions – chiefly on collateral points of English history – the ancient warder was naturally unable to reply; whereupon she always appealed to Lord Lambeth. But his lordship was very ignorant. He declared that he knew nothing about that sort of thing, and he seemed greatly diverted at being treated as an authority.

'You can't expect every one to know as much as you,' he said.

'I should expect you to know a great deal more,' declared Bessie Alden.

'Women always know more than men about names and

dates, and that sort of thing,' Lord Lambeth rejoined. 'There was Lady Jane Grey we have just been hearing about, who went in for Latin and Greek and all the learning of her age.'

'*You* have no right to be ignorant, at all events,' said Bessie.

'Why haven't I as good a right as any one else?'

'Because you have lived in the midst of all these things.'

'What things do you mean? Axes and blocks and thumbscrews?'

'All these historical things. You belong to an historical family.'

'Bessie is really too historical,' said Mrs Westgate, catching a word of this dialogue.

'Yes, you are too historical,' said Lord Lambeth, laughing, but thankful for a formula. 'Upon my honour, you are too historical!'

He went with the ladies a couple of days later to Hampton Court, Willie Woodley being also of the party. The afternoon was charming, the famous horse-chestnuts were in blossom, and Lord Lambeth, who quite entered into the spirit of the cockney excursionist,[84] declared that it was a jolly old place. Bessie Alden was in ecstasies; she went about murmuring and exclaiming.

'It's too lovely,' said the young girl, 'it's too enchanting; it's too exactly what it ought to be!'

At Hampton Court the little flocks of visitors are not provided with an official bellwether, but are left to browse at discretion upon the local antiquities. It happened in this manner that, in default of another informant, Bessie Alden, who on doubtful questions was able to suggest a great many alternatives, found herself again applying for intellectual assistance to Lord Lambeth. But he again assured her that he was utterly helpless in such matters – that his education had been sadly neglected.

'And I am sorry it makes you unhappy,' he added in a moment.

'You are very disappointing, Lord Lambeth,' she said.

'Ah, now, don't say that!' he cried. 'That's the worst thing you could possibly say.'

'No,' she rejoined; 'it is not so bad as to say that I had expected nothing of you.'

'I don't know. Give me a notion of the sort of thing you expected.'

'Well,' said Bessie Alden, 'that you would be more what I should like to be – what I should try to be – in your place.'

'Ah, my place!' exclaimed Lord Lambeth; 'you are always talking about my place.'

The young girl looked at him; he thought she coloured a little; and for a moment she made no rejoinder.

'Does it strike you that I am always talking about your place?' she asked.

'I am sure you do it a great honour,' he said, fearing he had been uncivil.

'I have often thought about it,' she went on after a moment. 'I have often thought about your being an hereditary legislator. An hereditary legislator ought to know a great many things.'

'Not if he doesn't legislate.'

'But you will legislate; it's absurd your saying you won't. You are very much looked up to here – I am assured of that.'

'I don't know that I ever noticed it.'

'It is because you are used to it, then. You ought to fill the place.'

'How do you mean, to fill it?' asked Lord Lambeth.

'You ought to be very clever and brilliant, and to know almost everything.'

Lord Lambeth looked at her a moment. 'Shall I tell you something?' he asked. 'A young man in my position, as you call it—'

'I didn't invent the term,' interposed Bessie Alden. 'I have seen it in a great many books.'

'Hang it, you are always at your books! A fellow in my position, then, does very well, whatever he does. That's about what I mean to say.'

'Well, if your own people are content with you,' said Bessie

Alden, laughing, 'it is not for me to complain. But I shall always think that, properly, you should have a great mind – a great character.'

'Ah, that's very theoretic!' Lord Lambeth declared. 'Depend upon it, that's a Yankee prejudice.'

'Happy the country,'[85] said Bessie Alden, 'where even people's prejudices are so elevated!'

'Well, after all,' observed Lord Lambeth, 'I don't know that I am such a fool as you are trying to make me out.'

'I said nothing so rude as that; but I must repeat that you are disappointing.'

'My dear Miss Alden,' exclaimed the young man, 'I am the best fellow in the world!'

'Ah, if it were not for that!' said Bessie Alden, with a smile.

Mrs Westgate had a good many more friends in London than she pretended, and before long she had renewed acquaintance with most of them. Their hospitality was extreme, so that, one thing leading to another, she began, as the phrase is, to go out. Bessie Alden, in this way, saw something of what she found it a great satisfaction to call to herself English society. She went to balls and danced, she went to dinners and talked, she went to concerts and listened (at concerts Bessie always listened), she went to exhibitions and wondered. Her enjoyment was keen and her curiosity insatiable, and, grateful in general for all her opportunities, she especially prized the privilege of meeting certain celebrated persons – authors and artists, philosophers and statesmen – of whose renown she had been a humble and distant beholder, and who now, as a part of the habitual furniture of London drawing-rooms, struck her as stars fallen from the firmament and become palpable – revealing also, sometimes, on contact, qualities not to have been predicted of bodies sidereal. Bessie, who knew so many of her contemporaries by reputation, had a good many personal disappointments; but, on the other hand, she had innumerable satisfactions and enthusiasms, and she communicated the emotions of either class to a dear friend, of her own sex, in Boston, with whom she was in voluminous correspondence. Some of her reflections, indeed, she attempted to impart to

Lord Lambeth, who came almost every day to Jones's Hotel, and whom Mrs Westgate admitted to be really devoted. Captain Littledale, it appeared, had gone to India; and of several others of Mrs Westgate's ex-pensioners[86] – gentlemen who, as she said, had made, in New York, a club-house of her drawing-room – no tidings were to be obtained; but Lord Lambeth was certainly attentive enough to make up for the accidental absences, the short memories, all the other irregularities, of every one else. He drove them in the Park, he took them to visit private collections of pictures, and having a house of his own, invited them to dinner. Mrs Westgate, following the fashion of many of her compatriots, caused herself and her sister to be presented at the English Court by her diplomatic representative – for it was in this manner that she alluded to the American Minister[87] to England, inquiring what on earth he was put there for, if not to make the proper arrangements for one's going to a Drawing Room.[88]

Lord Lambeth declared that he hated Drawing Rooms, but he participated in the ceremony on the day on which the two ladies at Jones's Hotel repaired to Buckingham Palace[89] in a remarkable coach which his lordship had sent to fetch them. He had on a gorgeous uniform,[90] and Bessie Alden was particularly struck with his appearance – especially when on her asking him, rather foolishly as she felt, if he were a loyal subject, he replied that he was a loyal subject to *her*. This declaration was emphasized by his dancing with her at a royal ball to which the two ladies afterwards went, and was not impaired by the fact that she thought he danced very ill. He seemed to her wonderfully kind; she asked herself, with growing vivacity, why he should be so kind. It was his disposition – that seemed the natural answer. She had told her sister that she liked him very much, and now that she liked him more she wondered why. She liked him for his disposition; to this question as well that seemed the natural answer. When once the impressions of London life began to crowd thickly upon her she completely forgot her sister's warning about the cynicism of public opinion. It had given her great pain at the moment; but there was no particular reason why she should remember it; it corresponded too little with any sensible reality; and it was disagreeable to Bessie to remember disagreeable things. So she was not haunted with the sense of a vulgar imputation. She was not in love with Lord Lambeth – she assured herself of that. It will immediately be observed that when such assurances become necessary the state of a young lady's affections is already ambiguous; and indeed Bessie Alden made no attempt to dissimulate – to herself, of course – a certain tenderness that she felt for the young nobleman. She said to herself that she liked the type to which he belonged – the simple, candid, manly, healthy English temperament. She spoke to herself of him as women speak of young men they like – alluded to his bravery (which she had never in the least seen tested), to his honesty and gentlemanliness; and was not silent upon the subject of his good looks. She was perfectly conscious, moreover, that she liked to think of his more adventitious merits – that her imagination was excited and gratified by the sight of a handsome young man endowed with such large opportunities – opportunities she hardly knew for what, but, as she supposed, for doing great things – for setting an example, for exerting an influence, for conferring happiness, for encouraging the arts. She had a kind of ideal of conduct for a young man who should find himself in this magnificent position, and she tried to adapt it to Lord Lambeth's deportment, as you might attempt to fit a silhouette in cut paper upon a shadow projected upon a wall. But Bessie Alden's silhouette refused to coincide with his lordship's image; and this want of harmony sometimes vexed her more than she thought reasonable. When he was absent it was of course less striking – then he seemed to her a sufficiently graceful combination of high responsibilities and amiable qualities. But when he sat there within sight, laughing and talking with his customary good humour and simplicity, she measured it more accurately, and she felt acutely that if Lord Lambeth's position was heroic, there was but little of the hero in the young man himself. Then her imagination wandered away from him – very far away; for it was an incontestable fact that at such moments he seemed distinctly dull. I am afraid that while Bessie's imagination was thus invidiously roaming, she cannot have been herself a very lively companion; but it may well have been that these occasional fits of indifference seemed to Lord Lambeth a part of the young girl's personal charm. It had been a part of this charm from the first that he felt that she judged him and measured him more freely and irresponsibly – more at her ease and her leisure, as it were – than several young ladies with whom he had been on the whole about as intimate. To feel this, and yet to feel that she also liked him, was very agreeable to Lord Lambeth. He fancied he had compassed that gratification so desirable to young men of title and fortune – being liked for himself. It is true that a cynical counsellor might have whispered to him, 'Liked for yourself? Yes; but not so very much!' He had, at any rate, the constant hope of being liked more.

It may seem, perhaps, a trifle singular – but it is nevertheless true – that Bessie Alden, when he struck her as dull, devoted some time, on grounds of conscience, to trying to like him more. I say on grounds of conscience, because she felt that he had been extremely 'nice' to her sister, and because she reflected that it was no more than fair that she should think as well of him as he thought of her. This effort was possibly sometimes not so successful as it might have been, for the result of it was occasionally a vague irritation, which expressed itself in hostile criticism of several British institutions. Bessie Alden went to some entertainments at which she met Lord Lambeth; but she went to others at which his lordship was neither actually nor potentially present; and it was chiefly on these latter occasions that she encountered those literary and artistic celebrities of whom mention has been made. After a while she reduced the matter to a principle. If Lord Lambeth should appear anywhere, it was a symbol that there would be no poets and philosophers; and in consequence – for it was almost a strict consequence – she used to enumerate to the young man these objects of her admiration.

'You seem to be awfully fond of that sort of people,' said Lord Lambeth one day, as if the idea had just occurred to him.

'They are the people in England I am most curious to see,' Bessie Alden replied.

'I suppose that's because you have read so much,' said Lord Lambeth, gallantly.

'I have not read so much. It is because we think so much of them at home.'

'Oh, I see!' observed the young nobleman. 'In Boston.'

'Not only in Boston; everywhere,' said Bessie. 'We hold them in great honour; they go to the best dinner-parties.'

'I dare say you are right. I can't say I know many of them.'

'It's a pity you don't,' Bessie Alden declared. 'It would do you good.'

'I dare say it would,' said Lord Lambeth, very humbly. 'But I must say I don't like the looks of some of them.'

'Neither do I – of some of them. But there are all kinds, and many of them are charming.'

'I have talked with two or three of them,' the young man went on, 'and I thought they had a kind of fawning manner.'

'Why should they fawn?' Bessie Alden demanded.

'I'm sure I don't know. Why, indeed?'

'Perhaps you only thought so,' said Bessie.

'Well, of course,' rejoined her companion, 'that's a kind of thing that can't be proved.'

'In America they don't fawn,' said Bessie.

'Ah! well, then, they must be better company.'

Bessie was silent a moment. 'That is one of the things I don't like about England,' she said; 'your keeping the distinguished people apart.'

'How do you mean, apart?'

'Why, letting them come only to certain places. You never see them.'

Lord Lambeth looked at her a moment. 'What people do you mean?'

'The eminent people – the authors and artists – the clever people.'

'Oh, there are other eminent people besides those!' said Lord Lambeth.

'Well, you certainly keep them apart,' repeated the young girl.

'And there are other clever people,' added Lord Lambeth, simply.

Bessie Alden looked at him, and she gave a light laugh. 'Not many,' she said.

On another occasion – just after a dinner-party – she told him that there was something else in England she did not like.

'Oh, I say!' he cried; 'haven't you abused us enough?'

'I have never abused you at all,' said Bessie; 'but I don't like your *precedence*.'[91]

'It isn't my precedence!' Lord Lambeth declared, laughing.

'Yes, it is yours – just exactly yours; and I think it's odious,' said Bessie.

'I never saw such a young lady for discussing things! Has some one had the impudence to go before you?' asked his lordship.

'It is not the going before me that I object to,' said Bessie; 'it is their thinking that they have a right to do it – a right that I should recognize.'

'I never saw such a young lady as you are for not "recogniz-ing". I have no doubt the thing is beastly, but it saves a lot of trouble.'

'It makes a lot of trouble. It's horrid!' said Bessie.

'But how would you have the first people go?' asked Lord Lambeth. 'They can't go last.'

'Whom do you mean by the first people?'

'Ah, if you mean to question first principles!' said Lord Lambeth.

'If those are your first principles, no wonder some of your arrangements are horrid,' observed Bessie Alden, with a very pretty ferocity. 'I am a young girl, so of course I go last; but imagine what Kitty must feel on being informed that she is not at liberty to budge until certain other ladies have passed out!'

'Oh, I say, she is not "informed"!' cried Lord Lambeth. 'No one would do such a thing as that.'

'She is made to feel it,' the young girl insisted – 'as if they were afraid she would make a rush for the door. No, you have a lovely country,' said Bessie Alden, 'but your precedence is horrid.'

'I certainly shouldn't think your sister would like it,' rejoined Lord Lambeth, with even exaggerated gravity. But Bessie

Alden could induce him to enter no formal protest against this repulsive custom, which he seemed to think an extreme convenience.

VI

Percy Beaumont all this time had been a very much less frequent visitor at Jones's Hotel than his noble kinsman; he had in fact called but twice upon the two American ladies. Lord Lambeth, who often saw him, reproached him with his neglect, and declared that although Mrs Westgate had said nothing about it, he was sure that she was secretly wounded by it. 'She suffers too much to speak,' said Lord Lambeth.

'That's all gammon,'[92] said Percy Beaumont; 'there's a limit to what people can suffer!' And, though sending no apologies to Jones's Hotel, he undertook in a manner to explain his absence. 'You are always there,' he said; 'and that's reason enough for my not going.'

'I don't see why. There is enough for both of us.'

'I don't care to be a witness of your – your reckless passion,' said Percy Beaumont.

Lord Lambeth looked at him with a cold eye, and for a moment said nothing. 'It's not so obvious as you might suppose,' he rejoined, dryly, 'considering what a demonstrative beggar I am.'

'I don't want to know anything about it – nothing whatever,' said Beaumont. 'Your mother asks me every time she sees me whether I believe you are really lost – and Lady Pimlico does the same. I prefer to be able to answer that I know nothing about it – that I never go there. I stay away for consistency's sake. As I said the other day, they must look after you themselves.'

'You are devilish considerate,' said Lord Lambeth. 'They never question me.'

'They are afraid of you. They are afraid of irritating you and making you worse. So they go to work very cautiously, and, somewhere or other, they get their information. They know a great deal about you. They know that you have been with those ladies to the dome of St Paul's[93] and – where was the other place? – to the Thames Tunnel.'[94]

'If all their knowledge is as accurate as that, it must be very valuable,' said Lord Lambeth.

'Well, at any rate, they know that you have been visiting the "sights of the metropolis". They think – very naturally, as it seems to me – that when you take to visiting the sights of the metropolis with a little American girl, there is serious cause for alarm.' Lord Lambeth responded to this intimation by scornful laughter, and his companion continued, after a pause: 'I said just now I didn't want to know anything about the affair; but I will confess that I am curious to learn whether you propose to marry Miss Bessie Alden.'

On this point Lord Lambeth gave his interlocutor no immediate satisfaction; he was musing, with a frown. 'By Jove,' he said, 'they go rather too far. They *shall* find me dangerous – I promise them.'

Percy Beaumont began to laugh. 'You don't redeem your promises. You said the other day you would make your mother call.'

Lord Lambeth continued to meditate. 'I asked her to call,' he said, simply.

'And she declined?'

'Yes, but she shall do it yet.'

'Upon my word,' said Percy Beaumont, 'if she gets much more frightened I believe she will.' Lord Lambeth looked at him, and he went on. 'She will go to the girl herself.'

'How do you mean, she will go to her?'

'She will beg her off, or she will bribe her. She will take strong measures.'

Lord Lambeth turned away in silence, and his companion watched him take twenty steps and then slowly return. 'I have invited Mrs Westgate and Miss Alden to Branches,' he said, 'and this evening I shall name a day.'

'And shall you invite your mother and your sisters to meet them?'

'Explicitly!'

'That will set the Duchess off,' said Percy Beaumont. 'I suspect she will come.'

'She may do as she pleases.'

Beaumont looked at Lord Lambeth. 'You do really propose to marry the little sister, then?'

'I like the way you talk about it!' cried the young man. 'She won't gobble me down; don't be afraid.'

'She won't leave you on your knees,' said Percy Beaumont. 'What *is* the inducement?'

'You talk about proposing – wait till I have proposed,' Lord Lambeth went on.

'That's right, my dear fellow; think about it,' said Percy Beaumont.

'She's a charming girl,' pursued his lordship.

'Of course she's a charming girl. I don't know a girl more charming, intrinsically. But there are other charming girls nearer home.'

'I like her spirit,' observed Lord Lambeth, almost as if he were trying to torment his cousin.

'What's the peculiarity of her spirit?'

'She's not afraid, and she says things out, and she thinks herself as good as any one. She is the only girl I have ever seen that was not dying to marry me.'

'How do you know that, if you haven't asked her?'

'I don't know how; but I know it.'

'I am sure she asked me questions enough about your property and your titles,' said Beaumont.

'She has asked me questions, too; no end of them,' Lord Lambeth admitted. 'But she asked for information, don't you know.'

'Information? Ay, I'll warrant she wanted it. Depend upon it that she is dying to marry you just as much and just as little as all the rest of them.'

'I shouldn't like her to refuse me – I shouldn't like that.'

'If the thing would be so disagreeable, then, both to you and to her, in Heaven's name leave it alone,' said Percy Beaumont.

Mrs Westgate, on her side, had plenty to say to her sister about the rarity of Mr Beaumont's visits and the non-appearance of the Duchess of Bayswater. She professed, however, to derive more satisfaction from this latter circumstance than she could have done from the most lavish attentions on the part of this great lady. 'It is most marked,' she said, 'most markcd. It is a delicious proof that we have made them miserable. The day we dined with Lord Lambeth I was really sorry for the poor fellow.' It will have been gathered that the entertainment offered by Lord Lambeth to his American friends had not been graced by the presence of his anxious mother. He had invited several choice spirits to meet them; but the ladies of his immediate family were to Mrs Westgate's sense – a sense, possibly, morbidly acute – conspicuous by their absence.

'I don't want to express myself in a manner that you dislike,' said Bessie Alden; 'but I don't know why you should have so many theories about Lord Lambeth's poor mother. You know a great many young men in New York without knowing their mothers.'

Mrs Westgate looked at her sister, and then turned away. 'My dear Bessie, you are superb!' she said.

'One thing is certain,' the young girl continued. 'If I believed I were a cause of annoyance – however unwitting – to Lord Lambeth's family, I should insist—'

'Insist upon my leaving England,' said Mrs Westgate.

'No, not that. I want to go the National Gallery[95] again; I want to see Stratford-on-Avon[96] and Canterbury Cathedral.[97] But I should insist upon his coming to see us no more.'

'That would be very modest and very pretty of you – but you wouldn't do it now.'

'Why do you say "now"?' asked Bessie Alden. 'Have I ceased to be modest?'

'You care for him too much. A month ago, when you said you didn't, I believe it was quite true. But at present, my dear child,' said Mrs Westgate, 'you wouldn't find it quite so simple a matter never to see Lord Lambeth again. I have seen it coming on.'

'You are mistaken,' said Bessie. 'You don't understand.'

'My dear child, don't be perverse,' rejoined her sister.

'I know him better, certainly, if you mean that,' said Bessie.

'And I like him very much. But I don't like him enough to make trouble for him with his family. However, I don't believe in that.'

'I like the way you say "however"!' Mrs Westgate exclaimed. 'Come, you would not marry him?'

'Oh no,' said the young girl.

Mrs Westgate, for a moment, seemed vexed. 'Why not, pray?' she demanded.

'Because I don't care to,' said Bessie Alden.

The morning after Lord Lambeth had had, with Percy Beaumont, that exchange of ideas which has just been narrated, the ladies at Jones's Hotel received from his lordship a written invitation to pay their projected visit to Branches Castle on the following Tuesday. 'I think I have made up a very pleasant party,' the young nobleman said. 'Several people who you know, and my mother and sisters, who have so long been regrettably prevented from making your acquaintance.' Bessie Alden lost no time in calling her sister's attention to the injustice she had done the Duchess of Bayswater, whose hostility was now proved to be a vain illusion.

'Wait till you see if she comes,' said Mrs Westgate. 'And if she is to meet us at her son's house the obligation was all the greater for her to call upon us.'

Bessie had not to wait long, and it appeared that Lord Lambeth's mother now accepted Mrs Westgate's view of her duties. On the morrow, early in the afternoon, two cards were brought to the apartment of the American ladies – one of them bearing the name of the Duchess of Bayswater and the other that of the Countess of Pimlico. Mrs Westgate glanced at the clock. 'It is not yet four,' she said; 'they have come early; they wish to see us. We will receive them.' And she gave orders that her visitors should be admitted. A few moments later they were introduced, and there was a solemn exchange of amenities. The Duchess was a large lady, with a fine fresh colour; the Countess of Pimlico was very pretty and elegant.

The Duchess looked about her as she sat down – looked not especially at Mrs Westgate. 'I dare say my son has told you that I have been wanting to come and see you,' she observed.

'You are very kind,' said Mrs Westgate, vaguely – her conscience not allowing her to assent to this proposition – and indeed not permitting her to enunciate her own with any appreciable emphasis.

'He says you were so kind to him in America,' said the Duchess.

'We are very glad,' Mrs Westgate replied, 'to have been able to make him a little more – a little less – a little more comfortable.'

'I think he stayed at your house,' remarked the Duchess of Bayswater, looking at Bessie Alden.

'A very short time,' said Mrs Westgate.

'Oh!' said the Duchess; and she continued to look at Bessie, who was engaged in conversation with her daughter.

'Do you like London?' Lady Pimlico had asked of Bessie, after looking at her a good deal – at her face and her hands, her dress and her hair.

'Very much indeed,' said Bessie.

'Do you like this hotel?'

'It is very comfortable,' said Bessie.

'Do you like stopping at hotels?' inquired Lady Pimlico, after a pause.

'I am very fond of travelling,' Bessie answered, 'and I suppose hotels are a necessary part of it. But they are not the part I am fondest of.'

'Oh, I hate travelling!' said the Countess of Pimlico, and transferred her attention to Mrs Westgate.

'My son tells me you are going to Branches,' the Duchess presently resumed.

'Lord Lambeth has been so good as to ask us,' said Mrs Westgate, who perceived that her visitor had now begun to look at her, and who had her customary happy consciousness of a distinguished appearance. The only mitigation of her felicity on this point was that, having inspected her visitor's own costume, she said to herself, 'She won't know how well I am dressed!'

'He has asked me to go, but I am not sure I shall be able,' murmured the Duchess.

'He had offered us the p – the prospect of meeting you,' said Mrs Westgate.

'I hate the country at this season,' responded the Duchess.

Mrs Westgate gave a little shrug. 'I think it is pleasanter than London.'

But the Duchess's eyes were absent again; she was looking very fixedly at Bessie. In a moment she slowly rose, walked to a chair that stood empty at the young girl's right hand, and silently seated herself. As she was a majestic, voluminous woman, this little transaction had, inevitably, an air of somewhat impressive intention. It diffused a certain awkwardness, which Lady Pimlico, as a sympathetic daughter, perhaps desired to rectify in turning to Mrs Westgate.

'I dare say you go out a great deal,' she observed.

'No, very little. We are strangers, and we didn't come here for society.'

'I see,' said Lady Pimlico. 'It's rather nice in town just now.'

'It's charming,' said Mrs Westgate. 'But we only go to see a few people – who we like.'

'Of course one can't like every one,' said Lady Pimlico.

'It depends upon one's society,' Mrs Westgate rejoined.

The Duchess, meanwhile, had addressed herself to Bessie. 'My son tells me the young ladies in America are so clever.'

'I am glad they made so good an impression on him,' said Bessie, smiling.

The Duchess was not smiling; her large fresh face was very tranquil. 'He is very susceptible,' she said. 'He thinks every one clever, and sometimes they are.'

'Sometimes,' Bessie assented, smiling still.

The Duchess looked at her a little and then went on – 'Lambeth is very susceptible, but he is very volatile, too.'

'Volatile?' asked Bessie.

'He is very inconstant. It won't do to depend on him.'

'Ah!' said Bessie. 'I don't recognize that description. We have depended on him greatly – my sister and I – and he has never disappointed us.'

'He will disappoint you yet,' said the Duchess.

Bessie gave a little laugh, as if she were amused at the

Duchess's persistency. 'I suppose it will depend on what we expect of him.'

'The less you expect the better,' Lord Lambeth's mother declared.

'Well,' said Bessie, 'we expect nothing unreasonable.'

The Duchess, for a moment, was silent, though she appeared to have more to say. 'Lambeth says he has seen so much of you,' she presently began.

'He has been to see us very often – he has been very kind,' said Bessie Alden.

'I dare say you are used to that. I am told there is a great deal of that in America.'

'A great deal of kindness?' the young girl inquired, smiling.

'Is that what you call it? I know you have different expressions.'

'We certainly don't always understand each other,' said Mrs Westgate, the termination of whose interview with Lady Pimlico allowed her to give her attention to their elder visitor.

'I am speaking of the young men calling so much upon the young ladies,' the Duchess explained.

'But surely in England,' said Mrs Westgate, 'the young ladies don't call upon the young men?'

'Some of them do – almost!' Lady Pimlico declared. 'When the young men are a great *parti*.'

'Bessie, you must make a note of that,' said Mrs Westgate. 'My sister,' she added, 'is a model traveller. She writes down all the curious facts she hears, in a little book she keeps for the purpose.'

The Duchess was a little flushed; she looked all about the room, while her daughter turned to Bessie. 'My brother told us you were wonderfully clever,' said Lady Pimlico.

'He should have said my sister,' Bessie answered – 'when she says such things as that.'

'Shall you be long at Branches?' the Duchess asked, abruptly, of the young girl.

'Lord Lambeth has asked us for three days,' said Bessie.

'I shall go,' the Duchess declared, 'and my daughter too.'

'That will be charming!' Bessie rejoined.

'Delightful!' murmured Mrs Westgate.

'I shall expect to see a deal of you,' the Duchess continued. 'When I go to Branches I monopolize my son's guests.'

'They must be most happy,' said Mrs Westgate, very graciously.

'I want immensely to see it – to see the Castle,' said Bessie to the Duchess. 'I have never seen one – in England at least; and you know we have none in America.'

'Ah! you are fond of castles?' inquired her Grace.

'Immensely!' replied the young girl. 'It has been the dream of my life to live in one.'

The Duchess looked at her a moment, as if she hardly knew how to take this assurance, which, from her Grace's point of view, was either very artless or very audacious. 'Well,' she said, rising, 'I will show you Branches myself.' And upon this the two great ladies took their departure.

'What did they mean by it?' asked Mrs Westgate, when they were gone.

'They meant to be polite,' said Bessie, 'because we are going to meet them.'

'It is too late to be polite,' Mrs Westgate replied, almost grimly. 'They meant to overawe us by their fine manners and their grandeur, and to make you *lacher prise*.'

'*Lacher prise*? What strange things you say!' murmured Bessie Alden.

'They meant to snub us, so that we shouldn't dare to go to Branches,' Mrs Westgate continued.

'On the contrary,' said Bessie, 'the Duchess offered to show me the place herself.'

'Yes, you may depend upon it she won't let you out of her sight. She will show you the place from morning till night.'

'You have a theory for everything,' said Bessie.

'And you apparently have none for anything.'

'I saw no attempt to "overawe" us,' said the young girl. 'Their manners were not fine.'

'They were not even good!' Mrs Westgate declared.

Bessie was silent awhile, but in a few moments she observed that she had a very good theory. 'They came to look at me!' she said, as if this had been a very ingenious hypothesis. Mrs Westgate did it justice; she greeted it with a smile and pronounced it most brilliant; while in reality she felt that the young girl's scepticism, or her charity, or, as she had sometimes called it, appropriately, her idealism, was proof against irony. Bessie, however, remained meditative all the rest of that day and well on into the morrow.

On the morrow, before lunch, Mrs Westgate had occasion to go out for an hour, and left her sister writing a letter. When she came back she met Lord Lambeth at the door of the hotel, coming away. She thought he looked slightly embarrassed; he was certainly very grave. 'I am sorry to have missed you. Won't you come back?' she asked.

'No,' said the young man, 'I can't. I have seen your sister. I can never come back.' Then he looked at her a moment, and took her hand. 'Good-bye, Mrs Westgate,' he said. 'You have been very kind to me.' And with what she thought a strange, sad look in his handsome young face, he turned away.

She went in and she found Bessie still writing her letter; that is, Mrs Westgate perceived she was sitting at the table with the pen in her hand and not writing. 'Lord Lambeth has been here,' said the elder lady at last.

Then Bessie got up and showed her a pale, serious face. She bent this face upon her sister for some time, confessing silently and, a little, pleading. 'I told him,' she said at last, 'that we could not go to Branches.'

Mrs Westgate displayed just a spark of irritation. 'He might have waited,' she said with a smile, 'till one had seen the Castle.' Later, an hour afterwards, she said, 'Dear Bessie, I wish you might have accepted him.'

'I couldn't,' said Bessie, gently.

'He is a dear good fellow,' said Mrs Westgate.

'I couldn't,' Bessie repeated.

'If it is only,' her sister added, 'because those women will think that they succeeded – that they paralysed us!'

Bessie Alden turned away; but presently she added, 'They were interesting; I should have liked to see them again.'

'So should I!' cried Mrs Westgate, significantly.

'And I should have liked to see the Castle,' said Bessie. 'But now we must leave England,' she added.

Her sister looked at her. 'You will not wait to go to the National Gallery?'

'Not now.'

'Nor to Canterbury Cathedral?'

Bessie reflected a moment. 'We can stop there on our way to Paris,'[98] she said.

Lord Lambeth did not tell Percy Beaumont that the contingency he was not prepared at all to like had occurred; but Percy Beaumont, on hearing that the two ladies had left London, wondered with some intensity what had happened; wondered, that is, until the Duchess of Bayswater came, a little, to his assistance. The two ladies went to Paris, and Mrs Westgate beguiled the journey to that city by repeating several times, 'That's what I regret; they will think they petrified us.' But Bessie Alden seemed to regret nothing.

'EUROPE'

I

'Our feeling is, you know, that Becky *should* go.' That earnest little remark comes back to me, even after long years, as the first note of something that began, for my observation, the day I went with my sister-in-law to take leave of her good friends. It is a memory of the American time, which revives so at present – under some touch that doesn't signify – that it rounds itself off as an anecdote. That walk to say good-bye was the beginning; and the end, so far as I was concerned with it, was not till long after; yet even the end also appears to me now as of the old days. I went, in those days, on occasion, to see my sister-in-law, in whose affairs, on my brother's death, I had had to take a helpful hand. I continued to go, indeed, after these little matters were straightened out, for the pleasure, periodically, of the impression – the change to the almost pastoral sweetness of the good Boston suburb from the loud, longitudinal New York. It was another world, with other manners, a different tone, a different taste; a savour nowhere so mild, yet so distinct, as in the square white house – with the pair of elms, like gigantic wheat-sheaves in front, the rustic orchard not far behind, the old-fashioned door-lights, the big blue and white jars in the porch, the straight, bricked walk from the high gate –that enshrined the extraordinary merit of Mrs Rimmle and her three daughters.

These ladies were so much of the place and the place so much of themselves that, from the first of their being revealed to me, I felt that nothing else at Brookbridge[1] much mattered.

They were what, for me, at any rate, Brookbridge had most to
give: I mean in the way of what it was naturally strongest in,
the thing that we called in New York the New England expression, the air of Puritanism reclaimed and refined. The Rimmles
had brought this down to a wonderful delicacy. They struck
me even then – all four almost equally – as very ancient and
very earnest, and I think theirs must have been the house, in
all the world, in which 'culture' first came to the aid of morning calls. The head of the family was the widow of a great
public character – as public characters were understood at
Brookbridge – whose speeches on anniversaries formed a part
of the body of national eloquence spouted in the New England
schools by little boys covetous of the most marked, though
perhaps the easiest, distinction. He was reported to have been
celebrated, and in such fine declamatory connections that he
seemed to gesticulate even from the tomb. He was understood
to have made, in his wife's company, the tour of Europe at a
date not immensely removed from that of the battle of Waterloo.[2] What was the age, then, of the bland, firm, antique Mrs
Rimmle at the period of her being first revealed to me? That is
a point I am not in a position to determine – I remember mainly
that I was young enough to regard her as having reached the
limit. And yet the limit for Mrs Rimmle must have been prodigiously extended; the scale of its extension is, in fact, the very
moral of this reminiscence. She was old, and her daughters
were old, but I was destined to know them all as older. It was
only by comparison and habit that – however much I recede –
Rebecca, Maria, and Jane were the 'young ladies'.

I think it was felt that, though their mother's life, after
thirty years of widowhood, had had a grand backward stretch,
her blandness and firmness – and this in spite of her extreme
physical frailty – would be proof against any surrender not
overwhelmingly justified by time. It had appeared, years
before, at a crisis of which the waves had not even yet quite
subsided, a surrender not justified by anything that she should
go, with her daughters, to Europe for her health. Her health
was supposed to require constant support; but when it had at
that period tried conclusions with the idea of Europe, it was

not the idea of Europe that had been insidious enough to prevail. She had not gone, and Becky, Maria, and Jane had not gone, and this was long ago. They still merely floated in the air of the visit achieved, with such introductions and such acclamations, in the early part of the century; they still, with fond glances at the sunny parlour-walls, only referred, in conversation, to divers pictorial and other reminders of it. The Miss Rimmles had quite been brought up on it, but Becky, as the most literary, had most mastered the subject. There were framed letters – tributes to their eminent father – suspended among the mementoes, and of two or three of these, the most foreign and complimentary, Becky had executed translations that figured beside the text. She knew already, through this and other illumination, so much about Europe that it was hard to believe, for her, in that limit of adventure which consisted only of her having been twice to Philadelphia. The others had not been to Philadelphia, but there was a legend that Jane had been to Saratoga.[3] Becky was a short, stout, fair person with round, serious eyes, a high forehead, the sweetest, neatest enunciation, and a miniature of her father – 'done in Rome' – worn as a breastpin. She had written the life, she had edited the speeches, of the original of this ornament, and now at last, beyond the seas, she was really to tread in his footsteps.

Fine old Mrs Rimmle, in the sunny parlour and with a certain austerity of cap and chair – though with a gay new 'front'[4] that looked like rusty brown plush – had had so unusually good a winter that the question of her sparing two members of her family for an absence had been threshed as fine, I could feel, as even under that Puritan roof any case of conscience had ever been threshed. They were to make their dash while the coast, as it were, was clear, and each of the daughters had tried – heroically, angelically, and for the sake of each of her sisters – not to be one of the two. What I encountered that first time was an opportunity to concur with enthusiasm in the general idea that Becky's wonderful preparation would be wasted if she were the one to stay with their mother. They talked of Becky's preparation – they had a sly, old-maidish humour that was as mild as milk – as if it were some mixture, for application somewhere, that she kept in a precious bottle. It had been settled, at all events, that, armed with this concoction and borne aloft by their introductions, she and Jane were to start. They were wonderful on their introductions, which proceeded naturally from their mother and were addressed to the charming families that, in vague generations, had so admired vague Mr Rimmle. Jane, I found at Brookbridge, had to be described, for want of other description, as the pretty one, but it would not have served to identify her unless you had seen the others. *Her* preparation was only this figment of her prettiness – only, that is, unless one took into account something that, on the spot, I silently divined: the lifelong, secret, passionate ache of her little rebellious desire. They were all growing old in the yearning to go, but Jane's yearning was the sharpest. She struggled with it as people at Brookbridge mostly struggled with what they liked, but fate, by threatening to prevent what she *dis*liked, and what was therefore duty – which was to stay at home instead of Maria – had bewildered her, I judged, not a little. It was she who, in the words I have quoted, mentioned to me Becky's case and Becky's affinity as the clearest of all. Her mother, moreover, on the general subject, had still more to say.

'I positively desire, I really quite insist that they shall go,' the old lady explained to us from her stiff chair. 'We've talked about it so often, and they've had from me so clear an account – I've amused them again and again with it – of what is to be seen and enjoyed. If they've had hitherto too many duties to leave, the time seems to have come to recognize that there are also many duties to *seek*. Wherever we go we find them – I always remind the girls of that. There's a duty that calls them to those wonderful countries, just as it called, at the right time, their father and myself – if it be only that of laying up for the years to come the same store of remarkable impressions, the same wealth of knowledge and food for conversation as, since my return, I have found myself so happy to possess.' Mrs Rimmle spoke of her return as of something of the year before last, but the future of her daughters was, somehow, by a different law, to be on the scale of great vistas, of endless aftertastes. I think

that, without my being quite ready to say it, even this first
impression of her was somewhat upsetting; there was a large,
placid perversity, a grim secrecy of intention, in her estimate
of the ages.

'Well, I'm so glad you don't delay it longer,' I said to Miss
Becky before we withdrew. 'And whoever should go,' I continued in the spirit of the sympathy with which the good sisters
had already inspired me, 'I quite feel, with your family, you
know, that *you* should. But of course I hold that every one
should.' I suppose I wished to attenuate my solemnity; there
was something in it, however, that I couldn't help. It must have
been a faint foreknowledge.

'Have you been a great deal yourself?' Miss Jane, I remember, inquired.

'Not so much but that I hope to go a good deal more. So
perhaps we shall meet,' I encouragingly suggested.

I recall something – something in the nature of susceptibility to encouragement – that this brought into the more
expressive brown eyes to which Miss Jane mainly owed it that
she was the pretty one. 'Where, do you think?'

I tried to think. 'Well, on the Italian lakes – Como, Bellagio,
Lugano.'⁵ I liked to say the names to them.

' "Sublime, but neither bleak nor bare nor misty are the
mountains there!" '⁶ Miss Jane softly breathed, while her sister
looked at her as if her familiarity with the poetry of the subject
made her the most interesting feature of the scene she evoked.

But Miss Becky presently turned to me. 'Do you know
everything—?'

'Everything?'

'In Europe.'

'Oh, yes,' I laughed, 'and one or two things even in America.'
The sisters seemed to me furtively to look at each other.
'Well, you'll have to be quick – to meet *us*,' Miss Jane resumed.

'But surely when you're once there you'll stay on.'

'Stay on?' – they murmured it simultaneously and with the
oddest vibration of dread as well as of desire. It was as if they
had been in the presence of a danger and yet wished me, who
'knew everything', to torment them with still more of it.

Well, I did my best. 'I mean it will never do to cut it short.'

'No, that's just what I keep saying,' said brilliant Jane. 'It would be better, in that case, not to go.'

'Oh, don't talk about not going – at this time!' It was none of my business, but I felt shocked and impatient.

'No, not at *this* time!' broke in Miss Maria, who, very red in the face, had joined us. Poor Miss Maria was known as the flushed one; but she was not flushed – she only had an unfortunate surface. The third day after this was to see them embark.

Miss Becky, however, desired as little as any one to be in any way extravagant. 'It's only the thought of our mother,' she explained.

I looked a moment at the old lady, with whom my sister-in-law was engaged. 'Well – your mother's magnificent.'

'*Isn't* she magnificent?' – they eagerly took it up.

She *was* – I could reiterate it with sincerity, though I perhaps mentally drew the line when Miss Maria again risked, as a fresh ejaculation: 'I think she's better than Europe!'

'Maria!' they both, at this, exclaimed with a strange emphasis; it was as if they feared she had suddenly turned cynical over the deep domestic drama of their casting of lots. The innocent laugh with which she answered them gave the measure of her cynicism.

We separated at last, and my eyes met Mrs Rimmle's as I held for an instant her aged hand. It was doubtless only my fancy that her calm, cold look quietly accused me of something. Of what *could* it accuse me? Only, I thought, of thinking.

II

I left Brookbridge the next day, and for some time after that had no occasion to hear from my kinswoman; but when she finally wrote there was a passage in her letter that affected me more than all the rest. 'Do you know the poor Rimmles never, after all, "went"? The old lady, at the eleventh hour, broke down; everything broke down, and all of *them* on top of it, so that the dear things are with us still. Mrs Rimmle, the night after our call, had, in the most unexpected manner, a turn for the worse – something in the nature (though they're rather mysterious about it) of a seizure; Becky and Jane felt it – dear, devoted, stupid angels that they are – heartless to leave her at such a moment, and Europe's indefinitely postponed. However, they think they're still going – or *think* they think it – when she's better. They also think – or think they think – that she *will* be better. I certainly pray she may.' So did I – quite fervently. I was conscious of a real pang – I didn't know how much they had made me care.

Late that winter my sister-in-law spent a week in New York; when almost my first inquiry on meeting her was about the health of Mrs Rimmle.

'Oh, she's rather bad – she really is, you know. It's not surprising that at her age she should be infirm.'

'Then what the deuce *is* her age?'

'I can't tell you to a year – but she's immensely old.'

'That of course I saw,' I replied – 'unless you literally mean so old that the records have been lost.'

My sister-in-law thought. 'Well, I believe she wasn't positively young when she married. She lost three or four children before these women were born.'

We surveyed together a little, on this, the 'dark backward'.[7] 'And they were born, I gather, *after* the famous tour? Well, then, as the famous tour was in a manner to celebrate – wasn't it? – the restoration of the Bourbons—'[8] I considered, I gasped. 'My dear child, what on earth do you make her out?'

My relative, with her Brookbridge habit, transferred her share of the question to the moral plane – turned it forth to wander, by implication at least, in the sandy desert of responsibility. 'Well, you know, we all immensely admire her.'

'You can't admire her more than I do. She's awful.'[9]

My interlocutress looked at me with a certain fear. 'She's *really* ill.'

'Too ill to get better?'

'Oh, no – we hope not. Because then they'll be able to go.'

'And *will* they go, if she should?'

'Oh, the moment they should be quite satisfied. I mean *really*,' she added.

I'm afraid I laughed at her – the Brookbridge 'really' was a thing so by itself. 'But if she shouldn't get better?' I went on.

'Oh, don't speak of it! They want so to go.'

'It's a pity they're so infernally good,' I mused.

'No – don't say that. It's what keeps them up.'

'Yes, but isn't it what keeps *her* up too?'

My visitor looked grave. 'Would you like them to kill her?'

I don't know that I was then prepared to say I should – though I believe I came very near it. But later on I burst all bounds, for the subject grew and grew. I went again before the good sisters ever did – I mean I went to Europe. I think I went twice, with a brief interval, before my fate again brought round for me a couple of days at Brookbridge. I had been there repeatedly, in the previous time, without making the acquaintance of the Rimmles; but now that I had had the revelation I couldn't have it too much, and the first request I preferred was to be taken again to see them. I remember well indeed the scruple I felt – the real delicacy – about betraying that *I* had, in the pride of my power[10] since our other meeting, stood, as their phrase went, among romantic scenes; but they were themselves the first to speak of it, and what, moreover, came home to me was that the coming and going of their friends in general – Brookbridge itself having even at that period one foot in Europe – was such as to place constantly before them the pleasure that was only postponed. They were thrown back, after all, on what the situation, under a final analysis, had most to give – the sense that, as every one kindly said to them and they kindly said to every one, Europe would keep. Every one felt for them so deeply that their own kindness in alleviating every one's feeling was really what came out most. Mrs Rimmle was still in her stiff chair and in the sunny parlour, but if *she* made no scruple of introducing the Italian lakes my heart sank to observe that she dealt with them, as a topic, not in the least in the leave-taking manner in which Falstaff babbled of green fields.[11]

I am not sure that, after this, my pretexts for a day or two with my sister-in-law were not apt to be a mere cover for

another glimpse of these particulars: I at any rate never went
to Brookbridge without an irrepressible eagerness for our customary call. A long time seems to me thus to have passed, with
glimpses and lapses, considerable impatience and still more
pity. Our visits indeed grew shorter, for, as my companion
said, they were more and more of a strain. It finally struck me
that the good sisters even shrank from me a little, as from one
who penetrated their consciousness in spite of himself. It was
as if they knew where I thought they ought to be, and were
moved to deprecate at last, by a systematic silence on the subject of that hemisphere, the criminality I fain would fix on
them. They were full instead – as with the instinct of throwing
dust in my eyes – of little pathetic hypocrisies about Brookbridge interests and delights. I dare say that as time went on
my deeper sense of their situation came practically to rest on
my companion's report of it. I think I recollect, at all events,
every word we ever exchanged about them, even if I have lost
the thread of the special occasions. The impression they made
on me after each interval always broke out with extravagance
as I walked away with her.

'*She* may be as old as she likes – I don't care. It's the fearful
age the "girls" are reaching that constitutes the scandal. One
shouldn't pry into such matters, I know; but the years and the
chances are really going. They're all growing old together – it
will presently be too late; and their mother meanwhile perches
over them like a vulture – what shall I call it? – calculating. Is
she waiting for them successively to drop off? She'll survive
them each and all. There's something too remorseless in it.'

'Yes; but what do you want her to do? If the poor thing *can't*
die, she can't. Do you want her to take poison or to open a
blood-vessel? I dare say she would prefer to go.'

'I beg your pardon,' I must have replied; 'you daren't say
anything of the sort. If she would prefer to go she *would* go.
She would feel the propriety, the decency, the necessity of
going. She just prefers *not* to go. She prefers to stay and keep
up the tension, and her calling them "girls" and talking of the
good time they'll still have is the mere conscious mischief of a
subtle old witch. They won't have *any* time there isn't any time

to have! I mean there's, on her own part, no real loss of measure or of perspective in it. She *knows* she's a hundred and ten, and she takes a cruel pride in it.'

My sister-in-law differed with me about this; she held that the old woman's attitude was an honest one and that her magnificent vitality, so great in spite of her infirmities, made it inevitable she should attribute youth to persons who had come into the world so much later. 'Then suppose she should die?' – so my fellow-student of the case always put it to me.

'Do you mean while her daughters are away? There's not the least fear of that – not even if at the very moment of their departure she should be *in extremis*. They would find her all right on their return.'

'But think how they would feel not to have been with her!'

'That's only, I repeat, on the unsound assumption. If they would only go to-morrow – literally make a good rush for it – they'll be with her when they come back. That will give them plenty of time.' I'm afraid I even heartlessly added that if she *should,* against every probability, pass away in their absence, they wouldn't have to come back at all – which would be just the compensation proper to their long privation. And then Maria would come out to join the two others, and they would be – though but for the too scanty remnant of their career – as merry as the day is long.

I remained ready, somehow, pending the fulfilment of that vision, to sacrifice Maria; it was only over the urgency of the case for the others respectively that I found myself balancing. Sometimes it was for Becky I thought the tragedy deepest – sometimes, and in quite a different manner, I thought it most dire for Jane. It was Jane, after all, who had most sense of life. I seemed in fact dimly to descry in Jane a sense – as yet undescried by herself or by any one – of all sorts of queer things. Why didn't *she* go? I used desperately to ask; why didn't she make a bold personal dash for it, strike up a partnership with some one or other of the travelling spinsters in whom Brookbridge more and more abounded? Well, there came a flash for me at a particular point of the grey middle desert: my correspondent was able to let me know that poor Jane at last *had* sailed. She had gone of a sudden – I liked my sister-in-law's view of suddenness – with the kind Hathaways, who had made an irresistible grab at her and lifted her off her feet. They were going for the summer and for Mr Hathaway's health, so that the opportunity was perfect and it was impossible not to be glad that something very like physical force had finally prevailed. This was the general feeling at Brookbridge, and I might imagine what Brookbridge had been brought to from the fact that, at the very moment she was hustled off, the doctor, called to her mother at the peep of dawn, had considered that *he* at least must stay. There had been real alarm – greater than ever before; it actually did seem as if this time the end had come. But it was Becky, strange to say, who, though fully recognizing the nature of the crisis, had kept the situation in hand and insisted upon action. This, I remember, brought back to me a discomfort with which I had been familiar from the first. One of the two had sailed, and I was sorry it was not the other. But if it had been the other I should have been equally sorry.

I saw with my eyes, that very autumn, what a fool Jane would have been if she had again backed out. Her mother had of course survived the peril of which I had heard, profiting by it indeed as she had profited by every other; she was sufficiently better again to have come down-stairs. It was there that, as usual, I found her, but with a difference of effect produced somehow by the absence of one of the girls. It was as if, for the others, though they had not gone to Europe, Europe had come to them: Jane's letters had been so frequent and so beyond even what could have been hoped. It was the first time, however, that I perceived on the old woman's part a certain failure of lucidity. Jane's flight was, clearly, the great fact with her, but she spoke of it as if the fruit had now been plucked and the parenthesis closed. I don't know what sinking sense of still further physical duration I gathered, as a menace, from this first hint of her confusion of mind.

'My daughter has been; my daughter has been—' She kept saying it, but didn't say where; that seemed unnecessary, and she only repeated the words to her visitors with a face that was all puckers and yet now, save in so far as it expressed an ineffaceable complacency, all blankness. I think she wanted us a little to know that she had not stood in the way. It added to something – I scarce knew what – that I found myself desiring to extract privately from Becky. As our visit was to be of the shortest my opportunity – for one of the young ladies always came to the door with us – was at hand. Mrs Rimmle, as we took leave, again sounded her phrase, but she added this time: 'I'm so glad she's going to have always—'

I knew so well what she meant that, as she again dropped, looking at me queerly and becoming momentarily dim, I could help her out. 'Going to have what *you* have?'

'Yes, yes – my privilege. Wonderful experience,' she mumbled. She bowed to me a little as if I would understand. 'She has things to tell.'

I turned, slightly at a loss, to Becky. 'She has then already arrived?'

Becky was at that moment looking a little strangely at her mother, who answered my question. 'She reached New York this morning – she comes on to-day.'

'Oh, then—!' But I let the matter pass as I met Becky's eye – I saw there was a hitch somewhere. It was not she but Maria who came out with us; on which I cleared up the question of their sister's reappearance.

'Oh, no, not to-night,' Maria smiled; 'that's only the way mother puts it. We shall see her about the end of November – the Hathaways are so indulgent. They kindly extend their tour.'

'For *her* sake? How sweet of them!' my sister-in-law exclaimed.

I can see our friend's plain, mild old face take on a deeper mildness, even though a higher colour, in the light of the open door. 'Yes, it's for Jane they prolong it. And do you know what they write?' She gave us time, but it was too great a responsibility to guess. 'Why, that it has brought her out.'

'Oh, I knew it *would*!' my companion sympathetically sighed.

Maria put it more strongly still. 'They say we wouldn't know her.'

This sounded a little awful, but it was, after all, what I had expected.

III

My correspondent in Brookbridge came to me that Christmas, with my niece, to spend a week; and the arrangement had of course been prefaced by an exchange of letters, the first of which from my sister-in-law scarce took space for acceptance of my invitation before going on to say: 'The Hathaways are back – but without Miss Jane!' She presented in a few words the situation thus created at Brookbridge, but was not yet, I gathered, fully in possession of the other one – the situation created in 'Europe' by the presence there of that lady. The two together, at any rate, demanded, I quickly felt, all my attention, and perhaps my impatience to receive my relative was a little sharpened by my desire for the whole story. I had it at last, by the Christmas fire, and I may say without reserve that it gave me all I could have hoped for. I listened eagerly, after which I produced the comment: 'Then she simply refused—'

'To budge from Florence? Simply. She had it out there with the poor Hathaways, who felt responsible for her safety, pledged to restore her to her mother's, to her sisters' hands, and showed herself in a light, they mention under their breath, that made their dear old hair stand on end. Do you know what, when they first got back, they said of her – at least it was *his* phrase – to two or three people?'

I thought a moment. 'That she had "tasted blood"?'

My visitor fairly admired me. 'How clever of you to guess! It's exactly what he did say. She appeared – she continues to appear, it seems – in a new character.'

I wondered a little. 'But that's exactly – don't you remember? – what Miss Maria reported to us from them; that we "wouldn't know her".'

My sister-in-law perfectly remembered. 'Oh, yes – she broke out from the first. But when they left her she was worse.'

'Worse?'

'Well, different – different from anything she ever *had* been, or – for that matter – had had a chance to be.' My interlocutress hung fire a moment, but presently faced me. 'Rather strange and free and obstreperous.'

'Obstreperous?' I wondered again.

'Peculiarly so, I inferred, on the question of not coming away. She wouldn't hear of it, and, when they spoke of her mother, said she had given her mother up. She had thought she should like Europe, but didn't know she should like it so much. They had been fools to bring her if they expected to take her away. She was going to see what she could – she hadn't yet seen half. The end of it was, at any rate, that they had to leave her alone.'

I seemed to see it all – to see even the scared Hathaways. 'So she *is* alone?'

'She told them, poor thing, it appears, and in a tone they'll never forget, that she was, at all events, quite old enough to be. She cried – she quite went on – over not having come sooner. That's why the only way for her,' my companion mused, '*is*, I suppose, to stay. They wanted to put her with some people or other – to find some American family. But she says she's on her own feet.'

'And she's still in Florence?'

'No – I believe she was to travel. She's bent on the East.'

I burst out laughing. 'Magnificent Jane! It's most interesting. Only I feel that I distinctly *should* "know" her. To my sense, always, I must tell you, she had it in her.'

My relative was silent a little. 'So it now appears Becky always felt.'

'And yet pushed her off? Magnificent Becky!'

My companion met my eyes a moment. 'You don't know the queerest part. I mean the way it has *most* brought her out.'

I turned it over; I felt I should like to know – to that degree indeed that, oddly enough, I jocosely disguised my eagerness. 'You don't mean she has taken to drink?'

My visitor hesitated. 'She has taken to flirting.'

I expressed disappointment. 'Oh, she took to *that* long ago.

Yes,' I declared at my kinswoman's stare, 'she positively flirted – with *me*!'

The stare perhaps sharpened. 'Then you flirted with *her*?'

'How else could I have been as sure as I wanted to be? But has she means?'

'Means to flirt?' – my friend looked an instant as if she spoke literally. 'I don't understand about the means – though of course they have something. But I have my impression,' she went on. 'I think that Becky—' It seemed almost too grave to say.

But *I* had no doubts. 'That Becky's backing her?'

She brought it out. 'Financing her.'

'Stupendous Becky! So that morally then—'

'Becky's quite in sympathy. But isn't it too odd?' my sister-in-law asked.

'Not in the least. Didn't we know, as regards Jane, that Europe was to bring her out? Well, it has also brought out Rebecca.'

'It has indeed!' my companion indulgently sighed. 'So what would it do if she were there?'

'I should like immensely to see. And we *shall* see.'

'Why, do you believe she'll still go?'

'Certainly. She *must*.'

But my friend shook it off. 'She won't.'

'She shall!' I retorted with a laugh. But the next moment I said: 'And what does the old woman say?'

'To Jane's behaviour? Not a word – never speaks of it. She talks now much less than she used – only seems to wait. But it's my belief she thinks.'

'And – do you mean – knows?'

'Yes, knows that she's abandoned. In her silence there she takes it in.'

'It's her way of making Jane pay?' At this, somehow, I felt more serious. 'Oh, dear, dear – she'll disinherit her!'

When, in the following June, I went on to return my sister-in-law's visit the first object that met my eyes in her little white parlour was a figure that, to my stupefaction, presented itself for the moment as that of Mrs Rimmle. I had gone to my room after arriving, and, on dressing, had come down: the apparition I speak of had arisen in the interval. Its ambiguous character lasted, however, but a second or two – I had taken Becky for her mother because I knew no one but her mother of that extreme age. Becky's age was quite startling; it had made a great stride, though, strangely enough, irrecoverably seated as she now was in it, she had a wizened brightness that I had scarcely yet seen in her. I remember indulging on this occasion in two silent observations: one to the effect that I had not hitherto been conscious of her full resemblance to the old lady, and the other to the effect that, as I had said to my sister-in-law at Christmas, 'Europe', even as reaching her only through Jane's sensibilities, had really at last brought her out. She was in fact 'out' in a manner of which this encounter offered to my eyes a unique example: it was the single hour, often as I had been at Brookbridge, of my meeting her elsewhere than in her mother's drawing-room. I surmise that, besides being adjusted to her more marked time of life, the garments she wore abroad, and in particular her little plain bonnet, presented points of resemblance to the close sable sheath and the quaint old headgear that, in the white house behind the elms, I had from far back associated with the eternal image in the stiff chair. Of course I immediately spoke of Jane, showing an interest and asking for news; on which she answered me with a smile, but not at all as I had expected.

'*Those* are not really the things you want to know – where she is, whom she's with, how she manages and where she's going next – oh, no!' And the admirable woman gave a laugh that was somehow both light and sad – sad, in particular, with a strange, long weariness. 'What you do want to know is when she's coming back.'

I shook my head very kindly, but out of a wealth of experience that, I flattered myself, was equal to Miss Becky's. 'I do know it. Never.'

Miss Becky, at this, exchanged with me a long, deep look. 'Never.'

We had, in silence, a little luminous talk about it, in the

course of which she seemed to tell me the most interesting things. 'And how's your mother?' I then inquired.

She hesitated, but finally spoke with the same serenity. 'My mother's all right. You see, she's not alive.'

'Oh, Becky!' my sister-in-law pleadingly interjected.

But Becky only addressed herself to me. 'Come and see if she is. *I* think she isn't – but Maria perhaps isn't so clear. Come, at all events, and judge and tell me.'

It was a new note, and I was a little bewildered. 'Ah, but I'm not a doctor!'

'No, thank God – you're not. That's why I ask you.' And now she said good-bye.

I kept her hand a moment. '*You're* more alive than ever!'

'I'm very tired.' She took it with the same smile, but for Becky it was much to say.

IV

'Not alive,' the next day, was certainly what Mrs Rimmle looked when, coming in according to my promise, I found her, with Miss Maria, in her usual place. Though shrunken and diminished she still occupied her high-backed chair with a visible theory of erectness, and her intensely aged face – combined with something dauntless that belonged to her very presence and that was effective even in this extremity – might have been that of some centenarian sovereign, of indistinguishable sex, brought forth to be shown to the people as a disproof of the rumour of extinction. Mummified and open-eyed she looked at me, but I had no impression that she made me out. I had come this time without my sister-in-law, who had frankly pleaded to me – which also, for a daughter of Brookbridge, was saying much – that the house had grown too painful. Poor Miss Maria excused Miss Becky on the score of her not being well – and that, it struck me, was saying most of all. The absence of the others gave the occasion a different note; but I talked with Miss Maria for five minutes and perceived

that – save for her saying, of her own movement, anything
about Jane – she now spoke as if her mother had lost hearing
or sense, or both, alluding freely and distinctly, though indeed
favourably, to her condition. 'She has expected your visit and
she much enjoys it,' my interlocutress said, while the old
woman, soundless and motionless, simply fixed me without
expression. Of course there was little to keep me; but I became
aware, as I rose to go, that there was more than I had supposed. On my approaching her to take leave Mrs Rimmle gave
signs of consciousness.

'Have you heard about Jane?'

I hesitated, feeling a responsibility, and appealed for direction to Maria's face. But Maria's face was troubled, was turned
altogether to her mother's. 'About her life in Europe?' I then
rather helplessly asked.

The old woman fronted me, on this, in a manner that made
me feel silly. 'Her life?' – and her voice, with this second effort,
came out stronger. 'Her death, if you please.'

'Her death?' I echoed, before I could stop myself, with the
accent of deprecation.

Miss Maria uttered a vague sound of pain, and I felt her
turn away, but the marvel of her mother's little unquenched
spark still held me. 'Jane's dead. We've heard,' said Mrs
Rimmle. 'We've heard from – where is it we've heard from?'
She had quite revived – she appealed to her daughter.

The poor old girl, crimson, rallied to her duty. 'From Europe.'

Mrs Rimmle made at us both a little grim inclination of the
head. 'From Europe.' I responded, in silence, with a deflection
from every rigour, and, still holding me, she went on: 'And
now Rebecca's going.'

She had gathered by this time such emphasis to say it that
again, before I could help myself, I vibrated in reply. 'To
Europe – now?' It was as if for an instant she had made me
believe it.

She only stared at me, however, from her wizened mask;
then her eyes followed my companion. 'Has she gone?'

'Not yet, mother.' Maria tried to treat it as a joke, but her
smile was embarrassed and dim.

'Then where is she?'

'She's lying down.'

The old woman kept up her hard, queer gaze, but directing it, after a minute, to me. 'She's going.'

'Oh, some day!' I foolishly laughed; and on this I got to the door, where I separated from my younger hostess, who came no further. Only, as I held the door open, she said to me under cover of it and very quietly:

'It's poor mother's idea.'

I saw – it was her idea. Mine was – for some time after this, even after I had returned to New York and to my usual occupations – that I should never again see Becky. I had seen her for the last time, I believed, under my sister-in-law's roof, and in the autumn it was given to me to hear from that fellow-admirer that she had succumbed at last to the situation. The day of the call I have just described had been a date in the process of her slow shrinkage – it was literally the first time she had, as they said at Brookbridge, given up. She had been ill for years, but the other state of health in the contemplation of which she had spent so much of her life had left her, till too late, no margin for meeting it. The encounter, at last, came simply in the form of the discovery that it *was* too late; on which, naturally, she had given up more and more. I had heard indeed, all summer, by letter, how Brookbridge had watched her do so; whereby the end found me in a manner prepared. Yet in spite of my preparation there remained with me a soreness, and when I was next – it was some six months later – on the scene of her martyrdom I replied, I fear, with an almost rabid negative to the question put to me in due course by my kinswoman. 'Call on them? Never again!'

I went, none the less, the very next day. Everything was the same in the sunny parlour – everything that most mattered, I mean: the immemorial mummy in the high chair and the tributes, in the little frames on the walls, to the celebrity of its late husband. Only Maria Rimmle was different: if Becky, on my last seeing her, had looked as old as her mother, Maria – save that she moved about – looked older. I remember that she moved about, but I scarce remember what she said; and indeed what was there to say? When I risked a question, however, she had a reply.

'But *now* at least—?' I tried to put it to her suggestively.

At first she was vague. ' "Now"?'

'Won't Miss Jane come back?'

Oh, the headshake she gave me! 'Never.' It positively pictured to me, for the instant, a well-preserved woman, a sort of rich, ripe *seconde jeunesse* by the Arno.

'Then that's only to make more sure of your finally joining her.'

Maria Rimmle repeated her headshake. 'Never.'

We stood so, a moment, bleakly face to face; I could think of no attenuation that would be particularly happy. But while I tried I heard a hoarse gasp that, fortunately, relieved me – a signal strange and at first formless from the occupant of the high-backed chair. 'Mother wants to speak to you,' Maria then said.

So it appeared from the drop of the old woman's jaw, the expression of her mouth opened as if for the emission of sound. It was difficult to me, somehow, to seem to sympathize without hypocrisy, but, so far as a step nearer could do so, I invited communication. 'Have you heard where Becky's gone?' the wonderful witch's white lips then extraordinarily asked.

It drew from Maria, as on my previous visit, an uncontrollable groan, and this, in turn, made me take time to consider. As I considered, however, I had an inspiration. 'To Europe?'

I must have adorned it with a strange grimace, but my inspiration had been right. 'To Europe,' said Mrs Rimmle.

FORDHAM CASTLE

Sharp little Madame Massin, who carried on the pleasant pension and who had her small hard eyes everywhere at once, came out to him on the terrace and held up a letter addressed in a manner that he recognized even from afar, held it up with a question in her smile, or a smile, rather a pointed one, in her question – he could scarce have said which. She was looking, while so occupied, at the German group engaged in the garden, near by, with aperitive beer and disputation – the noonday luncheon being now imminent; and the way in which she could show prompt lips while her observation searchingly ranged might have reminded him of the object placed by a spectator at the theatre in the seat he desires to keep during the entr'acte. Conscious of the cross-currents of international passion, she tried, so far as possible, not to mix her sheep and her goats. The view of the bluest end of the Lake[1] of Geneva – she insisted in persuasive circulars that it *was* the bluest – had never, on her high-perched terrace, wanted for admirers, though thus early in the season, during the first days of May, they were not so numerous as she was apt to see them at midsummer. This precisely, Abel Taker could infer, was the reason of a remark she had made him before the claims of the letter had been settled. 'I shall put you next the American lady – the one who arrived yesterday. I know you'll be kind to her; she had to go to bed, as soon as she got here, with a sick-headache brought on by her journey. But she's better. Who isn't better as soon as they get here? She's coming down, and I'm sure she'd like to know you.'

Taker had now the letter in his hand – the letter intended for 'Mr C. P. Addard'; which was not the name inscribed in the

two or three books he had left out in his room, any more than
it matched the initials 'A.F.T.' attached to the few pieces of his
modest total of luggage. Moreover, since Madame Massin's
establishment counted, to his still somewhat bewildered mind,
so little for an hotel, as hotels were mainly known to him, he
had avoided the act of 'registering', and the missive with which
his hostess was practically testing him represented the very
first piece of postal matter taken in since his arrival that hadn't
been destined to some one else. He had privately blushed for
the meagreness of his mail, which made him look unimport-
ant. That however was a detail, an appearance he was used to;
indeed the reasons making for such an appearance might never
have been so pleasant to him as on this vision of his identity
formally and legibly denied. It was denied there in his wife's
large straight hand; his eyes, attached to the envelope, took in
the failure of any symptom of weakness in her stroke; she at
least had the courage of his passing for somebody he wasn't, of
his passing rather for nobody at all, and he felt the force of her
character more irresistibly than ever as he thus submitted to
what she was doing with him. He wasn't used to lying; whatever his faults – and he was used, perfectly, to the idea of his
faults – he hadn't made them worse by any perverse theory,
any tortuous plea, of innocence; so that probably, with every
inch of him giving him away, Madame Massin didn't believe
him a bit when he appropriated the letter. He was quite aware
he could have made no fight if she had challenged his right to
it. That would have come of his making no fight, nowadays, on
any ground, with any woman; he had so lost the proper spirit,
the necessary confidence. It was true that he had had to do for
a long time with no woman in the world but Sue, and of the
practice of opposition so far as Sue was concerned the end had
been determined early in his career. His hostess fortunately
accepted his word, but the way in which her momentary attention bored into his secret like the turn of a gimlet gave him a
sense of the quantity of life that passed before her as a dealer
with all comers – gave him almost an awe of her power of not
wincing. She knew he wasn't, he couldn't be, C. P. Addard,
even though she mightn't know, or still less care, who he was;

and there was therefore something queer about him if he pretended to be. That was what she didn't mind, there being something queer about him; and what was further present to him was that she would have known when to mind, when really to be on her guard. She attached no importance to his trick; she had doubtless somewhere at the rear, amid the responsive underlings with whom she was sometimes heard volubly, yet so obscurely, to chatter, her clever French amusement about it. He couldn't at all events have said if the whole passage with her most brought home to him the falsity of his position or most glossed it over. On the whole perhaps it rather helped him, since from this moment his masquerade had actively begun.

Taking his place for luncheon, in any case, he found himself next the American lady, as he conceived, spoken of by Madame Massin – in whose appearance he was at first as disappointed as if, a little, though all unconsciously, he had been building on it. Had she loomed into view, on their hostess's hint, as one of the vague alternatives, the possible beguilements, of his leisure – presenting herself solidly where so much else had refused to crystallize? It was certain at least that she presented herself solidly, being a large mild smooth person with a distinct double chin, with grey hair arranged in small flat regular circles, figures of a geometrical perfection; with diamond earrings, with a long-handled eye-glass, with an accumulation of years and of weight and presence, in fine, beyond what his own rather melancholy consciousness acknowledged. He was forty-five, and it took every year of his life, took all he hadn't done with them, to account for his present situation – since you couldn't be, conclusively, of so little use, of so scant an application, to any mortal career, above all to your own, unless you had been given up and cast aside after a long succession of experiments tried with you. But the American lady with the mathematical hair which reminded him in a manner of the old-fashioned 'work',[2] the weeping willows and mortuary urns represented by the little glazed-over flaxen or auburn or sable or silvered convolutions and tendrils, the capillary flowers, that he had admired in the days of his innocence – the

American lady had probably seen her half-century; all the more that before luncheon was done she had begun to strike him as having, like himself, slipped slowly down over its stretched and shiny surface, an expanse as insecure to fumbling feet as a great cold curved ice-field, into the comparatively warm hollow of resignation and obscurity. She gave him from the first – and he was afterwards to see why – an attaching impression of being, like himself, in exile, and of having like himself learned to butter her bread with a certain acceptance of fate. The only thing that puzzled him on this head was that to parallel his own case she would have had openly to consent to be shelved; which made the difficulty, here, that that was exactly what, as between wife and husband, remained unthinkable on the part of the wife. The necessity for the shelving of one or the other was a case that appeared often to arise, but this wasn't the way he had in general seen it settled. She made him in short, through some influence he couldn't immediately reduce to its elements, vaguely think of her as sacrificed – without blood, as it were; as obligingly and persuadedly passive. Yet this effect, a reflexion of his own state, would doubtless have been better produced for him by a mere melancholy man. She testified unmistakeably to the greater energy of women; for he could think of no manifestation of spirit on his own part that might pass for an equivalent, in the way of resistance, of protest, to the rhythmic though rather wiggy water-waves that broke upon her bald-looking brow as upon a beach bared by a low tide. He had cocked up often enough – and as with the intention of doing it still more under Sue's nose than under his own – the two ends of his half-'sandy' half-grizzled moustache, and he had in fact given these ornaments an extra twist just before coming in to luncheon. That however was but a momentary flourish; the most marked ferocity of which hadn't availed not to land him – well, where he was landed now.

His new friend mentioned that she had come up from Rome and that Madame Massin's establishment had been highly spoken of to her there, and this, slight as it was, straightway contributed in its degree for Abel Taker to the idea that they had something in common. He was in a condition in which he

could feel the drift of vague currents, and he knew how highly
the place had been spoken of to *him*. There was but a shade of
difference in his having had his lesson in Florence. He let his
companion know, without reserve, that he too had come up
from Italy, after spending three or four months there: though
he remembered in time that, being now C. P. Addard, it was
only as C. P. Addard he could speak. He tried to think, in
order to give himself something to say, what C. P. Addard
would have done; but he was doomed to feel always, in the
whole connexion, his lack of imagination. He had had many
days to come to it and nothing else to do; but he hadn't even yet
made up his mind who C. P. Addard was or invested him with
any distinguishing marks. He felt like a man who, moving in
this, that or the other direction, saw each successively lead him
to some danger; so that he began to ask himself why he
shouldn't just lie outright, boldly and inventively, and see what
that could do for him. There was an excitement, the excitement of personal risk, about it – much the same as would
belong for an ordinary man to the first trial of a flying-machine;[3]
yet it was exactly such a course as Sue had prescribed on his
asking her what he should do. 'Anything in the world you like
but talk about *me*: think of some other woman, as bad and
bold as you please, and say you're married to *her*.' Those had
been literally her words, together with others, again and again
repeated, on the subject of his being free to 'kill and bury' her
as often as he chose. This was the way she had met his objection to his own death and interment; she had asked him, in her
bright hard triumphant way, why he couldn't defend himself
by shooting back. The real reason was of course that he was
nothing without her, whereas she was everything, could be
anything in the wide world she liked, without him. That question precisely had been a part of what was before him while he
strolled in the projected green gloom of Madame Massin's
plane-trees; he wondered what she *was* choosing to be and
how good a time it was helping her to have. He could be sure
she was rising to it, on some line or other, and that was what
secretly made him say: 'Why shouldn't I get something out of
it too, just for the harmless fun –?'

It kept coming back to him, naturally, that he hadn't the breadth of fancy, that he knew himself as he knew the taste of ill-made coffee, that he was the same old Abel Taker he had ever been, in whose aggregation of items it was as vain to feel about for latent heroisms as it was useless to rummage one's trunk for presentable clothes that one didn't possess. But did that absolve him (having so definitely Sue's permission) from seeing to what extent he might temporarily make believe? If he were to flap his wings very hard and crow very loud and take as long a jump as possible at the same time – if he were to do all that perhaps he should achieve for half a minute the sensation of soaring. He knew only one thing Sue couldn't do, from the moment she didn't divorce him: she couldn't get rid of his name, unaccountably, after all, as she hated it; she couldn't get rid of it because she would have always sooner or later to come back to it. She might consider that her being a thing so dreadful as Mrs Abel Taker was a stumbling-block in her social path that nothing but his real, his official, his advertised circulated demise (with 'American papers please copy'[4]) would avail to dislodge: she would have none the less to reckon with his continued existence as the drop of bitterness in her cup that seasoned undisguiseably each draught. He might make use of his present opportunity to row out into the lake with his pockets full of stones and there quietly slip overboard; but he could think of no shorter cut for her ceasing to be what her marriage and the law of the land had made her. She was not an inch less Mrs Abel Taker for these days of his sequestration, and the only thing she indeed claimed was that the concealment of the source of her shame, the suppression of the person who had divided with her his inherited absurdity, made the difference of a shade or two for getting honourably, as she called it, 'about'. How she had originally come to incur this awful inconvenience – *that* part of the matter, left to herself, she would undertake to keep vague; and she wasn't really left to herself so long as he too flaunted the dreadful flag.[5]

This was why she had provided him with another and placed him out at board, to constitute, as it were, a permanent *alibi*; telling him she should quarrel with no colours under which he might elect to sail, and promising to take him back when she had got where she wanted. She wouldn't mind so much then – she only wanted a fair start. It wasn't a fair start – *was* it? she asked him frankly – so long as he was always there, so terribly cruelly there, to speak of what she *had* been. She had been nothing worse, to his sense, than a very pretty girl of eighteen out in Peoria,[6] who had seen at that time no one else she wanted more to marry, nor even any one who had been so supremely struck by her. That, absolutely, was the worst that could be said of her. It was so bad at any rate in her own view – it had grown so bad in the widening light of life – that it had fairly become more than she could bear and that something, as she said, had to be done about it. She hadn't known herself originally any more than she had known him – hadn't foreseen how much better she was going to come out, nor how, for her individually, as distinguished from him, there might be the possibility of a big future. He couldn't be explained away – he cried out with all his dreadful presence that she *had* been pleased to marry him; and what they therefore had to do must transcend explaining. It was perhaps now helping her, off there in London, and especially at Fordham Castle – she was staying last at Fordham Castle, Wilts[7] – it was perhaps inspiring her even more than she had expected, that they were able to try together this particular substitute: news of her progress in fact – her progress on from Fordham Castle, if anything could be higher – would not improbably be contained in the unopened letter he had lately pocketed.

There was a given moment at luncheon meanwhile, in his talk with his countrywoman, when he did try that flap of the wing – did throw off, for a flight into the blue, the first falsehood he could think of. 'I stopped in Italy, you see, on my way back from the East, where I had gone – to Constantinople' – he rose actually to Constantinople – 'to visit Mrs Addard's grave.' And after they had all come out to coffee in the rustling shade, with the vociferous German tribe at one end of the terrace, the English family keeping silence with an English accent, as it struck him, in the middle, and his direction taken, by his new friend's side, to the other unoccupied corner, he found himself oppressed with what he had on his hands, the burden of keeping up this expensive fiction. He had never been to Constantinople – it could easily be proved against him; he ought to have thought of something better, have got his effect on easier terms. Yet a funnier thing still than this quick repentance was the quite equally fictive ground on which his companion had affected him – when he came to think of it – as meeting him.

'Why you know that's very much the same errand that took me to Rome. I visited the grave of my daughter – whom I lost there some time ago.'

She had turned her face to him after making this statement, looked at him with an odd blink of her round kind plain eyes, as if to see how he took it. He had taken it on the spot, for this was the only thing to do; but he had felt how much deeper down he was himself sinking as he replied: 'Ah it's a sad pleasure, isn't it? But those are places one doesn't want to neglect.'

'Yes – that's what I feel. I go,' his neighbour had solemnly pursued, 'about every two years.'

With which she had looked away again, leaving him really not able to emulate her. 'Well, I hadn't been before. You see it's a long way.'

'Yes – that's the trying part. It makes you feel you'd have done better—'

'To bring them right home and have it done over there?' he had asked as she let the sad subject go a little. He quite agreed. 'Yes – that's what many do.'

'But it gives of course a peculiar interest.' So they had kept it up. 'I mean in places that mightn't have so *very* much.'

'Places like Rome and Constantinople?' he had rejoined while he noticed the cautious anxious sound of her 'very'. The tone was to come back to him, and it had already made him feel sorry for her, with its suggestion of her being at sea like himself. Unmistakeably, poor lady, she too was trying to float – was striking out in timid convulsive movements. Well, he wouldn't make it difficult for her, and immediately, so as not to appear to cast any ridicule, he observed that, wherever great bereavements might have occurred, there was no place so

remarkable as not to gain an association. Such memories made
at the least another object for coming. It was after this recognition, on either side, that they adjourned to the garden – Taker
having in his ears again the good lady's rather troubled or
muddled echo: 'Oh yes, when you come to all the *object*s—!'
The grave of one's wife or one's daughter was an object quite
as much as all those that one looked up in Baedeker[8] – those of
the family of the Castle of Chillon and the Dent du Midi,[9] features of the view to be enjoyed from different parts of Madame
Massin's premises. It was very soon, none the less, rather as if
these latter presences, diffusing their reality and majesty, had
taken the colour out of all other evoked romance; and to that
degree that when Abel's fellow guest happened to lay down on
the parapet of the terrace three or four articles she had brought
out with her, her fan, a couple of American newspapers and a
letter that had obviously come to her by the same post as his
own, he availed himself of the accident to jump at a further
conclusion. Their coffee, which was 'extra',[10] as he knew and
as, in the way of benevolence, he boldly warned her, was
brought forth to them, and while she was giving her attention
to her demi-tasse he let his eyes rest for three seconds on the
superscription of her letter. His mind was by this time made
up, and the beauty of it was that he couldn't have said why. the
letter was from her daughter, whom she had been burying for
him in Rome, and it would be addressed in a name that was
really no more hers than the name his wife had thrust upon
him[11] was his. Her daughter had put *her* out at cheap board,[12]
pending higher issues, just as Sue had put him – so that there
was a logic not other than fine in his notifying her of what coffee every day might let her in for. She was addressed on her
envelope as 'Mrs Vanderplank', but he had privately arrived,
before she so much as put down her cup, at the conviction that
this was a borrowed and lawless title, for all the world as if,
poor dear innocent woman, she were a bold bad adventuress.
He had acquired furthermore the moral certitude that he was
on the track, as he would have said, of her true identity, such
as it might be. He couldn't think of it as in itself either very
mysterious or very impressive; but, whatever it was, her

duplicity had as yet mastered no finer art than his own, inasmuch as she had positively not escaped, at table, inadvertently dropping a name which, while it lingered on Abel's ear, gave her quite away. She had spoken, in her solemn sociability and as by the force of old habit, of 'Mr Magaw', and nothing was more to be presumed than that this gentleman was her defunct husband, not so very long defunct, who had permitted her while in life the privilege of association with him, but whose extinction had left her to be worked upon by different ideas.

These ideas would have germed, infallibly, in the brain of the young woman, her only child, under whose rigid rule she now – it was to be detected – drew her breath in pain.[13] Madame Massin would abysmally know, Abel reflected, for he was at the end of a few minutes more intimately satisfied that Mrs Magaw's American newspapers, coming to her straight from the other side and not yet detached from their wrappers, would not be directed to Mrs Vanderplank, and that, this being the case, the poor lady would have had to invent some pretext for a claim to goods likely still perhaps to be lawfully called for. And she wasn't formed for duplicity, the large simple scared foolish fond woman, the vague anxiety in whose otherwise so uninhabited and unreclaimed countenance, as void of all history as an expanse of Western prairie seen from a car-window,[14] testified to her scant aptitude for her part. He was far from the desire to question their hostess, however – for the study of his companion's face on its mere inferred merits had begun to dawn upon him as the possible resource of his ridiculous leisure. He might verily have some fun with her – or he would so have conceived it had he not become aware before they separated, half an hour later, of a kind of fellow-feeling for her that seemed to plead for her being spared. She *wasn't* being, in some quarter still indistinct to him – and so no more was he, and these things were precisely a reason. Her sacrifice, he divined, was an act of devotion, a state not yet disciplined to the state of confidence. She had presently, as from a return of vigilance, gathered in her postal property, shuffling it together at her further side and covering it with her pocket-handkerchief – though this very betrayal indeed but

quickened his temporary impulse to break out to her, sympathetically, with a 'Had you the misfortune to *lose* Magaw?' or
with the effective production of his own card and a smiling, an
inviting, a consoling 'That's who *I* am if you want to know!'
He really made out, with the idle human instinct, the crude
sense for other people's pains and pleasures that had, on his
showing, to his so great humiliation, been found an inadequate
outfit for the successful conduct of the coal, the commission,
the insurance and, as a last resort, desperate and disgraceful,
the book-agency business[15] – he really made out that she didn't
want to know, or wouldn't for some little time; that she was
decidedly afraid in short, and covertly agitated, and all just
because she too, with him, suspected herself dimly in presence
of that mysterious 'more' than, in the classic phrase, met the
eye. They parted accordingly, as if to relieve, till they could
recover themselves, the conscious tension of their being able
neither to hang back with grace nor to advance with glory; but
flagrantly full, at the same time, both of the recognition that
they couldn't in such a place avoid each other even if they had
desired it, and of the suggestion that they wouldn't desire it,
after such subtlety of communion, even were it to be thought of.

Abel Taker, till dinner-time, turned over his little adventure
and extracted, while he hovered and smoked and mused, some
refreshment from the impression the subtlety of communion
had left with him. Mrs Vanderplank was his senior by several
years, and was neither fair nor slim nor 'bright' nor truly, nor
even falsely, elegant, nor anything that Sue had taught him, in
her wonderful way, to associate with the American woman at
the American woman's best – that best than which there was
nothing better, as he had so often heard her say, on God's great
earth. Sue would have banished her to the wildest waste of the
unknowable, would have looked over her head in the manner
he had often seen her use – as if she were in an exhibition of
pictures, were in front of something bad and negligible that
had got itself placed on the line,[16] but that had the real thing,
the thing of interest for those who *knew* (and when didn't Sue
know?) hung above it. In Mrs Magaw's presence everything
would have been of more interest to Sue than Mrs Magaw; but

that consciousness failed to prevent his feeling the appeal of
this inmate much rather confirmed than weakened when she
reappeared for dinner. It was impressed upon him, after they
had again seated themselves side by side, that she was reaching
out to him indirectly, guardedly, even as he was to her; so that
later on, in the garden, where they once more had their coffee
together – it *might* have been so free and easy, so wildly foreign, so almost Bohemian – he lost all doubt of the wisdom of
his taking his plunge. This act of resolution was not, like the
other he had risked in the morning, an upward flutter into fiction, but a straight and possibly dangerous dive into the very
depths of truth. Their instinct was unmistakeably to cling to
each other, but it was as if they wouldn't know where to take
hold till the air had really been cleared. Actually, in fact, they
required a light – the aid prepared by him in the shape of a
fresh match for his cigarette after he had extracted, under
cover of the scented dusk, one of his cards from his pocket-book.

'There I honestly am, you see – Abel F. Taker; which I think
you ought to know.' It was relevant to nothing, relevant only to
the grope of their talk, broken with sudden silences where they
stopped short for fear of mistakes; but as he put the card before
her he held out to it the little momentary flame. And this was
the way that, after a while and from one thing to another, he
himself, in exchange for what he had to give and what he gave
freely, heard all about 'Mattie' – Mattie Magaw, Mrs Vanderplank's beautiful and high-spirited daughter, who, as he
learned, found her two names, so dreadful even singly, a combination not to be borne, and carried on a quarrel with them
no less desperate than Sue's quarrel with – well, with everything. She had, quite as Sue had done, declared her need of a
free hand to fight them, and she was, for all the world like Sue
again, now fighting them to the death. This similarity of situation was wondrously completed by the fact that the scene of
Miss Magaw's struggle was, as her mother explained, none
other than that uppermost walk of 'high' English life which
formed the present field of Mrs Taker's operations; a circumstance on which Abel presently produced his comment. 'Why

if they're after the same thing in the same place, I wonder if we shan't hear of their meeting.'

Mrs Magaw appeared for a moment to wonder too. 'Well, if they do meet I guess we'll hear. I will say for Mattie that she writes me pretty fully. And I presume,' she went on, 'Mrs Taker keeps *you* posted?'

'No,' he had to confess – 'I don't hear from her in much detail. She knows I back her,' Abel smiled, 'and that's enough for her. "You be quiet and I'll let you know when you're wanted" – that's her motto; I'm to wait, wherever I am, till I'm called for. But I guess she won't be in a hurry to call for me' – this reflexion he showed he was familiar with. 'I've stood in her light so long – her "social" light, outside of which every-thing is for Sue black darkness – that I don't really see the reason she should ever want me back. That at any rate is what I'm doing – I'm just waiting. And I didn't expect the luck of being able to wait in your company. I couldn't suppose – that's the truth,' he added – 'that there was another, anywhere about, with the same ideas or the same strong character. It had never seemed to be possible,' he ruminated, 'that there could be any one like Mrs Taker.'

He was to remember afterwards how his companion had appeared to consider this approximation. 'Another, you mean, like my Mattie?'

'Yes – like my Sue. Any one that really comes up to her. It will be,' he declared, 'the first one I've struck.'

'Well,' said Mrs Vanderplank, 'my Mattie's remarkably handsome.'

'I'm sure—! But Mrs Taker's remarkably handsome too. Oh,' he added, both with humour and with earnestness, 'if it wasn't for that I wouldn't trust her so! Because, for what she wants,' he developed, 'it's a great help to be fine-looking.'

'Ah it's always a help for a lady!' – and Mrs Magaw's sigh fluttered vaguely between the expert and the rueful. 'But what is it,' she asked, 'that Mrs Taker wants?'

'Well, she could tell you herself. I don't think she'd trust me to give an account of it. Still,' he went on, 'she *has* stated it more than once for my benefit, and perhaps that's what it all finally comes to. She wants to get where she truly belongs.'

Mrs Magaw had listened with interest. 'That's just where Mattie wants to get! And she seems to know just where it is.'

'Oh Mrs Taker knows – you can bet your life,' he laughed, 'on that. It seems to be somewhere in London or in the country round, and I dare say it's the same place as your daughter's. Once she's there, as I understand it, she'll be all right; but she has got to get there – that is to be seen there thoroughly fixed and photographed, and have it in all the papers – first. After she's fixed, she says, we'll talk. We *have* talked a good deal: when Mrs Taker says "We'll talk" I know what she means. But this time we'll have it out.'

There were communities in their fate that made his friend turn pale. 'Do you mean she won't want you to come?'

'Well, for me to "come", don't you see? will be for me to come to life. How can I come to life when I've been as dead as I am now?'

Mrs Vanderplank looked at him with a dim delicacy. 'But surely, sir, I'm not conversing with the remains—!'

'You're conversing with C. P. Addard. *He* may be alive – but even this I don't know yet; I'm just trying him,' he said: 'I'm trying him, Mrs Magaw, on you. Abel Taker's in his grave, but does it strike you that Mr Addard is at all above ground?'

He had smiled for the slightly gruesome joke of it, but she looked away as if it made her uneasy. Then, however, as she came back to him, 'Are you going to wait here?' she asked.

He held her, with some gallantry, in suspense. 'Are you?'

She postponed her answer, visibly not quite comfortable now; but they were inevitably the next day up to their necks again in the question; and then it was that she expressed more of her sense of her situation. 'Certainly I feel as if I must wait – as long as I *have* to wait. Mattie likes this place – I mean she likes it for *me*. It seems the right *sort* of place,' she opined with her perpetual earnest emphasis.

But it made him sound again the note. 'The right sort to pass for dead in?'

'Oh she doesn't want me to pass for *dead*.'

'Then what does she want you to pass for?'

The poor lady cast about. 'Well, only for Mrs Vanderplank.'

'And who or what is Mrs Vanderplank?'

Mrs Magaw considered this personage, but didn't get far. 'She isn't any one in particular, I guess.'

'That means,' Abel returned, 'that she isn't alive.'

'She isn't more than *half* alive,' Mrs Magaw conceded. 'But it isn't what I *am* – it's what I'm passing for. Or rather' – she worked it out – 'what I'm just not. I'm not passing – I don't, can't here, where it doesn't matter, you see – for her mother.'

Abel quite fell in. 'Certainly – she doesn't want to have any mother.'

'She doesn't want to have *me*. She wants me to lay low. If I lay low, she says—'

'Oh I know what she says' – Abel took it straight up. 'It's the very same as what Mrs Taker says. If you lie low she can fly high.'

It kept disconcerting her in a manner, as well as steadying, his free possession of their case. 'I don't feel as if I *was* lying – I mean as low as she wants – when I talk to you so.' She broke it off thus, and again and again, anxiously, responsibly; her sense of responsibility making Taker feel, with his braver projection of humour, quite ironic and sardonic; but as for a week, for a fortnight, for many days more, they kept frequently and intimately meeting, it was natural that the so extraordinary fact of their being, as he put it, in the same sort of box,[17] and of their boxes having so even more remarkably bumped together under Madame Massin's *tilleuls*, shouldn't only make them reach out to each other across their queer coil of communications, cut so sharp off in other quarters, but should prevent their pretending to any real consciousness but that of their ordeal. It was Abel's idea, promptly enough expressed to Mrs Magaw, that they ought to get something out of it; but when he had said that a few times over (the first time she had met it in silence), she finally replied, and in a manner that he thought quite sublime: 'Well, we *shall* – if they do all they want. We shall feel we've helped. And it isn't so *very* much to do.'

'You think it isn't so very much to do – to lie down and die for them?'

'Well, if I don't hate it any worse when I'm really dead—!' She took herself up, however, as if she had skirted the profane. 'I don't say that if I didn't *believe* in Mat—! But I do believe, you see. That's where she *has* me.'

'Oh I see more or less. That's where Sue has *me*.'

Mrs Magaw fixed him with a milder solemnity. 'But what has Mrs Taker against you?'

'It's sweet of you to ask,' he smiled; while it really came to him that he was living with her under ever so much less strain than what he had been feeling for ever so long before from Sue. Wouldn't he have liked it to go on and on – wouldn't that have suited C. P. Addard? He seemed to be finding out who C. P. Addard was – so that it came back again to the way Sue fixed things. She had fixed them so that C. P. Addard could become quite interested in Mrs Vanderplank and quite soothed by her – and so that Mrs Vanderplank as well, wonderful to say, had lost her impatience for Mattie's summons a good deal more, he was sure, than she confessed. It was from this moment none the less that he began, with a strange but distinct little pang, to see that he couldn't be sure of her. Her question had produced in him a vibration of the sensibility that even the long series of mortifications, of publicly proved inaptitudes, springing originally from his lack of business talent, but owing an aggravation of aspect to an absence of nameable 'type' of which he hadn't been left unaware, wasn't to have wholly toughened. Yet it struck him positively as the prettiest word ever spoken to him, so straight a surprise at his wife's dissatisfaction; and he was verily so unused to tributes to his adequacy that this one lingered in the air a moment and seemed almost to create a possibility. He wondered, honestly, what she could see in him, in whom Sue now at last saw really less than nothing; and his fingers instinctively moved to his moustache, a corner of which he twiddled up again, also wondering if it were perhaps only *that* – though Sue had as good as told him that the undue flourish of this feature but brought out to her view the insignificance of all the rest of him. Just to hang in the iridescent ether with Mrs Vanderplank, to whom he wasn't insignificant, just for them to sit on there together, protected, indeed positively ennobled, by their loss of identity, struck him as the foretaste of a kind of felicity that he hadn't in the past known enough about really to miss it. He appeared to have become aware that he should miss it quite sharply, that he would find how he had already learned to, if she should go; and the very sadness of his apprehension quickened his vision of what would work with her. She would want, with all the roundness of her kind, plain eyes, to see Mattie fixed – whereas he'd be hanged if he wasn't willing, on his side, to take Sue's elevation quite on trust. For the instant, however, he said nothing of that; he only followed up a little his acknowledgement of her having touched him. 'What you ask me, you know, is just what I myself was going to ask. What has Miss Magaw got against *you*?'

'Well, if you were to see her I guess you'd know.'

'Why I should think she'd like to show you,' said Abel Taker.

'She doesn't so much mind their *seeing* me – when once she has had a look at me first. But she doesn't like them to hear me – though I don't talk so very much. Mattie speaks in the real English style,'[18] Mrs Magaw explained.

'But ain't the real English style not to speak at all?'

'Well, she's having the best kind of time, she writes me – so I presume there must be some talk in which she can shine.'

'Oh I've no doubt at all Miss Magaw *talks*!' – and Abel, in his contemplative way, seemed to have it before him.

'Well, don't you go and believe she talks too much,' his companion rejoined with spirit; and this it was that brought to a head his prevision of his own fate.

'I see what's going to happen. You only want to go to her. You want to get your share, after all. You'll leave me without a pang.'

Mrs Magaw stared. 'But won't you be going too? When Mrs Taker sends for you?'

He shook, as by a rare chance, a competent head. 'Mrs Taker won't send for me. I don't make out the use Mrs Taker can ever have for me again.'

Mrs Magaw looked grave. 'But not to enjoy your seeing—?'

'My seeing where she has come out? Oh that won't be necessary to *her* enjoyment of it. It would be well enough perhaps if

I could see without being seen; but the trouble with me – for I'm worse than you,' Abel said – 'is that it doesn't do for me either to be heard *or* seen. I haven't got *any* side—!'[19] But it dropped; it was too old a story.

'Not any possible side at all?' his friend, in her candour, doubtingly echoed. 'Why what do they want over there?'

It made him give a comic pathetic wail. 'Ah to know a person who says such things as that to me, and to have to give her up—!'

She appeared to consider with a certain alarm what this might portend, and she really fell back before it. 'Would you think I'd be able to give up Mattie?'

'Why not – if she's successful? The thing you wouldn't like – *you* wouldn't, I'm sure – would be to give her up if she should find, or if you should find, she wasn't.'

'Well, I guess Mattie will be successful,' said Mrs Magaw.

'Ah you're a worshipper of success!' he groaned. 'I'd give Mrs Taker up, definitely, just to remain C. P. Addard with you.'

She allowed it her thought; but, as he felt, superficially. 'She's your wife, sir, you know, whatever you do.'

' "Mine"? Ah but whose? She isn't C. P. Addard's.'

She rose at this as if they were going too far; yet she showed him, he seemed to see, the first little concession – which was indeed to be the only one – of her inner timidity; something that suggested how she must have preserved as a token, laid away among spotless properties, the visiting-card he had originally handed her. 'Well, I guess the one I feel for is Abel F. Taker!'

This, in the end, however, made no difference; since one of the things that inevitably came up between them was that if Mattie had a quarrel with her name her most workable idea would be to get somebody to give her a better. That, he easily made out, was fundamentally what she was after, and, though, delicately and discreetly, as he felt, he didn't reduce Mrs Vanderplank to so stating the case, he finally found himself believing in Miss Magaw with just as few reserves as those with which he believed in Sue. If it was a question of her 'shining' she would indubitably shine; she was evidently, like the wife by whom he had been, in the early time, too provincially, too primitively accepted, of the great radiating substance, and there were times, here at Madame Massin's, while he strolled to and fro and smoked, when Mrs Taker's distant lustre fairly peeped at him over the opposite mountain-tops, fringing their silhouettes as with the little hard bright rim of a coming day. It was clear that Mattie's mother couldn't be expected not to want to see her married; the shade of doubt bore only on the stage of the business at which Mrs Magaw might safely be let out of the box. Was she to emerge abruptly *as* Mrs Magaw? – or was the lid simply to be tipped back so that, for a good look, she might sit up a little straighter? She had got news at any rate, he inferred, which suggested to her that the term of her suppression was in sight; and she even let it out to him that, yes, certainly, for Mattie to be ready for her – and she did look as if she were going to be ready – she must be right down sure. They had had further lights by this time moreover, lights much more vivid always in Mattie's bulletins than in Sue's; which latter, as Abel insistently imaged it, were really each time, on Mrs Taker's part, as limited as a peep into a death-chamber. The death-chamber was Madame Massin's terrace; and – he completed the image – how could Sue *not* want to know how things were looking for the funeral, which was in any case to be thoroughly 'quiet'? *The* vivid thing seemed to pass before Abel's eyes the day he heard of the bright compatriot, just the person to go round with, a charming handsome witty widow, whom Miss Magaw had met at Fordham Castle, whose ideas were, on all important points, just the same as her own, whose means also (so that they could join forces on an equality) matched beautifully, and whose name in fine was Mrs Sherrington Reeve. 'Mattie has felt the want,' Mrs Magaw explained, 'of some lady, some real lady like that, to go round with: she says she sometimes doesn't find it very pleasant going round alone.'

Abel Taker had listened with interest – this information left him staring. 'By Gosh then, she has struck Sue!'

' "Struck" Mrs Taker—?'

'She isn't Mrs Taker now – she's Mrs Sherrington Reeve.' It had come to him with all its force – as if the glare of her genius were, at a bound, high over the summits. 'Mrs Taker's dead: I thought, you know, all the while, she must be, and this makes me sure. She died at Fordham Castle. So we're both dead.'

His friend, however, with her large blank face, lagged behind. 'At Fordham Castle too – died there?'

'Why she has been as good as *living* there!' Abel Taker emphasized. ' "Address Fordham Castle" – that's about all she has written me. But perhaps she died before she went' – he had it before him, he made it out. 'Yes, she must have gone as Mrs Sherrington Reeve. She had to die to go – as it would be for her like going to heaven. Marriages, sometimes, they say, are made up there; and so, sometimes then, apparently, are friendships – that, you see, for instance, of our two shining ones.'

Mrs Magaw's understanding was still in the shade. 'But are you sure—?'

'Why Fordham Castle settles it. If she wanted to get where she truly belongs she has got *there*. She belongs at Fordham Castle.'

The noble mass of this structure seemed to rise at his words, and his companion's grave eyes, he could see, to rest on its towers. 'But how has she become Mrs Sherrington Reeve?'

'By my death. And also after that by her own. I had to die first, you see, for *her* to be able to – that is for her to be sure. It's what she has been looking for, as I told you – to *be* sure. But oh – she was sure from the first. She knew I'd die off, when she had made it all right for me – so she felt no risk. She simply became, the day I became C. P. Addard, something as different as possible from the thing she had always so hated to be. She's what she always would have liked to be – so why shouldn't we rejoice for her? Her baser part, her vulgar part, has ceased to be, and she lives only as an angel.'

It affected his friend, this elucidation, almost with awe; she took it at least, as she took everything, stolidly. 'Do you call Mrs Taker an angel?'

Abel had turned about, as he rose to the high vision, moving, with his hands in his pockets, to and fro. But at Mrs Magaw's question he stopped short – he considered with his head in the air. 'Yes – now!'

'But do you mean it's her idea to marry?'

He thought again. 'Why for all I know she is married.'

'With you, Abel Taker, living?'

'But I ain't living. That's just the point.'

'Oh you're too dreadful' – and she gathered herself up. 'And I won't,' she said as she broke off, 'help to bury you!'

This office, none the less, as she practically had herself to acknowledge, was in a manner, and before many days, forced upon her by further important information from her daughter, in the light of the true inevitability of which they had, for that matter, been living. She was there before him with her telegram, which she simply held out to him as from a heart too full for words. 'Am engaged to Lord Dunderton,[20] and Sue thinks you can come.'

Deep emotion sometimes confounds the mind – and Mrs Magaw quite flamed with excitement. But on the other hand it sometimes illumines, and she could see, it appeared, what Sue meant. 'It's because he's so much in love.'

'So far gone that she's safe?' Abel frankly asked.

'So far gone that she's safe.'

'Well,' he said, 'if Sue feels it—!' He had so much, he showed, to go by. 'Sue *knows*.'

Mrs Magaw visibly yearned, but she could look at all sides. 'I'm bound to say, since you speak of it, that I've an idea Sue has helped. She'll like to have her there.'

'Mattie will like to have Sue?'

'No, Sue will like to have Mattie.' Elation raised to such a point was in fact already so clarifying that Mrs Magaw could come all the way. 'As Lady Dunderton.'

'Well,' Abel smiled, 'one good turn deserves another!' If he meant it, however, in any such sense as that Mattie might be able in due course to render an equivalent of aid, this notion clearly had to reckon with his companion's sense of its strangeness, exhibited in her now at last upheaved countenance. 'Yes,' he accordingly insisted, 'it will work round to that – you see if it doesn't. If that's where they were to come out, and they *have* come – by which I mean if Sue has realized it for Mattie and acted as she acts when she does realize, then she can't neglect it in her own case: she'll just *have* to realize it for herself. And, for that matter, you'll help her too. You'll be able to tell her, you know, that you've seen the last of me.' And on the morrow, when, starting for London, she had taken her place in the train, to which he had accompanied her, he stood by the door of her compartment and repeated this idea. 'Remember, for Mrs Taker, that you've seen the last—!'

'Oh but I hope I haven't, sir.'

'Then you'll come back to me? If you only will, you know, Sue will be delighted to fix it.'

'To fix it – how?'

'Well, she'll tell you how. You've seen how she can fix things, and that will be the way, as I say, you'll help her.'

She stared at him from her corner, and he could see she was sorry for him; but it was as if she had taken refuge behind her large high-shouldered reticule, which she held in her lap, presenting it almost as a bulwark. 'Mr Taker,' she launched at him over it, 'I'm afraid of you.'

'Because I'm dead?'

'Oh sir!' she pleaded, hugging her morocco defence.[21] But even through this alarm her finer thought came out. 'Do you suppose I shall go to Fordham Castle?'

'Well, I guess that's what they're discussing now. You'll know soon enough.'

'If I write you from there,' she asked, 'won't you come?'

'I'll come as the ghost. Don't old castles always have one?'

She looked at him darkly; the train had begun to move. 'I *shall* fear you!' she said.

'Then there you are.' And he moved an instant beside the door. 'You'll be glad, when you get there, to be able to say—' But she got out of hearing, and, turning away, he felt as abandoned as he had known he should – felt left, in his solitude, to the sense of his extinction. He faced it completely now, and to himself at least could express it without fear of protest. 'Why certainly I'm dead.'

Glossary of Foreign Words and Expressions

à la bonne heure!: (literally) at the good time (French); about time!
à la chinoise: (literally) in the Chinese fashion (French), in a top knot
à l'Américaine: in the American way (French)
à l'Anglaise: in the English style (French)
abbé: (literally) abbot (French), priest.
air penché: leaning over with an expression of concentration (French)
allez: come on; *allons donc!*: oh, come on! (as dismissive phrase) (French)
amoroso: sweetheart (Italian)
au fait: up to date (French)
belle brune: beautiful brunette (French)
belle enfant: beautiful child (French)
bête: stupid, uncomprehending (French)
bêtises: foolish things (French)
bien élevée: well brought up (French)
bon temps: (literally) good times (French), good old days
bon-bons: sweets (French)
bosquet: in French gardens, a formal arrangement of trees of the same age and species, planted in rows (French, from Italian *bosco*, grove, wood)
bourgeoise: middle-class woman (French)
ça n'a pas de principes!: that's unscrupulous! (French)
cafés-concerts: cafés offering light music (French)
canaletto: a small canal or channel (Italian)
castel: a small castle (French)
cavaliere avvocato: (literally) gentleman lawyer (Italian); a minor official
ce génie-là: that genius (French)
chère belle: (literally) beautiful dear (French), my dear girl
chez vous: with you or in your country (French)
chignon: hair done up in a knot at the back of the head (French)
cicerone: tourist guide (Italian)

comme cela se fait: as it is done, as is right (French)

comme il faut: (literally) as it must (French); respectable

conversazione: a scheduled social meeting to discuss art or literature (Italian)

coup d'œil: (literally) stroke of the eye (French); all-encompassing glance

coupés: four-wheeled horse-drawn carriages (French)

cousine: (female) cousin (French)

couturière: dress designer (French), dressmaker

croûte aux fruits: fruit tart (French)

dame: woman, wife (French)

décolletées: dressed as for a party, wearing dresses with low-cut necklines (French)

demande en mariage: marriage proposal (French)

demi-tasse: (literally) a half cup (French); a small cup of black coffee

des hommes sérieux: serious people (French)

dévote: pious person (French)

du meilleur monde: (literally) of the better world (French), of the best society

d'une étourderie: scatter-brained (French)

d'une humeur massacrante: in a foul temper (French)

ecco!: there you are! (Italian)

elle s'affiche: (literally) she is putting up a poster of herself (French), hence she is publishing or making a spectacle of herself

en pied: (of a portrait), full-length, from head to foot (French)

entêtée: obstinate(French)

en train: in a better humour (French)

en ville: in town (French)

esprit: spirit, wit (French)

fait quelques folies: done some foolish things (French)

faux bonhomme: false fellow (French)

femme de chambre: chambermaid (French)

fête: a festival (French), civil or religious

fiacre: a small hackney carriage for public hire (French)

filles de haut lieu: young women of high social status (French)

fonds: groundwork (French)

frittata: (literally) something fried (Italian); a sort of omelette including cheese and sometimes meat or vegetables

galant homme: courteous man (French); *galant* on its own is a skirt-chaser

grand seigneur: a great lord (French), a man of dignified and aristocratic bearing *in extremis*: at the point of death (Latin)

inconduite: bad behaviour (French)

intime: intimate (French), familiar

intimité: (literally) intimacy (French), private life

J'adore la peinture!: I love painting (French)

jeune fille: young woman, virgin (French) *jeune homme*: young man (French)

jolie à croquer: pretty enough to eat (French)

la belle découverte!: what a great discovery! (French)

la senta: you decide (Italian)

la vieille galanterie française: the old French tradition of gallantry (French)

lacher prise: (literally) let go (French); give up

lingeres (or *lingères*): washerwomen (French)

loggia: an open-sided gallery (Italian)

marchese: marquis (Italian)

mauvais sujet: bad lot, troublemaker (French)

menus plaisirs: (literally) small pleasures, the finer things of life (French)

noblesse oblige: (literally) the obligation of nobility (French); i.e., the idea that privilege entails responsibilities

palazzo: not a palace but an imposing building (Italian)

Parisienne: (female) resident of Paris, hence, a sophisticated lady (French)

parti: marrying material, suitable match (archaic French)

partie: departed, left (French)

persiflage: mockery (French)

piazza: city or town square (Italian)

plaisanterie: joke (French)

potagers: vegetable gardens, kitchen gardens (French)

pour vous autres: (literally) for you others; for your sort (French)

prie-dieu: (literally) pray [to] God (French); a small, portable kneeler for prayer, consisting of a kneeling bar with a raised shelf in front for the arms

quatrième: the fourth-floor of an apartment building (French)

que sais-je?: (literally) what do I know? (French) what have you?

quelle existence!: what a life! (French)

quelle toilette!: what grooming! (French)

qui se passe ses fantaisies: (literally) who goes along with her fantasies (French), who acts according to her whims, who does what she wants

race: pedigree (French)

revanche: revenge (French)

ruche: (literally) beehive (French), a ruffled or pleated piece of fabric used for decoration.

sabots: clogs, wooden shoes (French)

salle à manger: dining room (French)

seconde jeunesse: (literally) second childhood (French), a new lease on life

sergent de ville: policeman (French)

silence de mort: the silence of death (French)

société de bonnes œuvres: (literally) an association of good works (French), a charity

soupe aux choux: cabbage soup (French)

tilleuls: lime trees (French)

ton: manner, tone (French)

tonnelle: arbour (French)

tournure: bearing, posture (French)

tout bonnement: quite simply (French)

trattoria: informal restaurant (Italian)

visage de croquemort: undertaker's face (French)

voilà les femmes, monsieur!: that's women for you, sir! (French)

voyons: let's see (French)

Notes

Sources for these notes include Karl Baedeker, *Switzerland, and the Adjacent Portions of Italy, Savoy, and the Tyrol* (1872) (*SIST*), John Murray's *Handbook for Travellers in France* (1864) (*HTF*), Murray's *Handbook to London as it Is* (1876) (*HL*), Murray's *Handbook for Travellers in Northern Italy* (1866) (*HNI*), Murray's *Handbook for Visitors to Paris* (1867) (*HP*), Murray's *Handbook for Rome and its Environs* (1867 and 1871) (*HRE 67, HRE 71*), Murray's *Handbook for Travellers in Switzerland, and the Alps of Savoy and Piedmont* (1865) (*HSA*), and the Oxford English Dictionary (*OED*). The texts of James's travel sketches are taken, where possible, from the original periodical publication, or from their reprinting in the relevant Library of America volume, rather than the heavily revised versions in *Italian Hours* (1909). James's letters are identified by date and recipient, and (where relevant) volume and page numbers in *The Complete Letters of Henry James* (*CLHJ*); where embedded in helpful comment, they are also cited by page number in Philip Horne, *Henry James: A Life in Letters* (*HJLL*). Where I refer by surname to authors of criticism or other editions, or to short titles of works, full references will be found in the list of further reading.

Translations of words and phrases in foreign languages are given in the Glossary on pp. 337–40, arranged alphabetically by first foreign word in each instance.

TRAVELLING COMPANIONS

1. *Last Supper ... at Milan*: the great wall painting (*c.*1495–7) – not actually a fresco, as the narrator goes on to call it – by Leonardo da Vinci (1452–1519) in the refectory of the Dominican

Convent of Santa Maria delle Grazie (in English, St Mary of the Graces), Milan. Because the painting was affixed to the inside of an outer wall of the building, damp began to attack it almost immediately. Over the years it had been patched up many times, before being desecrated by French revolutionary troops, who used the refectory as an armoury, and later as a prison. When the story is set it adjoins a garrison. Murray describes the painting as in a state of 'irreparable decay' (*HNI*, p. 201). When James first saw it in 1869, he wrote to his mother that it was 'horribly decayed – but sublime in its ruins. The mere <u>soul</u> of the picture survives – the form, the outline' (10 September) (*CLHJ*, II, p. 96).

2. *the reader will remember*: according to Leslie (p. 59), this phrase is a reminder that James's story was to come out in the *Atlantic*, which had published numerous essays on European art, and many of whose readers had travelled to Europe; in other words, that James was not writing a barely disguised travelogue for culturally naive readers, as many critics of 'Travelling Companions' have argued.

3. *Cenacolo*: literally, a supper room on an upper floor (Italian), from Latin *coenaculum*: a room where one ate; here a common name for the painting of the Last Supper before Christ's crucifixion.

4. *A single glance . . . American*: because she carries herself with a freedom socially impossible for Italian, and possibly other European, women; her identification as American is made more explicit seven paragraphs below: 'She was largely characterized by that physical delicacy and that personal elegance (each of them sometimes excessive) which seldom fail to betray my young countrywomen in Europe.'

5. *Tintoretto . . . Correggio*: Jacobo Comin (1518–94), nicknamed 'Tintoretto' (the cloth dyer), the Venetian Renaissance artist, a prolific painter of religious and civic scenes decorating public buildings in the city; Michelangelo di Lodovico Buonarroti Simoni (1475–1564), Renaissance painter, sculptor and architect, most famous for his statues of *David* in Florence and the *Pietà* in St Peter's Basilica, and for the frescos of the Creation and Last Judgement on the ceiling and altar wall of the Sistine Chapel, Vatican City; Antonio Allegri da Correggio (or 'from Correggio') (Italian) (1489–1534), flourished in Parma, a late Italian Renaissance painter of religious and classical themes. Of the last mentioned, James wrote to his sister Alice on 6 October 1869, 'He had a most divine touch – & seems to have been a sort of <u>sentimental</u> Leonardo – setting Leonardo

down as "intellectual". A couple of his masterpieces at Parma perfectly <u>reek</u> with loveliness' (*CLHJ*, II, p. 129).

6. *a door . . . entering the fresco*: this was cut in 1652, then later bricked up; its shape can still be seen in the form of a flat arch at the lower centre of the picture.

7. *piqué*: a close-textured fabric of cotton or silk.

8. *purple feather*: Leslie points out (p. 72) that 'to an American nineteenth-century readership, the colour purple was associated with the costume a woman would wear in her first year of mourning'. Presumably Miss Evans is still mourning her American fiancé killed in the Civil War. Later in Venice, when the narrator encounters her in the Basilica of St Mark's, she is wearing 'a black lace shawl and a purple hat'.

9. *Murray*: John Murray III (1808–1892), Byron's London publisher who invented the modern guidebook, began producing his *Murray's Handbooks for Travellers* in 1836. James himself admired the Murray handbooks and used them extensively. In his letter to his mother on 8 September 1869, he proclaimed, 'I think I can lay my hand on my heart (or on my <u>Murray</u>; they are now identical) & say that I know Milan' (*CLHJ*, II, p. 96).

10. *Interlaken*: the town in the German-speaking canton of Bern, Switzerland. Murray describes it as 'situated about half way between the lakes of Thun and Brienz, whence its name . . . signifying "between the lakes". Interlaken has of late become so completely a fashionable watering-place, that those who wish for quiet and economy resort to the pensions here, of which there are several' (*HSA*, p. 80).

11. *church of St Ambrose . . . Library*: the Basilica di Sant'Ambrogio (Italian), a very early church, built by St Ambrose (*c*.340–97) from 379 to 386, later completed in the Romanesque style in the first half of the twelfth century; Ambrosian Library: the Biblioteca Ambrosiana (Italian), founded by Cardinal Federico Borromeo (1564–1631) in 1609 in honour of St Ambrose.

12. *the Cathedral*: Duomo di Milano (Italian), a vast Italian Gothic structure begun in 1386 and not completed until 1935.

13. *that lovely Raphael in the Brera*: *Lo Sposalizio della Virgine*, or *Marriage of the Virgin*, by the high Renaissance painter Raphael, or Raffaello Sanzio da Urbino (1483–1520), was originally commissioned for a church in Città di Castello in northern Umbria, but by 1806 was in the Pinacoteca (picture gallery) di Brera, Milan. In 1869 James wrote to his mother: "Tis a great work & Raphael was an enviable fellow to have been able to see

things about him, as in that picture – let alone <u>do</u> them' (10 September, *CLHJ*, II, p. 96).

14. *Titian and Paul Veronese*: Tiziano Vecelli or Vecellio (1488/ 1490–1576) the Venetian painter; Paolo Caliari (1528–88), known as Veronese because he was born in Verona, Venetian Renaissance painter of religious and mythological subjects.

15. *Araminta, New Jersey*: a woman's name, but in New Jersey, a fictional town or city.

16. *Monte Rosa ... Simplon pass*: alpine features visible from a high point in Milan; Monte Rosa, at 15,203 feet the highest elevation in the Swiss Alps, and part of the watershed between northern and southern Europe, is permanently covered in snow and ice, even in mid-summer.

17. *mantillas*: lace veil worn by Mediterranean women as a head covering in the Catholic Church.

18. *Picturesque*: an aesthetic term for a view that combines the awesome precipices of the sublime with the rounded curves of the beautiful; a picture of contrasts. At a more basic level the term could simply mean like a picture. In his early writings on landscape, such as the 1870 essay on 'Lake George', James spoke of his 'pursuit of the picturesque'. 'I shall long remember a certain little farm-house before which I stayed my steps to stare and enjoy. If the pure picturesque means simply the presentation of a picture, self-informed and complete, I have seen nothing in Italy or England which better deserves the praise' (*Great Britain and America*, p. 743).

19. *Borromeus*: Carlo Borromeo, Cardinal Archbishop of Milan from 1564 to 1584; see note on Ambrosian Library, above.

20. *Stendahl*: the French novelist Marie-Henri Beyle (1783–1842), better known by his pen name Stendhal. In 1869 James wrote to his sister Alice from Rome: 'I have been reading Stendahl [sic] – a capital observer & a good deal of a thinker. He really knows Italy' (7, 8 November, *CLHJ*, II, p. 179).

21. *virginibus puerisque*: literally, concerning virgin girls and boys (Latin) – that is, the pictures are curtained from the eyes of the youth. The reference predates Robert Louis Stevenson's essay of that title on marriage in his *Virginibus Puerisque and Other Papers* (1881).

22. *Chartreuse de Parme* (or *The Charterhouse [Carthusian monastery] of Parma*): a novel by Stendhal, published in 1839, that traces the adventurous life of Fabrice del Dongo, a young Italian nobleman who runs away to enlist in Napoleon's army and

fights in the Battle of Waterloo, then moves with his beautiful and seductive aunt Gina, the Duchess of San Severino, to Parma, where they both become involved in numerous political and sexual intrigues. From Malvern, England, where he was taking the waters in March 1870, James wrote to his old friend, the art historian Charles Eliot Norton, 'I have just been reading [*The Charterhouse of Parma*] – with real admiration . . . It is certainly a great novel.' See *HJLL*, pp. 33 and 33n.

23. *Piazza die [dei] Signori*: a handsome square, formally the centre of power in Verona; also known as Piazza Dante because of the statue of Dante at its centre. In 1869 James described it to his mother as 'small, compact & elegant as if it were made for a lot of Picturesque Italians to play at the civic virtues' (10 September, *CLHJ*, II, p. 98).

24. *Dante*: Dante Alighieri (1265–1321), author of *The Divine Comedy*, written between 1308 and 1321, the greatest work of Italian literature, that established the Florentine vernacular as standard Italian.

25. *Palladio's palaces . . . Ruskin*: Andrea Palladio (1508–80), the sixteenth-century Italian architect, active in the Republic of Venice, promoted a classical style derived from Roman proportions; his *I Quattro Libri dell'Architettura* (*The Four Books of Architecture* (1570)) spread his influence throughout Europe. In his *The Stones of Venice* (1851–3) the Victorian art critic and social thinker John Ruskin (1819–1900) objected to Palladio's formulaic classicism, especially as applied to Christian churches, like San Giorgio Maggiore in Venice. Writing to his father from Venice on 17 September 1869, James, like Mr Brooke, recalled spending just one day in Vicenza on his way from Verona to Venice: 'It is easily described by saying that Vicenza is Palladio . . . What one looks at is the outsides of about a hundred palaces – the town swarms with 'em. I enjoyed them vastly, but since coming here & getting a hold of a vol. of Ruskin's Stones of V., I find that he pronounces Palladio infamous & must blot out that shameful day' (*CLHJ*, II. p. 105).

26. *Haroun-al-Raschid*: Harun al-Rashid (763 or 766–809), the fifth Abbasid Caliph; his rule from 786 to 809 was marked by great advances in Islamic art and music, as well as scientific and other cultural achievements. He and his court appear in many stories in the early eighth-century *Book of One Thousand and One Nights*. The stories are full of disguises and switched identities. James owned a copy of *The Thousand and One*

Nights, in England commonly called the *Arabian Nights' Entertainments,* trans. E. W. Lane (London: Knight, 1843). Allusions to the *Arabian Nights* appear in other of James's writings, including *Watch and Ward* (1871), *The Europeans* (1878) and *What Maisie Knew* (1897).

27. *Parmigianino*: Girolamo Francesco Maria Mazzola (1503–40), also known as Parmigianino ('the little one from Parma'), a sixteenth-century mannerist painter who worked in Parma, among other places.

28. *Hotel de l'Europe*: the Albergo dell' Europa, described in Murray's as 'close to the Piazza di San Marco . . . with a magnificent view over the Southern Lagunes' (*HNI*, p. 359), now the Hotel Europa e Regina.

29. *Piazzetta*: little square (Italian); in Venice the Piazzetta is at the east end of St Mark's Square (Piazza San Marco) running at right angles to it, past the Doge's palace to the Molo, or waterfront.

30. *Basilica*: St Mark's Cathedral, built between about 1073 and 1117, the great Italo-Byzantine basilica, at the eastern end of the Piazza San Marco, and the cathedral church of the Archdiocese of Venice. In 1869 James wrote to his brother William, 'St Mark's, within, is a great hoary shadowy tabernacle of mosaic & marble, entrancing you with its remoteness, its picturesqueness & its chiaroscuro – an immense piece of Romanticism' (15 [27] September, *CLHJ*, II, p. 120).

31. *great mosaic Christ . . . dome of the choir*: Murray writes: 'The interior of the Basilica is very rich . . . The vaulting is covered with mosaics upon a gold ground' (*HNI*, p. 367); the dome of the choir contains a mosaic bust of Christ surrounded by standing prophets, the four evangelists and the Virgin Mary, but if Miss Evans is looking forward to the apse at the end of the choir, her eyes would be fixed on the great seated Christ Pantocrator (all ruling), the focal point in St Mark's, as in so many Byzantine basilicas.

32. *the dark Baptistery . . . mosaic Crucifixion above it*: the mosaic crucifixion is above the altar in the Baptistery; Murray, quoting the traveller and writer Henry Gally Knight (1786–1846), warns that ' "The defect of the interior of St Mark's is that it is not sufficiently light. The windows are few in proportion to the size of the building. Rich, therefore, as the interior is, it is gloomy to a fault, in spite of the brilliant rays of a southern sun" ' (*HNI*, p. 366).

33. *George Sand*: pseudonym of Amantine-Lucile-Aurore Dupin (1804–76), French novelist; James greatly admired her work; see *HJLL*, p. 15n. Her novel *La Dernière Aldini*, published in *La Revue des Deux Mondes* in December 1837, was translated into English in 1847. As Leslie points out (pp. 82–4), some events in 'Travelling Companions' echo its plot. Nello is the gondolier of a widowed noblewoman, Bianca Aldini, and her daughter Alezia. Nello is in love with Bianca, but afraid to reveal his feelings. One night they are out in the gondola, only to get stuck in the marshes and be forced to spend the night together. They declare their love for one another. Nello wants to marry Bianca, not least to prevent a scandal, but at length decides that the social gap between them would make the match impossible, and so leaves Venice altogether. Much later, Nello changes his name, trains as a musician, and at length becomes a famous opera star. Without recognizing her, he falls in love with Alezia, now grown up. She reciprocates his love, but once he realizes who she is, still stuck in the difference in social rank between them, he persuades her to marry someone more suitable.

34. *John the Baptist . . . cover of the basin*: Murray writes: 'In the middle [of the Baptistery] is a basin with a bronze cover . . . on the top is a statue in bronze of St John the Baptist' (*HNI*, p. 368).

35. *Caffè Quadri*: in St Mark's Square, mentioned in Murray (*HNI*, p. 359) as 'the resort of the military and Austrians'; still going strong, it is now a popular meeting place for tourists and visitors to Venice. Writing to William Dean Howells's friend, the poet Edmund Clarence Stedman, to offer him advice on lodging in Venice, James mentioned having lived the previous spring in four rooms with a 'divine' view, but so 'meagrely & hideously furnished' that 'I had to feed out, entirely – in the Piazza: the best place is the Café Quaddri [sic]' (*HJLL*, p. 137 and 137n.).

36. *Florian's*: Caffè Florian, another legendary café in St Mark's Square – in fact, the oldest in the world – 'has long enjoyed what may be called an European reputation' (*HNI*, p. 359). Still flourishing today, Florian's, famously a meeting place for writers and artists, will later be the scene of a fateful encounter between Merton Densher and Lord Mark in James's *The Wings of the Dove* (1902).

37. *Bellini*: Giovanni Bellini (1430–1516), Italian Renaissance painter, the best known of a family of Venetian painters.

38. *Scuola di San Rocco*: built in the fifteenth century to provide offices and meeting halls for a Venetian confraternity, the Scuola Grande di San Rocco was provided with over forty paintings by Tintoretto and his assistants, as well as works by Titian and others. In his essay 'Venice', published in the *Century Magazine* in 1882, James would write: 'Solemn indeed is the place, solemn and strangely suggestive, for the simple reason that we shall scarcely find four walls elsewhere that inclose within a like area an equal quantity of genius ... It is not immortality that we breathe at the Scuola di San Rocco, but conscious, reluctant mortality' ('Venice', p. 19).

39. *women of Titian*: Titian (q.v.) was and remains famous for his pictures of alluring, but also respectable and imposing women.

40. *Grand Canal ... Lido*: the Canal is the widest of Venice's canals and at 2.38 miles also the longest; running in a reverse 'S' curve from the lagoon near the Santa Lucia railway station to St Mark's Basin, it provides the chief thoroughfare for Venetian boat traffic. The Lido is the sand bar across the Lagoon from Venice that shelters the city from the Adriatic Sea; since 1857 it has been a beach resort.

41. *Miss Evans was sitting on one of the Hebrew tombs*: in 1386 the Republic of Venice granted permission for the city's Jewish population to bury their dead in a property on the Lido; in 1516 the city authorities confined them to the first ghetto in Europe. Leslie points out (p. 83) that when Nello mulls over whether to leave Venice for ever in *La Dernière Aldini* (q.v.), he too sits on one of the tombs in the old Jewish cemetery on the Lido.

42. *Ducal Palace*: literal translation of the Italian Palazzo Ducale, but more often Anglicized as the Doge's Palace, the home of the supreme authority of the Republic; dating from the fourteenth century, the building is in the Venetian Gothic style, facing the Grand Canal; Veronese and Tintoretto were among those artists who decorated the ceilings.

43. *little church of San Cassiano*: the fourteenth-century church in the San Polo district of Venice; in the church there are three paintings by Tintoretto, who was a parishioner there, all completed between 1565 and 1568, including his *Crucifixion*, fully described below, which John Ruskin (q.v.) called the finest example of its subject in Europe (see *The Stones of Venice*, III, p. 289) and his *Resurrection of Christ*. In his essay, 'A European Summer. VII. From Venice to Strasburg', James wrote, 'I repaired

immediately to the little church of San Cassano [sic], which contains the smaller of Tintoret's two great Crucifixions; and when I had looked at it a while I drew a long breath and felt I could contemplate any other picture in Venice with proper self possession. It seemed to me I had advanced to the uttermost limit of painting; that beyond this another art – inspired poetry – begins.'

44. *campo*: literally, field (Italian), another, smaller kind of public square. Venice has many campi, but only one piazza, the Piazza San Marco.

45. *Rape of Europa*: by Veronese; in 'A European Summer' James writes, 'Mr Ruskin, whose eloquence in dealing with the great Venetians sometimes outruns his discretion, is fond of speaking even of Veronese as a painter of deep spiritual intentions. This, it seems to me, is pushing matters too far, and the author of "The Rape of Europa" is, pictorially speaking, no greater casuist than any other genius of supreme good taste. Titian was assuredly a mighty poet, but Tintoret – well, Tintoret was almost a prophet.'

46. *his solemn comrade*: that is, Tintoretto.

47. *Torcello*: now a quiet island at the northern end of the Lagoon, but in the tenth century it had a population of 10,000, by far the largest in the Republic, and could be said to be where Venice began.

48. *Padua*: just 25 miles to the west of Venice, home of a university already nearly 650 years old by the time of the story's setting, and a city of many treasured works of art.

49. *church of St Anthony*: or Basilica of St Anthony, Padua, begun in around 1232 and completed in 1310, it has been built in a number of architectural styles, including the Romanesque, baroque and, in its external appearance, Byzantine.

50. *chapel of Giotto*: the Cappella degli Scrovegni, or Scrovegni Chapel, the walls of which are covered with the astonishing fresco cycle completed in about 1305 by the early Renaissance Florentine Giotto (1266/7–1337), illustrating the life of Christ and the life of the Virgin. In describing the work to his sister Alice in 1869, James used almost the same words he would later give to Mr Brooke's narrative in the story: 'I have always fancied that to say anything about Giotto was to make more or less a fool of one's self & that he was the special property of the mere sentimentalists of criticism. But he is a real complete painter of the very strongest sort. In one respect he has never

been surpassed – in the faculty of telling a story – the mastery of dramatic presentation' (6 October, *CLHJ*, II, p. 127).

51. *Caffè Pedrocchi*: 'The Caffè Pedrocchi, celebrated all over Italy, is the best,' according to Murray; 'there is also a *restaurant*' (*HNI*, p. 339); still popular today.

52. *one possible sequel to our situation*: that is, for the man to offer to marry the compromised woman.

53. *Hotel Danieli*: then as now, a five-star hotel on the Lagoon just east of the Molo.

54. *Canalezzo* (or *Canalasso*): Venetian dialect for the Grand Canal.

55. *Ca' Doro* (or Ca' d'Oro): literally, Golden House (Italian), the Palazzo Santa Sofia, a large palace built in the Venetian Gothic style, facing the Grand Canal.

56. *Hawthorne*: Nathaniel Hawthorne (1804–64), the American novelist, author of *The Scarlet Letter*; his short story, 'Rappaccini's Daughter', published in his 1844 collection *Mosses from an Old Manse* concerns the daughter of a Padua scientist who tends her father's poisonous herbs long enough to become immune to them, but also to poison other plants and animals with whom she comes in contact.

57. *I think I know*: that is, that her father has insisted to Brooke on his obligation to marry his compromised daughter.

58. *German philosopher*: Philip Horne (private communication) suggests convincingly that Brooke means that she is strenuous, theoretical, abstract and forever making distinctions.

59. *Blue Grotto . . . tarantella*: The Blue Grotto is a sea cave on the coast of Capri, the walls of which are bathed in blue light when sunlight enters the cavern filtered up through the water within it; the Tiberian ruins are probably the remains of the Villa Jovis (Villa of Jupiter), the largest of the twelve villas to be built by the Roman Emperor Tiberius (42 BC–AD 37) on Capri, and the one in which he lived and reigned from its completion in 27 till his death ten years later; the tarantella is a fast southern Italian folk dance.

60. *Campagna*: the countryside around Rome, around 800 square miles in area and during the eighteenth and nineteenth centuries the most painted landscape in Europe; Murray offers: 'The Campagna, or the undulating country which extends on all sides around Rome, includes portions of ancient Latium and Etruria . . . The Sabine Mountains surround like an amphitheatre the whole expanse of the north-eastern Campagna;

while the more picturesque mountains which bound the plains of Latium on the S.E. are studded with villages, each representing some site of classical interest. Along the plain from N. to S. the Tiber winds as a long yellow line, marking the ancient boundary between Latium and Etruria' (*HRE 71*, pp. 11–12). 'The Campagna alone,' wrote James in *William Wetmore Story* (1903), 'for the satisfaction at once of sense and soul, for rides (most of all), drives, walks, excursions of whatever sort, feasts *al fresco*, pictures, *ad infinitum*, archaeology lively or severe ... the Campagna was an education of the taste, a revelation of new sources both of solitary and of social joy' (p. 347).

61. *dishonoured plain ... funereal desert*: seems to take its tone from the fact of classical ruins in the Campagna. See Robert Browning's 'Two in the Campagna' (1855) in which the male lover, surrounded by impersonal nature and all too aware of his mortality, laments the natural barriers to his understanding and their emotional union.

62. *St Peter's*: the great basilica in Vatican City, the largest and greatest Renaissance cathedral in the world, and a gathering place for Catholics from all over the world.

63. *recent Council*: probably the First Council of the Vatican (1870), which, among other things, proclaimed the Pope's infallibility.

64. *Caffè Greco*: established in 1760 by a Greek owner (Greco is Italian for Greek), then and now a favourite meeting place for artists, writers, politicians and other people of note.

65   *Borghese ... Titian*. The Borghese Gallery, in the Villa Borghese on the Pincian Hill, Rome, contains a collection of paintings, sculpture and antiquities begun by Cardinal Scipione Borghese (1577–1633), nephew of Pope Paul V; the picture described is Titian's *Sacred and Profane Love*; opinion is still divided as to which woman represents the sacred and which the profane.

66. *Pamfili-Doria Villa*: the Villa Doria-Pamphilj, a seventeenth-century villa within the largest landscaped park in Rome.

MADAME DE MAUVES

1.   *terrace ... Saint-Germain-en-Laye*: Saint-Germain-en-Laye is a prosperous suburb of Paris, just under 12 miles north-west from the city centre; the 'terrace' is not an artefact but a flat landform above and bordering a shore – in this case of the River

Seine. The painting by the French impressionist Alfred Sisley (1839–99) *The Terrace at Saint Germain, Spring, 1875* (The Walters Art Museum, Baltimore, Maryland) gives an idea of the view.

2. *Brébant*: the Café le Brébant was, and remains, a fashionable brasserie on the Boulevard Poissonnière, Paris. Murray writes, 'From their number and splendour the cafés of Paris are one of the characteristic features of the city; and being the daily resort of Frenchmen of all classes, they deserve to be visited by strangers, even independently of the attractions which they furnish for his accommodation, being unlike anything to be found at home' (*HP*, p. 32).

3. *Gymnase*: the Théâtre du Gymnase, or the Gymnase Dramatique, a theatre in the Boulevard Bonne-Nouvelle, 'for short comedies and vaudevilles', according to Murray (*HP*, p. 240), known then for its plays of domestic manners; among its playwrights were Émile Augier (1820–89) and George Sand (q.v.). In a letter to his sister Alice in 1870, James wrote: 'It is half-past midnight & I have just come in from the <u>Gymnase</u> theatre where I have had a very exquisite pleasure. A new play by name <u>Froufrou</u> (if you can read it) & a new actress, Mlle. Desclée who has suddenly scrambled to the top of the histrionic heap. The play very clever – the actress – superlative! The whole thing admirable for finish & delicacy' (25 January, *CLHJ*, II, p. 274). Aimée-Olympe Desclée spent only a short time at the top of the histrionic heap; only four years after James saw her perform, she died at the age of 38.

4. *American ... perceived*: see note on 'Travelling Companions', p. 342.

5. *Wall Street*: running for under a mile from Broadway to South Street in lower Manhattan; then as now, the centre of the financial district in New York City.

6. *Hôtel de l'Empire*: then and now a luxury hotel in the Rue de l'Arbre Sec, midway between the Louvre Museum and what is now the Pompidou Centre.

7. *Exiled Stuarts*: after being overthrown by the Glorious Revolution of 1688 and the accession of William and Mary, the Catholic King James II of England exiled himself to Saint-Germain-en-Laye, dying there in 1701.

8. *Homburg*: later Bad Homburg, a German town just over 15 miles north of Frankfurt; established in the Middle Ages, from the mid nineteenth century it was a fashionable spa with a

casino. James stayed there for his health in the summer of 1873, just a year after the recently united German government had closed down the gambling there (the ban was later reversed). His 'Homburg Reformed', a light-hearted appreciation of the place, was published in *The Nation* of 28 August 1873 and later collected in *Transatlantic Sketches* (1875). Writing to his parents on 14 August 1873, James declared his health much improved, and said, 'I yesterday dispatched a tale in III parts to the *Galaxy* – with regret, as it is the best written thing I've done' (*HJLL*, pp. 56 and 56n). The tale was 'Madame de Mauves'; he felt the 'regret' because he would have preferred to place it in *The Atlantic Monthly*.

9. *Nice*: founded probably as a Greek colony around 350 BC, after 1860 a French city highly popular with tourists, offering a Mediterranean climate, including a mild winter, together with numerous sophisticated cultural events and shopping opportunities.

10. *Madame la Vicomtesse*: that is, the wife of a *vicomte*, or viscount.

11. *Euphemia*: derived from classical Greek roots, the name means well spoken of, of good repute.

12. *Ultramontane*: literally, [from] the other side of the mountain[s] (Latin); figuratively, relating to central – that is, Vatican – supremacy over national or diocesan authority of the Roman Catholic Church.

13. *Legitimist*: a royalist supporting the dynastic succession of the Bourbon Kings, who were overthrown in the July Revolution, 1830.

14. *Paladins*: the twelve knights represented in various early French romances as companions of Roland, later of Charlemagne (Old Fr.).

15. *Joinville and Commines*: Jean de Joinville (1224–1317), medieval historian, and Philippe de Commines (1447–1511), writer and commentator on the contemporary political scene in the courts of Burgundy and France.

16. *Auvergne*: the mountainous region in south central France.

17. *Château de Mauves*: as the *castel* was called; *château* (French) is another word for *castel*.

18. *gentilhomme*: gentleman (French); not just a polite or decent man as in English usage, but an aristocrat, man of noble birth.

19. *Quixotic*: extravagantly chivalrous or romantic, after the fanciful knight Don Quixote, in the novel of that name (two vols., 1605 and 1616) by Miguel de Cervantes (*c*.1547–1616).

20. *Figaro*: *Le Figaro*, founded in Paris as a satirical weekly in 1826, became a daily paper in 1866; it is a newspaper of record, of conservative leanings, and the oldest national newspaper in France.

21. *M. le Baron*: the Baron (French) – that is, Richard de Mauves.

22. *Jeannot and Jeannette*: a series of ballads that became particularly popular during the American Civil War (1861–5) about an army conscript bidding farewell to his sweetheart, first published as sheet music in 1840s Philadelphia.

23. *Baronne de Mauves*: that is, Euphemia's title once she is married.

24. *Fates*: apparently Euphemia is conflating the three fates (*Moirai*) of Greek mythology, who spun, measured and cut the thread of people's lives, and the Romano-medieval goddess Fortuna, who spun her wheel to determine the fate of those lives fixed on it.

25. *Havre*: or Le Havre, literally, the harbour (French), the great seaport on the Normandy coast where the River Seine enters the Atlantic. 'Originally Havre de Grace, from a small chapel of Notre Dame de Grace which stood on its site . . . It is quite a modern town, owing its foundation to Francis 1' (Murray, *HTF*, p. 63), in 1517.

26. *pavilion*: probably in the sense of *OED* definition 7: A projecting subdivision of a building or facade, distinguished by more elaborate decoration, or by greater height and distinction of sky-line.

27. *twenty rods*: a rod, also a perch or a pole, an English surveyor's unit of measurement dating back to the sixteenth century, measuring 16.5 feet; so twenty rods would be 330 feet.

28. *furbelows*: ruffles or flounces on a garment.

29. *Gérôme in painting, and for M. Gustave Flaubert in literature*: Jean-Léon Gérôme (1824–1904) was a French painter in the academic style, working with historical topics. In 1875 and 1876 James would discuss him at some length in his letters to the *New York Tribune*, collected as *Parisian Sketches*. He was dubious about his work, for example judging his *Chariot Race* set in the Roman Circus Maximus (now in the Art Institute of Chicago) to be obsessed with curious architectural detail which the modern viewer is unfit to judge: 'What the ordinary observer sees is that the painter has mastered a vast amount of curious detail, and, after all, unless the ghost of some old Roman man about town comes back for the purpose, I do not see who is to prove that M. Gérôme's ingenious reconstruction

is either a good likeness of the actual scene or a poor one' (Letter 10). Gustave Flaubert (1821–80), author of *Madame Bovary* (1856–7) was the leading French realist novelist and a great stylist. James was later to review his *The Temptation of St Anthony* (1874) for *The Nation* in 1874. James admired the novelist's art but was unsettled 'by bodily details in fiction, with moral and physical ugliness as the centre of artistic vision' (Kaplan, p. 166). Later still in Paris James got to know Flaubert and his circle. Writing to his mother on 11 January 1876, he recalled sitting 'with him a couple of hours, chattering famously & greatly liking him. He is an excellent old fellow, simple, naif & convaincu, in his own line, & extremely kind and friendly, not to say affectionate' (*CLHJ*, III, p. 40).

30. *Van Eyck and Memling, Rubens and Rembrandt*: Jan van Eyck (*c*.1390–1441), Hans Memling (*c*.1430–94), Peter Paul Rubens (1577–1640) and Rembrandt Harmenszoon van Rijn (1606–69) – that is, the Flemish or Dutch painters whose works were to be seen in the Low Countries, where Longmore was supposed to have joined Webster.

31. *Alfred de Musset*: Alfred Louis Charles de Musset-Pathay (1810–57), French poet, novelist and dramatist. In the *Atlantic Monthly* for September 1870, James reviewed an anthology of Musset's work edited and translated by Sarah Butler Wister, and in *The Galaxy* for June 1877, published a long essay on the author, reflecting on his affair with George Sand (q.v.) and judging him to be 'not the poet of nature, of the universe, of reflection, of morality; he was the poet simply of a certain order of personal emotions'. Both essays are collected in *LCFW*, pp. 592–618.

32. *Bois de Boulogne*: the large park on the western edge of Paris.

33. *sibyl . . . Roman king*: a sibyl was an oracular woman believed to possess prophetic powers; Madame Clairin alludes to the old Roman legend that when the Cumaean Sibyl offered Tarquinius, the last king of Rome, the nine books of her indispensable prophecies, he refused her on the grounds that she was asking too high a price for them.

34. *Chénier*: André Chénier (1762–94), French poet, said to be the precursor of the Romantic movement.

35. *Tuileries gardens*: between the Louvre Museum and the Place de la Concorde, a public garden since the French Revolution.

FOUR MEETINGS

1. *four times*: in a letter of 21 March 1879 to Mrs F. H. Hill about her review of 'Daisy Miller', 'Four Meetings' and 'An International Episode' he referred to the second of these as 'the 3 Meetings'. Edel suggests that this slip indicates that James was thinking of 'Three Meetings' (1852), a short story by Ivan Turgenev (Edel, II. p. 219n). 'Three or four of [Turgenev's] <u>Nouvelles,</u> I think,' James wrote to Henry Wadsworth Longfellow in May 1870, 'are the best short stories ever written' (*CLHJ*, II, p. 356). James later wrote extensively on Turgenev, in the *North American Review* in 1974, in the *Atlantic Monthly* in 1884, and elsewhere; these pieces have been collected in *LCFW*, pp. 968–1034.

2. *some seventeen years ago*: hence around 1860.

3. *sun-picture*: an outdoor scene focused on silver salts that blacken in the light; hence (in 1850s and 1860s American usage) a photograph.

4. *Castle of Chillon*: an eleventh-century castle at the eastern tip of Lake Geneva, built to control the road from Burgundy to the Grand Saint Bernard Pass over the Alps, then as now a popular tourist attraction. From 1530 to 1536 the Dukes of Savoy used it to imprison the Genevan libertine, politician and sometime monk François de Bonivard (or Bonnivard) (1493–1570) for opposing the Savoyards' control of his homeland. 'The ring by which he was attached to one of the pillars still remains,' writes Murray (*HSA*, p. 185), 'and the stone floor at its base is worn by his constant pacing to and fro.' 'The Prisoner of Chillon' (1816), by George Gordon, Lord Byron (1788–1824), tells a version of the story. To reinforce his point about the worn floor, Murray quotes from Byron's sonnet on Bonivard, placed before the main body of the poem:

> Chillon! thy prison is a holy place,
>   And thy sad floor an altar; for 'twas trod
> Until his very steps have left a trace
>   Worn, as if the cold pavement were a sod, ['thy' in Byron; 'the' in Murray]
> By Bonnivard! May none those marks efface!
>   For they appeal from tyranny to God.

5. *Europe was getting sadly dis-Byronized*: presumably in that it was becoming less moved by heroic action in pursuit of romantic ideals, the overthrow of political and social conventions.

6. *picturesque*: see note on 'Travelling Companions', p. 344.

7. *Havre*: see note on 'Madame de Mauves', p. 354.

8. *circular notes*: letters of credit from one's home banker to bankers abroad, an early version of traveller's cheques.

9. *place of convenience*: Murray (*HTF*, p. 63) notes that the city 'has no fine buildings nor historical monuments; its streets are laid down chiefly in straight lines, and at right angles with one another, and they are grouped around the basins, or docks'.

10. *ancient fortress*: the round tower built by Francis I to defend the entrance of the harbour. J. M. W. Turner (1775–1851) painted it in or around 1832; so did Eugène Boudin (1824–98), whose *Le Havre: La tour François*, done around 1854, brings out the similarity to the Castle of St Angelo most clearly.

11. *Francis the First*: King of France from 1515 until his death in 1547, Francis I (1494–1547) founded Le Havre in 1517; he was a great patron of the arts, who worked to standardize the French language.

12. *castle of St Angelo*: or Castel Sant'Angelo (Italian), that other circular fortress, on the Tiber in Rome; originally built as the mausoleum of the Emperor Hadrian (d. 138), later rebuilt as a Papal fortress, residence and prison.

13. *lately been demolished*: the tower was demolished in 1861, to enlarge the entrance to the harbour. Since this story begins in around 1860 (see note 2, p. 356) and another three years and some months have elapsed since that *conversazione* in Grimwinter, it's unlikely that Caroline Spencer could have seen the tower even if she hadn't got straight back on the steamer. Had James himself ever seen it? Perhaps only in the paintings of Turner and Boudin.

14. *Rue Bonaparte*: in the Bohemian 6th Arrondissement (municipal borough) on the Left Bank of the River Seine, the site of the École des Beaux Arts, the haunt of artists; and the birthplace of the French painter Édouard Manet (1832–83).

15. *Raphaelesque or Byronic attire*: referring to the late Renaissance painter Raphael Sanzio di Urbino (1483–1520) and to Lord Byron, so presumably the cousin's physique suits neither classical nor romantic dress.

16. *Gérôme*: see note to 'Madame de Mauves', p. 354.

17. *Hôtel des Princes* ... *Belle Normande* (beautiful Norman Woman): unlike the hotels in 'Travelling Companions', these inns appear to be fictional.

18. *'carry-all'*: American folk etymology for *carriole* (French), a light, covered carriage.

19. *mezzotint*: literally, half tone (Italian); a print made from an engraved copper or steel plate, the surface of which has been scraped and polished to give the effect of light and shade; a popular method of reproducing paintings in the eighteenth and nineteenth centuries.

20. *French novel*: at the time notorious in the Anglo-American world for romantic, often sexually suggestive adventures.

DAISY MILLER

1. *Vevey*: a town in the French-speaking canton of Vaud, on the north shore of Lake Geneva; by the nineteenth century already a popular tourist resort; James visited the town in the summer of 1869.

2. *Newport*: the fashionable seaside resort on Aquidneck Island, 23 miles south of Providence, the state capital of Rhode Island; in the 1880s some of America's wealthiest families would build their summer homes there, the mansion-sized 'cottages' in which to entertain their social equals during the summer season. James knew it well from an early age, since his parents lived there on and off for a number of years, from the 1850s. James's first essay on it, in *The Nation* for 15 September 1870, speaks of its wonderful combination of 'an abundance of society with an abundance of solitude' and its 'charming broad-windowed drawing-rooms, on their great seaward piazzas, within sight of the serious Atlantic horizon' (*Great Britain and America*, pp. 759–66, 766).

3. *Saratoga [Springs]*: a popular spa town in upstate New York; when James visited it in 1870, he wrote an essay for *The Nation* for 11 August 1870, remarking on its 'two monster hotels which stand facing each other along a goodly portion of [the] course of Sixth Avenue' all contributing to 'a quite momentous spectacle; the democratization of elegance' (*Great Britain and America*, pp. 750–1, 753).

4. *'Trois Couronnes'*: Three Crowns (French), on the lake; then as now a luxury hotel in Vevey, described by Baedeker as 'spacious and comfortable' (*SIST*, p. 194).

5. *Ocean House*: built in 1868, this is still an elegant ocean-front hotel in Newport.

6. *Congress Hall*: then a fashionable hotel in Saratoga Springs; now a casino, though still a historical landmark.

7. *secretaries of legation*: wear ambassadorial dress when they stand in for the head of legations.

8. *Dent du Midi . . . Castle of Chillon*: Baedeker lists the spectacular views from any hotel on the shore at Vevey: 'To the E. the Tour de Peilz, Clarens, Montreux, and Chillon are visible; next, Villeneuve and the mouth of the Rhone; in the background the Alps of Valais, the Dent de Midi, Mont Velan (adjoining the Great St Bernard) and Mont Catogne (the 'sugar loaf')' (*SIST*, p. 194). Dent (or Dents) du Midi, literally, teeth in/of the south (French), a mountain in the Valais Canton, across Lake Geneva from Vevey, 3,257 metres high, with a jagged top made up of seven summits. For the Castle of Chillon: also visible across the lake; see note on 'Four Meetings', p. 356.

9. *metropolis of Calvinism*: Geneva had already embraced the Reformation by the time the Protestant reformer Jean Calvin (1509–64) arrived there in 1536, but later there he was to found the Geneva Academy as a school of Protestant theology, and to clarify and codify the tenets of his theology to the point where the city popularly came to be known as the Protestant Rome.

10. *put to school . . . gone to college there*: the James family were in Geneva during the winter of 1859–60, when the sixteen-year-old Henry himself was 'put to school' at M. Rochette's École Préparatoire aux Écoles Spéciales, to follow a course in mathematics that he didn't like. Later he was set free to attend lectures at the Academy, by then part of the University of Geneva, along with his elder brother William.

11. *knickerbockers*: trousers gathered at the knee, plus-fours. Up to the beginning of the First World War American boys who wore short trousers in the summer wore knickerbockers in winter.

12. *alpenstock*: literally, Alp stick (though the German is *Bergstock*, or mountain stick), a long wooden staff with an iron spike at one end; a sort of walking stick for negotiating icy surfaces.

13. *fellow-countryman*: because he pronounces 'har-r-d' with that American fronted 'r'.

14. *Simplon*: the mountain pass between Brig in the Valais in Switzerland and Domodossola in Italy, originally built between 1801 and 1805 on the orders of Napoleon, to get wheeled cannon and heavy military transport across the Alps.

15. *her cards*: her formal calling cards, *cartes de visite*.

16. *Schenectady*: a thriving manufacturing town in upstate New York, and a pioneer in higher education (James's father had been to Union College there), with good trade connections via the Mohawk and Hudson Rivers and the Erie Canal, and early railroad links.

17. *in the cars*: on the train.

18. *inconduite*: misconduct, loose behaviour (French); in the New York Edition this word was revised to the slightly more sinister *arrière-pensée* – that is, ulterior motive (French); see Horne, *HJR*, pp. 238–9.

19. *more than once*: when he visited the Castle of Chillon in 1872, James was discouraged by the crowd: 'When I went, Baedeker in hand, to "do" the place, I found a huge concourse of visitors waiting the reflux of an earlier wave. "Let us at least wait till there is no one else," I said to my companion. She smiled in compassion of my naïveté, *"There is never no one else,"* she answered. "We must treat it as a crush or leave it alone" ' ('Swiss Notes', *Transatlantic Sketches*, pp. 56–70, 66).

20. *courier*: better-off travellers on the continent employed couriers, who made all the relevant arrangements for travel, accommodation and local tours.

21. *furbelows*: see note on 'Madame de Mauves', p. 354.

22. *rouleaux*: cylindrical coils (French) formed by curlers or rollers; a fashionable hairstyle at the time.

23. *Homburg*: see note to 'Madame de Mauves', p. 352.

24. *Comanche*: the Native American tribe from the Great Plains, famous for their horsemanship.

25. *table d' hôte*: literally, the guests' table (French), where the hotel guests sit together; the New York Edition revises this to Daisy's demotic 'the common table' – i.e., the ordinary hotel dining room, where meals were served at set times; the implication is that Mrs Costello has her meals served in her rooms, the more expensive and exclusive alternative to the table d'hôte.

26. *dark old city*: that is, Geneva.

27. *as our ancestors used to say, of sensibility*: the capacity for perceiving and responding to the feelings of others, and to the aesthetic influences of the arts or imaginative literature; it is traced back to 'our ancestors' because from the publication of John Locke's *Essay Concerning Human Understanding* (1689), it was central to the thinking about how we perceive the world and construct reality; it was also at the heart of the

eighteenth-century English cult of the sentimental novel, like Henry Mackenzie's *The Man of Feeling* (1771), in which characters displayed their moral superiority by their hypersensitive feelings, often fainting, or weeping over occurrences that others would find insignificant; the title of Jane Austen's *Sense and Sensibility* (1811) questions the sentimental novel by posing its opposite quality as equally, morally efficacious, if not more so.

28. *what metaphysicians term the objective cast*: that is, anchored in the assumption that things exist in reality, outside the emotions or intellectual biases of the perceiver – as opposed to the subjective. The metaphysicians alluded to are probably Immanuel Kant (1724–1804), for the subjective side of the argument, and Gottlob Frege (1848–1925) for the objective.

29. *oubliettes*: secret dungeons under trap doors, where prisoners could be kept out of sight and out of mind; from Fr. *oublié*, forgotten.

30. *unhappy Bonivard*: see note 4 on 'Four Meetings', p. 356.

31. *Rome towards the end of January*: Poole (pp. 188–9) notes that 'many of the tourist sights and venues in the second half of ["Daisy Miller"] had already featured in James's writing, in his first full-length novel, *Roderick Hudson* (1875), and his five essays that made their debut in American periodicals in 1873, were gathered for the concerted volume of *Transatlantic Sketches* (1875), and many years later revised for reissue in *Italian Hours* (1909). Of these, it is particularly valuable to read alongside this tale "A Roman Holiday" and "From a Roman Note-Book".' Also worth noting is his letter to Alice James, written over two days, 7 and 8 November 1869, just a week after he arrived in Rome on his first visit to the city alone (*CLHJ*, II, pp. 171–82), giving his impressions of the galleries, the Baths of Caracalla, the Pantheon, the churches, the Campagna, the Vatican and St Peter's. 'It's a place in which you needn't in the least feel ashamed of a perpetual reference to <u>Murray</u>: a place in which you feel emphatically the value of "culture." '

32. *'Paule Méré'*: *Paule Méré* (1864), a novel by the Geneva-born Victor Cherbuliez (1829–99), in which a man like Winterbourne meets a young woman who, though innocent, scandalizes society with her spontaneous independence; after the man rejects her when discovering her in what he takes to be a compromising situation, she dies of a broken heart. James clearly knew the novel, which he described in the *North American Review* for

October 1873 as 'an attempted exposure, rather youthful in its unsparing ardour, of the narrowness and intolerance of Genevese society. How true the picture is, we are unable to say; but the story is admirably touching' (*LCFW*, pp. 185–6); so he could have found in it a source for the plot of 'Daisy Miller'.

33. *the American Banker's*: in an essay on the topic, published in *The Nation* for 3 October 1878, James wrote that a good way of acquiring a collective impression of Americans abroad 'is to go and sit for half an hour in the waiting room of any European banker upon whom Americans hold letters of credit' ('Americans Abroad', *Great Britain and America*, pp. 786–92, 790). Murray notes that 'Messrs. Packenham and Hooker, 20, Piazza di Spagna ... conducts a large portion of the American business' in Rome (*HRE 71*, p. xix).

34. *Via Gregoriana*: just south of the Spanish Steps, an area where artists and intellectuals then lived; much favoured by better-off visitors to the city.

35. *the infant Hannibal*: the great Carthaginian military leader Hannibal Barca (247–*c*.181 BC), learned early to hate Rome, and vowed to destroy it, being the son of the Hamilcar Barca (275–228 BC), who led the Carthaginians in the First Punic War.

36. *He means the ship*: launched early in 1873, the *City of Richmond* was a 450-foot-long steamship, yet fully rigged as a sailing vessel; she carried passengers between New York and Liverpool from 1874 until 1890.

37. *the Pincio*: on the Pincian Hill, just north of the Spanish Steps, at the western end of a large complex of gardens extending from the Villa Borghese; its paths were and are popular for strolling and its balustraded western promontory a favourite place, especially at sunset, for gazing out over the Piazza del Popolo below, and St Peter's across the River Tiber beyond. Murray notes that of all the city's public walks, the promenade on the Pincio 'is the most fashionable and frequented at Rome, especially during the fine afternoons of winter and spring (*HRE 71*, p. 99).

38. *You'll get the fever*: See note on the' villainous miasma' below, p. 365.

39. *penny-a-liner*: hack journalist.

40. *cavaliers*: literally, knights (Italian), but here used for any gallant young gentlemen.

41. *victoria*: a light four-wheeled, one-horse carriage; with a collapsible top, it has two seats, plus one for the driver.

42. *wall of Rome*: the Aurelian Walls, built between 271 and 274 to keep out the barbarians, by the Emperors Lucius Domitius Aurelianus (214 or 215–75) and Marcus Aurelius Probus (232–82), incorporated the Pincio within their bounds, which are today marked by the Viale Muro Torto, or Boulevard of the Crooked Wall (Italian).

43. *Villa Borghese*: see note on 'Travelling Companions', p. 351.

44. *barber's block*: wooden head for storing or displaying a wig.

45. *the Golden Age*: in Greek mythology the first age of human-kind, when nature provided so abundantly that no one had to work, and everyone lived to a healthy old age, but Mrs Costello means, simply, a time without social constraints.

46. *marchese*: marquess (Italian); ranks between a count and a prince.

47. *Corso*: literally, a race (Italian); one of the main streets of Rome, it is a long, straight thoroughfare running south from the Piazza del Popolo to the centre of the city, so called because from the fifteenth century it was the course of an annual race of riderless horses. As Murray points out, 'The Corso, which in its N. portion, follows the line of the ancient Via Flaminia . . . divides the principal district of modern Rome into 2 parts; that on the E . . . is the quarter where foreign visitors chiefly reside; it contains the best streets and the most modern houses, and is one of the healthiest parts of the city' (*HRE 71*, p. 2).

48. *Doria Palace*: the Palazzo Doria Pamphilj, which fronts on the Via del Corso, from the sixteenth century, a gallery of statuary and paintings, as well as a private residence.

49. *Innocent X . . . picture of a different kind*: Horne notes that Pope Innocent X had founded the Pamphilj family. Though Diego Velásquez (1599–1660) worked mainly in Spain, he painted the Pope's portrait while visiting Rome in 1651. When he saw the painting on his 1869 tour of Italy, James wrote to Grace Norton on 11 November that the portrait was a 'really great picture – one of those works which draw heavily on your respect, & make you feel the richer for the loss' (*HJLL*, p. 30 and 30n). Familiar to modern gallery-goers as the source for the series of 'Screaming Popes' by Francis Bacon (1909–92) in the 1950s, the painting, still in the Gallery of the Doria Palace, shows the Pope's expression as calculating, even cynically scheming – anything but 'innocent'; a 'cabinet' here is a small room in a gallery.

50. *Palace of the Cæsars . . . Palatine*: the Palatine Hill, the oldest and most central of the seven ancient hills of Rome, immediately

above and to the south of the Roman Forum, thought to be the site of the Lupercal, the cave named for the she-wolf ('lupa' in Italian) who nourished Remus and the city's mythical founder Romulus as babies. The Palatine is where the Emperor Domitian chose to build his imperial palace, which formed the extensive ruins of the so-called 'Palace of the Caesars'.

51. *Cælian Hill*: another of the seven ancient hills of Roman settlement, to the east of the Palatine and south of the Colosseum.

52. *Arch of Constantine*: one of the largest and best preserved of the triumphal arches in Rome, built in AD 315 to celebrate the victory of the Emperor Constantine (272–337) over the Emperor Maxentius (c.278–312); spanning the Via Triumphalis, the wide road followed by the emperors when they entered the city in triumph, it stands between the Palatine and the Colosseum.

53. *Colosseum*: the four-tiered, oval amphitheatre at the north-east corner of the Roman Forum, so called because it had been built next to a huge bronze statue of Nero based on the Colossus of Rhodes. Seating between 50,000 and 80,000 spectators, it was used for gladiatorial contests, re-enactments of mythical scenes, mock battles, animal hunts and the executions of criminals by exposing them to wild animals. Pope Pius V (1504–72) recommended that devout Christians should collect the sand from the arena as a relic, because it had been soaked in the blood of Christian martyrs. In 1749, Pope Benedict XIV (1675–1758) declared the Colosseum to be a sacred place where early Christians had been martyred. There are, however, few early Christian records supporting the later Church's view that Christians were martyred in the Colosseum; it was in the Circus Maximus, the ancient Roman chariot racing arena, that the Christian martyrs' blood really did flow.

54. *the picturesque*: see note on 'Travelling Companions', p. 344.

55. *Byron's famous lines*: Winterbourne is doing what Murray suggests all tourists should do on their visit to the Colosseum, recall the lines in Byron's dramatic poem 'Manfred' (1817), taken from Manfred's soliloquy in Act III, scene iv: 'I stood within the Coliseum's wall,/'Midst the chief relics of almighty Rome . . . /But the gladiators' bloody circus stands/A noble wreck in ruinous perfection,/While Caesar's chambers and the Augustan halls,/Grovel on earth in indistinct decay./And thou dids't shine, thou rolling moon, upon/All this, and cast a wide and tender light.' Murray cites these lines, calling them 'the only description which

has ever done justice to the wonders of the Coliseum' (*HRE 71*, p. 53). As Poole remarks acutely, 'Murray quotes Byron freely to induce the appropriate "romantic" response to the ruins of empire' (p. 192).

56. *villanous miasma*: malaria, or Roman fever, also called *la perniciosa*, 'the deadly' (Italian), was then thought to be caused by the damp air of the low-lying areas of the city; the literal meaning of malaria, the common medical name for the disease, is 'bad air' (Italian). In fact, the disease is caused by a parasite carried by mosquitoes of the genus *anopheles* that bred in the waters of swamps and on the banks of the river in the city, and were especially active at night.

57. *great cross*: commemorates the Christian martyrs supposedly sacrificed there, set up in the centre of the arena in the eighteenth century, removed in 1874, then reinstated in 1927. Gooder quotes a letter that William James sent to their father when he and his brother Henry visited Rome in 1868 (actually 1873) expressing his horror of the Colosseum, 'with that cold sinister half-moon and hardly a star in the deep blue sky – it was all so strange, and, I must say, inhuman and horrible, that it felt like a nightmare ... Anti-Christian as I generally am, I actually derived a deep comfort from the big black cross that had been planted in the damned blood-soaked soil' (p. 275).

58. *splendid pills*: Eugenio's pills were probably a compound of quinine, often carried by nineteenth-century travellers in the form of either pills or a powder to be dissolved in water (the 'tonic' in gin and tonic is a late descendant of this specific). Derived from the bark of the South American cinchona tree, quinine was used as an anti-malarial drug from the late seventeenth century to the 1940s, to alleviate the symptoms of the disease. It would certainly not prevent its onset, as Daisy and even Winterbourne seem to believe.

59. *Protestant cemetery*: or Cimitero Acattolico (non-Catholic cemetery) as it's called in Rome, is close to the Porta San Paolo and next to Rome's only pyramid, the tomb of the tribune Caius Cestius, south of the Aventine Hill. Many artists and writers are buried there, including John Keats (1795–1821), Percy Bysshe Shelley (1792–1822), the Scottish novelist R. M. Ballantyne (1825–94) and the American sculptor William Wetmore Story (1819–95), whom James knew well and would later commemorate in his *William Wetmore Story and his Friends* (1903). Story's *Angel of Grief* decorates the tomb that he shares with

his wife Emelyn (1820–95). Murray contrasts 'the silence and seclusion of the spot' with 'the tomb of the ancient Roman and with the massive city walls and towers which overlook it' (*HRE 71*, p. 321).

AN INTERNATIONAL EPISODE

1. *Broadway*: the oldest thoroughfare in New York, Broadway follows the old Native American Wickquasgeck Trail, running the length of Manhattan Island, into the Bronx, finally ending north of Sleepy Hollow in Westchester County – a distance of 33 miles in all. Passing just west of Times Square, as it crosses West 45th to West 48th Streets, it goes through the theatre district, leading to Broadway becoming a metonym for live theatre in New York. For James as a child, as he explained at the beginning of chapter 6 of *A Small Boy and Others* (1913), 'Broadway was the feature and the artery, the joy and the adventure of one's childhood, and it stretched, and prodigiously, from Union Square to Barnum's great American Museum by the City Hall.'

2. *horse-cars and other democratic vehicles*: horse-cars were trams drawn by horses or mules, streetcars on rails; they were democratic in the sense that anyone could board and ride on them for a small fare. James knew that the horse-cars were among the first of the New World shocks to be encountered by European visitors, who were accustomed to getting around cities by cabs or private carriages, rather than conveyances in which they would (literally) have to rub shoulders with *hoi polloi*.

3. *Union Square*: the public square in lower Manhattan, New York, only three city blocks from where the James family lived, at 58 West 14th Street, from 1847 to 1855, when Henry was from four to twelve years old, and well known to him. When James was a child the Square was largely residential, and enclosed – 'encased in iron rails', as he was to put it in *A Small Boy and Others* (1913). Later it was opened out and as Poole notes (pp. 184–95), had become increasingly commercialized after the Civil War of 1861–65.

4. *monument to Washington*: a large bronze equestrian statue by Henry Kirke Brown (1814–86); unveiled in 1856, and the first public statue erected in New York since the equestrian statue of George III in 1770.

5. *pater patriæ*: father of [his] country (Latin); in English, not Latin, the expression is the most common American epithet for George Washington.

6. *low latitude*: New York is roughly at the same latitude as Naples; this also accounts for its 'strong, crude light' in summer, as mentioned in the first paragraph of the story.

7. *square, without any palings*: that is, as opposed to London, where many squares were surrounded by iron palings, and some even closed except to key-holding residents living around them.

8. *street-cars*: American for trams.

9. *Pompadour-looking dresses*: that is, after the style of Madame de Pompadour (1721–64), mistress of Louis XV of France, a fairly low-cut dress, tightly cinched in at the waist, often fronted by an embroidered or otherwise decorated 'stomacher', and a very full skirt.

10. *thingumbob*: English slang, first occurring *c.*1870–5, for something for which the speaker does not know, or has forgotten the name; variants include thingum and thingummy.

11. *Belgrave Square*: dating from the 1820s, one of the largest squares in London, consisting of four grand residential terraces surrounding a private garden fenced off with palings and reserved for the use of residents; today many national embassies and high commissions occupy the surrounding buildings. James revised this detail for the New York Edition, changing 'Belgrave' to 'Grosvenor'. At the time of the story Grosvenor Square in Mayfair was also fenced off and reserved for residents, with the added irony that from the days of John Adams (1735–1826) it was where the American Mission, later Embassy, to the Court of St James, was situated.

12. *absorbing ... promiscuously*: the relative openness of American hotels seems to be the issue here, also the fact that people come and go off the street for business meetings or other encounters, not necessarily to stay the night.

13. *portmanteaux*: large leather suitcases that open out into two compartments. By contrast to the passers-by wandering 'promiscuously' in and out, these are travellers who have come to stay.

14. *citizens*: again (see note 12 above) the democratic tone and utility of the American hotel are stressed.

15. *the Fifth Avenue*: Fifth Avenue runs in a north-easterly direction from Washington Square in Lower Manhattan. James recalls 'The Old Fifth Avenue' as part of 'a pleasanter, easier, lazier past' in chapter 2 of *The American Scene* (1907), 'New

York Revisited', but as Poole points out (p. 195) by the time of the story's setting, Fifth Avenue was 'famed for its high society and culture, exclusive clubs, luxurious hotels, and elegant shops'. It was also where the wealthiest New Yorkers, like the Vanderbilts and the Astors, had their town houses.

16. *cave of Æolus*: in Homer's *Odyssey* Aeolus, god of the four winds, held captive the winds of all directions in a cave on the floating island of Aeolia, letting them free as directed by the gods.

17. *hackney-coach*: from mid-seventeenth-century London, a four-wheeled taxi cab drawn, usually, by two horses with seating for up to six passengers. In 1823 a smaller, lighter conveyance with two wheels and one horse was introduced in London; called a cabriolet, it was the origin of today's term cab, though in New York the word hackney persists in the phrase hack-stand for a taxi stand.

18. *hydraulic elevator*: a lift raised or lowered by a piston in a cylinder into which fluid is pumped underneath the passenger car; it was a new development replacing the more standard elevator raised and lowered by a cable attached to the top of the structure, but only until buildings grew too tall for the hydraulic option.

19. *sherry-cobblers*: a popular summer drink, consisting of dry sherry and citrus juice poured over sugar and crushed ice, sipped through a straw. Originating in the United States, it began to catch on in Great Britain too, after the eponymous hero of Charles Dickens's *The Life and Adventures of Martin Chuzzlewit* (1843–4) swallows his first glass of sherry-cobbler in America: 'Martin took the glass with an astonished look; applied his lips to the reed; and cast up his eyes once in ecstasy. He paused no more until the goblet was drained to the last drop. "This wonderful invention, sir," said Mark, tenderly patting the empty glass, "is called a cobbler. Sherry Cobbler when you name it long; cobbler, when you name it short."' The straw was as much a novelty as the drink itself.

20. *Newport*: see note on 'Daisy Miller', p. 358.

21. The 'Russia': the Cunard line's first single-screw express liner sailed between Liverpool and New York; from 1867 it briefly held the speed record for the Atlantic crossing, for a run from New York to Queenstown (later Cobh), Ireland, in 8 days and 25 minutes.

22. *gnats*: What the English used to call mosquitoes.

23. *the Tennessee Central*: since the real-life Tennessee Central Railway was not established until 1893, it's unlikely that James had an actual railway in mind for the time in which the story is set, but Poole is clearly right to suggest the reference to another company with a shared name: 'James is picking up on business opportunities much in the air in the late 1870s. The Tennessee and Pacific Railroad had operated between Lebanon and Nashville from 1871 before its finances collapsed in 1877' (pp. 196–7). This failure has presumably prompted the lawsuit that Beaumont's clients are considering initiating.

24. *Boston . . . intellectual town*: as one who had lived in both New York and Ashburton Place, Boston, James was acutely aware of the actual and symbolic contrast between the two cities. If New York was increasingly America's business centre, Boston was its intellectual. As the seat of many universities – Harvard, Boston University, MIT, and others – not to mention the home of the Unitarians, transcendentalists, abolitionists, early feminists and other high-minded reformers of the Church, education, politics and the social order, Boston had garnered a reputation for being the intellectual centre of the US.

25. *Miss Alden*: Bessie Alden's surname may have been suggested by Henry Mills Alden (1836–1919), and from 1869, Editor of *Harper's*, or by that near legendary Massachusetts settler, John Alden (*c.*1599–1687), a crewman on the Plymouth Separatists' *Mayflower*, who decided to remain in New England and marry Priscilla Mullins, rather than return to England on the ship, later serving in a number of important positions in the new colony.

26. *passengers . . . ladies and very young children*: because the sea air was thought to be good for young children, and women and children were customarily sent on holiday while the men remained behind in the City to work.

27. *'real mean'*: very cruel; Percy is ironically imitating the American vernacular; 'mean' in English usage means stingy.

28. *Valenciennes lace*: a type of lace in which the pattern sits in a net-like ground, both woven at the same time; originating in Valenciennes in northern France, the craft moved to Belgium; by the nineteenth century Valenciennes lace was machine made.

29. *fête champêtre*: literally, a pastoral festival or country feast (French), *fêtes champêtres* were, in fact, elegant garden parties of the sort enjoyed by the French court, in a landscaped park like that at Versailles.

30. *bowieknife*: long-bladed fighting knife commonly associated with the American Wild West.

31. *basket-phaetons*: lightly sprung, open carriages of wicker-work, mounted on four large, light wheels, drawn by one or two horses.

32. *chalet*: in the Swiss Alps, a square, wide-fronted wooden house with a gently sloping roof and projecting eves. According to the art critic John Ruskin (q.v.), the chalet, while 'occasionally picturesque, frequently pleasing, and, under a favourable con-currence of circumstances, beautiful . . . is not, however, a thing to be imitated; it is always, when out of its own country, incon-gruous' (*The Poetry of Architecture*, p. 46).

33. *knocked up*: British slang for worn out, as opposed to the American usage, made pregnant.

34. *Ocean House*: see note 5 to 'Daisy Miller', p. 359.

35. *piazza*: not Italian for town square but archaic American usage for a large porch, or veranda, as in Herman Melville's *Piazza Tales* (1856).

36. *great wit*: the American writer and artist Thomas Gold Apple-ton (1812–84), was famous for his witticisms, the best known of which was 'Good Americans, when they die, go to Paris'. Later Oscar Wilde (1854–1900) would pick up the joke in Chapter III of *The Picture of Dorian Gray*: (1891), with a sting in the tail for the bad Americans:

> 'They say that when good Americans die they go to Paris,' chuck-led Sir Thomas . . . 'Really! And where do bad Americans go to when they die?' inquired the Duchess. 'They go to America,' mur-mured Lord Henry.

37. *Dover Street*: a quiet street in Mayfair, London, close to the Green Park, noted for its exclusive clubs and hotels. Poole (p. 198) is probably right to conjecture that Jones's Hotel is a thinly disguised Brown's Hotel, a quiet and expensive favourite with Americans since it opened in 1837.

38. *with all our imperfections on our heads*: in Shakespeare's *Ham-let* the ghost of his father complains to Hamlet that he had been murdered with 'No reck'ning made, but sent to my account/With all my imperfections on my head' (Act I, scene v, lines 78–9).

39. *country life . . . ruins . . . estates*: in his *Hawthorne* (1879) country houses are among those things that James lists as lack-ing in America; see Introduction, p. xiv.

40. *Kingsley's novels*: Charles Kingsley (1819–75), novelist, historian and priest in the Church of England, was best known for *Westward Ho!* (1855), *The Water Babies* (1863) and *Hereward the Wake* (1866). In various essays and reviews James praised Kingsley's work, for example writing in his obituary for *The Nation* for 28 January 1875, 'If we picked out half-a-dozen modern English novels for the use of posterity . . . one of the first would certainly be 'Westward Ho!' (*LCAEW*, p. 1105). There are plenty of coastal scenes in *Westward Ho!*, with its action swinging from Elizabethan north Devon to the Caribbean, but it's not clear what coasts Miss Alden is thinking of here.

41. *Thackeray and George Eliot*: William Makepeace Thackeray (1811–63), satirical novelist of English social mores, and George Eliot: pen name of Mary Ann Evans (1819–80), journalist, editor and a highly serious novelist of sharply realistic insights into her characters' psychological responses to social and political change. Poole points out (p. 199) that George Eliot's *Middlemarch* (1871–2) and *Daniel Deronda* (1874–6) would have been much more to Miss Alden's taste than the work of Dickens, for instance.

42. *Mrs Gore*: Catherine Grace Frances Gore (1799–1861), British novelist and playwright, who wrote numerous novels of fashionable English life. Her prodigious output was a favourite of James's paternal grandmother, along with other 'promptly pirated' English 'fiction of the day', as he recalls of his infancy in Albany at the beginning of *A Small Boy and Others* (1913).

43. *the long avenue*: The Avenue was then Newport's main street, where visitors and summer residents went to be seen.

44. *'Peerage', like the people in Thackeray*: that is, a reference book, like Debrett's *The New Peerage* or Burke's *Peerage*, a guide to the blood lines and connections of British holders of hereditary titles. In Thackeray's *Vanity Fair* (1847) Sir Pitt Crawley is described as 'a selfish boor . . . unworthy of his title' despite being in Debrett's.

45. *peer*: one who holds any of the five grades of the British nobility, listed in descending order: duke, marquis, earl, viscount and baron.

46. *Countess of Pimlico*: a countess is one rank lower than marquis; as for her title, Poole (p. 199) quotes Tintner (p. 33) to the effect that the South London district of Pimlico becomes the basis of several of Thackeray's parodic and satiric names, such as Lady Pimlico, Amethyst Pimlico and a little Lord Pimlico.

47. *'fast girl'*: socially or sexually forward young woman.
48. *blue-stocking*: an educated, intellectual woman; the term origin-
     ates in the Blue Stockings Society, led by the critic Elizabeth
     Montagu (1718–1800). Later the term could acquire pejorative
     connotations, as in *OED*, definition 2, 'transferred sneeringly
     to any woman showing a taste for learning, a literary lady'.
49. *livings*: property or income to dispense to a clergyman.
50. *'associations'*: mental connections; according to the American
     novelist and essayist Washington Irving (1783–1859) in 'The
     Author's Account of Himself', in *The Sketchbook of Geoffrey
     Crayon, Gent.* (1819–20), Europe offered 'the charms of stor-
     ied [historical] and poetical association' that America lacked;
     see introduction, p. xviii.
51. *picturesque*: see note on 'Travelling Companions', p. 344.
52. *Duke of Green-Erin*: another title verging on the comic. 'Erin'
     was the term used by poets and Irish nationalists during the
     nineteenth century as a romantic name for Ireland – also called
     (poetically) the 'Emerald Isle'.
53. *Season*: that time of year, from April to August, when the aris-
     tocracy left their country houses to take up residence in their
     London mansions, to engage in politics and fashionable social
     events.
54. *Ascot races*: the most fashionable of the various horse-racing meet-
     ings on the flat – that is, as opposed to steeplechase racing, which
     is run over hedges and other hurdles – and a fixture in the season.
     Founded in 1711 by Queen Anne (1665–1714), the Ascot races in
     Berkshire have always enjoyed royal patronage, not least because
     the course is only around six miles from Windsor Castle.
55. *Hansom cab*: a cabriolet, a light, one-horse, two-wheeled car-
     riage for hire, it could seat two people – three at a squeeze – with
     the driver seated above and behind the passenger compartment
     (see note 17, above, p. 368).
56. *Bond Street and Regent Street*: then as now, among the most
     fashionable shopping areas in London.
57. *Westminster Abbey*: the large Gothic church in Westminster,
     begun in 1245 by Henry III, traditionally the place where Brit-
     ish monarchs are crowned and buried; then as now one of the
     chief sites on the tourist itinerary.
58. *the Tower*: the Tower of London, on the north bank of the
     River Thames in central London; it was founded in 1066 as part
     of the Norman Conquest of England, later expanded in the

twelfth and thirteenth centuries. A royal palace, the Tower was also used as a prison and place of execution, and is the place where the Crown Jewels of England are kept; like Westminster Abbey, the Tower was and remains a popular tourist attraction.

59. *Madame Tussaud's*: the wax sculptor Marie Tussaud (1761–1850) first brought her collection of waxworks to London in 1802. By the time of Mrs Westgate's visit the museum would have been moved to Baker Street, Marylebone, London, though by 1884 Marie's grandson had opened the much larger gallery still known today, round the corner in the Marylebone Road. Early waxworks included victims of the French Revolution and (in a separate 'Chamber of Horrors') notorious murderers in the news, but figures of the British Royal family and notables like Horatio Nelson and Sir Walter Scott soon joined the collection. As with the Tower and the Abbey, Madame Tussaud's was and remains a staple of the tourist itinerary.

60. *Beacon Street*: the major thoroughfare in Boston, later extended westwards to suburbs like Brookline and Newton.

61. *Charing Cross Hotel*: in front of and above Charing Cross railway station. Opened in 1865, a year after the station itself, the hotel presents an ornate frontage in the French Renaissance style in the Strand, London, between Trafalgar Square and Covent Garden.

62. *the 'German'*: the cotillon, or cotillion, a sort of square dance involving numerous couples and sometimes party games.

63. *'in the English style'*: possibly in the sense that he was dressed by London tailors, as opposed to – say – Christopher Newman in James's *The American* (1877), who first appears in 'an exposed shirt-front and a cerulean cravat'.

64. *the scene of Lady Jane Grey's execution*: Lady Jane Grey: (1536/1537–54), great-granddaughter of Henry VII and first cousin once removed of Edward VI; reputed to be the most learned woman in England, she was a devout Protestant who was nominated by the dying Edward VI as successor to the crown, in order to block the succession of his half-sister, the Catholic Mary (and incidentally his other half-sister Elizabeth); Lady Jane was actually the *de facto* monarch from 10 July until 19 July 1553, until the Privy Council changed its mind and decided to back Mary. Lady Jane was imprisoned in the Tower and eventually executed for treason, along with her husband, Lord Guildford Dudley.

65. *Hyde Park ... Rotten Row*: Hyde Park is one of the largest public parks in London. Henry VIII created it for hunting in 1536. When William III moved his residence to Kensington Palace in 1689, he had a drive laid out for his exclusive use along the park's south side, to allow his carriage to drive from Kensington Palace to the Palace of Whitehall in Westminster. Originally designated the *route du roi* (French for the king's road), its name was corrupted to Rotten Row, and in the eighteenth and nineteenth centuries it became a place for the upper classes to be seen riding.

66. *Morning Post*: a London paper, founded in 1772 and Conservative in sympathies, that recorded the comings and goings, and other activities, of the prominent and wealthy.

67. *Thackeray*: see note 41, p. 371. The *Morning Post*'s gossip about the rich and famous comes within Thackeray's satirical orbit, though he himself wrote for the paper in his early career; see, for example, *The Newcomes* (1855), a work that James knew well, in which Clive Newcome says to his cousin Ethel, 'Oh, Ethel, what a standard we folks measure fame by! To have your name in the *Morning Post* and to go to three balls every night.'

68. *Punch*: *Punch or The London Charivari* was the illustrated British weekly magazine of humour, satire and politics; established in 1841, it introduced cartoons, engravings and later photographs into its display; reaching its peak of circulation in the 1940s, it closed in 1992.

69. *they are pinned back*: that is, the 'blue flounces'.

70. *an hour ago*: this is not a joke; in the 1870s London had an hourly postal delivery.

71. *Hurlingham*: the exclusive sporting and social club in Fulham, London, founded in 1869, where the gentry shot pigeons and where polo was first played.

72. *Piccadilly*: at just under a mile in length, Piccadilly was the main thoroughfare in London, running east–west from Piccadilly Circus to Hyde Park Corner; at the time of the story it was a street of mansions, bookshops and publishers. Dover Street, site of the ladies' hotel, meets Piccadilly at right angles.

73. *Hampton Court*: the royal palace on the River Thames at Richmond, Surrey, just under 12 miles south-west of the centre of London; acquired and revamped in 1514 by Cardinal Thomas Wolsey (*c.*1473–1530), it was later taken over and enlarged by his patron Henry VIII (1491–1547); like Madame Tussaud's (q.v.), the Tower and Westminster Abbey (q.v.), Hampton Court

was and remains firmly on the tourist itinerary. An early scene in *A Passionate Pilgrim* (1871), James's first fiction set in England, takes place there.

74. *Windsor*: Windsor Castle, the royal residence in Windsor, Berkshire, on the River Thames, just under 25 miles to the west of London; built by William the Conqueror in the eleventh century, it was and remains a popular tourist attraction.

75. *the Dulwich Gallery*: the Dulwich picture collection, based on a gift from the Shakespearean actor and theatre manager Edward Alleyn (1566–1626), then greatly enlarged and opened to the public in 1817 in a purpose-built gallery with natural lighting designed by the Regency architect Sir John Soane; Dulwich Village is some 5½ south and across the river from central London, but partly because for some years it was the only public gallery in the country, it was on the American visitors' must-see list.

76. *Rosherville Gardens*: a pleasure garden in Gravesend, Kent, down the River Thames, just over 27 miles east of London; laid out over 17 acres, with Greek temples, an archery lawn, theatres and other amusements, it was a favourite venue for Londoners, who travelled down the river in steamers to land at the pier built specially for the Gardens. Poole notes (p. 201), 'Not a normal destination for tourists, and certainly too vulgar for Lord Lambeth and the circles he moves in.'

77. *I never speak*: as a hereditary peer, Lord Lambeth would have the right to attend and speak in the House of Lords, the upper house of the British Parliament in the Palace of Westminster; the Lords' role was to revise and consent to bills passed by the lower house, the House of Commons. After the Reform Bill of 1832, which widened the franchise of the Commons, and which the Lords rejected, Prime Minister Earl Grey (1764–1845) persuaded King William IV (1765–1837) to appoint eighty new reform-minded peers to weaken the upper house's resistance; so by the time of the tale, Lord Lambeth's influence would have been much reduced, even if he did deign to speak in the Lords.

78. *Lord Chamberlain*: the senior officer of the Royal Household; usually a peer, he managed the business of the Household and arranged ceremonial events, and from 1737 until well after the time of the story, could vet and prevent new plays from being performed.

79. *Emperor of Russia*: in other words, an absolute ruler; Article 1 of the Fundamental Laws of the Russian Empire stated that

the 'Emperor of All Russia is an autocratic and unrestricted monarch'.

80. *'trap'*: a light, two-wheeled vehicle pulled by a single horse or pony, seating two to four persons.

81. *donjon*: a massive inner tower in a medieval castle, in this case the Tower of London.

82. *beefeater*: yeoman warder of the Tower, officially to look after prisoners and guard the Crown Jewels, but also available as guides; their popular name may derive from the traditionally large ration of beef allowed them at court.

83. *crimson doublet*: the ceremonial dress of the beefeater.

84. *cockney excursionist*: that is, a vulgar tourist from the city – especially London.

85. *Happy the country*: Bessie's joke borrows the form of the Latin tag *beatus ille* (happy is the man), first used in the Second Epode of the Latin poet Horace (65–8 BC), as in (in John Dryden's translation of 1685). 'How happy in his low degree,/How rich in humble Poverty, is he,/Who leads a quiet country life!' The formula was much imitated by classical and renaissance historians.

86. *ex-pensioners*: that is, those who had enjoyed her hospitality in America.

87. *American minister*: that is (after 1893), the American Ambassador. At the time the tale was first published, the American minister was John Welsh (1805–86), a prominent Philadelphia merchant.

88. *Drawing Room*: in nineteenth-century English usage, the smartest room in the house, where visitors may be entertained, a salon.

89. *Buckingham Palace*: in Westminster, London; from 1837, with the accession of Queen Victoria, the official London residence and workplace of British Kings and Queens; Mrs Westgate's invitation to the palace would have been arranged by the American minister, a service long since expired due to the number of Americans in London.

90. *gorgeous uniform*: in the nineteenth century, where appropriate, the nobility were expected to wear the regalia proper to their order of chivalry, such as the Order of the Bath, the Order of the Thistle, the Order of the Garter, etc., on visits to the Palace.

91. *precedence*: the order of precedence, the British social hierarchy which runs from the monarch down through dukes, earls,

viscounts, the gentry (including knights), to esquires and gentlemen; women follow men, from royalty, through ladies and dames, to wives and daughters of peers and wives and daughters of younger sons.

92. *gammon*: slang for nonsense.

93. *dome of St Paul's*: designed by Sir Christopher Wren (1632–1723), the Anglican cathedral of St Paul, the seat of the Bishop of London, sits on Ludgate Hill in the City of London; consecrated in 1697, it replaced an older, medieval cathedral gutted in the Great Fire of London (1666); its dome, which rises to 365 feet, was and remains a popular tourist attraction, accessible from inside by a series of steps.

94. *Thames Tunnel*: designed and built by Marc Brunel (1769–1849) and his son Isambard Kingdom Brunel (1806–59), the Thames Tunnel opened in 1843 running under the River Thames for the 1,300 feet between Rotherhithe on the south bank and Wapping on the north; it was the first tunnel to have been completed successfully under a navigable river, and although it never made a living as a carriageway, it proved an enormous pedestrian attraction for tourists paying a penny each and visiting the numerous elegant gas-lit shops in its many arcades. By 1869 the East London Railway Company was running trains through it, and it is now used as a link in the London Overground railway.

95. *National Gallery*: founded in 1824, at first in Pall Mall, then moving in 1838 to a purpose-built gallery at the top of Trafalgar Square in the heart of London, the National Gallery soon became, and remains, the chief attraction for those wanting to see a wide range of paintings from all over Europe.

96. *Stratford-on-Avon*: or Stratford-upon-Avon; the market town in Warwickshire, about 22 miles south-east of Birmingham, renowned as the birthplace of William Shakespeare.

97. *Canterbury Cathedral*: founded in 597, it was and remains the seat of the Archbishop of Canterbury, head of the Anglican Church.

98. *We can stop . . . Paris*: Canterbury is on the road from London to Dover, where they will catch the steam packet for France.

'EUROPE'

1. *Brookbridge*: an imaginary 'suburb' of Boston; the name com-
    bines those of two 'real' suburbs, Brookline and Cambridge,
    Massachusetts, the latter of which might conform to the
    description offered in the story. (James's notebook entry for
    27 February 1895 mentions an old Mrs Palfrey, aged 95, of
    Cambridge as the inspiration for his tale.)
2. *date . . . Battle of Waterloo*: that is, 18 June 1815, when an
    allied force of British and Prussian troops, led by the Duke of
    Wellington and Gebhard Leberecht von Blücher, crushed the
    French army commanded by Napoleon.
3. *Saratoga*: see note on 'Daisy Miller', p. 358.
4. *gay new 'front'*: normally applied to an item of male clothing;
    OED (definition 8d) gives, 'that part of a man's shirt which
    covers the chest and is more or less displayed'.
5. *Como, Bellagio, Lugano*: Como and Bellagio (or Bellaggio) are
    cities in Lombardy, Italy, on Lake Como, Lugano on Lake
    Lugano in Ticino, southern Switzerland; all three are fashiona-
    ble tourist attractions, and were on James's itinerary in August
    and September 1869, when he hiked over Switzerland into Italy.
    From Cadenabbia, on the west shore of Lake Como, he wrote to
    his sister Alice on 31 August 1869, 'In its general presentment &
    contour the Lake of Como strikes me as hardly superior to the
    finest Swiss lakes – but it's when you come to the details – the
    swarming shimmering prodigality of the landscape – that you
    stand convinced & enchanted before Italy and summer' (*CLHJ*
    II, p. 85).
6. *'Sublime . . . there'*: This description – actually of the moun-
    tains around Lake Como – comes from the play *Philip van
    Artevelde: A Dramatic Romance* (1835), by Sir Henry Taylor
    (1800–86), but Miss Jane probably encountered the lines in
    HSA, which reprints a fuller excerpt on p. 319:

> 'Sublime, but neither bleak nor bare,/Nor misty are the mountains
> there,/Softly sublime – profusely fair,/Up to their summits clothed
> in green,/And fruitful as the vales between,/They lightly rise, And
> scale the skies,/And groves and gardens still abound;/For where
> no shoot could else take root,/The peaks are shelved, and terraced
> round.'

7.   *'dark backward'*: from Shakespeare's *The Tempest* (1611), Act I,
     scene ii. On the island, where they have been marooned, Pros-
     pero urgently needs to fill in his daughter Miranda's vague
     memories of their past back in Milan; when she dimly remem-
     bers having been served by 'four or five women', he asks, 'What
     seest thou else/ In the dark backward and abysm of time?'

8.   *restoration of the Bourbons*: in April 1814, following the fall of
     Napoleon, the House of Bourbon was restored to the French
     Throne in the person of Louis XVIII, who inaugurated a period
     of conservative, albeit constitutional, monarchy; on his death in
     1824 he was succeeded by his more reactionary brother,
     Charles X. The Restoration ended with the July Revolution of
     1830.

9.   *awful*: that is, awesome.

10. *pride of my power*: the phrase may have been suggested by
     Leviticus 26: 19, when God is telling Moses what he will do to
     the Israelites if they don't keep His commandments: 'And I will
     break the pride of your power; and I will make your heaven as
     iron, and your earth as brass.'

11. *Falstaff babbled of green fields*: In Act II, scene iii of Shake-
     speare's *Henry V* (1599). As the King is embarking on a
     supposedly heroic war in France, Falstaff, his old drinking com-
     panion and lord of misrule, whom he has finally rejected at the
     end of *Henry IV, Part 2* (1596–9), dies in the room of a tavern;
     as the tavern hostess tells the story:

     after I saw him fumble with the sheets and play with flowers and
     smile upon his fingers' ends, I knew there was but one way; for his
     nose was as sharp as a pen, and a' [he] babbled of green fields.

FORDHAM CASTLE

1.   *bluest end of the Lake*: the only end of lake Geneva to afford
     views of the Castle of Chillon and the Dent du Midi, as is
     claimed on p. 323 of the tale, would have to be the eastern. The
     James family had lived in Geneva from 1856 to 1860, and James
     had visited Vevey in 1869 (see notes on 'Daisy Miller', p.
     358 and p. 359). In 1872 he stayed in a hotel that might have sug-
     gested Madame Massin's establishment, the 'charming Hotel
     Byron at Villeneuve, the eastern end of the lake, of which I have

retained a kindlier memory than of any of my Swiss resting-places' ('Swiss Notes', *Transatlantic Sketches*, p. 61). It was on this trip that he went 'Baedeker in hand' to tour the Castle of Chillon (see note on 'Daisy Miller', p. 359).

2. *old-fashioned 'work'*: Reeve notes that 'The custom of making memorial ornaments from locks of the deceased's hair – "hair-work" – was popularized from the mid-1850s by *Godey's Lady's Book*, a journal based in Philadelphia. The hair would be boiled in soda water for ease of working, arranged in delicate patterns, and enclosed in a glass-covered medallion or jewellery casing.'

3. *first trial of a flying-machine*: the Wright Brothers, Orville (1871–1948) and Wilbur (1867–1912) had made the first powered flight in December 1903, less than a year before the publication of 'Fordham Castle', but they and others had been experimenting with manned gliders for some years before.

4. *'American papers please copy'*: a phrase typically attached to an obituary notice on an international wire service like Reuters, of an American abroad. Conversely, American wire services like the Associated Press or United Press reporting on the death of – say – an Irish immigrant would attach the phrase 'Irish papers please copy'.

5. *dreadful flag*: that is, his name.

6. *Peoria*: the city in Illinois, on the Illinois River, incorporated as a village in 1835, now a prosperous and populous middle-western city; in American popular culture Peoria is a bye-word for middle American, or American mainstream culture, dating from Horatio Alger, Jr.'s popular novel, *Five Hundred Dollars; or, Jacob Marlowe's Secret* (1890), in which a group of actors 'play in Peoria'; since the vaudeville era of the late nineteenth and early twentieth centuries the phrase 'Will it play in Peoria?' has been a figure of speech to express the question of whether a particular book, play, movie or advertising idea will appeal to a wide spread of the American demographic.

7. *Fordham Castle, Wilts*: one of James's many imaginary names for the various English country houses in his fiction; 'Wilts' is short for the county of Wiltshire in south-west England, noted for (among other things) real country houses like Longleat and Stourbridge.

8. *Baedeker*: the widely used travel guides, published from 1827 by the German press Verlag Karl Baedeker. Though James used

Baedeker's *SIST* when visiting the Castle of Chillon (see note 19 on 'Daisy Miller" p. 360.), he also depended on Murray's guides.

9.   *Castle . . . Midi*: see notes to 'Daisy Miller', p. 359.

10. *'extra'*: that is, not included in the price of full board at the hotel.

11. *thrust upon him*: in Shakespeare's *Twelfth Night* (1602) Sir Toby Belch, Sir Andrew Aguecheek and Maria concoct a spoof letter to Malvolio, supposedly from Olivia, the Lady of the house, that she is secretly in love with him. Part of Olivia's flattering praise of Malvolio is that 'Some are born great, some achieve greatness, and some have greatness thrust upon 'em' (Act II, scene v, lines 144–5).

12. *cheap board*: inexpensive lodging with meals.

13. *drew her breath in pain*: in Shakespeare's *Hamlet* (1599/1601), as Hamlet lies dying he says to Horatio, 'If thou didst ever hold me in thy heart,/Absent thee from felicity awhile/And in this harsh world draw thy breath in pain/To tell my story' (Act V, scene ii, lines 351–4). As Reeve points out, James was fond of the phrase, using it 'in Chapter 16 of *The Tragic Muse*, where the atmosphere surrounding Mr Carteret made Nick Dormer "draw his breath a little in pain" (NYE vii. 294), in "The Beast in the Jungle" (' "he gazed, he drew breath, in pain", NYE xvii. 125), only two years prior to writing "Fordham Castle", and would use it again, in revising *The American* for the New York Edition ("drew his breath awhile in pain", NYE ii.537).'

14. *car-window*: the window of a train carriage.

15. *the book-agency business*: a book agent was not a literary agent, but a relatively humble door-to-door salesman of books, or of subscriptions to forthcoming books. To give a sense of the contemporary status of the occupation, Reeve cites another work by Horatio Alger, Jr., (cf. the note on Peoria, above), the Preface to *The Young Book Agent, or Frank Hardy's Road to Success* (1905): 'It is the custom of many persons in ordinary life to sneer at a book agent and show him scant courtesy, forgetting that the agent's business is a perfectly legitimate one and that he is therefore entitled to due respect so long as he does that which is proper and gentlemanly' (p. iii).

16. *placed on the line*: as Reeve points out, 'The principal paintings by the best-known artists at the annual summer exhibition at the Royal Academy in London were placed 'on the line', i.e. in a

central row on the wall, with the bottom edge of the frame eight feet from the ground, the painting tilted towards the viewer.'

17. *sort of box*: kind of predicament.

18. *real English style*: presumably in received pronunciation rather than a regional and/or lower-class accent.

19. *I haven't got any side*: Abel's finished sentence might have been 'I haven't got any side that she finds presentable'.

20. *Lord Dunderton*: a typically Jamesian fictional name, but a character of this name appears in *The Guards*, an anonymous satirical novel of 1827.

21. *morocco defence*: refers to her 'large, high-shouldered reticule', which was presumably made of morocco, an expensive leather made from goatskin.

PENGUIN CLASSICS

THE BOSTONIANS
HENRY JAMES

'There was nothing weak about Miss Olive,
she was a fighting woman, and she would fight him to the death'

Basil Ransom, an attractive young Mississippi lawyer, is on a visit to his cousin
Olive, a wealthy feminist, in Boston when he accompanies her to a meeting on
the subject of women's emancipation. One of the speakers is Verena Tarrant,
and although he disapproves of all she claims to stand for, Basil is immediately
captivated by her and sets about 'reforming' her with his traditional views. But
Olive has already made Verena her protégée, and soon a battle is under way for
exclusive possession of her heart and mind. The Bostonians is one of James's most
provocative and astute portrayals of a world caught between old values and the lure
of progress.

Richard Lansdown's introduction discusses *The Bostonians* as James's most
successful political work and his funniest novel. This edition contains extracts from
Tocqueville and from James's 'The American Scene', which illuminate the novel's
social context. There are also notes and a bibliography.

Edited with an introduction by Richard Lansdown

PENGUIN CLASSICS

THE EUROPEANS
HENRY JAMES

'They are sober; they are even severe ... But we shall cheer them up'

Eugenia, an American expatriate brought up in Europe, arrives in rural New England with her charming brother Felix, hoping to find a wealthy second husband after the collapse of her marriage to a German prince. Their exotic, sophisticated airs cause quite a stir with their affluent, God-fearing American cousins, the Wentworths – and provoke the disapproval of their father, suspicious of foreign influences. To Gertrude Wentworth, struggling against her sombre puritan upbringing, the arrival of the handsome Felix is especially enchanting. One of Henry James's most optimistic novels, *The Europeans* is a subtle and gently ironic examination of manners and morals, deftly portraying the impact of experience upon innocence.

Part of a series of new Penguin Classics editions of Henry James's works, this edition contains a chronology, further reading, notes and an introduction by Andrew Taylor exploring the novel's shifting patterns of opposites and James's portrayal of personal and national identity.

'This small book, written so early in James's career, is a masterpiece of major quality' F. R. Leavis

Edited with an introduction and notes by Andrew Taylor
Series editor Philip Horne

PENGUIN CLASSICS

WASHINGTON SQUARE
HENRY JAMES

'Why, you must take me or leave me ... You can't please your father and me both; you must choose between us'

When timid and plain Catherine Sloper acquires a dashing and determined suitor, her father, convinced that the young man is nothing more than a fortune-hunter, decides to put a stop to their romance. Torn between a desire to win her father's approval and passion for the first man who has ever declared his love for her, Catherine faces an agonizing choice, and eventually becomes all too aware of the restrictions that others seek to place on her freedom. James's masterly novel deftly interweaves the public and private faces of nineteenth-century New York society, and is also a moving study of innocence destroyed.

Part of a series of new Penguin Classics editions of Henry James's works, this edition contains a chronology, suggested reading, notes and an introduction discussing the novel's lasting influence and James's depiction of the quiet strength of his heroine.

'Perhaps the only novel in which a man has successfully invaded the feminine field and produced a work comparable to Jane Austen's' Graham Greene

Edited with an introduction and notes by Martha Banta
Series editor Philip Horne

PENGUIN CLASSICS

THE MILL ON THE FLOSS
GEORGE ELIOT

Edited with an introduction by A. S. Byatt

Brought up at Dorlcote Mill, Maggie Tulliver worships her brother Tom and is desperate to win the approval of her parents, but her passionate, wayward nature and her fierce intelligence bring her into constant conflict with her family. As she reaches adulthood, the clash between their expectations and her desires is painfully played out as she finds herself torn between her relationships with three very different men: her proud and stubborn brother, a close friend who is also the son of her family's worst enemy, and a charismatic but dangerous suitor. With its poignant portrayal of sibling relationships, *The Mill on the Floss* is considered George Eliot's most autobiographical novel; it is also one of her most powerful and moving.

In this edition writer and critic A. S. Byatt provides full explanatory notes and an introduction relating *The Mill on the Floss* to George Eliot's own life and times.

PENGUIN CLASSICS

THREE AMERICAN POETS: MELVILLE, TUCKERMAN AND ROBINSON

> 'They said that Fame her clarion dropped
> Because great deeds were done no more –
> And Glory - 'twas a fallen star!
> But battle can heroes and bards restore'

From out of the shadow cast by the Civil War emerged three unique American voices. Herman Melville explored the effect of the war on America's youth and the death of heroism in a series of intense narrative poems, which are represented here along with his later, more introspective verse. A similar strain of loss marks the work of Frederick Goddard Tuckerman, who was also grieving for the death of his wife, and whose haunting lyrics were influenced by his friendship with Tennyson. Two-time Pulitzer prize-winner Edwin Arlington Robinson's work was characterized by his masterly use of the sonnet form and his penetrating character study. His most famous poems are gathered here alongside some less familiar verse.

This new anthology contains a general preface, along with individual introductions to each poet, a table of dates and suggestions for further reading.

Edited by Jonathan Bean